BADWATER

BADWATER

THE FORENSIC GEOLOGY SERIES
BOOK 2

TONI DWIGGINS

All characters and events portrayed in this work are fictitious. Certain geographical features have been slightly altered.

Cover design: Wicked Good Book Covers

— To be notified of new releases, sign up for my mailing list:

https://eepurl.com/GtdZn

— Contact me at:

Website: tonidwiggins.com

Facebook: facebook.com/ToniDwigginsBooks

"Before outsiders changed our valley, it was described in the names of the places that were important for our survival here. Many are the names of springs. ... If the Manly Party, who traveled across our valley in 1849, had known our stories and trails, they would have found water, and *Tumpisa* ("red rock") might not be known as a Valley of Death."

— The Timbisha Shoshone Tribe

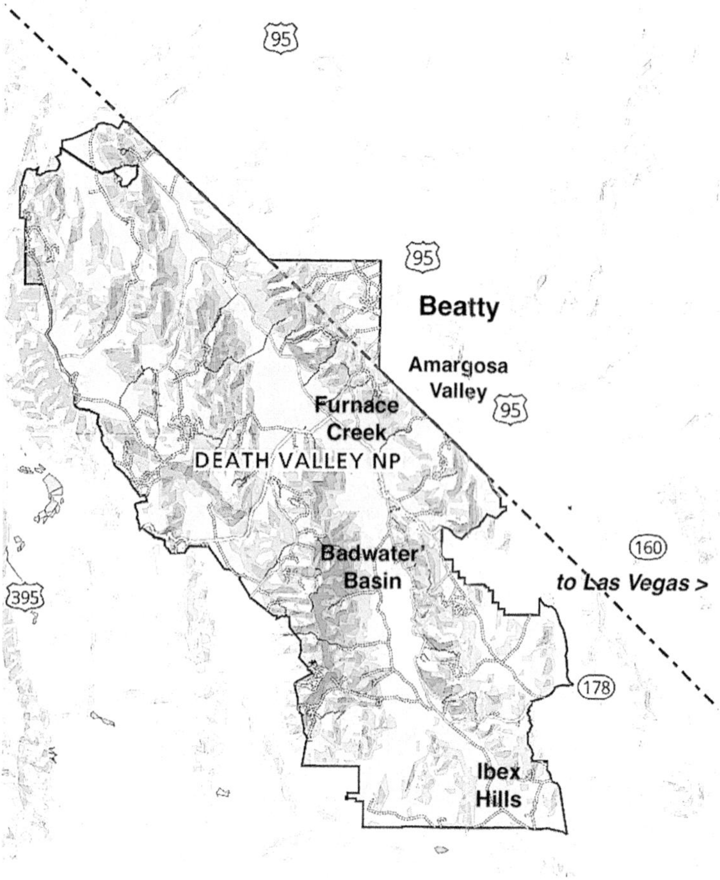
95
95
Beatty
Amargosa
Valley
95
Furnace
Creek
DEATH VALLEY NP
160
Badwater
Basin
to Las Vegas >
395
178
Ibex
Hills

1

THE FIGURE COMING down the dark road was bulky, and it took me a moment to realize he was dressed in hazmat.

I suddenly felt a little naked out here.

Walter, beside me, crouching to stow the donut bag in his field pack, had not yet noticed.

We were at the intersection of the highway and an offshoot side road that climbed uphill, and our view from here was limited. The only thing visible, way uphill, were emergency spotlights cracking the night.

"Our man's coming," I told my partner. "And he's in hazmat."

Walter looked up. "*That* wasn't mentioned."

"No kidding."

The oncoming man was moving slowly—perhaps due to the muddied condition of the graded road. I glanced at the sky, where a cloud roof glowed faintly beneath a hidden moon. Presumably, there'd been a summer thunderstorm here, wherever precisely *here* was.

It had been clear an hour ago in Mammoth, our home base in the eastern Sierra Nevada mountains. We run a two-person lab called Sierra Geoforensics and what we do for a living is read earth evidence at scenes of crime and crisis. This job had begun truly in the dark--it was four a.m. when Walter picked up a call on our after-hours number from an FBI field officer who urgently requested our services. Walter had then phoned me, jolting me out of my four a.m. stupor. It took us ten minutes to consult, speculate, and sign onto the case. Fifteen minutes later an agency helicopter collected us and we headed east from Mammoth and crossed another mountain range, which meant we'd passed from California into Nevada, then bellied down to this dark desert highway, coming in well short of the scene. The pilot deposited us with a *good luck* and then the chopper lifted off and disappeared into the night.

And here we waited.

"One good thing," I said, "our man's not wearing a breather."

Walter peered. "You have young eyes."

"Hey, it's more a question of what jumps out at you."

"Cassie, what jumps out at me in the dark belongs in the realm of bad poetry." He added, "Night vision goes to hell as one ages."

I nudged his arm. "Yeah, you predate the dinosaurs."

"At times I feel I do."

We fell silent, as the Special Agent drew up to join us.

Indeed, he was bare-faced. The hazmat suit encased him from booties to plastic collar line. Above that, he was unprotected. He had graying hair in a salon cut and a beaky face with aristocratic lines. He gave us a nod. "I am Hector Soliano with the FBI." The voice had a faint Spanish accent. "Mr. Walter Shaws, Ms. Cassie Oldfield, I appreciate that you have come on such short notice."

"The situation appeared to warrant it," Walter said. He added, "And your colleague should have informed us that we would need to suit up."

"When she contacted you, there was no need."

"And now?"

"A precaution. The situation evolves."

A vein began to throb in my neck.

"Mr. Soliano," Walter said, "I don't guess well. Not on five hours sleep. A cup of coffee would help. Barring that, I would like to know what the devil is going on."

Hector Soliano gave a curt shrug. "And I, who have had three hours sleep, would wish to know this as well."

Walter's eyebrows lifted.

"On the surface," Soliano said, "the attempted hijacking, the shooting...my colleague should have explained this."

"She did," Walter said. "And the evolution?"

"And the evolution has led us to err on the side of extreme caution."

And it's like pulling teeth, I thought, for the FBI to share details with non-agency people. I said, "And?"

"It is best you see for yourself. But first I am most anxious to have you suit up." Soliano started up the side road.

We fell in.

Walter said, "Where, precisely, are we?"

We were, as best I could tell by the castoff of emergency lights, on an alluvial fan leading into the hacked-up foothills of a gaunt range that loomed above.

"We are just off Nevada state highway 95," Soliano said, "southwest of the town of Beatty. A passing motorist saw what appeared to be a vehicle chase turning onto this road and notified the Beatty Sheriff, who investigated and notified federal responders. I came out here and determined that we wanted a forensic geology consult. We have you on file. I am told you are worth your fee."

"We are," Walter said. "Let's go put our eyes on the scene."

As we tramped uphill we topped a small rise and got a better view. Ahead, big vehicles clogged the road. Adjacent to the road, the scene was spotlighted. Yellow rope zoned off a large chunk of desert where a semi-trailer truck lay on its side. It appeared to have tumbled down an incline and come to rest in the desert scrub. Well uphill of the crash site was another roped and spotlighted area, occupied by a hulking crane.

On the road directly ahead of us there was a big white van, lettered RERT, and Soliano led us toward its open door.

I asked, "What's RERT?"

"An acronym..." Soliano touched his brow—the difficulty of acronyms in a non-native language. "With the Environmental Protection Agency."

My attention jumped back to the spotlighted crash scene, which was uphill of us and the white van. Suited figures had now come into view, poking around the scrub brush near the truck. The figures wore hoods and masks and air tanks.

Soliano snapped his fingers and turned to me. "R-E-R-T. Radiological Emergency Response Team."

I nodded. Made sense.

And then some.

Emergency evolving.

2

Scotty Hemmings held open the top of the coveralls as if he were holding an evening coat.

I'd already got the suit up to my waist but it was cramped quarters inside the RERT van and the material was stiff. I wormed into the arms and then started to pull on a latex glove.

"Whoa Cassie," Scotty said, "inflate it first. You don't want a blown-out glove."

No, I didn't want that.

I listened intently to Scotty Hemmings, wishing to dress exactly as the RERT chief dressed. He had an easygoing air with looks to match—shaggy blond hair and a big square dimpled smiling face—and we were already on a first-name basis. But there was nothing laid-back about his instructions.

Walter, I noticed, was taking exquisite care in the assembly of his own suit.

I blew my gloves into fat balloon hands and checked for leaks.

Scotty handed me rubbery over-gloves. The bar-code sticker said Wal-Mart.

The RERT chief shops discount? I took a closer look at the

equipment racks. Indeed, much of this stuff would be at home in Walter's garage: brooms, shovels, hoses, portable vacuum. Some belonged in an anal-retentive kitchen: fancy scrub brushes, bottles of sodium carbonate and trisodium phosphate. And then there were the defensive items: suits and tanks and probes and meters, the only one of which I recognized was a Geiger counter.

There was also a thermos of coffee but Scotty warned against a full bladder in hazmat.

The van door opened and a white-suited red-haired man came in. He held up a meter with its battery compartment open and Scotty jerked a thumb at the shelves.

The logo on the man's suit said CTC. Then he wasn't with RERT. He was with another set of initials. My head ached.

The red-haired man gave Walter and me the once-over, then spoke to Scotty. "Pinch me coach, am I dreaming or are you sending civilians out there?"

"The name's Scotty," Scotty said, "and what business is it of yours?"

"Funny you should ask. It *is* my business. My gig's radiation protection." The man made us a little bow. "Hap Miller, chief health physicist with the CTC radioactive waste facility—known in the vernacular as *the dump*. Shipment outside was headed for my facility. Which is why I respectfully asked Scotty here why he's sending you innocents out there."

Walter introduced us and explained our business.

For a long moment Miller's deep-set blue eyes held steady on us and then he said, "Not my call," and turned back to the shelves.

I looked at Scotty, whose call it was.

"Hey," Scotty said, "we got some weirdness going on with the truck outside and everybody's jumpy."

"What weirdness?"

"I'm gonna let the FBI fill you in on that."

Evolving-situation weirdness, I assumed.

"My job's just to get you ready." Scotty ripped yellow tape from a wide roll. He taped my gloves to my sleeves.

I nodded. Ready's good. "So, I understand this shipment isn't, uh, irradiated hospital waste. Booties and gloves and such."

Hap Miller snorted.

"Fraid it's a lot nastier than that," Scotty said. "According to the manifest, the load is ion-exchange resin beads. Cleans radionuclides from the cooling water at the nuke plant. Beads absorb the rads—that's why this load was on its way to get buried. I mean, these beads pick up some pretty active puppies."

"Such as?" Walter asked.

"Well, the reactor gets whacked by stray neutrons and you get, say, cobalt-60."

Cobalt-60? That vein started up in my neck again.

"And, you get leaks from the fuel rods. Fission products."

Walter looked at me, and I looked at him.

"You know, the cesiums and the strontiums..." Scotty bent to tape my rubber booties to my coverall legs. "And americium, plutonium..."

Miller turned. "Also known as Oh-My-God-iums." His thin mouth turned down in a curbed smile.

I wetted my lips. "Just how hot are these resin beads we have out there?"

Scotty glanced up at me. "We're not talking irradiated booties."

Walter was watching me. He wore the solicitous look he used to throw at me when I was a kid doing scutwork in his lab and he'd take me out to a real crime scene, the look he'd wear when I'd signed on officially after grad school and the scenes became more gritty. The look he still gives me, when it gets truly nasty. Although it's the geology that brings us to the crime scenes, often enough the evidence is lodged on a body—we're not spared the impact of human mayhem.

Scotty took his tape and moved to Walter.

I threw Walter a look of my own. Six months ago he had a transient ischemic attack—a starter stroke, as his doctor bluntly put it. A sign of things to come if he does not knock off the donuts and pace himself at the scenes, and the risk grows with increasing age.

Walter rotated his wrists so that his gloves could be taped to his sleeves.

And this isn't just another day at the office, is it?

"Okey-doke," Scotty said when he'd finished taping Walter, "to be on the safe side you're gonna used canned air." He helped me, then Walter, into tank harnesses and then passed us face-pieces. "Kinda like scuba gear. Either of you dive?"

I said, "I've snorkeled."

"Hey, that's cool. Me, I surf. Learned on the swells at San Onofre State Beach." Scotty dimpled. "In front of the old nuke plant."

I noticed the Saint Christopher medallion around Scotty's neck. Patron saint of surfers, as I recalled from my beach days at UCLA, worn to protect the wearer from harm.

"Last thing," Scotty said, "we're gonna slap dosimeters on you. Keep track of any exposure to radiation. Anybody asks for a reading, hold it up to the light and sing out the millirems." He passed us the pen-like objects. "Clip it somewhere between the neck and the waist. Over the heart's good."

Easy to find my heart, since it was drumming. "We might be exposed?"

"No worry, procedure. We've metered the area you'll be going into and it's just low-level background rad."

"Where are the casks?"

"Still rounding them up. But they're in another area—not

the one you're going into. You don't go near the casks. Even though they're shielded, some gammas leak through. And like I said, this is a hot load."

Hap Miller snapped a battery into his meter. "Hotter than you think, coach."

"The name's *Scotty* and what the hell's that mean?"

"Means it came from a real nasty cleanup site, Scotty."

I spoke. "How hot?"

Miller regarded me. "You eat salsa?"

I nodded.

"You like it hot?"

"Medium-hot. What is that, some kind of health physics metaphor?"

"Should be. Resins, metaphorically, work like salsa, depending on the radionuclides they pick up. They come in mild, medium, hot, or..." Miller blew on his fingers, "triple-X."

"Christ," Scotty said. He turned for the door.

"Well then, ever hear of Fukushima?"

Scotty froze. Surfer dude whose waves just went flat.

Walter said, "The Japanese nuclear plant?"

"Yowza." Miller nodded. "Plant that got hammered by the quake and tsunami. Reactors going Godzilla. Spent-fuel pools leaking."

Scotty said, "What's that got to do with this?"

"Frame of reference—for those who don't eat salsa." Miller gave me a wink. "Resins used to clean the Fukushima contaminated water were hot as can be."

I said, faintly, "And the resins we have outside?"

"That hot."

3

Roy Jardine stood frozen in the desert-night furnace and thought about his life.

It was a life of one crap job after another.

In his workaday career he had mastered the details of seventeen crap jobs, and on the eighteenth crap job the details tried to kill him.

So he'd taken job eighteen rogue.

And look what happened. It had not gone as planned. In fact, things went way out of control. They had a saying for this, in job eighteen. Going critical. Things had really gone critical tonight and Jardine needed a new plan, fast. He was not good at this—thinking on the fly. He liked to chew on a plan for as long as it took. So after the truck crash he'd gone home to lay low. And he'd chewed. Two hours later he had a bellyful of undigested plan. The problem, he'd realized, was making a plan in a vacuum. He needed to know what was happening.

So he'd gone out to reconnoiter.

He'd driven back close to the crash site and pulled off the highway onto the desert hardpack. Then he'd climbed up a knoll and raised his binoculars to scope the site. Hells bells, the place was swarming. Everybody was masked and hooded but he imagined their faces. Their expressions. Serious.

He liked that.

For the first time since things went critical, he recaptured his grand vision. He came alive. If he had not been afraid of being heard, he would have howled.

Footsteps sounded.

He froze. The sounds were at a distance. That gave him hope. At a distance, in the dark, he'd look like a post. The joke was, Roy Jardine was so skinny that if he turned sideways all you'd see was his shadow. As a matter of fact, Shadow was his nickname. He'd earned it on job number three, refrigeration mechanic, shadowing his supervisor's every move in order to get it right. He'd once read up on his personality type and diagnosed himself as borderline obsessive-compulsive. No sidewalk-crack counting or anything. Just a need to master the details.

The sound came closer and now he identified it. Claws on hardpack dirt. Coyote. If it started to bark he'd howl in relief along with it.

He found he'd sweated through his shirt.

He plucked the shirt away from his ribs. He swiped the back of his neck, lifting aside his ponytail. It was a thick black snake that made people look twice. He'd grown the ponytail on his first crap job—one-hour photo clerk—to look like he was in on the joke. He'd kept it because females liked to braid it and dudes noticed it instead of his perfectionism. And after the incident on job eighteen it gave them something to look at instead of his face.

Shadow, the long lean dude with the outlaw tail.

Go for it, dude.

He knew what he had to do. Recover control. There was already a plan in place: the grand vision, the mission, a long careful time in the making with attention paid to the details.

And it was still an excellent plan. But now he needed to make adjustments, adapt to the new situation. He told himself: you can do that, Roy. What happened tonight changed things. You have new enemies. The cops are in it now. They're going to try to stop you. Don't let them, dude.

I won't, he promised.

He hooked his thumbs in the loops of his jeans and strolled back to the pickup.

He turned on the engine, revving it. That sounded ace.

But as he drove onto the highway he worried that somebody might have heard and he lectured himself for being cocky and even though he saw no other cars he made himself sick on adrenaline.

He'd overreacted. As he drove past the crash site nobody came to chase him. He was just another drive-all-night roadie going about his business.

He tooled along highway 95, riding high now, and he gave himself another lecture. Listen Roy, you're doing good. You're incognito for now but very soon you're going to step out of the shadows. They won't call you Shadow, then.

He pressed his shoulders against the seat. He felt his chest swell. He'd heard of people doing this, being thrown out of their comfort zone and growing stronger. That's what he was doing right now: growing into his destiny. He was like the outlaws of the Old West who start out being ordinary dudes going through their crap days and then some villain kicks them in the comfort zone and they turn into outlaws. Not low-down outlaws. Outlaws with a mission.

He suddenly wondered if he should have a hideout. Just in case.

Yeah.

He knew just the place. It was already set up for the mission but there was plenty of space he could make his own. He liked that so much he decided to name it. He put on his thinking cap. He was a history junkie and since he was now an outlaw he wanted to name the hideout after a famous Old West outlaw lair. It came to him: *Hole-in-the-Wall*. That's where famous outlaws like the Wild Bunch had their base of operations. That wasn't just in the movies, that was a real place, up a narrow pass, hidden in the rock, impossible for the enemy to approach without being seen. Jardine's hideout was like that. If the enemy got on his tail, he'd make a stand at *Hole-in-the-Wall*.

The Long Lean Dude was back in the saddle.

Getting ready to take on the enemy.

He'd never counted sidewalk cracks but now he counted his chances.

4

SCOTTY HEMMINGS LED the way out of the van, touching his neck where the Saint Christopher medallion hung beneath his suit. Walter followed, adjusting the tank harness belt where it cut across his belly.

As I squeezed past Hap Miller, who did not give me an inch, he grinned. Not the same species as Scotty's good-natured smile. It was a toxic grin, as though Miller had leached up a few too many contaminants.

"Hold on," Miller told me, "you look a mite stressed. Allow me to send you forth with the health physics blessing."

I paused.

He used his meter probe to outline a cross over my chest. "In the name of alpha, beta, gamma, and *holy* neutron, go with low dose."

"Okay."

"You know dose? Amount of radiation absorbed. Potential for damage."

Yeah, I knew dose. I said, "Thanks for the good wishes."

Miller put on his facepiece, adjusting the head straps, electrifying his curly red hair. "Ladies first," he said, indicating the door.

Outside the van, Miller set off on his own course and I joined Walter and Scotty.

"Listen up, folks," Scotty said, "like I said in the van, there're places you *can* go, and places you *can't* go. Up ahead, where it's roped, is the hot zone. Zone runs alongside the road, waaay uphill. Some areas have been metered and okayed—like the area we're going into, where the truck is. We'll call that Area One. The area you're *not* going into is uphill of that, where the crane's working—Area Two. That's where the casks got thrown. Questions?"

Only one: what's the weird thing you and Soliano are saving up for us? I held my tongue. We'd find out soon enough.

"Okey-doke," Scotty said, "let's mask up."

We fitted our facepieces and raised our hoods and opened the regulator valves and the air flowed. We headed up the road to Area One, the crash site, where Hector Soliano awaited us. Masked-up now, like us, features obscured, like ours, he was nonetheless readily identifiable by his height and his ramrod FBI posture.

Scotty led the three of us through the control point into the hot zone.

Spotlights showed a path already tramped by other feet in the muddied soil. I felt bulky, moving with a truly odd gait in my rubber booties. I carried the field kit in my balloon-tested hand. I scanned Area One for stray casks. Nothing. Nothing but desert, no worry, just the everyday naturally occurring background radiation emitted by the native soil and rock, to which I never give a thought unless I'm doing a chem analysis for a soil profile.

We came to the semi-trailer. It was, in essence, a delivery truck. But for the lead shield between the cab and the trailer unit, it could have been delivering refrigerators. The battered rig had come to rest on its right side, belly facing us, wheels painfully skewed. I pictured it rolling, shooting out refrigerators as it tumbled.

Soliano gathered us. "I will first explain what we know."

His voice came tinny over the speaker in my facepiece. I had to ignore the hiss of my air tank and my own Darth Vader breathing.

Soliano continued. "The vehicle is owned by Alliance Freight. Alliance reports that it was following the correct route, according to its transponder. It was en route to the CTC waste repository, five miles ahead, off highway 95."

Highway 95 was just visible, the dark strip that bisected the desert.

"Skid marks indicate the hijacker forced the truck off the highway, onto this side road. Tire marks take the vehicles farther uphill, where the truck went over the edge. The trailer portion took the brunt and was breached, scattering its cargo. The vehicle continued to tumble downhill and came to rest here."

I looked uphill, where the truck had gouged something of a bobsled run.

"Footprints suggest the hijacker left his vehicle and followed on foot."

"Hijacker, singular?" Walter asked.

"A single series of prints, which we attribute to the hijacker."

"On what basis?"

"Location. Direction." Soliano shrugged. "The scene is difficult—everyone who left a print was wearing protective booties. Including, presumably, the hijacker, since there are bootie prints around his vehicle's tire marks."

"Hijacker, male?" I asked.

Soliano waved a hand—his default assumption. "Hijacker, homicidal. The driver has been shot."

I gazed up at the dented cab. "Maybe the intent was homicide, not hijacking."

"The intent reaches beyond homicide."

So now we came to it.

Soliano led the way to the back of the trailer. I steeled myself for something hideous—there were things beyond murder that qualified—but the first thing I noticed on the crippled back panel was the standard radiation placard. Black fan-bladed symbol in a yellow triangle, RADIOACTIVE in black. The only thing unfamiliar to me was the red Roman numeral III and the number 7. So okay, we rank our soils, they rank their rads.

I thought, there's nothing weird about a rad symbol on a radwaste truck.

And then Soliano pointed and we moved in closer and what I had thought was mud smears resolved into a drawing. The first thing I noticed was that I could read the drawing without tipping my head. Which meant it had been done after the crash, with the trailer on its side.

Walter made a sound, tinny in my earpiece. Astonishment.

It was a crude sketch in black marker. Radiating lines fell from the fan blades, like rain. Like fallout. The lines fell onto a stick figure, who was running. Behind the figure was a skull and crossbones. Over my canned breathing I could hear Scotty mutter, "Goddamn weird-ass game."

I turned to Soliano. "This is what you meant by the situation evolving?"

"Yes. It was initially overlooked."

I could understand why. Unless you looked closely, you'd assume it was smeared mud from the truck's tumble down the hill.

Soliano said, "Our hijacker leaves us a message. The radiation..." He seemed to search for the words. He found them. "Escapes control."

"Yup," Scotty said, grim. "That promises a bad nuclear day."

I focused, hard, on the scene at hand. "Has anything here been touched?"

Soliano led us around to the front of the truck. "My evidence technicians have processed the scene. Photos, serology, fibers, prints. They recovered bullet casings, nine millimeter. We have established from the entry angle that the weapon was fired through the windshield from here." He pointed to a patch of ground marked by orange cones. "The soil evidence is untouched. I lack the budget for a full-time geologist."

Yes, that keeps us in business.

"However, I am most anxious that you see the driver." Soliano gestured to a ladder leading up to the cab. "The driver is encased in mud."

Walter eyed the ladder. "Why don't you take the driver, Cassie?"

I shifted. Walter doesn't think he can get up the ladder? I've seen him climb far worse, but not in bulky hazmat. And not, I calculated, since the starter stroke.

He opened his field kit. "And why don't I begin with the tires."

I grabbed my kit and nodded, as if it was after all no big deal. But it was. As I crabbed up the ladder I worried it—what if Walter's field days are numbered?—and then I reached the cab and my worry made way for focus.

I leaned against the bent frame and set my field kit on the side of the cab. I got the flashlight and shined it through the broken window, panning the interior. There was a garbage dump on the caved-in downhill side. Crumpled brown bags. Grande Starbucks cup. Spilled tool kit. A paperback. I angled the light; *Don Quixote*. Son of a gun. Attached to the visor was a credential with the driver's name, Ryan Beltzman, and next to that a red-lettered sign: *Engage Brain Before Engaging Engine*.

I came back, finally, to the driver, around whom I'd been peering.

Ryan Beltzman was still strapped in, slumped rightward. His legs were jammed under the dashboard. Even hanging from the seat belt, he showed the stiffness of early rigor. He was blond, like Scotty, although his hair was longer. The side of his head was dented, like the cab itself. He'd been shot. I couldn't tell how many bullets it had taken to deconstruct his face. Gunshot wounds weren't my field but I'd seen enough of them at other crime scenes to think that what happened to Beltzman, here, was overkill.

Perp's a marksman, I thought. With a temper.

I got my cell phone and turned on the camera and photographed the scene. I selected and laid out my tools: specimen dishes, scoops, scalpel.

Then I took a big Darth Vader inhale and set to work.

Beltzman was coated with mud—Soliano got that right. Jeans, T-shirt, back of the head. I picked up the scalpel, clumsy in gloved fingers. I chose a thick skin of mud on the left shoulder and pried a chunk free. Not a pretty piece of work. Probably didn't matter—this guy had clearly rolled in the mud and I was not going to be finding any neat sequences of deposition. I deposited the mud chunk in a specimen dish. I took two more samples and then something caught my eye, in his shirt pocket. I poked with the scalpel. Mud flaked. It was a joint.

Great. The radwaste driver's a pothead.

I would have liked to get to his shoe soles but I'd have to climb in with him. I did not really care to do that. I packed up my kit and climbed down and told Soliano I'd need Beltzman's shoes and access to the cab to finish my collection when they righted the truck.

My attention turned to Walter. He was squatting at the right front tire, prying mud from the treads. For a long moment I just watched him work, and his balance was fine and his motor skills were fine and I took that in and stored it up against the ladder thing, balancing the scales of doubt and hope.

I moved to the coned area and knelt for a close look. Just eyeballing the soil here—a fine-grained alluvium—I'd have to say it was a poor match to the mud on Beltzman. So where did he pick it up? Once I got the stuff under the scopes I'd do a profile but it helped to consider likely neighborhoods. The most obvious would be a rest stop along his route. So let's say the hijacker jumps Beltzman at the rest stop, and they wrestle in the mud. And the driver gets away that time, but the hijacker follows and forces the truck off the road here, and Beltzman doesn't get away this time. I'd want a geophysical map of the land along his route. It was a workable theory, the sort of thing I prefer to call an educated guess, and Walter calls my onageristic estimate.

An onager is a wild ass. I had no wild-ass guess on what the hijacker had in mind next: the intent in black marker.

Maybe the stick figure knew—running for its life. Who wouldn't try to escape those radiating lines? And who was the poor stick figure supposed to be? Man, woman? Or did the figure stand in for people in general? I shivered. Let's make it just one person. Let's make it a him. Let's wish him a clean escape.

"Geologists?" Soliano hovered.

I rose. "I'd like to collect samples up the road."

Soliano said, "I will lead you."

Soliano and I tramped farther up the graded road, paralleling the yellow-rope line, leaving Area One behind. When we reached the big flatbed trucks bearing the CTC logo I saw we'd come alongside Area Two—the area we were not going into. Nevertheless, we paused to watch the suited figures at work. The slope gentled here, which was why, I supposed, the casks had come to rest here. I saw only one cask, in the grip of a portable crane. It looked, more or less, like a mammoth tin can.

It should look scarier.

Soliano leaned close. "It pulls on the mind, yes?"

Yes.

We edged around the trucks and continued up the road. We brought out the flashlights because the steeper hillside up ahead was not lighted. This was one of the areas, according to Scotty, that had already been checked and okayed.

Soliano used his flashlight to illuminate a hodgepodge of tire tracks. He pointed out two sets: the smaller vehicle in pursuit of the larger vehicle. And then, still farther uphill, the road took a hook and the larger tracks veered wildly over the edge. I pictured Ryan Beltzman fighting the wheel, losing. I pictured the tailgating hijacker. Male, in Soliano's default description--not that it mattered.

What mattered was the gleam of intent in his eyes.

The hijacker's tire tracks continued to a wide spot and turned around. Here, he got out of his vehicle. Three distinct bootie-prints, marked by orange cones, led over the edge. Two had been casted and lifted. I photographed the ground, then sampled the uncasted print and the tire tracks. Some telling mineral might have transferred. A long shot. It was the mud on Ryan Beltzman that was going to tell the story, if I could read it.

Soliano, waiting at the road edge, called me over. He'd made a discovery. He pointed his flashlight down where the slope wrinkled into a small ravine. There were more bootie prints, these coming up the slope.

We decided to go down and have a look.

At the ravine, I was mentally comparing the size of the prints to those up on the road, and declaring them a match, when I stumbled and peered at the uneven ground under my own booties and thought, what's this?

"Hey," I said.

Soliano aimed his light.

I got a better look now at the stuff on the ground, the bone-white ashy trail that led down the ravine, and then Soliano painted his light along the white trail—downhill to a tangle of scrub brush where a cask was nearly concealed like an overlooked Easter egg—and it seemed to me that when this cask was thrown free it must have cracked like an egg upon impact and spilled its contents, rolling downhill until caught by the brush. As the alarm was going off in my head I seized on what Scotty had said—he'd said *beads*, resin beads not ash—but I thought, radwaste gets incinerated too doesn't it?

Scotty had said, back in the van, that a cask cannot fully shield the radwaste. And if a lead cask can't stop all the gammas, and the stuff was now under my feet, how much protection did my protective clothing give?

Not enough.

5

OLD HORROR-FLICK SCENES reeled through my brain.

Lab-coated scientists with Einstein hair pouring the wrong flask of purple liquid into the wrong vat. Repentant scientists—the victims usually being rogue scientists who repent too late, or vapid pretty girls—writhing while their skin blisters and their pores ooze purplish blood. Tiny mutant monsters flailing in incubators. Post-apocalyptic landscapes stripped of vegetation—not unlike the landscape I stood in—while legions of giant insects stride across land that has been bequeathed to the quickly adaptable.

I watch too many dumb movies.

Scotty Hemmings bounded up. He had a meter in one hand and a pancake-shaped wand in the other. "Stand still," he snapped.

I'd been running. Lumbering. I halted. Sweat cascaded down my flanks.

I glanced around. Soliano came to a halt nearby. We had nearly reached the road and if someone hadn't stopped us we would likely have kept going to put another stretch of distance between us and the spill. Suited figures were converging on the area. A figure with binoculars jammed against his face plate was shining a spotlight across the slope to the ravine. Two others, down below, shined lights on the cask in the scrub brush.

I turned back to Scotty. "You said..."

"Hang on a sec."

Long as you want.

He began at my feet, tracing my boots with the wand.

I stared at his bent hood, my heart hammering.

He shook his head and stood.

"Scotty?"

"Stand straight. Feet apart. Arms out, palms up. Stand still."

I complied, straining to hear the Geiger counter. Was it crackling? Was it screaming bloody murder?

Scotty skimmed the probe along my body. He did my arms first and then jumped to the top of my head, zigzagging across my face, then switchbacking down my torso. He took his time, agonizingly slow, and he was stone silent and everyone, I noticed, was stone silent. Soliano, a silent statue like me, was being metered by a suit with the RERT logo.

"Turn around," Scotty told me. "Feet apart. Arms out."

I turned. Two suited figures were nearby. I identified Hap Miller by the yellow tape on his tank with his last name in black marker. He was monitoring one of the CTC workers—in his health physics capacity, I assumed. Miller spoke, loud enough to break the eerie silence. "Enlighten me, Jenkins, why you came charging into a contaminated zone before it's been stabilized?"

The worker extended his middle finger. "Wasn't roped."

"You're living proof," Miller said, "that Mama Jenkins slept with a jackass."

And then all was quiet again. I listened to the voice in my head going over every wrong step until I thought I would scream. I wished Scotty would speak. Anything at all. I turned my head and said, "How'd you get into this business?"

"Stand still."

I froze.

He was silent for so long I thought he wouldn't answer, and then he did. "Was a lifeguard at San Onofre, beach in front of the nuke plant. Plant had a spill and RERT showed up. Lifeguards in hazmat. I thought cool job, no sharks."

"Just rads, huh?"

"Huh." He said no more so I shut up. I'd gotten used to the hiss of my air and the wheeze of my breathing and I listened to that until he banged me on the shoulder and said, "No worry."

I turned fully to face him. "So I'm not...?"

"You're not crapped up." He was reading his meter. His frown showed through the mask. "But I gotta say this is real weird. We gotta figure this out real fast. I mean, this stuff should be *hot* and you walked right through it and I didn't get *any* reading off your booties."

"Scotty!"

We turned. The guy with the binoculars approached, signaling. Scotty took the binocs and for the first time turned his attention to the spill. He yelled, "Shine another spot!" A second spotlight hit the spill, turning the white ashy powder even whiter.

"That's not resin beads," Scotty said. "What in hell's going on here?"

6

I STOOD at the edge of the newly-roped hot zone but in truth I'd already crossed over.

There is a line, in working a case, that separates the professional from the personal and in most cases I've worked the personal seeps in here and there. A victim who looks like a guy I dated in high school. A microwave in the kitchen at the scene that is the same make as the microwave in my kitchen. And that's fine, that familiarity, that human link. That's fine unless the personal balloons to blot out the professional and gets in the way of doing the job. When I'd stepped in what I thought was the shit fifteen minutes ago the personal had swelled nearly to bursting.

I needed to get back on the safe side of the line. I needed to find out what I'd stepped in. Put a name to that white ashy stuff, objectify it, and get it the hell out of my personal space. And so I waited while the hazmat professionals secured the scene so Walter and I could take our turn.

Hap Miller was out there, taking charge of the CTC dump property in the scrub brush. Miller metered the breached cask and called out, "*Not hot*," shaking his head like he did not believe it.

I had a clear view of the cask. Ashy stuff spilled out near the lid. Looked just like the stuff I'd stepped in earlier, uphill in the ravine. The stuff trailed from the ravine down to the cask, where it had come to rest in the brush. I pictured, again, the radwaste truck tumbling down this hill, shooting out casks. This cask must have been breached upon impact, trailing white ash as it tumbled.

This cask was supposed to contain highly radioactive resins. But it did not. So said Hap Miller's Geiger counter. So said Scotty Hemmings, when he took his first look at the spill: *that's not resin beads.*

This cask was an enigma.

Scotty was now examining the lid, which jutted askew. "Looks like the hold-down bolts came loose. Could be the top wasn't torqued." He gave Walter and me his considered thumbs-up.

I gave a glance downhill where CTC workers were recovering another cask. So far—so Miller had said—the other casks held precisely what they should.

I returned my attention to the enigma cask. Walter and I approached.

What had I been thinking? It looked nothing like a tin can.

It was a steel cylinder, about four feet long and three feet in diameter. It had flanged collars and lifting lugs. A severed tie-down cable spooled from one of the lugs. I could not help reading the yellow labels on the steel skin: IXResin, Radioactive III. Contents: Cs-137, Co-60, Pu-239, Sr-90, Be-7. Whoa. The labels said this stuff was triple-X hot but, in fact, the contents were not as advertised.

Whatever it was, it was not hot and we were encased in protective clothing and therefore there was no worry.

I squatted at the breached lid assembly.

Scotty was behind me. "What in hell is that stuff?"

Big spotlights washed the scene. The lid opened like a surprised mouth, baring rubbery gasket gums. White ashy stuff spewed from the mouth and dusted the ground. Stuff that had nearly given me heart seizure. Now, as I studied it, I knew what it was. And it made no sense. I fumbled my loupe out of the kit and looked through the high-power lens.

"What is it?" Miller this time.

Trivial to ID but just to be sure I looked again. Pearly, with a nonmetallic luster. Walter was beside me with his own lens, shaking his head like he could not believe it.

"Geologists?" Soliano now.

I said, in wonder, "It's talc."

On the way back to the RERT van Walter said, "Characteristics?"

Straight to work, then. Good enough. So, what do the characteristics of talc tell us about this scene?

I began. "Firstly, of course, talc is the softest mineral." Baby soft; I could vouch for that. "Streak white, luster pearly, cleavage basal, fracture lamellar, particle size...uh, extremely fine..." And what did this tell us so far? "I've got nothing useful," I admitted. Too much adrenaline. Too little sleep. Thoughts scattering like a puff of talc.

Well then, how about *dispersion* for a defining characteristic? I knew it well. Me, age seven, choking on a talc cloud, backing away from the changing table. Mom dusting my baby brother Henry's butt so the diaper won't rub a sore on his delicate skin. Won't lead to a bleed.

I shook off the memory. Yeah, talc's highly dispersible. Tell me something I don't know.

Walter and I walked on toward the van. Booties scattering gravel.

Memories still rolling, my little brother always good for a wallow. Me, age eleven, taking Henry, age five, for a walk. And I'd let him wear his flip-flops and his toes met a rock. Blood. Screams. A crowd gathering. I pocket the rock, hide it. Phone home. Mom and Dad speeding up in the Ford, scooping up my brother. Walter's there; crowd's just outside his lab. Walter's just some adult I've seen around town but my parents know him and they pass me off. The Ford squeals away toward the hospital. Walter shepherds me into his lab. I'm awkward with this old guy —he was early middle-age back then but to me at age eleven, he was old. And the old guy listens when I do a core dump—guilt, resentment, worry. I bring out the rock. Call it a shitkicking rock. In actuality, Walter says, that's basalt. He washes off the blood. He puts it under the microscope. By the time Mom calls from the hospital—Henry's bleeding stopped, send Cassie home—I don't want to leave. I want to find out how that rock came from a volcano. And in the weeks that follow I want to find out how a rock is evidence that helps to solve a crime.

And then two months after the stubbed toe, Henry has another accident—this one not survivable—and I find true solace in Walter's lab, where good things get done.

And now, eighteen years later, I've got a double masters in geology and criminalistics but at heart I'm still the eager beaver Walter created in his lab. I want to repair the rip in the safety net that allows us to go about our daily lives.

I want to find out if this talc evidence will help solve this crime.

In the RERT van we began to strip down to our street clothes.

"We have a puzzle," Soliano said, easing off his gloves. "And we have here a collection of people with unique expertise. Shall we put our heads together?"

Was that a request? Soliano didn't strike me as the type to request. More like the type to require.

"Our puzzle," Soliano continued, "begins with a truck leaving the nuclear plant, carrying a shipment of radioactive resin beads. The truck is bound for the CTC waste repository. En route, there is a crash. I am called to the scene. I make my initial evaluation—attempted hijacking. Mr. Hemmings and his RERT colleagues arrive to monitor the area for radiation hazards. CTC sends its people to recover their property, and its health physicist Mr. Miller to protect its people. My geologists arrive. We investigate. We find, by accident, that one of the casks does not contain resin beads. It contains talc." He regarded us, one by one, with the same exacting focus. "How is this possible?"

"Alchemy?" Miller said.

"Thank you for the levity," Soliano said, without a smile. "Let us consider, instead, that we have a 'dummy cask'—to cover the theft of a resin cask."

"Jesus," Scotty said, "you mean a swap?"

"This is possible?"

"Swapped where?"

Soliano considered. "Perhaps at the nuclear plant. Perhaps somewhere along the driver's route. With the driver, possibly, an accomplice. How would this be done?"

"To start with," Scotty said, "they'd need a crane to handle the casks."

"Very well. What else would be needed?"

Walter said, "Talc, evidently. It's chemically inert, easy to handle..." He glanced at me.

Yeah, okay, I'm on it—characteristics of talc. What else do they tell us?

"And where does the perp acquire this talc?" Soliano asked.

I said, "You don't get that much talc just anywhere. You'd need a source like a mine." I pictured it. The perp shoveling up talc to fill a radwaste cask—which is a damn misuse of the geology. What kind of scumbag thinks that up?

"And how does the perp acquire the empty cask, to fill with the talc?" Soliano eyed Miller. "This is your cask, I am told."

Miller raised his palms. "*Mine*? Comes from the dump where I *work*. We supply the casks to the nuke plant. They fill 'em, then they ship 'em back to us. Cask isn't mine in the sense of bought and paid for."

"You quibble. I mean yours in the sense of responsibility."

"Yowza, I quibble. Responsibility-wise, it's Milt Ballinger's cask. He's dump manager."

"Christ," Scotty said, "who cares who's in charge? If it's a swap then we've got a cask of hot resins running around out there."

Miller grinned. "On little cat feet?"

"You could try taking this damn serious, Miller."

Soliano snapped, "Gentlemen."

Miller bowed and unzipped his suit, rolling it down. I was able to smile and Walter chuckled and Scotty scowled. Soliano studied Miller's street clothes with distaste. Soliano himself was FBI informal in khakis and a short-sleeve linen shirt. Walter and I wore our lightweight summer gear. Scotty's street clothes were snug black jeans and a green polo shirt. Miller was in a league of his own. He wore baggy shorts in screaming yellow-orange plaid and his T-shirt had a drawing of Bart Simpson with the caption *There's No Way You Can Prove Anything*. Miller didn't look anything like bug-eyed buzz-cut Bart. Miller had wild red hair, a pale heart-shaped face, and blue eyes set deep as cave pools. But Miller and Bart did share that same no-shit look.

"To complete the scenario..." Soliano waited until he'd regained our attention. "Had the crash not occurred, the driver would have made his delivery of the dummy talc cask—along with the rest of the shipment—to the dump. And the swap would have gone undetected." He regarded Miller. "This is possible?"

"Perp'd need some serious mojo."

Walter said, "There might be a way to test the theory."

"Yes?" Soliano said.

"If the perp does have the necessary know-how," Walter said, "perhaps he tried the swap before. On a previous shipment. And that time things went as planned and the talc cask *did* arrive at the dump. In which case, it could be located?"

Miller shook his head. "Too late now. Casks get buried right away, way down deep where the sun don't shine."

My gut constricted, down deep. I hated Walter's idea. Because if the perp tried the swap only once, tonight, and screwed it up—as he clearly screwed up tonight—then there was some hope he'd fail at whatever plans he had for that cask of hot resins.

I got a crazy vision of the cask on little cat feet chasing the stick figure. The stick's not laughing. Stick's scared shitless.

I wasn't laughing either. I dearly hoped the perp was a one-shot screwup. Because if he'd tried this before, and succeeded, that level of competence did not bode well for our side. I hated Walter's theory but it was a good one, and testable. I had to give due credit to my mother and brother. I said, "Ever put talcum powder on a baby?"

Silence. Nobody had, it seemed.

Come on, I thought, it's a defining characteristic. "Talc's

highly dispersible. It gets on the changing table too." I pictured white talc on steel cask skin. "And then you track it all over the place."

7

JERSEY WOULDN'T SIT STILL.

When Roy Jardine had returned home two hours ago from his reconnoiter, Jersey as usual bounced like a windup toy. He'd petted her, fed her, welcomed her onto his lap when he settled into his Lazy-boy. But she wouldn't calm down. He'd finally had to set her on the floor so he could work.

She paced. She felt his jumpiness. Normally he'd appreciate that, her understanding him. Poodles were smart as pigs and his bitch Jersey was the smartest poodle he'd ever owned.

"Sit, girl," he said, and she quieted, giving him her adoring look.

It was like normal—Roy and Jersey holed up at home. His place was a tidy little homestead, a pink stucco box of a house with a red tile roof. Colors like Jersey's belly. His place was isolated, at the far end of town. And Beatty was a desert town with nothing around it. He blessed hick towns.

Of course once you left Beatty you went into the action zone. Six miles down the highway from Beatty was the CTC dump and beyond that, another six miles or so, was the crash site. Lights, action, busy busy busy.

He got up, checked the front door lock, sat back down. Jumpy as Jersey. He didn't feel safe at home anymore. Maybe he'd better go to the hideout in case things went critical again.

And they would, one way or another.

Jersey barked. He shushed her. He had work to do.

He picked up the yellow notepad. For the past two hours he'd been chewing over what he had learned at the crash site. Now he was ready to draw up a plan. He made two columns, one marked *Enemy* and the other marked *Roy's Action Items*.

In the *Enemy* column he wrote *Sheriff, Fire Department, RERT, CTC, seven unmarked vehicles, one FBI helicopter.*

In the *Roy* column, he wrote *Find Out What They Know About Roy Jardine. Find Out What They Are Going To Do Next.*

He put aside the notepad in disgust. He'd learned almost nothing. His action items lacked implementation details. Find out *how*?

He went into the kitchen and got a pint of strawberry ice cream.

Jersey was on his heels.

He took the pint back to his Lazy-boy and fed the first spoonful to Jersey. Pink ice cream on pink dog tongue. He took the next spoonful. Technically, sharing the spoon was unhygienic but he'd been sharing with Jersey for years and never got sick. Of course he bathed her every other day and never let her into anything disgusting like the trash can. He fed her two more bites and then no more. He didn't want to upset her stomach. "Mine now, girl," he said, and the smart bitch stopped begging. The ice cream cooled his mouth and sugared his belly and by the time he'd worked his way through the pint he knew what to do.

More recon. Reconnoitering, he meant, but he liked calling it recon. It would have been foolish to write some Rambo action in his *Action Item* column, just to look ace. He bet outlaws reconned in detail before they launched an operation. At least, the smart ones in the history books did.

The limitation of his recon at the crash site, he realized, was that he'd been too far away. He needed to get close where things were happening to get actionable information. And things would sure be happening at the dump. He pictured it. He'd worked at the dump for three crap years—job eighteen—and he knew exactly what everybody would be doing at any given time. Except this morning. This wouldn't be a regular morning, this would be an emergency morning. So how should he act? Normal, he thought. Just go into work and act normal. But in reality, doing recon.

Was that doable?

The ice cream soured his gut. What if he was already a suspect? What if the cops were at the dump waiting for him?

Jersey whined. When he didn't pet her, she started barking.

"Enough, girl." He had to smack her, lightly, on the rump to shut her up.

Now *think* Roy. He thought.

He picked up the phone and called his shift mate—not a buddy, Jardine didn't have buddies—but a dim dude who sometimes swapped shifts with him. *Sorry it's so early but would you mind taking my shift this morning?—I'm hungover.* Jardine wasn't, he'd never been, but this was an excuse any of the guys would buy. What the excuse bought Jardine now was an info dump from his shift mate. *Oh Roy, man, ya gotta come in cuz Ballinger's callin' in everybody cuz—shit man you dunno?*—and then the dimwit went on to tell Jardine what three other guys had told him.

Roy Jardine concluded he was presumed as innocent as the next guy.

He went to the kitchen and rinsed out the ice cream carton and put it in the trash and washed his spoon and put it in the drainer. Jersey followed, nosing around the trash. "No, girl." She knew something was up. She knew he wasn't going to bed and so she wasn't going to be curling up in her nice dog bed on the floor beside him.

He went back to his Lazy-boy and picked up the yellow pad. Under *Roy's Action Items,* he wrote *Undercover Recon At The Dump.*

Then he moved into action. He packed up supplies—his Buck knife, extra clothing, toothbrush, toothpaste, soap, deodorant, washcloth, all the things he'd need at the hideout if he had to stay long. The hideout was already stocked with the basics: sleeping bag, freeze-dried food, bottled water, flashlight, first-aid kit, emergency backup supplies.

Jersey sat on his pack and wouldn't get off.

He squatted beside her. He ruffled her curly topknot and scratched under her chin. He wished he could take her along but she'd hate the hideout. Too cold, too dark, no soft bed. No ice cream. Easy to get lost. Easy to get hurt. He wished he knew how long he'd be there. He couldn't leave her alone in the house, and he had no friends, no neighbors, who would take care of her. And he did *not* want anyone asking questions.

He lifted her off his pack and set her on the floor.

He gathered his supplies and went out back and stowed his stuff in the pickup.

He came back in and got the carrier and opened the top and put in a soft towel and said, "In, girl."

Jersey whined. Only time he put her in the carrier was to take her to the vet in Las Vegas, because Beatty's vet was substandard. She hated the long drive. But she loved him. She gave him a pleading look. He pointed, sternly, and she jumped in. He unsnapped her collar and pulled it off. She didn't understand. He scratched her behind the ears. He closed the carrier. He picked it up and cradled it, like he was just cradling his dog.

He went outside to the pickup and put the carrier in the passenger seat and shut the door. He locked up the house. He got in the driver's seat. Jersey whined. "It's okay, girl," he said.

It wasn't.

He drove into town and took a side street and then another and another--he didn't know where he was, he'd never been in this part of town--and finally he found a quiet area where there was nobody in sight. He parked and got out and opened the passenger door and picked up the carrier and set it on the ground, in the shade of a pine tree. He stuck his forefinger through a vent hole and found her curly topknot. He gave her a scratch. He said, "Somebody will pick you up and you'll be theirs."

She whined.

He left. No more time for sentiment. He got in the driver's seat and closed the door and drove away as quietly as possible, not feeling ace at all, taking back roads out of Beatty.

Some day he might get another poodle. A big one, a standard. Definitely not a toy. That would be sacrilege. There could never be another Jersey.

When he hit the highway, he gunned the engine and hightailed it.

By the time he reached the dump he had put his feelings in order.

Heartsore, but back in the saddle.

The Long Lean Dude was going undercover.

8

I OPENED the door of the van and stepped out into the ninety-degree glimmer of Tuesday's dawn at the radioactive waste dump.

With daybreak I could see that we were on a high plain dotted with creosote and sage, which already stung my nose. To the east and west were bald mountain ranges. To the north and south ran highway 95. I toed the ground. A gravelly soil, nearly dry now. No talc seams here. If I found talc at the dump it wouldn't be native. It would have hitched a ride.

Walter remained in the van, where we had set up a rudimentary lab. He'd said you have the talc—and the heat—and I'll have the driver's mud and the air conditioning.

How does he do that? Make it sound like I'm doing him a favor.

But he'd read me right. I wanted that talc.

We'd convoyed here from the crash site—RERT vans, FBI vans, Soliano's big SUV, Miller's little CTC sedan. I watched everybody pile out, fan out. FBI agents and Scotty's RERT team to scour the dump for the missing resin cask, on the theory the perp panicked and dumped it here. Soliano had already called for a Department of Energy helicopter to search from the air, measuring for radionuclides.

Miller came over and gave me a bow. "Welcome to Nowheresville."

"Not to me. I like the desert."

"I see that by your hands. I admire a woman who uses her hands."

My hands are chapped, nicked, the unpolished nails cut blunt. I put them in my pockets. Miller's gaze moved to my face. I fought the urge to wipe away the sweat. Even a good washing, though, would not erase the marks that the years in the field were beginning to leave, despite my devotion to hats and sunscreen. Still and all, if I had to rate my looks on the geological scale, I'd say I was in the uplift phase. I gave Miller a smile.

Soliano joined us and Miller led the way. I trailed them, gawking at the scenery.

Earthen embankments rose twenty feet high and extended in rows beyond my field of view. The nearest horizon was a six-foot chain-link fence topped by barbwire. Directly in front of us were the kind of crackerbox buildings that make staff think Nowheresville. Right now, everything glowed. Sunup gilded the dump.

I spotted the CTC logo on a low-slung warehouse with titanic doors. Underneath, the logo was decoded: *Closing The Circle Of The Atom*.

I got it. I wasn't sure I believed it, though. There's at least one cask of radioactive resins deserving of closure that's not getting buried. And if the swap theory's right, the perp stole a cask from here to fill with talc. And nobody here even noticed, until the swap was derailed with the crash. This place did not inspire great confidence in me. Maybe it was just the stress of the past few hours but I was thinking, this place promises what it cannot deliver. Closing the circle of the atom? They unleash the power of the atom and then try to put it back into the ground but it's a sitting duck, there waiting for something to go wrong. What kind of earthquake protection do they have? What kind of scumbag protection?

We passed an embankment with an open trench. It was lined with wooden crates and metal drums six rows deep and ten layers high. A forklift crawled along the trench with a fresh box in its tines, hunting for space for one more.

"That's the low-rad stuff." Miller winked. "Booties and gloves and such."

We moved on.

Ahead was an inner fence with a sign that said *Restricted Area, Controlled Access*. Miller signed us in at the guardhouse and passed out dosimeters.

Passing through the gate was like going from kindergarten to college. Now, it got serious. The open trench here was lined with concrete vaults. The package being lowered into the nearest vault was hung on the end of cables. Miller steered us behind a huge wheeled crate full of earth. It was labeled *Portable Shield*.

Good idea.

"Here's the man," Miller said, waving, "here's Mister Radwaste himself. Cassie Oldfield, Hector Soliano, I give you the dump's own manager—Milton Ballinger."

A compact man with the bantam stride of a nervous rooster approached. "Put it away Hap, these people aren't looking to be entertained, they came with a problem and I got it covered." Ballinger was middle-aged and boyish-looking. Egg bald, smooth tan from the scalp down, jawline firm to its sharp chin. He could have been an advertisement for the uranium health cures the atomic enthusiasts used to promote.

Miller said, "Milt himself came up with our dump motto—closing the circle. Wowza. That made him a rock star with the honchos."

"We just go by the initials. You know, CTC." Milt Ballinger's small eyes shone bright as new pennies.

Roy Jardine was having trouble paying attention to his job. Nerves. Well, he bet outlaws got nervous sometimes.

He needed to keep up with his recon.

He watched Ballinger come over to where Miller was. There were two strangers with Miller. A tall snooty-looking male and a female dressed like she was going for a hike. They must be plainclothes cops. That made sense. He bet they came here looking for the resin cask.

As long as they weren't looking for him. How could they be? None of them were paying attention to him. The cops were listening to Miller.

He wondered what Miller was saying. Some joke. Miller thought he was so much better than everybody, so he mocked them. One time when this dude contaminated a finger on a crapped-up wrench, Miller said he'd have to meter the dude's nose and crotch too. Ha ha.

But Jardine had to admit, when Miller mocked Ballinger, Jardine liked it.

Ballinger was talking to the cops now. He was probably bragging how he rushed to work to make sure no terrorists were launching an attack, or something. Mr. Whoop-de-doo General Manager. Jardine wondered what they'd think if they knew what Ballinger's nickname was around the dump. It was the password he used online: *Hot-Boy*. He told his bigmouth assistant it meant *hot* as in *rad*, and she told everybody. Everybody knew that when he logged onto his porn sites he didn't mean *rad*.

Jardine watched Hot-Boy bullshitting the cops.

Milt Ballinger jabbed a finger at the CTC flatbed from the crash site. "Just unloading the last package."

Indeed, only one of the casks recovered from the crash remained on the flatbed. The truck was parked within a coned-off zone. A crane loomed.

Soliano eyed the cask. "It contains what it should contain?"

"Hundred percent," Ballinger said.

"You know this how?"

"Because it's hot," Miller put in. "Notice how we're remote-handling it?"

I watched as the remote-operated crane attached a grappling device to the cask. Here's where it happened, if the perp tried this before and succeeded. Here's where the dummy cask got craned off the truck and, maybe, got jostled and, perhaps, shed grains of talc. I was going to have to get up there in the unloading zone. Up there where it's too hot to touch. I had my own monitor—I wore the laser spectrometer slung over my shoulder like a purse—but it was not remote-operable.

Ballinger nudged Soliano. "See that gal over there with the tallywhacker?"

We looked at the suited figure poking a long telescoping wand into the cask lid assembly. Only way to tell she was a *she* was by the color of her booties, hot pink.

"She's not doing it long distance for grins."

"And what," Soliano said, "does this tallywhacker tell her?"

"She's reading the surface dose rate." Ballinger hooked his thumbs into his belt buckle, a brass horseshoe. "See, these're high-gamma resins, gonna throw off some serious dose."

"How often do you receive these serious resins?"

"Often as somebody has nasty messes to clean up."

I spoke. “What happens if the serious resins—the ones that are missing—get loose in the environment?”

“Depends.” Ballinger shifted. “If they get cleaned up in time.”

“In time for what?”

“Before they release their rads.”

“Into the air?”

“Yeah. Air, soil, water, that’d be the worry.”

Hap Miller sighed. “And then, by and by, we’d get John Q Public asking what’s your plutonium doing in my coffee?”

I stared. “Are you serious?”

“Now and then,” Miller said.

“C’mon,” Ballinger said, “we got *one* missing cask. You find it, we’ll bury it.”

Soliano’s face sharpened. “You are certain this has not happened before?”

“Darn right. We keep track of every shipment.”

“How?”

“Gal over there with the tallywhacker matches her readings to the numbers on the shipping manifest. Manifest says what’s in the load—types of rads, curie count, tracking numbers, the whole shooting match.”

Soliano frowned. “The manifest cannot be altered?”

“Doesn’t matter. Even if some knothead diddled it, we’ll catch it. See, the shipper sends us an electronic copy to check against the papers that go in the truck. Got that crypto stuff, real secure.”

“Not in my experience.”

“Sure, fine, nothing’s foolproof but we take all reasonable precautions.” A stitch of sweat appeared on Ballinger’s lip. “This...incident...this is a first.”

“Your facility has had no problems before?”

Ballinger licked the sweat off his lip. "No more'n anybody else's."

"Anti-nuclear agitation?"

"Nah nah, we don't get that crap here."

"Right," Miller put in, "the locals love us. We employ them. And once a year the feds make the good citizens of Beatty pee in a cup, just to keep us honest."

"Listen," Ballinger said, "I myself grew up in Beatty and there was real competition for jobs here. Course, you need serious training if you wanna go far in this biz."

I wondered if some local was upset about not getting a job here, if this was a question of sour-grapes sabotage. My attention caught on a suited figure checking the mechanics of a truck filled with sand. He kept glancing at us, like he expected Ballinger to come correct him. I wondered if he was new on the job. He abruptly turned his back. Name on his tape was Jardine. My attention returned to the issue at hand. I said, "Mr. Ballinger, I'd like to check the unloading area."

"For what?"

"Talc. On the chance our perp tried this before. And succeeded."

"Missy, that's frigging nuts."

I flushed. I was beat, out of my element, and not a little hungry. I said, "I'd still like to monitor."

"Oookay, but you're not going out there unsupervised and you're sure not going right now."

I did not really care to go out there right now. The suited figures, retreating behind a portable shield, did not care to be out there either. The sand truck guy, Jardine, threw us another glance. I fought the urge to wave. I folded my arms and watched the delicate dance of the crane boom as it lifted the cask from the flatbed. The operator directed this dance with a handheld remote, guided by a camera mounted on the boom. I held my breath. I guessed he held his.

"What puzzles me," Soliano said, "is why the perp filled the dummy cask with talc—the cask we found at the crash site. Why not simply leave it empty?"

"Nah nah," Ballinger said, "that'd set off alarm bells. Package gotta weigh what the manifest says it weighs—that's how we adjust the crane boom angle."

"I see. He is clever."

"No he's not. Because he's not gonna sneak it past us. Not today, not last week, not ever. See, it's gonna get metered and if it contains talc we're gonna say, well that cask isn't throwing off any gammas. Then we're gonna sample and find out why not."

"Who is going to say? The woman with the tallywhacker?"

"Her, today. Another day, whoever on the cask team signs up." Ballinger blew a shot of air onto his moist upper lip. "How's it matter?"

"You tell it to me. We have ruled out the manifest, which is possible to diddle. It is possible to spoof the weight, with talc. But it is not possible for a cask of talc to give off gammas, as you explain." Soliano lifted his palms. "Consequently, the person metering the cask is a key player. That person could falsely report, yes?"

Ballinger turned to Miller.

"Moi? The site radiation safety officer god? Falsely report?"

"You join the cask team, Hap? Criminy, just go get the roster."

I watched Hap Miller saunter off, feeling a little naked without the radiation safety officer god on immediate watch. And then my attention returned, like a grappling hook had got hold of it, to the unloading zone. The crane boom swung slowly, so slowly that if it were moving a bucket of water not a drop would spill. It came to a halt over the trench, bobbed, and the cask sank into its concrete coffin.

Almost time.

Jardine was doing better now. Doing the job. Handling the recon.

He came back to the unloading zone and checked the hydraulics on the boom lift truck then gave the operator the okay, and the operator back-filled the cask caisson with sand, and Jardine watched the procedure like he cared.

What he cared about was why Miller had suddenly left. Did something happen?

And now Ballinger and the cops were watching Jardine and Jardine's skin prickled and it wasn't just the sweat inside his suit. But if they knew something they would have already come for him.

Still, maybe it was time to go. He put his tools in the caddy and casually strolled past the enemy toward the security gate.

"Yo, Roy!" Ballinger called out.

Jardine nearly died.

"Come on over here."

"Roy's a little hoity-toity," Ballinger confided.

The man slowly came our way.

"This here's Roy Jardine," Ballinger said. "Roy, these people are helping out with the incident. Need you to assist the lady. Go ahead and unmask."

Jardine unhooded and threaded the straps of his facepiece over a long braided ponytail. He pushed up the facepiece.

I tried not to stare but... Holy moly.

Soliano spoke, low, to Ballinger. "Mr. Jardine's...this is significant?"

"His *face*? Nah nah. See, awhile back there was a little, uh, incident with a cesium-137 source. You know, kind they use for gauges, or cancer treatments? Was a prank that went out of control." Ballinger clapped Jardine on the shoulder. "Okay by you, Roy, I tell them what happened?"

"You just did, Mr. Ballinger."

It didn't sound okay by Jardine. He had a nasal voice that broke as it rose. And it didn't look okay by him. He held his head high. He had a high forehead, skin pulled tight by the skinned-back hair in the tight ponytail. Wide-set brown eyes, down-turned at the corners. Flattened nose, spreading at the nostrils. Long horsey jaw in which the small mouth got lost. Large irregular oval on his left cheek, with a mottled interior and a rim that wormed around the crater.

I was not bothered by the scar. My little brother Henry had scars. The last one, which I remember best, was a dent like a jack-o-lantern grin below his knee where the joint lining had been excised. So Jardine's scar didn't bother me. It was his expression that hurt. He looked so very sad.

Soliano asked, "Who played this prank?"

"Never found out," Ballinger said. "Called in the Sheriff but no luck. Still, CTC officials put their trust in me to handle things and that's what I did. Ran a lessons-learned session for all my people. Attendance mandatory. And I made dead sure the company covered Roy's medicals. Pain and suffering, to boot."

Soliano turned to Jardine. "This resolution satisfied you?"

"Yeah."

I watched his scarred face. I've seen lesser insults be motive for mayhem.

Soliano pulled out his wallet and showed Jardine his ID. "Mr. Jardine, may I inquire as to your whereabouts last night?"

Jardine said, slowly, "Home in bed."

"Alone?"

Jardine went scarlet. He nodded.

"And your job here is?"

"Maintenance."

"Have you ever worked on the cask team?"

"No."

"Do you wish to?"

Jardine shrugged. "Takes a lot of training."

Ballinger nodded. "Darn right."

"I see." Soliano regarded Jardine. "Thank you for your time."

So that's it? I thought Jardine warranted a few more questions but I couldn't come up with any. I agreed with Soliano that the key player was whoever metered the cask. Jardine might have motive, but not the training or the opportunity. He was likely just one of those unfortunates who swallowed the insult and collected his compensation.

"All right then, Roy," Ballinger said. "Lady wants to poke around out there. I need somebody to go with her. Make sure she doesn't whack her head or trip or... Liability stuff."

Jardine turned to me and his gaze fixed on the spectrometer hanging from my shoulder. He said, in that nasal complaint, "What are you?"

I said, "Geologist."

He pursed his little mouth.

I didn't really mind having a keeper, going out there. Jardine led the way, punctiliously skirting the sand truck to prevent, I guessed, me whacking into it. My attention shifted to the ground. Here's where it happened, if the swap was run before—if the dummy cask arrived and shed grains of talc. Of course, any talc spilled here would have been scuffed into invisibility. Not, however, invisible to the laser eye of my spectrometer. I selected the chemical fingerprint for talc and began the scan. The laser illuminated the soil, scattering its constituents into their spectral wavelengths.

Jardine closed in behind me. I saw him by the long morning shadow he cast, which dogged my every move. I grew distracted, almost missing the spectrometer's chirp. I stared at the screen, at the jagged wavelength line. "Huh," Jardine said, at my ear, "how's that thing work?" It doesn't, I thought. It doesn't happen this way—first place I stick my nose and bingo. That's more than luck. That's a red flag. I said, "Give me some space." He backed off. I reset the spectro. It scanned and chirped the news. So okay, I got lucky. I shook my head and expanded the searchable grid. "There it is," Jardine said, with me again. He'd recognized the wavelength before the meter chirped. By the time I'd covered the loading zone he acted like it was his show. "Can it tell you where the stuff came from?" he wanted to know. "No," I said, huffier than I'd intended, "that takes doing geology."

As we returned from the scan, Hap Miller was returning with the roster. He gave Jardine a look. Cartoon eyes. "Hey there, Roy. You helping the purty lady?"

Jardine's face pit purpled.

"That's right," I said, "he was." Jardine had been, actually, getting on my nerves but it cost me nothing now to include the guy. "We found talc. It's all over the place." I waited for them to get it. I waited for Ballinger to object—nah nah, knothead can't sneak in a cask full of talc. I waited for Miller to make a joke.

Soliano got it first. He spun on Ballinger. "How many casks are missed from your inventory?"

"You people are making this case bigger'n it is."

I bristled. No we're not. We'd just proved Soliano's swap theory was correct. More than that—not only could the perp engineer such a swap but he'd damn well done it before. The dump manager may not like the theory but it fit the facts. So this case was getting bigger than any of us liked.

I stared at the logo on Ballinger's shirt and thought, there wouldn't even *be* a case if you CTC people did what that motto promised, closing the damn circle of the atom.

Just keep your plutonium out of my coffee.

Jardine was choking.

He tried to chew over what he'd just learned but he couldn't swallow it all. The female with her meter had found the talc and now they all knew that last night wasn't the first time and they...

He stopped. He told himself not to get ahead of himself. How far could that meter take her? The trail stopped here, at the dump.

He edged away from the little group, filling in the forms on his clipboard like he was interested. They didn't even see him any more. Snooty Mister FBI had dismissed him. He focused on the others. That bastard Ballinger. Miller the mocker. The know-it-all female.

Purty lady. His face flamed and his scar burned. She pitied him. He hated pity. Almost as much as he hated Miller's mockery.

Miller mocked everybody but what stuck in Jardine's throat was the time Miller mocked about the *prank*. Jardine's first day back on the job, bunch of them were in the break room and Miller told the Three Pigs joke. First little pig builds a house of paper. Big bad Mr. Alpha Wolf tries to get in but even a paper wall stops him. Then big bad Mr. Beta Wolf comes along and he blows right through the paper and fries the pig. Second little pig builds a house of plastic, shielding enough to stop both Alpha and Beta wolves. But along comes Mr. Gamma Wolf, who's pure penetrating energy, and he goes through those walls and fries the second pig. Third little pig builds his house of thick earth with concrete siding and steel doors, which almost stops Gamma Wolf. Still, it's not possible for Gamma to be completely stopped and so a whisker and a couple of teeth get through. Third pig doesn't even notice the nibbling.

Jardine had sat stone-faced.

The real pigs were the ones who'd snuck in while he was napping—after pulling a sixteen-hour double shift!—and planted a sealed cesium source under his pillow. Source turned out to be leaking. A beta- and gamma-emitter. Nibbled a hole in his face. *Unintended consequence*, Ballinger's incident report said, *prank that went out of control.*

He thought, now, there are always consequences.

He crawled out of the memory and continued his recon.

The group shifted and the female waved and Jardine saw a newcomer approaching. Gray-haired fellow. Dressed like he lived in the desert, same as the female. The old fellow started talking but it was the female Jardine fixed on. Not fixated—that was different, that was obsessive. Fixed just meant he'd watched her work, up close, and noticed how she paid attention to her details.

But now that he was fixed on the female he had to say she was comely. Her auburn hair was sun-kissed—he was sure the light streaks were natural, not bottle. Her eyes were soft gray, round and innocent, but her cheekbones and jaw were sharp and strong. She had a good height—he was five foot eight and her head just reached his chin. She had a good shape, a female's curves but trim. She made him think of an Old West schoolmarm. Strict but fair, resourceful in harsh circumstances. And underneath, a raw untamed streak. He wondered what it would be like to have the female braid his ponytail.

She hadn't pitied him, he decided. It had been sympathy.

He edged in closer so he could hear. They never noticed.

The old fellow was complaining how he didn't like being rushed, how he couldn't do his best work that way—and Jardine agreed, you should never rush your work—and then Jardine's heart stopped. "Tremolite" the fellow was saying and then "talc" and then he slapped hands with the female and then Mister FBI started asking questions.

Jardine didn't need it explained.

The geologists were saying they could figure out where the talc came from.

He had to get out of here now.

His legs worked first—keeping it to a stroll, just another crap worker on his way to another crap outpost of the workday. His heart raced on ahead, pumping out that adrenaline. But he kept strolling and his mind caught up to his heart and told it to slow down and finally he reached a point where he could think.

He needed to take back control. The enemy was coming. A whole posse he was sure but the biggest threats right now were the old fellow and the female.

He'd been weak, for a moment, about the female. He needed to see her clearly.

The enemy had hair the color of a worn saddle and eyes like brushed steel and dirt under her fingernails.

9

I SAID, hopefully, "I could use some breakfast."

Soliano looked at his watch.

I thought, Soliano's the kind of cop who gets so consumed with a case that he forgets to eat. He'd struck out at the dump, questioning the cask team without producing a suspect. He'd left behind two agents to follow up and now he turned his attention to the hunt for the missing radwaste. He clearly did not want to strike out again.

Nor did I. But I never forget to eat.

We'd come to Beatty to gear up. Beatty was a hamlet tucked into the high desert hills, home to trucker cafes and jazzy casino buffets and most dump employees, including Hap Miller and Milt Ballinger. Soliano had drafted them both—Miller for his health physics expertise and Ballinger as the CTC official who would take possession, and responsibility, when we tracked down the stolen property.

We were, officially, a team now: Soliano and his FBI agents, Scotty and his RERT crew, two geologists, two radwaste reps. We were a thrown-together team of contentious egos but we had a single purpose. Find the missing resin casks.

And therein, in my view, lay a mystery. Ballinger had checked inventory and found that two casks—along with two portable cranes and one shielded trailer—were missing. This certainly confirmed the theory that the swap was run twice. Once last night, interrupted. Once at an unknown earlier date, to completion. The thing was, all that talc I'd found made me think that more than one dummy cask had made it to the dump. But...only two casks were missing. It bugged me.

Soliano said, "A take-away breakfast."

Ballinger said, "Egg McMuffin's always good."

Good didn't look to enter into it but right now I'd settle for egg anything.

Ballinger and I hit the McDonald's, Miller went home for his favorite tech-tools, Scotty resupplied at the Beatty Wal-Mart, and Soliano went to borrow a Blazer from the Sheriff for Walter and me to use in our field work.

While the others scattered, Walter and I holed up in our makeshift lab in the RERT van and wolfed the McMuffins I'd bought and built ourselves a map. The perp had left one hell of a trail in talc. The dummy cask. The unloading zone. The mud from the radwaste driver, Ryan Beltzman, which Walter had found to be ripe with talc. We hoped the map would point us to the place the swaps were made, and if we got real lucky there we would find the two missing resin casks.

That place was talc country.

An hour later the team was ready to go.

There was a hard moment when Walter made to get behind the wheel of our borrowed Blazer. Doctor orders say he does not drive until another six months without another transient ischemic attack. I said, "I'll drive." Walter, jaw set, detoured to the passenger side.

Resupplied, ill-fed, cranky, we hit the road.

Our convoy backtracked on highway 95 past the dump, past the crash site, then continued another forty miles of straight asphalt through stunning high desert to the road-stop town of Lathrop Wells. There, we turned due south onto highway 373. We followed that baked desert road across the state line—373 becoming 127—back into California through mud hills and eroded buttes and a couple of cinder-block towns.

We were taking the same route the radwaste truck had traveled, in reverse. A route that, right here, cut between two of the richest talc deposits in eastern California.

Which might explain why the perp used talc to fill the dummy casks. There was a huge supply to choose from.

Walter and I had seven mines on our list, which I'd downloaded from the California Division of Mines. Seven mines that tap into schistose rock and produce a talc high in the mineral tremolite—seven candidates to produce the talc to match our evidence.

I wanted to find the source mine, more than I wanted a cold lemonade or a long hot bath, and I wanted those a great deal.

I said, "Let's go this way."

Walter, Soliano, Ballinger, Miller, and Scotty turned their heads in unison to look beyond the sandy wash to the spiky sand-plastered hills.

Our convoy was parked on the shoulder of highway 127. It was time to make a choice. Time to leave the asphalt.

Soliano said, "You prefer to turn right?"

It was, actually, a tossup. There were likely deposits to the right of highway 127, and to the left. Either way was going to take us on primitive roads.

"Yup," I said, "let's go right."

"Why?" Miller lowered his aviator shades and gazed at me. "Why does a geologist decide to turn right?"

On a hunch. On consideration of the geography as well as the geology. On a look at the starred attractions on the Google map, a reminder of what's where. From Beatty to here, for over seventy miles, our route—the radwaste driver's route—bordered a place that had attracted its share of schemers.

"To the right," I jerked a thumb, "is Death Valley."

10

IT WAS HOT.

August-in-the-desert triple-digit hot.

Moisture from last night's rain was gone and the soil and the scrub brush and my skin were sucked dry.

I yanked the water bottle from its sling and sipped. My summer field wear was made to foil heat and sun—quick-dry nylon pants and shirt, ventilated desert boots, polarized UVP shades, a Sahara hat that shaded my neck—and still I baked. Walter, ahead of me on the sandy trail, had sweated through his quick-dry shirt. Soliano looked astonishingly crisp in his khakis; he'd bought a straw cowboy hat in Beatty. Scotty was dying in black jeans and a black Australian bush hat—stylish as hell but hot, I guessed, as hazmat. Ballinger wilted in polyester and a baseball cap. Miller had switched his shorts for flaming orange parachute pants. Bart Simpson stayed. Miller's redhead skin was shaded by a wide-brim fedora that was surprisingly un-cartoonish.

We'd turned right off highway 127 onto a dirt road and then bumped across a salt-encrusted delta up into the Ibex Hills.

Striped in sedimentary layers like a tabby cat, the hills showed blazes of pure white.

It was a short steep hike up a sandy trail to the mine entrance. The hillside was littered with old timbers and the ruins of a long chute. White tailings spilled down the slope.

I envisioned the perp with a shovel.

Walter and I divided our labor. He sampled the soil, looking for a match to the radwaste driver's coating: the place he had rolled in the mud. I went for the mine, looking for the mother lode: a match to our tremolite talc.

Scotty preceded me into the tunnel, metering for gases or gammas. When he reappeared and raised a thumb, I headed inside to grab an unweathered dishful of talc.

We were hotter, wearier, grumpier, and the shadows were longer. Thunderclouds had gathered. The convoy, visible down below, was parked in a flood plain. I kept an eye on the cloud-to-blue-sky ratio, knowing how fast summer storms could brew up.

Mine number four on our list was a ragged mouth rimmed with snow-white crystals shining like teeth.

Easier access to this mine than the first two, should that count with the perp.

Scotty trudged in, trudged out, thumbs-up.

A decaying sign post guarded the entrance, warning: *Trespassers Will Be Prosecuted.* A bullseye target completed the thought.

I went inside and shined my light.

A tall straight tunnel shot into white depths. A pepperminty smell stung my nose. The ceiling moved. I shifted my beam and it caught splintery old timbers hung with pale furred bodies.

Leathery wings flared. I let the beam plummet, revealing piles of guano on broken ore tracks.

"Here's the deal," I said, "I leave you alone and you leave me alone."

The ceiling settled down and I turned my attention to the walls. A slash of very dark rock caught my eye—diabase, a much older intruder than the bats. The diabase, eons ago, had plunged into the carbonate rock, ripping out oxides and replacing them with magnesium and silicon, and thus rudely metamorphosed the carbonate rock into talc.

I plucked a white crumb and slid it between thumb and forefinger. It flaked apart, like filo dough.

I liked it.

I got my phone and turned on flash and photographed the walls and floor.

I took five samples near the entrance. Scotty had only metered the main tunnel; there were offshoots right and left and likely down. I was no more likely to charge deeper into this mine than I was to start tap dancing, and it wasn't the bats that deterred me.

Outside, Soliano watched while I set up my little field lab. I did a quick hand-lens study then moved to the spectrophotometer. It was a cousin of the meter I'd used at the dump, the meter that so interested Roy Jardine. This one would impress him more because it'll tell me not only what I have, it'll tell the concentration. Talcs differed according to the parent rock from which they formed and the minerals that grew alongside—like tremolite.

It will tell me if I've found the source.

I mixed my sample with a pillow of indicator compound then inserted it into the SP. I recorded the numbers that came up on the window. I repeated the process with my evidence talc. Same numbers came up.

I sat back to savor it. This was what I dreamed of, when I dreamed of work, which was more often than was probably healthy. The moment of capture, the moment when I'd grab hold of a piece of the earth and give it an identity. A name, a set of vital statistics, and—the holy grail of forensic geology—an address. I tracked you down, pal. I know where you hang. You're mine.

I told Soliano, "We're here."

He produced his cell phone. While he talked, demanding every piece of data recorded on the Serendipity Talc Mine, I opened my water bottle and drank long and deep. Not cold lemonade but it would do.

Scotty went down to the RERT vans and returned with two team members, the three of them dressed out. They paused at the mine entrance to set their facepieces and breathers, then lumbered in.

I saw Walter come out of a van and start up the hill.

Hap Miller sat down beside me. He lifted his fedora and poured water over his head. His hair darkened to hematite, a match to the red bandana tied around his hat. "Hot enough for you, Buttercup?"

"Buttercup?"

"Nickname I picked out for you. Now, you ask why I'd name a brunet with gray eyes after a yellow flower?"

I bit. "Okay, why?"

"It's due to the egg yolk dripped on your shirt."

It took all the will I possessed not to look down.

"And please do call me by *my* nickname. Hap, short for Happy. Happy to look out for your well-being, ma'am."

For all his joking, he didn't strike me as particularly happy.

Well, I didn't strike me as a yellow flower, either. "Thanks," I said, "Hap."

Walter topped the trail and made a beeline for us. I studied his face. Red, but so's everyone else's. Streaming sweat, but sweat's good—he's hydrated. I said, "Where are you going?"

He tried to speak, then lifted the little ice chest. It had come with the Blazer; we were putting it to work.

"Beer?" Hap said.

"Soil samples," I said. "Sorry."

"No problemo. Anyway, I got snacks." Hap unshouldered his day pack and pulled out a bag of chips.

Walter joined us and Hap offered the chips. They were greenish-brown.

"Seaweed," Hap said. "Taste like Doritos only good for you. Full of alginic acid, which binds itself with any strontium-90 we mayhap pick up in the course of our travels."

I stared. "How about not picking any up?"

"How about being prepared? Boy Scout motto."

"I know the motto. I was a Girl Scout."

Hap grinned. "Guess that means we're meant for one another!"

Walter slid me a look; Walter thought not. Walter already worried about my flighty love life. And Walter, frowning at me, was clearly thinking the last thing I needed right now was to take a fancy to an ex-Boy Scout warning me about the risks of radiation. I slid my own look at Hap Miller. Never met anyone quite like him. I said, "What's up with strontium-90?"

"Just a for-instance." Hap shrugged. "For instance, it's a nuclide that resembles calcium. Get yourself a dose and your body sucks it to the bone, like it's calcium. And it sits there happy as a clam emitting radiation for its entire half-life. You two know the half-life of strontium-90, mayhap?"

I said, "Not offhand."

"Twenty-eight point nine years. I'd guess that's close to your own age."

Twenty-nine point three, actually. I saw where Hap was going with this. I didn't want to follow. I didn't need a health physicist to tell me what excessive radiation could do to the reproductive system. I was well-versed in that lesson.

"Mr. Miller," Walter said, "you might limit your advice to the strictly useful."

"Sure thing. Might it be useful to point out that a man your age is at special risk? Your cells are already in the decay mode, if I'm not taking too much liberty to say so."

"That you are."

I glanced at Walter. In the brutal summer light, his face looked eroded--compressed by the forces of the years and folded by the weight of the job.

I said, to Hap, "You trying to scare us?"

"Just encouraging you to pay attention." He held out the chip bag. "And Walter, please do call me Hap."

Happy to look out for our well-being. Fine, I guessed it could use looking out for. I took a chip. The brine puckered my tongue. It wasn't Doritos but I urged Walter to try one. He did, and made a face. I wondered how many radioactive isotopes Walter had absorbed over the years. A good deal more than I had because he'd been around a good deal longer. I offered him another chip.

We were finishing off the seaweed when Soliano joined us. "We have a development. We have an owner. She lives in Shoshone, that previous town which we passed through. She will be joining us," he glanced at his watch, "within the hour. In the meanwhile, I have obtained a telephone search warrant for the Serendipity."

It took me a moment. "This is an active mine?" I'd been thinking the perp chose an abandoned mine, where he could take what he wanted and go about his business in private. But we had an owner.

"That is not all," Soliano said. "We have a primary suspect."

We waited for it.

"Roy Jardine."

11

"CRIMINY," Milt Ballinger said, "*Roy's* the knothead?"

"Suspected knothead." Soliano did not smile. "My agents report that he left work approximately four hours ago, shortly after our own departure. Taken sick. He is not at his home, or at Beatty's medical facilities."

I felt suddenly sick myself. The heat. The McMuffin I'd wolfed. The memory of Roy Jardine. It was a tactile memory, his hazmat sleeve swish-swishing against my nylon shoulder as he tracked my hunt for talc.

"Left sick?" Ballinger said. "That's all?"

"No, that is not all. My agents have learned that Mr. Jardine's maintenance job includes the calibration of instruments. He spot-checks meters, an on-going basis. He is the only maintenance worker with this expertise. His co-worker reports that he volunteered for this duty, which often required overtime. Presumably, on a day of his choosing, he could choose to spot-check the meter of the person monitoring an incoming dummy cask. He could, for that moment, become the key player." Soliano regarded Ballinger. "You did not know the scope of his job?"

Ballinger wiped the sweat from his skull. "Hey, I got over a hundred employees. Don't have time to get into everybody's nitty-gritty."

"I have the time," Soliano said. "I have issued a be-on-the-lookout for a blue Ford pickup registered to Roy Jardine. From you, I will require his work records."

"You got fingerprints or anything?"

"Unfortunately, the hijacker, at the crash site, appears to have been a fastidiously careful man. He wore booties. He perhaps also wore a full suit, since my techs have recovered no prints, hair, fiber, or DNA—other than the driver's. Nevertheless, we will do a collection at Mr. Jardine's residence."

Ballinger shrugged.

"You appear reluctant to accept him as suspect."

"Nah nah, it's just...that'd mean Roy's a killer."

"Anybody's a killer," Hap said, "if they're pushed."

Walter said, "That's a fallacy."

I recalled Jardine's offended reaction when Hap teased him about helping the 'purty lady.' I wondered if Hap was worrying about having pushed Roy Jardine.

The dented white SUV peeled around the parked vans and gunned up the hill and jammed to a stop in an eruption of dust.

A woman swung out and stumped toward us. She was barrel-shaped and dressed in white—white shirt, white bandana, white jeans, white cowboy boots—a white barrel cactus of a woman. She wore a white straw cowboy hat akin to Soliano's and she carried, clamped by one arm, a shotgun. She barreled up to Soliano. "This is private fuckin property, what the hell you people doin here?"

Soliano showed his ID. "Christine Jellinek? My name is

Hector Soliano, I am FBI, and you will if you please place the weapon on the ground."

She didn't budge. "I got a fuckin permit."

"If you please." Soliano's hands flexed. "Now."

She spat. She turned and stumped to her SUV and stowed the shotgun. She came back, whipping off her hat to wipe her brow.

"Whooeee," Ballinger whispered, "she won't win no beauty contest."

Her face was like unfired clay that's been left in the sun. Her eyes were nearly hidden under slumping lids. It was hard to tell her age but her hair was yellow-streaked gray. Her skin, desert-varnish brown, looked like it might crack at the slightest touch. She caught us staring and clamped her hat back on, yanking its brim low.

My own skin scorched. I wouldn't welcome scrutiny, either, not after all my days in the field.

She halted in front of Soliano and said, "Now you can all fuck off."

"I am afraid not, Ms. Jellinek."

"You wanna address me, you address me by the name I go by which is not la-dee-da miss anything. I go by Chickie."

What is it with all the nicknames? I wondered. Is it the heat? Is it the solar radiation? Do people around here forget who they are?

Soliano watched Chickie intently. "You are not curious about us?"

"You're all fuckin rangers far as I care. This is my property and you got no right to go in there."

"I am curious about you. How is it that you are allowed to mine in a national park wilderness area?"

Walter cleared his throat. "Actually, Hector, she couldn't stake a new claim here but if her claim is pre-existing, it's valid."

Chickie nodded. “Damn right.”

“Providing,” Walter added, “that she meets Park Service conditions.”

“Fuckers’re killin me with their conditions.”

“Then perhaps,” Walter said, “you’d best abandon your claim.”

She raised a middle finger.

Perhaps she’d thought she had an ally in Walter, but she was damn wrong. Walter loves to poke around old mines and he finds the geology of precious ores an absorbing hobby—and, once, key to a case—but he prefers to see the geology left in place in national parks and wilderness areas.

"Chickie," I said, "you have a colony of nesting bats in your mine.”

“So the fuck what?”

“You start blasting, you’ll disturb them. Aren’t they protected?”

“Lotsa mines in the park got bats.”

“Yes but does the Park Service know about yours?”

Her eyes narrowed. And then suddenly widened—she was looking past me to the mine entrance, where Scotty and his team had appeared. They looked like some kind of futuristic miners from the depths.

Scotty came our way, shaking his head.

Soliano turned to me—they all turned to me—and I said, “All I can tell you is, this is as perfect a match for the talc as I could want.” I watched Chickie. She didn’t ask what I meant, didn’t ask about the hazmat suits and the Geiger counters, and she didn’t, oddly, ask what Scotty and his team were hunting in her mine.

I would have asked, in her place.

Soliano said, “Ms. Jellinek, talc has been found at the scene of a crime. Our geologist has identified it as originating here.”

Chickie glared. "She's wrong."

"Do you know a man by the name of Roy Jardine?"

"Never heard of him."

Soliano took out his cell phone and showed her a digital photo. "Do you know this man?"

"Never saw him."

"Did you sell your talc to this man?"

"Can't sell it to nobody."

"You are having difficulty with the approval process?"

She spat. "I got a fuckin mine's not bringin in a fuckin cent cuz the fuckin backpackin whale-watchin bat-lovin assholes got the government by the short hairs and they're stealin my rights. So somebody wants to pay me for my fuckin talc I'll fuckin well sell it."

Soliano pounced. "Then someone did buy talc from you?"

"No, someone didn't. Maybe your fucker stole it. I can't afford a guard, I can't even afford to fix up this old shit." She jerked a thumb at the crumbling ore chutes and bins. "But I will. I been workin other people's mines for twenty years." She jutted her chin. "You see this face? I got this face workin sunup to sundown and I earned it. This face is a *mine owner's* face, now. This is a proud face, fuckers."

I'd sure give her that. And I wondered what role pride might have played. If Jardine chose this mine because it was easier access here than to others nearby, he likely would have assumed—as we had—that this place was abandoned. And then the woman in white showed up with her shotgun. A woman whose mine, and pride, were not to be trifled with. I asked her, "If you caught someone stealing, would you report him?"

Her venomous look swung to me.

"Or, you could tell him to pay or you'll call the cops. A market of one is better than none. Right?"

She studied me. "Don't need no thief money, girly. I got a big market lined up. Know what it is?"

Sweat sluiced down my back.

She came closer, tipping her hat brim back, bringing her face up to mine. "You wanna know?"

I could not look away. She had that effect, like a desert sidewinder. You wouldn't want to turn your back.

She raised her index finger. She opened her mouth, emitting an overripe odor like fruit that has turned. She licked her finger. It glistened in the sun. It hit me like a snake strike, scoring my left cheek, and then withdrew.

My skin shriveled where the wet trail evaporated into the triple-digit air.

Chickie examined her finger. "Dirt," she said.

I stiffened. What's wrong with dirt?

Her own face was shiny clean. "Ever wear makeup?"

I said, tight, "Yes."

She bared her teeth, white as her hat. "Then stick your nose down out of the air, girly. You're my market."

Hap gave me the bandana from his fedora. I wiped her touch from my face. I wanted to disinfect it. I tried to return the bandana but Hap put up his hands: a gift.

And then I thought, maybe this was not a market question at all. Maybe Chickie was an accomplice. Maybe Chickie was counting on another source of income while waiting for Park Service approval to sell her talc.

"Ms. Oldfield," Soliano said, "you are certain the talc originates here?"

"You want certain, go with DNA. I can give you probability. I can tell you the proportion of tremolite to talc, down to parts per billion, in the evidence talc. I can tell you it's consistent with the talc here, and it's inconsistent with the three other mines I sampled. I can't promise there's no other location it could have come from. Maybe there's a mine out there with talc as good a match as this one." I pocketed the bandana. "And maybe pigs can fly."

Soliano turned to Scotty. "Let us look again here."

Scotty groaned.

Walter said, "In the meanwhile, I have soils to sample around here."

I nodded. It was, actually, within the realm of possibility that our evidence talc did not come from this mine—leaving flying pigs aside—and I'd be a whole lot happier if Walter could match the mud samples from Ryan Beltzman to this place. I moved to follow Walter, to lend a hand. I caught Chickie watching me. Her hooded eyes had slitted to emit a whitish gleam. It was, I thought, a truly pissed look and it was directed at me, the fucker who'd claimed to trace the talc to her mine.

That look convinced me I'd found the right address.

12

WALTER and I followed the geology and our noses around the hill to the backside of Chickie's mine. Here was another entrance, a back door. Just outside this tunnel, white mine tailings spilled to mix with the native soil.

I photographed. Walter knelt to sample.

It didn't take a forensic genius to read the story. Marks in the dried mud—knees, elbows, one unmistakable butt print, bootprints hither and thither—showed one hell of a fight and chase.

Walter agreed. "Preliminary," he said, peering through the hand lens, "but I suspect the driver acquired his mud here."

I glanced at the rough road that ran down to join the road our convoy had taken. Not fit for the radwaste truck but a more nimble vehicle could navigate it. In fact, there were faint tire tracks. I looked back to the tunnel. Gated, with a padlocked chain. I wondered if Roy Jardine had a key.

Chickie was astonished that some fucker changed the lock on

her gate and she grudgingly gave permission for Scotty to use bolt cutters.

It didn't take Scotty long to meter the tunnel. "Not hot," he said, "but you won't believe what's in there."

I swallowed. What's in there?

Soliano went in. Then he summoned Walter and me, Hap and Ballinger.

The tunnel was wide and straight and dead-ended in a large room, like a driveway into a garage. A two-car garage. The vehicle on the left looked like it belonged here. It was dented and scratched and mud-spattered—a high-clearance offroader with a winch and cable drum mounted on the front bumper. All four tires were flat.

Soliano shined his flashlight at the right front tire, illuminating a ragged hole.

I registered the tire damage, and the mud, which I was going to want to sample, only right now the tires were not the main event.

The main event was the trailer behind the offroader.

It was a brutish beast. Big enough to haul a hefty payload. Tough, clearly, with big-knuckle bolts and beefy tires, now flat. Built for crazy guys on testosterone weekends hauling their gear where the pavement doesn't go. Built for a crazy guy hauling stolen resin casks. The back of the trailer was gated with a fold-up steel ramp. A vaulted steel cover hung open and wide, like a clamshell.

The vehicle parked beside it was another beast entirely.

Half forklift, half crane, all business. It had a telescoping crane boom with its grappling arms wide open, as if for a hug. Slotted into one side were attachments: hooks, fork tines, a scoop. It had pneumatic tires with deep treads. It looked like it could go anywhere.

Arrayed against the mine wall were open crates of protective gear. Gloves, booties, suits, silvery tarps.

Hap whistled—surprise, marvel. “Lookee here. Boy’s got his own setup.”

Soliano eyed Ballinger. “This equipment is from your facility?”

Ballinger gaped. “Knothead helped himself to the store.”

One thing I knew for certain—Roy Jardine was in no way a knothead. Or, despite the events of last night, a screwup. This setup showed a level of competence that put me on high alert.

Soliano made a slow survey of the room. “I believe we have found the place of the swap. Mr. Ballinger, tell me how it is done.”

Ballinger jerked. “Me?”

“Easy Milt,” Hap said, “Hector just wants you to role-play. Pretend you’re Roy.”

“No frigging way.”

“If you please,” Soliano said. “You know this equipment, Mr. Ballinger. I wish your perspective.”

Ballinger gave Soliano a cautious look, then a nod.

Soliano returned the nod. "And so. You steal a cask, bring it here—perhaps in your blue Ford pickup. And here you fill it with talc, using this...forklift?”

“Telehandler,” Ballinger said sourly. “Roy could’ve.”

“Very good. So now you have a cask of talc. Meanwhile, your partner Ryan Beltzman approaches on the highway—that is the radwaste truck route?”

“That little twerp,” Ballinger said, “he was in on it?”

“Difficult to make the swap on your own, yes?”

“Wouldn’t know.”

Soliano’s face incised into a smile. “Let us put it all together. It is late night, little traffic, so Mr. Beltzman pulls just off the highway so the transponder will not show anything odd. And there he waits. Can you deliver the talc cask to him?"

"Sure I can." Ballinger's chest roostered out. "I mean, Roy can. Telehandler holds the cask like a baby. Drives like a dream. Go right out that tunnel down to the highway. Set the talc cask on the flatbed, pick up the resin cask." Ballinger warmed to it. "I'd do it remote for the hot load—telly's remote-operable. Then drive it back up here and set the resin cask in that trailer. Trailer'll handle it."

Soliano was nodding. "And then what?"

"Then the twerp takes the dummy cask with the shipment to the dump, and the knothead takes the resin cask wherever he frigging takes it."

"The *depot*, we will call it. Where would you site the depot?"

"With that rig," Ballinger indicated the offroader-trailer, "I'd be going somewhere off in the wild."

"What would you do when you got there?"

"Unload the frigging cask. With a telly. Remember, knothead stole two of my telehandlers."

Soliano kept nodding. "And then?"

"Come back here."

"Ah yes. Ready for the second swap, when the time comes. Last night. Which, to your dismay, went wrong."

Ballinger snorted. "Maybe I'm not such a hotshot."

"More than a mistake, I think. You, or your partner, shot out the tires. To stop the proceedings, yes?"

"Why I'd do that?"

"Cold feet? Change of plans?" Soliano flipped a hand. "In any case, there follows the chase—Mr. Beltzman in his truck, Mr. Jardine in his pickup."

Soliano, I noticed, had just switched to calling the perp Jardine, instead of putting Ballinger in that role. Ballinger seemed to notice too.

"And then," Soliano said coolly, "we come to the end of the scenario. The crash, the shooting."

"Almost," Ballinger said, easy now. "Then Roy comes into *work* this morning. That's just nutso."

Maybe, I thought. But Jardine had learned something at work, hadn't he? He learned he was leaving tracks. In talc. I'd made that plain enough, letting him know who was the geologist and who wasn't.

"If this scenario is correct," Walter said, "where is the resin cask now?"

We looked, as one, at the telehandler with its open arms empty. We'd seen the talc cask at the crash site. More than seen. So that meant the resin cask was here, last night, snuggled in the telly's arms like a toxic baby. So at some point Jardine came back to retrieve it? I figured I knew when: while we were shopping and eating and going about our business in Beatty. I said, chilled, "Jardine got the jump on us."

Hap whistled again. "Boy's got cojones."

"That he has." Soliano regarded Hap. "And what does a boy with cojones do with this cask?"

"My turn to be Roy?" Hap shuddered. "Depends on his motive. Who knows? That guy's brain-pan is beyond my ken."

I said, "What about the drawing on the radwaste truck?"

"You asking," Hap said, "what if he unleashes the beads?"

I nodded.

Hap ducked.

We had no idea where Jardine had gone from here. We had no soils from his blue Ford pickup to trace. So Walter and I went to the offroader rig: here was something we might be able to follow. Find the depot where he stored his toxic babies.

Walter opened the field kit.

Soliano herded the others out, promising to return with his trace analysis techs.

I doubted the techs would have much more luck here than they'd had at the crash site. Jardine was surely equally fastidious in here. It was protocol, certainly, to wear protective clothing when you're playing swap with radioactive waste. And even when you panic. I could see Jardine—couple hours ago? Spooked, rushing, but protocol says you suit up first. I hoped, fervently, that he'd worked up a nasty sweat. I no longer pitied him, with his sad face. I wanted to put him away, down deep somewhere where the sun don't shine. I wanted to find his toxic cargo and see it buried where it belonged and it damn well didn't belong running around on little cat feet out in the environment.

I yanked open my field kit and spilled half the contents.

Walter looked. "Focus, Cassie."

I inhaled, exhaled. That Zen thing.

We set to work. Walter began with the trailer and I took the offroader.

The treads of all the tires were ripe with dried mud but that didn't set my heart racing. Oh, we'd likely be able to ID it but there'd be no way to tell in what order the mineral components had been acquired. With every rotation of the wheels, the tires would have mashed the stuff, mixing the new with the old.

I decided to start on the fenders, where there should be something worth having. Tires mash soil but they also kick up glop onto the underside of fenders, which preserve and protect, one layer after another. I squatted at the right rear fender and shined my flashlight deep underneath. It was lovely. I made three cuts then slid my scalpel down to the metal and pried out a fine wedge of soil. I placed it gently in the specimen dish so as not to spoil the sequence of deposition.

The trailer, unfortunately, had no fenders. Walter made do with the tires.

We came out of the tunnel with our little ice chest packed with samples and told Soliano we'd need a few hours in our makeshift lab to build a soil map.

Hap was stretched out in the shade. "Map?" He lifted his fedora. "Where you going?"

"To hell." Chickie spat. She sat on the tailings heap. She'd claimed to have no knowledge of what was stored in her unused tunnel, and there was no evidence linking her to Jardine. No probable cause for Soliano to detain her. Still, she remained, keeping watch on her mine.

Walter said, mildly, "Hell is not on the itinerary."

I presumed not.

"Jardine left a trail," Walter said. "We'll be following it."

Soliano looked at his watch. "Good. Alert me before you leave. My agents and Mr. Hemmings' team will be expanding the search around here. We must select a place to rendezvous, at the end of the day." He thought. "We will establish headquarters at park headquarters—Furnace Creek. Check in at the ranger station."

We were huddling like high-school freshmen to exchange cell phone numbers when I reminded myself to ask Scotty if he could spare a couple gallons of Wal-Mart water for our field trip.

13

Roy Jardine had a problem.

There was hot cargo in the bed of his pickup, and his pickup was registered in his name, Roy Jardine, and that was not being incognito.

Last night, sitting at home in his Lazy-boy, he had wrestled with the problem of the resin cask. After the showdown with Beltzman, after things went critical, he had decided the safe thing was to leave the cask where it was, in the talc mine. Then this morning, Jardine had gone undercover at the dump to do recon—and that turned out to be a real smart decision. He'd learned what the enemies were up to. He'd had a bad moment when Mister FBI questioned him, but he'd played that real cool. The real danger was the geologists with their talc-sniffing noses.

That changed everything. He'd barely had time to get to the mine and recover the cask.

But he'd aced it.

And then he had to decide what to do with it.

He couldn't deliver it for use in the grand mission because he needed the trailer rig, and that loser Beltzman had crippled it.

This cask was an orphan now.

Orphaned cask. New enemies. The math was clear. The only thing that wasn't clear was how and when he would use it against his enemies. Until that became clear, he needed to store it.

So here he was traveling this two-lane road with a hot cargo, checking the rearview mirror so often his neck hurt. Nobody on this road but jackrabbits. And him. He checked the rearview. The cask rode low because he had loaded it on its side so it would look incognito under the tarp. He was proud how he'd improvised. He'd used a lead curtain from the supply box—and the curtain had grommets! And he had bungee cords in his toolbox! And *voila*, as snooty people say. And the tarp did more than just shield the cask. He'd filled the pickup bed with talc, for more shielding, and the tarp kept the talc from flying away. Tarp and talc, two layers of shielding. In job eighteen redundancy was a lifesaver that he'd taken to heart. He would have liked to stay dressed out—that was triple redundancy—but that wouldn't be incognito.

Where he was going, he had to look normal.

He needed a safe place to store the pickup and its cargo and then he needed to rent a car. He needed to do these two things without drawing attention. The best place to do this, he'd decided, was Las Vegas.

He took jackrabbit roads when he could. When he hit the highway he drove the speed limit.

When he reached Vegas all went smoothly. The clerk at the self-storage warehouse didn't give a crap what was under the tarp. The clerk at the Hertz didn't give a crap who he was, didn't notice that his name was fake because he'd planned weeks ago that he'd need a cover and he'd spent time on the details of the perfect fake ID.

How about that. The skills of his eleventh crap job—clerk at the DMV—turned out to be useful all these years later.

After leaving Vegas he tooled along the highway riding high. Incognito in his crap rental car, with his ponytail tucked up under the Budweiser ball cap he'd bought at the Rite-Aid. He'd be at his hideout in a few hours and when he got there he'd treat himself to a sponge bath.

He made a call on his cell phone. Nothing new, he was told. Call me when there is, he said. He hung up; it was illegal to talk on the phone while driving.

He drove all the way into Death Valley, just another tourist in his cheap rental car, and he parked at the Ranch motel in Furnace Creek in plain sight with all the other rental cars. From there, he had a long hike ahead of him. His nerves were strung tight until he cleared the settlement and disappeared into the canyons.

He hiked up to a ridge top for good cell reception and phoned again. It rang and rang. Okay, that just meant no privacy to answer his call. He'd try again in five minutes.

It sure was hot. He opened his pack and selected a foil bag but he couldn't tear it open with sweaty fingers.

He got out the Buck knife.

He'd had it forever. It was a clip-point hunting knife he'd bought the first time he went camping. He'd gone alone, sixteen-year-old kid setting out from home, sixteen-year-old man when he returned. He'd hunted and skinned a squirrel for his dinner. He'd whittled a stick to roast marshmallows. He'd cut rope to hang his food away from animals. It was a useful knife.

He suddenly tensed, remembering the last time he'd used the knife, angling the sharp point to pry a nasty thorn out of Jersey's paw. She'd let out a yip, and then she'd licked his face in thanks.

She wouldn't mind if he used it again.

He knifed open the foil bag and tapped out a handful of pink chunks. He ate them all at once. Hideous. Tasted nothing like strawberry. Tasted nothing like ice cream. But he began to cool off. He understood this was a mental thing—the words on the bag carried their own power. *Ice cream.* Even *freeze-dried* cooled him, a bit.

He'd live on kibbles if he needed until his grand vision was fulfilled.

He checked his watch. Four minutes gone. He decided waiting the full five would be obsessive. He called.

It was answered on the first ring. *What took you so long?*

He didn't want to sound worried. He said, real cool, "I was eating ice cream."

A muffled sound. A laugh.

He ignored that. "What did they say?"

They know who you are.

He went rigid. "How?"

You fucked up.

"You don't want to address me that way."

Get real.

Roy Jardine maintained a frigid silence.

You there?

He should make some smarty joke but he couldn't think of one so all he said was, "Keep me posted."

He shut the phone. He picked up his Buck knife and held it blade out—not that anybody was going to storm the ridge but no harm in the practice. The knife calmed him. So they know. So what? They'll never find you, Roy. You're a shadow. You're ace. You're going to sit here and finish your ice cream and wait for the next call and then you're going to ground, at *Hole-in-the-Wall*. You're really an outlaw now, Roy Jardine.

He straightened his back.

He wondered what the female geologist thought about him now. Females could get swept off their feet by outlaws—look at Etta Place and the Sundance Kid. That wasn't just a movie. That was in the history books. He closed his eyes. He'd worked side by side with the female, partners almost. Close enough to smell her. Sweat, sure, but something else. Some kind of female shampoo. Strawberry?

He put a chunk of strawberry ice cream on his tongue.

And now the female smiled at him and he smiled at her and offered her real strawberry ice cream and then suddenly it was Jersey, and not the female, begging him, and the stuff in his mouth turned back to paste.

His phone rang.

He opened his eyes and answered the call.

Guess what they just found?

"I don't guess. Tell me."

He listened—at first not understanding—and then finally when he understood he bent over and vomited up strawberry chunks.

What's that sound? You there? Say something.

He couldn't. He was too sick to talk. He wiped his mouth, heartsick.

This is bad, you get it?

He said he'd have to call back. He said the signal was breaking up.

It was Roy Jardine who was breaking up. Panicking. He couldn't believe they could figure out stuff like that. From dirt under the fenders?

He rested his head on his knees and when his insides stopped crawling he put himself back together. It's not a real map, he told himself. It's dirt. They'd have to be magicians to follow that dirt. His head swam. His grand vision was flickering like one of those desert mirages. If he didn't do something his vision was going to disappear.

He said, out loud, the geologists are not magicians.

But you have to make sure. Put on your thinking cap, Roy.

He put it on. And the answer came.

14

"LOOK," I said, "do you see something moving out there?"

Walter looked up from the map in his lap and peered out his window.

We were driving north on the West Side Road—so named because it hugged the western side of the long Death Valley basin. Forty miles since we'd left the talc mine and the only moving thing we'd seen was the occasional car. And that was across the saltpan from us on the Badwater Road, which hugged the eastern side of the basin.

But it wasn't a car I'd seen out on the saltpan. It was something else.

"I suppose," Walter said, turning back to his map, "I've missed it."

Walter was breaking my heart. If he couldn't drive, he was going to be of use navigating.

As if we could get lost driving this road through open desert.

The basin floor swept before us, south to north, like an unrolling carpet of sand and salt. Where it rolled off into the far horizon, I thought I could see the curve of the earth. To the west and east the basin floor met walls of fault-scarped mountains—the view so wide I could see the floor tilt.

What I couldn't see, now, was that thing on the saltpan. Nothing moved out there.

Well, the earth shimmied as heat boiled up.

I checked the gas gauge. I asked Walter to check our cell phone signals. I glanced at Scotty's water jugs in back. There's a reason they named it Death Valley. There's a reason nobody's out and about, not in a Death Valley summer.

I'd been here only once before, and that was in the spring. My scout troop came to see the wildflowers. Fourth grade, pre-Walter, pre-geology. The only geological samples I'd got were sand in my boots and dirt in my sleeping bag. I'd been more interested in the Boy Scouts in the next campsite. A mental picture formed of little Hap in a scout uniform, all knobby knees and big bandana. Very cute. A mental picture formed of big Hap, all lean angles and a backdoor grin. I blinked. What am I doing?

Walter said, "What did it look like?"

"What?" Oh, my thing on the saltpan. "I only got a glimpse. Just a...shape."

"A mirage."

"No, it was moving."

"Temperature turbulence makes the image vibrate. And you superimpose your own thoughts upon it."

My thoughts had just been on Hap and I didn't see Hap vibrating out there now. So what was I thinking of five minutes ago, when I first saw the shape? The thing that's been in my mind, upfront or lurking, since I saw the drawing on the radwaste truck last night: the running man. I tried, now, superimposing that stick figure on the shape I'd glimpsed on the saltpan. Heat rays shimmer down like fallout and the stick runs and the salt underfoot crackles like a carpet of resin beads. No. What

I'd seen was something else. Something creeping. I almost wished it was my stick. He seemed, now, an old friend. Don't worry, old stick, we'll find the missing beads and see them buried and no scumbag's going to unleash them on you. So you can stop running. Sit down. It's hot out there. You must be tired.

"Of course," Walter said, "the scientific explanation doesn't capture the charm of a mirage."

Charm? All right. I said, "When were you last here, mirage-watching?"

"Eons ago."

"Back when the desert was a lake?"

"Before that. Back in the Precambrian."

"Cool. You *do* predate the dinosaurs."

He smiled.

I smiled, and relaxed into the Death Valley summer.

The road curved to round the apron of an alluvial fan, a fan so perfect it drew an *ahhh* from Walter. Rainwater washes earth out of the mountains and the debris comes to rest at the canyon mouths, fanning onto the valley floor. Here's the heart of Death Valley: a mammoth basin, faulted and dropped deep below sea level, bordered by knife-ridged mountains which spill their guts, here and there, in coquettish fans.

It is a huge bathtub. Things flow into it. Nothing flows out.

I began to think about water.

Water wet the soils that spattered up and pasted themselves beneath Roy Jardine's offroader fenders.

We'd spent a good three hours in our makeshift lab in Scotty's RERT van with our noses in the fender soils, trying to patch together the layers. Some layers were defined. Some weren't. The soil map at this point was a roughed-in outline. Our map, actually, resided in specimen dishes in the little ice chest in the back seat.

I said, "Let's talk about the itinerary."

Walter grunted, unhappy with the thinness of the itinerary.

"So," I said, "Roy Jardine starts up his offroader rig and..."

As if Walter could, after all, resist. "Well. The first layer says he proceeds along the dirt road, or roads, near the talc mine. And then a break—pavement."

I waved a hand at the West Side Road. "Or an oiled road."

"Keep your hands on the wheel, Cassie. Yes, a hardpack surface. However, he could have driven a few miles, or hundreds of miles, before leaving the hardpack to pick up layer two. Coarse-grained alluvium suggests he drives upon an alluvial fan."

"So somewhere in the Basin and Range." This was all Basin and Range country, valley and mountain, on and on like waves from the Sierras to the Rockies.

"Today we'll confine ourselves to Death Valley, considering the proximity of the talc mine. And it fields a few lovely candidates."

I nodded. I was liking Death Valley more and more.

"Now," Walter settled happily into it, "layer three narrows Jardine's trail a smidge. It's fine-grained alluvium, playa mud and sand. Hence, we have him crossing a riverbed or a canyon wash."

Water. I nodded.

"Layer four is more forthcoming. A grayish soil, weathered I believe from a Cambrian marine dolomite."

"The canyon we're heading for? One of your candidates?"

"The closest."

"And layer five?"

"Layer five, layer six..." He grunted. "We need more time."

I was feeling it myself. Time. Jardine killed his partner. He was on the run. He might still have the resin cask with him. "So why's he heading up your canyon?"

"There are mines."

Of course. He based his swap in a mine. Makes sense that he chose another mine to hide his stolen radwaste. A mine would provide the shielding. Surely, he would think about shielding. I pictured him, his scar, his long horsey face. So sad. So sick.

I shook him off. Focus on the itinerary. I had my own reservations, beyond the sketchiness of the map. Oh, we'd been meticulous, if rushed, in analyzing the soils. But something didn't sit right. And I couldn't put my finger on it. Like our map had an unconformity, a crucial missing piece. Like the road had been cut and below was an abyss.

Walter cranked up the air-conditioning to freeze.

I punched the outside-air-temp button and the reading showed 119 degrees. The sun was trending westward toward the Panamint Range alongside us. Sink, I urged it. But then, of course, we lose our light.

Walter said, "Up ahead. How about that?"

A massive fan spilled from the Panamints. There had to be a canyon up there but it was not visible from down here because the fan looked to extend a good two miles from toe to head and rise several hundred feet.

I stopped the car and we got out. The heat slammed me. Chilled by Walter's freezer, I thought I was going to crack.

We were at the intersection of two stitches in the basin floor: the West Side Road and the rough route angling up the giant fan. I knelt and scooped samples of the alluvial deposits. If we were on the right track, they'd match the evidence dish marked *Layer Two* in the ice chest.

"What's that?" Walter suddenly said. "You hear something? A car?"

I listened. Nothing. I scanned the West Side Road, officially closed in summer. Nothing.

"I'm certain I heard a car," Walter said.

I'm seeing things, he's hearing things. Well, my young eyes

may have 20/20 vision but Walter's old ears have never plugged in an iPod. He hears like a twenty-year-old. We're both certain.

But all was silent and still.

Even so, I couldn't resist another look at the saltpan. I noted the channel that drained our canyon into the basin, curving like a sidewinder's path. No mysterious shapes out there. Nothing moved but the ground, liquid with heat.

I turned back to the Blazer, liquid with heat myself.

"Did you check the radiator," Walter asked, "before we left the mine?"

"Did *I*?"

He said, "It's the driver's responsibility."

"It's always been you who takes care of the car."

"Always been?"

Yikes. You nag somebody out of the driver's seat, you better take on the rest of the job. Forget mirages. Pay attention to the real threats, like an overheated car in the desert. I gathered my dignity and went to open the hood.

15

THE RADIATOR DRANK A PINT. Walter and I came to an accord. Shut off the air conditioning and roll down the windows.

I turned the Blazer onto the road up the fan toward the rugged front of the Panamint Mountains. The twisted strata were weathered into pinks and purples and winey reds. The fan was a gray gravelly tongue, cracked by dry stream channels. We bumped along, sending up a rooster tail of dust. I checked my rearview mirror—the West Side Road was empty. At the canyon mouth, the fan road dropped into a wash. We paused to grab a sample and then pushed on. As the road roughened into the canyon, the Blazer gave a lurch and I wrestled the wheel and Walter folded his arms and looked out the window.

Out the window, rock formations lined the walls like shelved books. We passed a few million years of history and a couple of branching side canyons, and when we'd plunged still deeper into the geological record and come to the gray and orange banded dolomites of the Bonanza King formation, I stopped the car.

We got out. Wicked hot but the canyon walls threw shade

and my bones were no longer rattling. I felt, suddenly, giddy. "Hey pardner," I said, "you fixin to rustle up a piece of that geology?" Walter chuckled. As he opened the field kit and laid out his tools, he broke into song: "In a cavern, in a canyon, excavating for a mine..." I joined in. "Lived a miner, forty-niner, and his daughter Clementine."

He knew all the verses. We filled our specimen dishes, exhausting Clementine.

A coyote screamed.

I was casting about for a coyote tune—and the thought was forming that it's too hot and too early for coyotes—when Walter said, "Someone's in trouble."

We went rigid, listening.

It came again, unmistakable this time. *Help.*

The thought was forming that it's Roy Jardine up there somewhere—stewing in his vat of radionuclides and hearing us—but the cry was high-pitched and he surely wasn't looking to be found.

Help, again, urgent.

The sound came from above. Over the rim into the next side canyon? Sound in a canyon is a tricky thing.

"Which way?" Walter said.

"I don't know. I don't like it." I got my cell to dial Soliano. Roaming. Nothing. In a cavern in a canyon, got no service for my phone. The cry came again. Walter tried his phone, which proved as useless as mine.

Help. A scream.

Walter yelled back, then started downcanyon.

I stopped him. "What are you doing?"

"Let's try that side canyon."

"Okay, let's drive."

"We can't drive up that side canyon, Cassie."

"I don't like it."

He said, "What if it's snakebite?"

Lord. Snakebite. Walter's only real fear. The canyon floor was sparsely haired with sage. Do sidewinders hole up in sage? I got the first aid pouch from our field kit, grabbed a water bottle, and we started downcanyon.

I recalled two side canyons, one branching off in each direction. We rounded a bend and came to the fork. We yelled, and waited for the cry that could not be pinpointed. Silence, now. Walter plunged into the north canyon. I followed. The canyon was narrow, sage climbing its slopes, and as we gained elevation it steepened and twisted. We yelled, rounding every twist. All I heard in reply was blood pounding in my ears.

Walter stumbled. I caught his arm. "Slow down."

He didn't, but it didn't much matter because within a few minutes the canyon dead-ended in a wall of trilobite-speckled shale.

Walter's face was beet red. Mine felt on fire. I drank then passed the water bottle to him. His hands shook. I thought, there's things worse than snakebite. There's the mini-strokes, which hit Walter twice in the last six months, numbing his legs and slurring his speech, making him ask silly questions. He said, now, "Shall we go?" which was not in the least a silly question.

We retraced our route in silence.

In the main canyon, Walter glanced at the south-branching fork.

"We're going back," I said, "and turning the car around and when we get onto the fan we'll try the cell again, and if it doesn't have service we'll drive all the way into Furnace Creek and find a ranger."

"All right." His voice was dry as sandpaper.

We trudged upcanyon, my worry deepening. Snakes, strokes, surprises.

I thought, there's hundreds of old mines in Death Valley so

what's the chance the first canyon on our list is the right one? Tiny, minuscule. Point oh five percent.

We rounded the bend and I saw that I was wrong.

16

THE HOOD WAS up on the Blazer and the doors were open. It looked like the car had come into the canyon for a tuneup. But the mechanic was a vandal.

Our things littered the ground. Field kit, packs, cell phones, maps, my purse. Stomped, smashed, dumped, ripped. Our gallon-jugs of water were knifed open. The soil was still wet.

Walter bent over the exposed engine. "Wires are cut." Voice drier than sandpaper.

There came a sound, somewhere downcanyon, of an engine.

I hissed, "She carries a shotgun," and we tumbled into the Blazer. I turned the ignition key. Nothing. We flattened ourselves onto the hot vinyl seats.

"She?" Walter whispered.

At last, it became too hot to breathe.

Seventeen minutes gone, by my watch. "Shall we?" I said.

Walter nodded.

We sat up. Nothing moved outside. We slowly opened the

doors, and that movement did not draw gunfire. We got out, wobbly. We stumbled to the wedge of shade cast by the canyon wall and collapsed on the baking ground.

I offered water.

Walter shook his head. The quart bottle was half-empty.

I said, "Does us no good in the bottle." Don't argue, partner. It's water in the body that'll keep us alive.

In the end, we drank.

Ten more minutes gone. I thought about moving.

Walter whispered, "Why do you think it was her?"

"Purse." My voice, like his, was sandpaper.

We studied the purse, lying beside the front tire. Walter gave it to me last Christmas—a creamy leather backpack purse, feminine and practical. Now it was gutted from flap to bottom, contents dumped.

Walter said, "Could have been Jardine."

"Look at my compact."

Shattered, the pressed powder cratered. My face prickled, where she'd run her wet finger. Ever wear makeup? It hadn't got that personal, with Jardine. Had it?

Walter said, "The compact could simply have broken."

"Shit," I said. "Shit."

The back seat was empty. I went cold in the overheated air. The perp had taken the ice chest, which meant the perp knew what our business was. And the only people who knew what was in the ice chest were the people at the talc mine. Nearly everyone at the mine knew because we'd spouted off about fender soils and maps and following the trail of Jardine's offroader.

"He has what he wants," Walter said. "He'll leave us alone now."

"He?"

"Or she. Take your pick."

"She," I said. For now.

I made an inventory. We had less than a third of a quart of water. We had a granola bar that had dropped under the seat, the first-aid kit, stuff from the violated field kit—scalpels and tweezers seeming the most useful. I was thankful that we'd left the valuable equipment, the spectrometers and the scopes, in Scotty's van.

Walter picked through the kit. "My knife's gone." He stared at the sliced water jugs, and then the exposed engine where the wires were cut. With his knife.

We returned to the shade and slumped against the wall.

Minutes passed, then Walter spoke. "We're vulnerable here."

"What do you want to do?"

"Take another side canyon," he said. "Find a place to hide."

"How long?"

"Until we can walk out under cover of darkness." He wetted his cracked lips. "Until it's not so damnably hot."

"What about Soliano?"

He blinked.

"Walter? Shouldn't we look for Soliano?"

He said, "I hadn't thought that far."

I sagged. How could he not think that far? Soliano had called while we were on the West Side Road. Walter had put his cell phone on speaker. We'd told Soliano our plans, that when we'd finished here we planned to catch the Greenwater Valley Road and check a couple of candidates over there, and then rendezvous when it got dark at Furnace Creek. Unless we phoned to say otherwise. How could Walter not think of Soliano?

He cleared his throat. "Of course. We must get down to the road. We must be visible."

I relaxed an inch.

We sat five minutes more, gathering ourselves.

I wondered when Soliano would take note that he hadn't heard from us, whether he'd check his watch and calculate that we must, by now, be over in Greenwater Valley, in which case the most direct route from the talc mines was not via the West Side Road. If he didn't find us elsewhere, though, sooner or later he'd surely come this way. Two people on the West Side Road would stick out like sore thumbs.

That is, until it got dark.

I roused myself and got the flashlight from the tire-changing cubby.

Walter rose, gathering our meager belongings. He stuffed them into my emptied pack.

I took my field knife and Hap's bandana from my pocket. I sawed the cloth in half, then dipped the halves in the radiator water. The red cloth darkened to hematite. I gave Walter one half and he understood. We squeezed the water over our heads and bodies, repeating the process until the radiator was dry, then draped the wet bandanas around our necks.

"You are a genius," he said.

"Girl Scouts."

We had to laugh.

He recovered his hat and shades.

I put on mine. I cleared my throat. “Well, pardner?”

“Let’s vamoose.”

I scooped a handful of dolomite-weathered soil and put it in my pocket. We’d come up here for samples and I was not leaving without a sample.

17

WE HEADED DOWNCANYON.

At the fork there were scuffed prints heading into the south canyon. Further down, around a gentle bend, there were tire tracks. Not ours. Smart place to stop, because there was room enough to turn around.

I said, "You *did* hear a car on the West Side Road."

"We should have waited."

Wouldn't have helped. The perp, tailing us, wanted to remain unseen. She comes around that curve, sees our car stopped beside the saltpan, backs her car up. Rolls down her window. Waits until she hears our engine start again. Then creeps around the curve, sees our rooster-tail going up the fan. Follows when it's safe. Comes just shy of the bend, gets out to walk. Takes the south fork and climbs its ridge. Maybe she sees us; maybe she just hears us. We don't hear her because we're singing our fool heads off. She gets inspired. Yells for help. We head downcanyon. And she scrambles down from the ridge and does her business. Then, while we're up the north fork, she escapes downcanyon with her prize: the ice chest, the soil map, all our work. She gets in the SUV, does her three-point turn, and exits the canyon.

At least I had to hope she'd exited.

We followed her tire tracks out of the canyon. At the head of the fan we paused, scanning the landscape below. No white SUV. No FBI-RERT convoy, either.

We started down.

The giant fan was veined with channels, some several feet deep, in which a person could flatten herself and her shotgun and not be seen from the road that cut down the center. I did not brood on that for long. I did not have the strength. I brooded instead on the heat that rose from the desert pavement and sucked the radiator water from my clothes. The ground was paved in rock chips mortared with sand. We could fry an egg on that hot smooth pavement, had we an egg. We could bake a quiche—the rock surface had collected a coating of iron and manganese oxides and that black desert varnish reflected heat like a convection oven.

Frying eggs. Egg McMuffin. My stomach turned.

We tramped down the road until our faces were varnished red and then Walter croaked "need a break" and I croaked "okay."

We left the road and cut across the desert pavement to the nearest channel. It was blessedly unvarnished, washed clean by floodwaters. We climbed down into the sandy gravel bed and huddled against the southwest wall, which cast a lip of shade. We could see just over the rim. The Badwater basin spread below us. If I saw a car anywhere in the basin, other than the white SUV, I planned to get up and wave.

We drank the water down to a trickle.

When my saliva had thickened, I put a pebble in my mouth. I passed one to Walter. "Suck on it."

After a time, Walter mumbled, "Could've shot us. Didn't."

I thought that over. "Good."

He was silent. I turned. His Sahara hat was pulled low and all I could see was his jaw working.

I said, "So you *do* think it's her? Shotgun."

He removed his pebble. "Men carry guns too."

True. But whoever it was evidently got what he wanted. She wanted. Therefore we didn't have to worry any more? I spat out my pebble. "Perp might still shoot us."

"Then I'd be wrong."

We had no more heart for talk.

Five times, we saw cars on the Badwater Road across the saltpan and I roused myself and stood and signaled. The sixth car, I didn't bother. We sat until shadows reached the head of the fan. The sun dipped behind the peaks above, reddening the clouds. We removed our hats and sunglasses and brooded on the nuclear sunset.

"We must go," Walter finally said.

I nodded. Going to get dark. Nobody going to see us up here.

We rose, shaky. I shouldered the pack. We crossed the desert pavement to the fan road. There came a hot breeze that lifted the sweat-plastered hair from my scalp. The breeze went away. My feet swelled with each step. The ventilating mesh did not ventilate enough. I feared my boots would burst. We descended and, astonishingly, reached the West Side Road.

We collapsed and sucked the last drops from the water bottle.

An eternity passed. Three more cars passed on the other side of the basin.

I tried to speak but my tongue had stiffened. I elbowed Walter, and pointed across the saltpan at the Badwater Road. We rose, shakier than before. I tried to estimate the distance. Couple of miles? Five? More? Who knows? Everything looks closer than it is out here.

We broached the saltpan.

Life clung at the edge. We bypassed bristling shrubs and scuffed through sand and silt and then passed onto blisters of salt. Still, there was life. Rubbery plants, here and there. Pickleweed. Stems like stacked pickles. You want to break one off and pop it in your mouth. We Girl Scouts tasted it. Puckery. Walter fingered it, in passing. *Adaptable*, he mouthed. I nodded. My mouth was sealed. Nothing to say. No spit to say it with. No sound out here but the crackle of salt beneath our boots. We walked on meringues awhile and then the ground hardened and smoothed. Floodplain. White and flat, a frozen lake. Looked like hell froze over.

Not even pickleweed out here. Nothing adaptable enough to live out here.

My tongue quilted. We were in a giant bathtub but there was no water. Too hot. Water had evaporated and left bathtub rings. Rings of salt. Saltpan shimmered in the dying light. Looked like water. My throat swelled. I thought I might drown.

I thought of the thing I'd seen from the car, eons ago. Well, hours ago. Hotter than hell on the saltpan then. What living thing would be out here? Creeping through hell.

Must have been a mirage.

"Rest," Walter croaked.

We sank onto the hard pan. I touched the salt and licked my finger. Sodium chloride. I giggled. If I had an egg I'd salt it.

"Look." Walter was pointing back to the West Side Road.

I looked. It was so near. We'd come through rings of salt—carbonates and sulfates and now we were in the zone of table salt and yet we hadn't come far at all. Salt rings. They rang around my head. Telling me something. I reached for the rings and they shattered. Grains of salt now. What was it I was reaching for?

"Look," Walter said, still pointing.

The road. That's it. We're mired in salt rings and we haven't come far at all. I would have cried if I'd had water for tears.

"Plants."

I did not care.

"Faults," he said.

It took me a very long time to process this, to look again where he was pointing and see the dark smudges at the foot of the fans, here and there. I projected the line of the smudges upfan, to the offset of the fault scarps. I thought this over. Faults grind rock. Faults build dams. Faults trap runoff. Faults make springs.

Smudges grow around springs.

I licked my lips. What kind of smudges? Salt-loving smudges? No. Not that salt-loving or they'd be on the pan.

I rasped, "You are a genius."

We rose, on hope. We angled southwest, aiming for the closest smudge. By the time we'd waded back across the floodplain to the pickleweed, night had edged in. We left the saltpan. The smudges resolved into shrubby trees with droopy branches. They gave off a smell in the hot night air.

My nose pinched. Mesquite. Dad grilling burgers. Somebody's birthday. Beer and sodas and sparkling waters in a trash can of ice.

We reached the stand of mesquite. I stared at the sandy ground. There was no beer. No sodas. No Evian or Arrowhead or Crystal Spring. There was no spring.

Walter fell to the ground and began to dig.

I came down beside him.

The sand grew damp. I ransacked the pack and then we dug with spatulas, seeing by flashlight. And then when it took more energy to dig than we had to spend, we sat back and waited for the seep to percolate through the sandy soil and find our hole.

After a time, Walter slumped.

Digging digging and then in wonder I was unearthing diamonds. They winked and disappeared. I dug harder and now I saw white worms among the diamonds, and now I laughed recognizing my own white fingers. Just keep digging. Greedy for diamonds. And now Walter was beside me, and I was willing to share with him but he got greedy too and scooped up diamonds and brought them to his mouth and sucked them up and I thought, oh Walter that is so crude. But then I was sucking diamonds too, crude as Walter, sucking up the salty wet diamonds until our fortune was spent.

We dozed.

Something was caressing me. I slapped my neck and came away with a crackling mess that gave off a bitter smell that cleared my head. I knew what to do. I wiped my hand clean, rolled to the dig, and scooped a palm of water. The silt had nearly settled out and it tasted less salty now. It left my hand silky smooth. When I had guzzled enough, I tied Hap's bandana over the mouth of the water bottle and sank it in the muddy seep. What a fine gift Hap had given me. Then I slept again, dreaming of salt rings and abysses and vibrating shapes and a woman powdering my face with talc until I could not breathe.

Walter woke me and said, "Look."

We stared across the saltpan, that great white starlit belly, to the Badwater Road where a pair of white eyes traveled north. It's them. They're looking for us.

We capped the water bottle and drank one last time from our oasis and then once again we broached the saltpan.

The night air was velvet now, not brutal, and we walked lightly across the crackling ground, and I thought we'd make the Badwater Road in no time at all. Except it was taking forever to reach the floodplain. Walter's shuffle was slowing us down. My rubber legs were slowing us down. There came another pair of eyes on the Badwater Road, and that spurred us onward, and at last we waded onto the floodplain. And then the saltpan changed again, bunching up, and we walked on tufts of salt that grew and grew as we picked our way deeper through this miniature forest.

There came a shriek.

We turned and Walter's flashlight caught it and I knew *that's* what I'd seen from the car and then I ducked because this was no mirage.

Walter stumbled.

I grabbed his arm. We went down together and I sliced my palm on a fin of salt.

It came at us low, skimming the tufts and then wheeling to avoid a pinnacle, and then it tumbled, wing over wing, and hit the pan.

We froze.

It picked itself up, pale wings unfolding. It screeched and came our way.

I kicked a chunk of rock salt free and heaved it and the bat shrank back, and then, insanely, came at us again. Not creeping. Attacking. Like it was rabid. Walter tried to blind it with his flashlight and in the beam the bat eyes shone red. It stopped. Mouth opened to let loose another shriek and the teeth shone, bloodied. We shoved ourselves up and took off, scrambling through the salt forest until we reached another floodplain and our legs gave out.

We sat back-to-back, Walter sweeping the flashlight beam to and fro, me listening for bat wings.

Someone bent over Walter.

I reached for the flashlight, which had rolled away, its beam now dimmed.

She turned to me.

The moon was up behind her, silhouetting her. Her face was in shadow. All I could make out was her long black hair, feathered like a shawl. She crouched, one hand cradling Walter's head, her lean body twisted toward me, other hand braced on her knee. She was still. She was a pillar of salt.

I croaked, "Who are you?"

From her shadow face came a high young voice. "An alien."

And she turned back to Walter. She lifted his head and took a water bottle from the sling around her hips and put it to his mouth. "Drink, Grandfather."

18

I HEARD WATER RUNNING. Splashing.

I dove into the cold pool below the waterfall. It was heaven.

"If you're happy and you know it, clap your hands."

I lay on a cloud. I fought through fog.

"If you're happy and you know it, croak like a frog. Rrrribit, rrribit."

I opened my eyes.

Hap Miller leaned over me. His heart face was inches above mine. "Welcome back. Long time no see."

"Where am I?"

"You're in fantasyland, Buttercup."

I made a slow survey. I was in a Spanish villa: sand-colored walls, arched stone fireplace, carved-wood furniture. I lay in a cloud of soft pillows under a heavy flowered spread. I began to remember being carried on a litter, transferred to this bed. A needle. My left arm lay on top of the spread, needle in my vein. Tubing ran up to an IV bag hung on the brass bedstead. Ceiling fan sent down a warm breeze. It wasn't enough. I pushed back the spread and breeze tickled my bare skin. I smelled of sweat and salt. I was in my underwear. I yanked up the spread.

Hap grinned. "Ladies at the pool wear a whole lot less."

I burned, beneath the covers. I now heard shouts. Kids. I turned my head. Two big windows, bristling palm trees outside.

Hap said, "We're in the playground of the rich and richer. This time of year, mostly foreigners. Why them furriners jess love the wild west--cain't get enough of our deserts. And heat! Gotta come see for theyselves jess how hot hot is."

"Hap." My throat felt scraped raw. "Where is this?"

"Welcome to the Furnace Creek Inn."

"Walter?"

"Doing fine. Right next door in a corner suite. With a private veranda for if he wants to catch himself some fresh air with his morning latte." Hap sighed. "As for poor me, I share a room with Milt. I do fear he'll snore."

"Why are we here?"

"Headquarters. The FBI, in the dapper person of Hector Soliano, negotiated a sweet deal. A German here and there had to be relocated but otherwise all are happy—except the taxpayers footing the bill. Then again, they'll never find out so all's well."

"I need to talk to him."

"All in good time. Doctor Hap needs to make sure you're up to it."

"You're a doctor?"

His eyes went flat. "You sound like my daddy." He gave the IV bag a squeeze. "My daddy tried to send me to Harvard med school but damn, they didn't want me. So I went to Podunk U and got me an EMT certificate. That's Emergency Medical Technician, ma'am. That didn't satisfy daddy so I went into the nuke biz and got me a health physics degree. I thunk daddy'd be impressed by all them alphas and betas and gammas under the supervision of his manly son. Daddy wudn't." Hap shrugged. "But hey, Milt was happy to hire a guy who can do radiation protection and, on the side, patch people up. You okay being tended to by a part-time EMT?"

I thought, Daddy sounds like poison. I said, "Thanks."

"You're welcome." He took my hand and checked my pulse. He put a blood pressure cuff on my IV arm and pumped it up. He brushed the sticky hair off my forehead. Cool hands.

I let my heavy eyes close. The pressure cuff pinched. The sheet abraded my tender feet. My left hand stung. My skin felt sticky. I tasted grit. I didn't care because I could summon enough saliva to swallow. I located an ache in my stomach that I identified as hunger. It was good to be alive.

There was a crash and I opened my eyes.

Hap held my arm steady. "Just thunder."

Rain came in a rush, clattering so loud my ears rang.

"More on the way, Hector says. That is, Hector says the clerk at the front desk says. Hurricane off Baja California and we get the whiplash." Hap fanned himself. "Cool us off."

I wetted my lips. "There was a girl."

He jerked a thumb. "Outside. Least she was, checking out the little bitty thongs on the ladies at the pool. Disapproving, I'd say. Methinks she is a Puritan."

"Who is she?"

"She told Hector she's an alien." Hap held his nose. "In need of a bath."

I smelled my own rank smell. "How'd she find us?"

"Took awhile to figure out you needed finding. We were at the talc mines way late, and when Hector couldn't raise you on the cell he figured you were up some canyon but next time he tried he got a mite worried. So he called Furnace Creek and they sent a ranger out rangering but he didn't find you on the West Side Road so he went on over to the Greenwater Road because that's where you said you were going next. Ranger found somebody'd seen a car like yours, so we all thought you were up some canyon over there. We didn't drag our sorry butts to Furnace Creek until after dark."

"What about Chickie?"

"Miss Chick left her mine in a huff not long after you left." Hap cocked his head. "Course, Milt left around about the same time. Went home to pack some necessities for him and me, shop for the others. Since it seemed we were gonna have a sleepover."

"When did Milt get here?"

"Late. Gotta say, though, don't see Milt as much of a suspect. Hasn't got the imagination to bushwhack you."

What it took was gall.

"Anyhoo, we all end up here at the Inn having a tailgate party, and a tip comes in—backpackers came across your car. So Hector dispatches some of his manly agents to find you."

"What about the girl?"

"Right there, listening in. We did attract a little crowd. Best I can make out, she's local and sees herself as Miss Alien Desert Rat and damned if she isn't because she went out and beat the FBI to the rescue."

I thought, bless her.

Hap checked his watch, then disconnected the IV and gently pulled the needle from my arm. "Feel okay, Cassie?"

Like I'd been resurrected. "You do good work."

"Uh-oh." Hap took my left hand. "Doctor Hap missed something." He rummaged in his kit. He squeezed a worm of ointment on my cut palm. He studied it. "Make a cool sketch." He gestured at a sketchpad sticking out of his kit. "I draw hands. Fact, I've drawn most of the hands at the dump. Get me some down-time and I gotta fill it. Did a real cool one for this deconner who blew out his gloves—little necrosis of the tissue." Hap made a face. "But it made for a Jackson-Pollocky sort of avante-garde effect."

"Like Roy Jardine's face?"

"Not that avante-garde." He bandaged my cut and released me. "Tell me, find anything out there afore you got bushwhacked?"

"No."

"Heard about your loss. That's a bitch."

"Loss?"

"The ice chest. Your soil map. Walter's been having a cow about that."

Me too.

"Cheer up. Start again, right? Go get more dirt off that rig?"

He's asking if I can? Why's he so interested? I thought, suddenly, just because Chickie and Ballinger left the mine early doesn't make them the only ones with the opportunity to bushwhack us. Jardine could have done it himself, if he knew where we were going. Who knew our plans, at the mine? Just about everybody. Hap certainly; he'd been the one who first asked. Or it could have been one of Soliano's agents who overheard, and phoned Jardine. Not Soliano himself, though, I couldn't buy that. But what about Scotty, or someone from Scotty's team? Shit, I was getting paranoid. Yeah, but paranoid's good.

Hap put away his band-aids. "From now on, take care out there."

"Sure."

"I'm not talking bushwhacking."

"So I'll wear a dosimeter. That what you're talking about?"

"You know what you are? You're like every other pragmatist who figures the odds. I'm trying to keep you out of the doodoo and you're thinking odds are you won't step in any."

"I understand odds."

"You're not listening. Story of my life. Hey, you know Homer? Homer Simpson, works at the nuke plant?" Hap wore a new T-shirt. He stretched it to show off the caption: *Trust Me, I'm Here to Help*. He sighed. "Nobody listens. I tell everybody I gotta frisk them slow so the reading's accurate and everybody bitches because they're under the gun to get stuff done. So I say sure, let's turbo-frisk, and you can take some home to the kids."

"I get your point, Hap."

He wouldn't stop. "And you know what's the real hoot?"

I shook my head.

"The numbers. Any idea how the experts came up with their numbers?"

"What numbers?"

"Numbers that say you got a so-and-so chance of getting cancer, or a scratch on the DNA. They don't rightly know what dose is gonna do it. So they take a guess. And that's where they get the numbers they feed into the equations."

"Will you please stop?"

He seemed to recoil. "Sure thing." He unhooked the empty IV bag and folded it around the needle and neatly coiled the tubing. He dropped the package in a wastebasket and tied off the plastic liner. He moved to me, at last, and eased the pressure cuff down my sticky arm, catching the hairs. "Sorry."

"It didn't hurt."

"Then sorry about the lecture. I do go on and on."

"It's not that."

"Bad breath?"

I laughed. "No. It's just...a long story."

He took off his watch and cocked his head.

"Starts with my grandmother."

"Doesn't it always?"

I laughed again. "Okay, you asked for it. She—my mother's mother—was at NTS way back when they were doing the atomic tests. Nevada Test Site. I'm sure you're familiar with it." Of course he was; NTS was almost next door to the dump. "She was a reporter, which was a big deal for a woman back then. Just for the local rag but since local was Vegas, covering the tests was local news. And it was always a big party. I mean, people went to the hotel roofs to watch the mushroom clouds. So when my grandmother gets sent to the test site to cover the story, she wants to make it entertaining. She stations herself in one of the phone booths and does a you-are-there report. She's dictating as the bomb goes off. The concussion knocks the booth over and shatters the glass. And my grandmother is lying on the ground, cuts all over, the blast wave blowing dirt in her face—and she doesn't miss a beat. The receiver's still live so she keeps reporting. She just lies there in the fallout and talks on the phone. Scoop of a lifetime. My grandmother dined out on that story for years. My mom told it around our dinner table. I thought it was exciting, until I got bored with it. And then my baby brother was born with hemophilia. That's when your blood won't clot and... Well I'm sure you know." Of course he knew; he must have learned it in EMT school; might need to tend a bleeder. "Since hemophilia is a genetic disorder, my folks tried to figure out where it came from. But there was no family history of it. So that kind of left the mutagenic factor. We figured Grandma got zapped. No way to prove it, but... She only had one kid—my mom. My mom had three kids. Fifty-fifty chance she was going to pass on that damaged gene each time. My older brother got a pass. My younger brother didn't." Poor little Henry, bleeding into his joints, bleeding out, bleeding all over my homework. "That's when my mom learned she was a carrier. Women don't express the trait, they just carry it and pass it on. We don't know about me—there's no definitive test to determine my carrier status. Only sure way to find out is to have a kid." I shrugged. "So that's why I got bitchy about your radiation lesson."

Hap had paled, beneath his freckles. "What happened to your brother?"

"He died. Bumped his head. Bleeding into the brain."

Hap folded the pressure cuff and tucked it away in his kit. He said, at last, "Goddamn."

I watched the ceiling fan spin. My throat ached. I'd sure done a core dump here. I blamed it on the case, which was scratching around my buried bone like a gamma scratch on the DNA. Normally, I keep it buried deep. Normally, I'm not thinking about my brother, although he's always there to be plumbed. Normally, I'm not thinking about having a kid, or the fear of losing a kid—it's something that drifts into my thoughts now and then and I wait until it drifts away. Unless Walter brings it up, worrying that my love life consists of hit and run, warning that I'm consigning myself to a future alone. And I cling to my cowardice and wait until Walter tires of the effort. My leg muscles twitched. I sat up, holding the bedspread to my chest, glancing around the room for my clothes. "I should get going."

Hap went to the closet and pulled out a big robe. He back-stepped to me, dropping the robe on my feet. "Give a hoot when you's decent."

I smiled. "Thanks but I'll just use my own clothes."

"Can't," he said to the wall. "Sent them to be laundered."

I dropped the bedspread. "I had soil in my pockets."

"That's why I sent 'em, Buttercup."

"It was *evidence.*"

"Whoops."

19

Hap held the door open and I—wearing the voluminous robe and matching terrycloth slippers—stepped out to a roofed walkway supported by stone pillars. The walkway bordered an astonishing lawn.

Hap said, "Wait'll you see the pool!"

We waded into the steaming grass. The rain had stopped and the sun already blistered through black clouds. We passed white-clothed tables and turquoise-cushioned chairs shadowed by fat umbrellas. We went to the edge of the lawn and stopped at the low stone wall. Stone stairways and meandering paths terraced down to a lower level of red-clay tennis courts and there, directly below, was Hap's slate-decked pool with its splashing kids and sunning thonged ladies—and gentlemen—on turquoise air floats, and the pool was edged by a wall of stone arches and a stone beehive fireplace, and beyond the stone arches was more lawn, and tall palms, and then the astonishing green ended and the real world of desert gravel began.

"Like I told you," Hap said, "fantasyland."

I turned to look back at the Inn buildings, which climbed right up against a mountain face. The red tile roofs and ocher adobe walls reflected the maroons and browns of the native rock.

"Those mountains are called the Funerals. Guess that makes this heaven."

Close enough, I thought.

"And that down there—if you'll turn around again—is the low-rent district."

I turned. The Inn sat up at the head of a giant fan. Down below at the fan's foot were dark radial lines, like crevices between toes. I recognized those smudges—stands of mesquite. This fan had some significant subsurface drainage. Potable water maybe. I stored the thought, although if one were stranded on this fan all one need do for a drink was stick out one's thumb and hitch a ride with one of the cars traveling the blacktop that ran from the Inn downfan to the oasis.

"Low-rent district's known as the village of Furnace Creek." Hap pointed at the oasis. "Maybe not so low-rent. There's the Ranch, which is a motel with a pool bigger'n ours. And then there's gift shops and restaurants and the museum and the stables and the date orchard and the visitor center and the ranger station and the airstrip and..." he swung an imaginary club, "let us not forget the golf course! Ain't it grand? Hundred and ten in the shade and they got acres of dewy green."

My vision suddenly swam.

Hap's arm went around my waist. "Steady, there."

I leaned into him.

"Now heaven's complete."

My breath caught. Not sure how to take that. Not sure how I wanted to take it. With a large grain of salt. I was suffocating in my robe. I whispered, "I need to get out of the sun."

He steered me back to the walkway. In the shade it was borderline cooler. I straightened up. He let me go.

There were eight rooms along this side of the building.

The girl sat against the wall of the corner room next to mine. There was the same black feathered hair I remembered, and her face was still in shadow. She wore cutoff jeans and a dirty white T-shirt. She hugged her legs. Her arms and legs were lean and brown. She had big puppy feet, brown toes curling over the ends of her sandals.

Hap bowed. "Miss Alien, might I introduce Ms. Cassie Oldfield, whose poor desiccated carcass you found. Whose life you nobly saved."

She tipped up her head.

Her face was childishly round. It hadn't thinned out like the rest of her. Her eyes were black under straight black brows. Her mouth was wide and curvy. She's going to get prettier, I thought.

I cleared my throat. "I want to tell you how enormously grateful I am."

She did not respond.

I began to feel alien, myself. "I don't even know where it was you found us. On the saltpan somewhere but..."

"Devil's Golf Course," Hap offered.

I said, "Good name."

She spoke. "Bad name."

I did not know what to say, so I asked, "What's your name?"

She stared at me.

Hap stepped in again. "How old is youse, Miss Alien?"

I thought she'd ignore him, or give him a number in Klingon years, but she said "fourteen" in her girlish voice and then pointedly looked beyond me to the black and blue sky.

Hap leaned in close to me and whispered, "Kids are scary."

20

THE AIR CONDITIONING blasted in Walter's suite.

Scotty Hemmings and Milt Ballinger were iced side by side on a wicker loveseat. Hector Soliano, in a deep winged chair, sipped iced tea. Hap Miller leaned against the stone fireplace.

The team was reassembled. But I had to wonder, now, did we all share the same goal?

I recalled what Hap said about Ballinger leaving the talc mine early, and I pictured the cocky little man cutting engine wires, slashing water jugs, ripping my purse. Maybe. But Ballinger reveled in his position as dump manager, the small-town boy who made good, the rock star who came up with the CTC dump motto—Closing the Circle of the Atom. So why would he join forces with Roy Jardine and jeopardize all that? He wouldn't, I thought. Unless he was pushed.

Scotty, with his dimpled grin and surfer hair, was so upfront about his lifeguard ethics. But Scotty had little tolerance for anybody he thought didn't measure up, who joked about serious matters. Like Hap. Maybe Scotty's disdain was for dump workers, in general. But then he wouldn't join forces with Jardine, would he?

Soliano, I couldn't see as anything but dedicated to his job. He was the foreigner who became a top cop in the heart of America's law enforcement community. So driven he'd barely stop to eat. And he didn't know an alpha particle from a gamma ray before this job.

Hap did, though. Hap with his barbs about radiation dose and turbo-frisking. But Hap didn't joke about the victims—not about my brother, anyway. I just couldn't see him misusing the triple-X resins, even to make some point about Homer Simpson incompetence.

Bottom line, I just couldn't tie any of these people to Roy Jardine.

So I went to Walter, the team member who mattered to me.

Walter stretched on a turquoise chaise, wearing a robe that matched mine. He took hold of my unbandaged hand, his papery skin cold. I scrutinized him. His eyes were inflamed. His color was off. If we'd been alone I would have asked some technical question that required a clear and present mind. Or maybe just, what day is this? Actually, I had to think about that one myself. Wednesday.

He said, "You look better than one would expect."

I had to smile. He was his normal self.

"Hey," Scotty said. "You guys gave us some major worry."

"Hell of a thing," Ballinger said.

I warmed to the sympathy, and took the winged chair beside Soliano's. These were the good seats, in front of the table. There were buttery pastries, tall sandwiches, a coffee urn, pitchers of iced liquids. Breakfast? Lunch? I checked my watch; nine-thirty. Brunch. There was the lemonade I'd been craving but first I craved water. I poured, slowly, so as not to spill a drop, and drank down half the glass. I took a sandwich, faint with desire. I bit through strata of bread and turkey and ham and cheese and sweet ripe tomato. Nobody else was eating. Hap opened his sketchpad. I wondered whose hands he was going to draw. Mine, maybe. Tomato juice dripped down my wrist. I fought the urge to lick it.

Soliano said, when my mouth was empty, "If you are able...?"

"I'm able. Bring in Chickie."

"When we locate her. We investigate any and all leads. We run the prints from your vehicle but it appears the perp wore gloves."

Of course she did. He did.

Soliano continued, "We still have the Department of Energy's aerial team out searching. I am told they have some 'real neat toys' that will 'sniff out' any nuclide of interest down on the ground."

I said, "Unless it's in a mine."

Scotty spoke. "Then we're blind."

"Geologists," Soliano said, "how long to replace your lost soil map?"

Walter rubbed his face. "Half a day. At the least."

"You will feel equal to the task? We either wait for you to..." He let it die.

Or we get someone who doesn't get stranded in the desert and lose their map. Soliano was wondering how long it would take to locate another geologist or two and chopper them here and bring them up to speed. Well, there is no other geologist as formidable as Walter Shaws. As for me, I learned something out there in the desert. Fear lasts only so long. I met Walter's gaze. His hair was mussed, his face mottled. His bushy eyebrows lifted--you with me? I nodded--let's nail her. Him. Them. I turned to Soliano. "We're good, Hector."

Soliano steepled his fingers and tipped them to me. "Then let us move on. We have a development. CTC opened an email early this morning, from Mr. Jardine. It was routed through a re-sender in Bulgaria. Hence, untraceable. He demands ten million —wire transfer to an account in the Cayman Islands."

Ballinger snorted. "Knothead's dreaming."

Soliano regarded Ballinger. "CTC shares your opinion."

"Knothead give a deadline?"

"Friday, noon."

"Or what?"

"He threatens contamination."

"Jesus," Scotty burst in, "of what?"

"Of *the priceless*," Soliano said. "Whatever this is."

Walter said, "Life."

"Yeah," Scotty said, "couple resin casks could ruin somebody's day."

Whose day, I wondered? My thoughts switched from possible partners to possible targets. Jardine conceivably bore a lot of grudges—against Hap, Ballinger, the guys in the break room, CTC honchos, and perhaps even Chickie. So he wanted his revenge in dollars? The threat to contaminate something, or someone, was certainly alarming enough.

But still, the two missing casks bugged me. Jardine went to the considerable trouble of running the swap two times. Two chances of getting caught. Why not cut the risk in half? Surely, one cask of triple-X salsa would suffice.

No, this scenario was wrong. Something was off. But I couldn't see what. I was still fuzzy-headed, weak. I took another bite of sandwich. The tomato slipped out. The ham slid on the cheese, where the tomato had been. I stared. A word formed in my fuzzy brain: unconformity. In geology, it's a place between two strata where there's a missing piece in the record of time. Where the deposition of rock-forming muds or silts was interrupted, or the rock was eroded away. I'd used that image on the West Side Road, trying to figure what was wrong with our fender soil map. I'd seen its opposite on the saltpan—rings of salt, layer after layer, unbroken. We'd been trying to patch together the fender-soil layers to make rings of salt—unbroken layers, a complete map. But we couldn't. Our map had unconformities. Missing pieces. Cuts in the road. I suddenly thought I understood. My stomach dropped like I'd just taken a tumble into that abyss. I set down my sandwich. "Hey."

They'd all been talking. Speculating. They'd gone on without me. Now, they stopped.

I said, "I think we got it wrong. About the missing casks."

Soliano's face sharpened. "What are you saying?"

"I'm saying we didn't get the chance to separate all the layers of the fender soils. Every trip Jardine took he'd accumulate a layer, but it wouldn't be complete. Pick up mud here and not there, because it was raining here and not there. And on other trips it's dry as toast and nothing clings to the fenders."

"Why numerous trips? Only two casks are missed. This does not fit."

I glanced at Walter. Walter lifted a hand to me. My theory. Or was this a wild-ass guess? Either way, I ran with it. "It fits if you look at it another way. He makes numerous swaps—but he doesn't need to steal a new cask every time."

Soliano frowned. "He steals two casks. This is what he needs?"

"No. All he needs is one."

Soliano's frown deepened.

"Just try this on. He steals two empty casks from the dump. Let's say he puts one aside for some reason—call it the Spare Cask." I took a water glass from the table and set it aside, on the floor. "Let's call the other empty cask he steals the Swap Cask." I picked up another glass. "So he takes this Swap Cask to the talc mine and fills it." I reached for the salt shaker.

Walter smiled. "May I?" He unscrewed the top from the shaker and passed it to me.

"Thanks." I poured the salt into my glass. "Then when Ryan Beltzman comes with the radwaste truck, they make their swap. The Swap Cask, now containing talc," I held up my glass of salt, "for a resin cask from Beltzman's radwaste shipment."

Walter was already filling a glass with pepper.

We swapped glasses.

I continued. "So now Beltzman, with the Swap Cask full of talc in his truck, continues on to the dump. Where the cask gets buried."

Walter set his glass of salt on the table and covered it with a napkin.

Oh yeah, I loved this man. "Meanwhile, the resin cask," I held up my glass of pepper, "awaits Jardine in the offroader's trailer. So Jardine now drives his rig to his depot. A mine, let's say." That place we're going to find when we build ourselves a new map.

Soliano was nodding.

"But instead of storing the resin cask at his depot, Jardine dumps out the beads." I grabbed the nearest thing at hand, a wastebasket, and dumped in the pepper.

Hap chuckled.

I held up my now-empty glass. "Now Jardine has an empty cask. And he can take it back to the talc mine and fill it with talc." Walter already had another salt shaker open. I poured the contents into my glass. "And this now becomes the Swap Cask for the next exchange, when Beltzman next comes with a shipment of hot resin casks."

"Ongoing?" Soliano said. "This is what you mean?"

That's what I meant. "Talc for resins, talc for resins, and so on and so on."

Scotty sat forward. "And he dumps the resins, at the depot, every time?"

"Yeah, he'd have to."

"Into what?"

"Good question." Where, in the depot mine, is he stockpiling those resin beads? Not in a wastebasket, that's for sure. It would overflow.

"Then..." Scotty said, white, "that means all the beads are uncasked."

There was a long silence, in which shouts from the pool filled the vacuum. No one moved. No one recapped the salt and pepper shakers. No one touched the wastebasket containing stockpiled pepper. It might as well have held resin beads.

"And so," Soliano finally said, "his ongoing swap comes to an end Monday night. This means that the resin cask in the talc mine—which Mr. Jardine came to fetch—that is the last cask exchanged?"

"It'd have to be."

"How long do you theorize this swap has been running?"

I looked to Ballinger. "How long has the dump been taking the hot resins?"

Ballinger's face took on a sickly hue.

"Well," Hap said, "we get resins from reactor cleanups, spent fuel pools, messes at legacy sites." He whistled. "Boy could've stockpiled one hell of a shitload of stuff."

"And what," Soliano asked, "could he contaminate with such a quantity?"

"A shitload of the priceless."

"A shitload," Scotty said. "How the hell much is a shitload? How the hell is my team supposed to handle that? This is unbelievable. You guys let this clown steal this stuff for God knows how long and it's out there. Jesus Christ." He ran his hands through his hair. "And don't forget the Spare Cask. Why'd he steal that one? What's that for?"

I shrugged. Good question.

"Let me have a go at it," Walter said. "Let us say, on one of his swaps, he does not empty the resin beads into his stockpile. He sets that resin cask aside. For a rainy day." Walter selected an unopened pepper shaker, and set it aside. "Then, to keep the swap going, he will need a new empty cask. So he steals another —the second cask missing from the dump." Walter picked up the empty glass I'd set on the floor. "The Spare Cask, which now becomes the cask used for the ongoing swap. And the swap continues."

"So he's got his shitload of loose resins in the depot," Scotty said, "*and* he's got this rainy-day resin cask somewhere? Jesus H. Christ."

"Well what's the frigging rainy-day cask *for*?" Ballinger asked.

"What is *any* of it for?" Soliano snapped. "Find it. Before it matters." He checked his watch. "We have fifty hours until his deadline."

Walter said, "Cassie, there's something else."

With an effort, I nodded. What the hell else could there be?

"A message was sent, about finding our car."

"Backpackers. Hap told me."

Hap looked up from his sketchbook. "Told her what the message said."

"The wording is irrelevant," Soliano said. "The provenance is telling. It was a text message, routed through a re-sender in Bulgaria."

It took me longer than it should have. "Jardine?" I went cold. "But why?"

"The message means that he knew about, or carried out, the attack. Presumably his purpose was to interrupt your work, steal your samples. That achieved," Soliano shrugged, "perhaps he did not wish to accrue another murder charge."

"Jeez," Ballinger said, "that makes him some kinda twisted guardian angel."

The hairs rose on my forearms.

"Don't look like the hands of an angel," Hap said.

We all turned.

Hap was studying his sketchpad. "Look real earthly, to me." He reversed the pad, showing us. "Roy's hands."

The sketch was surprisingly detailed, considering the short time Hap had given it. Roy Jardine's hands looked ready to move. The long fingers flexed, showcasing big knuckles. The nails were short, squared. There was a signet ring on the right pinkie.

I said, "What's that engraving on the ring?"

"Beats me. I'm drawing it from memory."

Scotty peered. "The ocean, and a beach."

Walter moved closer. "No, it's the desert."

Hap beamed. "How about it's a Rorschach test? You know, the ink blots where everybody sees what they want to see? So Scotty wants to be surfing, and Walter's right where he belongs, the desert rat. How about the rest of you? Milt? Ever notice Roy's ring?"

"No, but I'd like to wring his disloyal neck."

"Hector? Give it your best shot. Could be a clue."

Despite himself, Soliano edged in for a look. "Desert," he said finally.

"Cassie?"

I said "Death Valley" although it could equally well have been the Great Rift Valley in Tanzania. I wished Jardine in Tanzania.

"Then desert it is, with a prejudice toward Death Valley." Hap studied his sketch. "Now the hands. You notice that little callus on the right middle digit? That's maybe Glock finger. Not so angelic. That's what you get when you shoot a lot and your finger rubs against the trigger guard." He glanced at us. "I used to shoot."

Walter threw me a look. Men carry guns, too.

"So what?" Scotty said. "We already figured Jardine shot Beltzman."

"Yeah but we haven't figured why." Hap shut the sketchbook. "I have a theory."

Soliano gave him the long look. "You are being very helpful, Mr. Miller."

"Doin my best, which you might mention to the CTC honchos in case the subject of rewards comes up." Hap grinned. "Anyhoo, I call it the one-thing-leads-to-another theory. Goes something like this—Ryan effs up some little thing and Roy yells at him. Ryan gets his feelings hurt and then, by and by, the gun comes out. Don't know whose gun, who shoots the tires, but at the crash site the gun ends up in the hand of the guy with Glock finger, Roy Jardine." Hap whistled, sound like a falling skyrocket. "The oops factor."

Soliano frowned. "The what?"

"Human frailty, Hector. Murphy's Law."

"You make a point, Mr. Miller?"

"Murphy's Law--that's when everything that can go wrong does go wrong, in the worst possible way." Hap cocked his head. "Surely you experienced that? You make a mistake that leads to another mistake, that leads to a real big miscalculation?"

My ears rang. Coyote scream, a cry for help. It almost had gone wrong, in the worst possible way. I nodded. Yeah, I knew Murphy's Law.

Walter looked, suddenly, older than his years. "We take your point, Hap."

Hap turned to Scotty. "Scotty me boy? Any miscalculations on your watch?"

"Yeah, lost track of a guy's dose rate once. He went over the limit. Anybody doses over again, on my watch, I go back to surfing and the sharks." Scotty glared. "That answer your question, Miller?"

"Honorably." Hap turned to Soliano. "Hector? Miscalculations?"

"On occasion. I am human."

"Me too! That's why I live in utter mortal dread of screwing the pooch, so to speak." Hap patted his T-shirt. "Homer and I know you don't wanna screw the pooch when you're in charge of the gents."

"Who are the gents?" Soliano asked.

"Mr. Alpha, Mr. Beta, Mr. Gamma. The gentlemen like to play real rough." Hap smiled. "Let me get philosophical for a minute. Ionizing radiation is by nature unstable, and people are like radionuclides. Unstable. It's like you said, Hector, we're human. So we jess cain't help it—we gotta eff up, now and again. And when you put your unstable people in charge of your unstable atoms..." He rolled his eyes. "Ooops."

It struck me that Hap had not asked about any screwups on Ballinger's watch. Then again, I guessed we were living one right now.

21

WALTER and I were making space in his suite to set up our lab when someone pounded on the door.

I opened it to the sound of shrieking. The girl was inches from me. My height. Weedy. Eyes wild. I took a step back. Shrieks came again, somewhere outside.

Walter came over. The girl grabbed his hand. "Hurry, Grandfather. Trouble."

I followed them outside and down the walkway that led from our annex.

Again, the shrieking.

I broke into a run, passing them both.

There were paths leading in four different directions, and steps going up a level and down a level. I glanced down at the pool. Nobody there. A woman in a peach uniform rushed past and I stopped her but before I could ask she said "aqui aqui" and took off. I followed.

The path rounded the hip of a building and dropped down into cascading palm gardens on a grassy hillside. I stared in some wonder at the stream bubbling down to the pond, which was carpeted in water lilies. I thought I heard a frog croak.

I hurried down.

There was a good-sized crowd under the palms—in bathing suits, shorts, sundresses, housekeeping uniforms—guests and staff shoulder-to-shoulder all pressing in on something and then, as one, heaving backward in a renewed hail of shrieks. I picked out Milt Ballinger's bald head, twisting to have a long look at the bare thonged behind of a blond woman tanned to mahogany.

I tightened my robe and wormed into the crowd.

I saw bits of green between sunburnt shoulders and Hawaiian shirts, as if these people had gathered in mass heat-stroke delusion to stare at the lawn. The hot air smelled of sweat and coconut oil. I tried to work my way through the throng but a mahogany-chested blond man—the match to Milt's thonged woman—blocked my way. He suddenly noticed me. "Kleine fledermaus," he said, and popped me up to the front of the crowd.

I thought I was the one with heat stroke. It followed me, I thought.

No question of mirage, this time.

The bat canted in the grass, one leathery wing dug into the thatch, the other wing half-folded. The little body was raw with sores. One translucent ear was bent and cemented to the head by a yellowish crust. The creature had left a mark of its progress, a thin black trail of feces that culminated, where it now crouched, in a red-tinged seep. Suddenly the mouth opened to reveal a bloodied tooth hanging from its gums. The bat emitted a shrill cry.

The crowd cried back.

I saw, at the far end of the crowd, Walter and the girl. He had a hand on her shoulder. I wanted to go over and ask if he thought it was the same bat we'd seen on the saltpan, if it gave him a shiver like it gave me, but at that moment Scotty pushed through the crowd.

"Get back, get back, raus everybody, vaya vaya, merci people, get yourselves the heck outta the way!" Scotty ran one hand through his blond hair, spiking it, and with his other hand raised his cell phone. "Jasper, get yourself into a suit now and bring a Geiger and a collection box..." He looked around. "Some kinda gardens. Next to the pool."

The bat opened its mouth and the dangling tooth dropped like a tiny spear into the grass. A Japanese woman began taking pictures. Scotty tried to block her view and a Japanese man complained.

Soliano brushed past me, whispering to a white-haired ranger.

Passing along the cover story, I guessed. We are, officially, an EPA team monitoring the health of the local ecosystem.

"Show's over, folks," the ranger shouted, flapping his hands, and the gawkers reluctantly fell back.

Scotty was on the phone again, standing sentinel between the bat and the departing crowd, sparing more than a few glances for the retreating behinds.

I moved to Soliano, whose attention was fixed on the bat. "We saw a bat last night."

He flinched.

"Didn't mean to startle you."

"It is just..." He touched his forehead. "I am reminded."

"Of what?"

"A dying dog. And the heat."

I asked, anxious to figure out Soliano, "What happened?"

He angled toward me, although his eyes never left the bat. "I was a boy in a family of wealth. Our estate was in the mountains, for the coolness. I was driven to school by a chauffeur. A small sedan, so as not to draw attention. The windows were tinted, so that no one might see inside. My family wished to avoid trouble. Once, unfortunately, trouble found us on the drive to school. A man and a dog lay in the road, blocking our way. They had been shot. Bandits. My chauffeur was fearful. He was fearful to turn around and take me home because his job was to deliver me to school. He was fearful to bring the wounded man into the car...all the blood. He was fearful to get out and move the man out of the way...bandits, he feared. He was fearful of the dog, which showed its teeth. My chauffeur could not drive around the man and the dog. The road was narrow, ditches on each side. He was fearful to drive over the man, afraid for his own mortal soul. The consequence was that we waited in the car. It grew stifling." Sweat bloomed, now, on Soliano's face. "At last the man appeared to have died. My chauffeur drove onward. I felt a bump. That was all." Soliano made his gesture, hand to brow. "I looked out the back window. The man was crushed. But the dog, remarkably, lifted its head. I saw the teeth. I knew I was going to have dreams of those teeth. The sun must have lighted the teeth but I feared it was God's doing. I thought the dog had been resurrected to exact revenge because we did not act."

After an excruciating half-minute in the stifling vacuum, I had to say something. "You were just a kid."

Soliano gave a curt nod.

"The chauffeur was in charge."

Another nod.

The bat opened its eyes. They were a solid milk of cataracts.

Soliano flicked aside his khaki shirttail, reached into his waistband holster, and brought out a small pistol. He fired and the bat somersaulted backward, leaving a new trail of blood. It did not move again.

This time, I said nothing. He'd done the right thing—people had to be protected, and the creature surely needed to be put out of its misery—but I felt I was intruding on Soliano's peculiar path to action.

"Hector." Scotty was suddenly with us. "You got a lab in Vegas can do a necropsy?" He eyed the carcass. "Looks a whole lot like ARS."

I knew those initials but Soliano had to ask.

"Acute radiation sickness," Scotty answered.

22

Roy Jardine woke up bright and early Wednesday morning.

Well, it wasn't bright because he was deep inside the hideout, and eight a.m. wasn't that early. But he'd deserved a good night's sleep.

He ate his freeze-dried Eggs Ranchero with satisfaction, as if they were real eggs.

He dressed with satisfaction. He wore his shirt with the cowboy pockets and pearl buttons, Levi jeans, and concho-strap boots. Although he could not see himself—there was no mirror in the hideout, that would be vain—he knew he looked ace. A pity nobody was here to see him in this outfit.

Today, he dressed for himself. For the occasion: Strike Day.

He assessed his mental state. Ready? Yes. Rested? Yes.

Come to terms with the events of yesterday?

Yesterday—Tuesday at three p.m. precisely—he'd had his brainstorm. How to stop the geologists. And it worked. They were stopped. Their dirt map was destroyed. They were left to the mercy of the desert.

He'd retreated to *Hole-in-the-Wall* in relief.

And there he'd turned his efforts to the mission. He worked

on the plan for hours, well into the night, but when he rechecked his work he'd been disappointed. Too many details left out. Too much left to chance. He'd berated himself. Then forgiven himself. He was exhausted. He'd been without sleep for almost two days.

And he was missing Jersey.

That's when he'd let his guard down.

Somehow, in his weary soul, his bitch got mixed up with the female geologist. He was driving her in his pickup--he'd given her a ride! But then he realized he couldn't take her with him, where he was going, so he had to leave her by the side of the road. She'd have to hitchhike. But that wasn't safe. She was better off hiking into the desert, where nobody could find her. And then he'd allowed himself a better fantasy: himself coming to the rescue, finding her, scooping her in his arms and carrying her into the shade and laying her down and sharing his water. She'd been so thirsty. He'd cupped her head so she could drink from his bottle.

Then his fantasy turned dark. She'd died in the desert. He was glad. She was the enemy.

And then his rational self had intervened. If the geologists died in the desert, Mister FBI would bring in somebody to replace them. Snap his fingers like in a snooty restaurant. Waiter! My wine has spilled. Bring me another! And Roy Jardine would not get the opportunity to study a replacement, up close. He needed to keep *these* geologists. He felt he knew them. He could plan ahead, predicting what they would do.

He'd decided there was no need for the geologists to die. He could not count on them to save themselves, or get found, and so he'd saved them himself. He'd texted the message. Pretended it was from backpackers, a real smart detail. Then he had sent another message, this one to CTC, telling them what was required of them.

His work for the night at last done, he'd gotten into his sleeping bag and slept the sleep of the just.

And now, Wednesday morning, a new day. Strike Day.

Refreshed, dressed for the occasion, he turned again to the mission plan. His desk was a crate and his tools were pencil and paper. In this humble workplace, he would launch the mission. A year in the planning, it was a good plan. He need adjust only a few details to deal with the enemy.

Fresh start. He crumpled last night's pages and flung them away.

Jersey's collar hung on a nail. He touched it for good luck.

He drew up his new timetable. The mission had two stages. He could choose the timing of Stage One. In fact, he had just chosen. Today.

But Stage Two—the consummation, the grand finale—was harder to schedule. That depended upon forces beyond his control: the trigger event. He could only estimate when that would happen. That's why, in his email to CTC, he'd given the deadline of Friday noon. That gave him over two days. That should be enough.

He worked a good four hours adjusting the details. Travel times. Setup times. Tools needed. And then he went over everything again.

When he finished, he collected his tools and packed his pack. He added three water bottles and more freeze-dried junk because the Stage One strike would take many hours. And then, regretfully, he changed his clothes. The jeans were fine but he needed hiking boots, not high-heeled cowboy boots. He replaced the cowboy shirt with a stained green T-shirt and tucked his ponytail under the Budweiser ball cap.

Incognito, he went outside.

It was hot as an oven. He didn't care. It was a good day because it was Strike Day.

He set off, hiking full of joy. He arrived at the site at one thirty-five p.m., ten minutes ahead of schedule.

He waited, incognito, watching for vehicles. Watching for other hikers.

It was too hot. There was nobody around.

He took the booties out of his pocket. He knew, now, how the geologists could track dirt. He probably had dirt from the hideout in his boots, and he knew what happened with dirty footwear. Every day when he came home from work at the dump, he had dump dirt on his shoes, and he'd have to stamp his shoes on the porch to clean them, and then he'd sweep up the dislodged dirt, and then he'd take off his shoes before going into the house because he could never get them clean enough and he hated, just hated, tracking in dirt. Now, of course, stamping his feet wasn't enough. She would put her nosy nose right to his bootprints and find something. He smiled. Not this time, he told her. He pulled on his booties, covering his dirty hiking boots.

He hiked up the ridge to the gate.

He unlocked the gate. His was a duplicate key, made to fit the Park Service lock. He went inside, shutting the gate behind him, reminding himself to leave it unlocked when he left. He moved deeper inside and then unslung his pack and got out the flashlight.

Dark in here. Of course he knew his way. He'd been here before, two weeks ago, setting up Stage One of the mission. At that point, of course, he had no idea things would go critical. But it really did not matter because the details still worked. The name of the operation still fit: *The Trial*. He had one adjustment to make, and that's why he was here again now. It was a brilliant adjustment. It would put the enemy on the run.

He took out the rest of his gear.

As he dressed out, he thought about the female. No fantasies now. His thoughts hardened. The geologists had suffered in the desert. Not just physically—the mental was more important. The geologists were good. And now they were wounded. In their predictable brains there had been planted an invader. Fear.

He finished dressing out and started down the tunnel.

An hour later he was up at the observation post.

When he'd settled in, he got out his laptop and sent another message. Telling them it was time. Telling them where to come. An invitation. He liked putting it that way. So polite. Of course, they would not refuse. They would come. And then *The Trial* would commence.

23

I SAID, "We're going to have to go back up the canyons."

Walter had his nose in the Munsell color charts, ranking the hue of layer five. His tongue was anchored between his teeth. He was showered, shaved, dressed, and looking little worse for the wear.

I was showered and dressed.

Walter put up a hand: let me finish. Color is subjective. Most soils are adulterated with gray, so the question is: is layer five's gray a departure from the neutral, or not?

I waited. It matters. Color is a signpost of source. I hoped he'd find a lead. I sure had nothing new. In the four hours since Soliano had shot the bat, we'd struggled to reassemble our map. While Walter set up our lab, I'd been choppered to the talc mine to take new samples. When I returned, we began anew the task of creating definable layers out of the odds and ends of fender soils. After two hard hours, the only new thing I had was a craving for ham-and-tomato sandwiches. I said, finally, "Anything?"

"Same thing I found yesterday."

"It's a start."

"A restart. We've lost a full day." Walter closed his chart and swiveled to face me. "As to the canyons, Hector's offered an escort."

We'd lost more than a day. We'd lost our freedom in the field. I curled my hands, where the cut palm stung. I focused on Walter's hands, which rested on his thighs. Hands marked by the years and the sun and the rocks in the field. Blunt-fingered corded hands, still strong. Hap should draw those hands. There was a thin white scar on his right pointer, courtesy of his pocket knife. I had my own knife scar—right thumb, from peeling crystals of mica. And now of course I had a fresh palm wound, although I couldn't blame that on normal wear and tear. I regarded our four hands. Not a Glock callus in sight. We were sitting ducks. I said, "Good idea."

We worked another half-hour and then there came a knock at the door.

"Will you get that?" Walter said, nose in his soils. "It may be Pria."

"Who's Pria?"

"Our girl. She appears to spend her free time around here."

I rose. "You know her name."

"Shouldn't I?"

There was another knock—pounding this time—and I thought, not only do we require babysitting, we're becoming babysitters, and I reached the door and opened it before she could pound again. But it wasn't Pria, it was Hap.

He said, "We got mail."

We left the Inn by convoy.

Walter and I rode with Soliano and Hap and Ballinger in a

green Jeep that Soliano had appropriated from the Park Service. RERT vans tailed us.

We took highway 190 around the back of the Inn and up the stem of the fan into the mountains. The road followed a wide gravelly wash, which climbed gently between two parallel ranges. To our left continued the abrupt face of the Funerals. To our right began the Black Mountains, which ran southward between the saltpan and the Funerals. We were wedged between two mountain faces as different as Walter's and—it came to me—Pria's. The cavernous Funerals were folded in sunburnt browns and somber grays and the gentle Blacks were furred in pastel mudstones. We passed a beard of white issuing from the fault zone along the base of the Funerals. Travertine deposits, I hazarded. Old dry springs.

Indeed, we were traveling up a long drainage ditch. I saw how the waters that drained from the Funerals and Blacks would collect in the gravelly wash, which would channel those waters with their sediment load down to spill onto the fan. I saw how the fan was still being built.

I'd keep that flood channel in mind, what with these hurricane-spawned storms. I had checked the weather report and learned that the hurricane off Baja California, according to Monday's forecast, would be throwing storms our way all week. I'd keep in mind the Park Service's Doppler radar scan, which provided a detailed flood risk index.

I peered at the sky. Broken clouds.

"Dolomite up there," Walter said, peering at the Funerals.

I saw. Dolomite in fender layer four. How coy of Jardine if he'd stashed his radioactive booty in the Funerals.

Our destination, however, was in the Black Mountains. We turned off 190 onto the graded road that cut into Twenty-Mule-Team Canyon. The jumbled badlands were naked of any shrub, their eroded contours shaded in mustard and cream and purple and pink. Black-mouthed burrows pockmarked the hills.

Walter checked his map against the GPS coordinates in Jardine's email.

You are cordially invited, Jardine had written. And then he gave the time and place. And then he set the hook: *A package awaits you inside the borax mine.*

And we bit. We couldn't pass up the chance to recover at least some of the stolen radwaste. Of course, we had to consider that it might be a trap, which was why we planned to proceed with all due care. Or, maybe, nothing awaited us in the mine, and this was a hoax—Jardine running us around the desert, deflecting us from our job of following the evidence.

The road climbed and curved and I stopped admiring the geology and started worrying about the mine we'd been invited to. The mudstone was now shot with snowy veins of borate ore. I knew my mining geology—anyone who worked with Walter had to know her mining geology. An ancient lake once filled this area, collecting alluvia from the surrounding mountains, some of whose rocks contained boron. And then the lake dried up and the borates were precipitated out, and then people came along to mine it, and then Roy Jardine came along to defile the already cored-out hills.

We rounded the bend and Walter said, "Here."

The convoy stopped. We piled out and flinched, hammered by the heat.

There was a small ridge above us and footprints led up the hillside. We paused to examine them. They were fresh, made after this morning's thundershower. We'd seen their like before, at the crash site: dimple-soled rubber prints, bootie prints. Roy Jardine's prints. Very smart, Roy. So you really were here. I shivered.

Scotty took the lead. In his board shorts and Hawaiian shirt he looked like the surfer dude he'd been. But he was RERT chief now with instruments strapped over each shoulder. We went single-file along the spine of the ridge, a beaten path in the crumbly soil. If I were making a movie starring the badlands of Mars, I'd film it here. Where clouds shadowed it, the soil looked bruised, but it nonetheless threw up waves of heat. I took small breaths, hoping to cool the air before it seared my lungs. Mars-breathing.

Ahead, the ridge dead-ended in the flank of a hill. Scotty metered the area and then gave us a thumbs-up.

We followed the bootie prints to the adit that cored into the hillside. The adit was about six feet high and wide enough for a couple of fat mules. Nothing fancy, no timbers, no rails, just a gate barring entrance and a warning sign: *DANGER: Loose rock. Decaying explosives. Bad air. Rattlesnakes.*

To say nothing of whatever Jardine had left for us in there.

Hap read the sign. "Whew, no bats."

Scotty turned to Soliano. "Hey, what about the bats?" Scotty had found and collected the bat on the saltpan and handed off both carcasses to a lab in Vegas that could do a radioanalysis necropsy, fast.

Soliano squinted, as if fighting a vision of sunlit teeth. "Radiation sickness."

We digested that. Nobody voiced the thought that two bats, somewhere within their range, had encountered a lethal source of high-rad resins. Nobody said aloud, maybe somewhere is here.

Soliano had a Park Service key but he didn't need it—the gate nudged open.

Walter said, "Look at those."

Tire tracks, faint but unmistakable, inside the adit. I looked back along the ridge but if there had been tracks incised there, rain or wind had obliterated them. Still, whatever rolled into this tunnel must have come up that path. Narrow, but doable—fit for a Mars-roving telehandler.

No way to know when the telly was here but I figured I knew the *why*. To transport a cask. Any thought that our summons was a hoax wilted in the hot adit mouth.

"Okey-doke," Scotty said, "let's get to it."

Soliano started. "But you are not yet suited."

"Checking for gas, first, Hector. Carbon monoxide, dioxide. Collects in old mines near the floor. We walk around much and we'll stir it up."

I felt monumentally relieved that Scotty knew this. That he was prepared for whatever mother nature, along with Roy Jardine, had in store for us.

Scotty took his meters into the tunnel. After a full minute, he emerged. "Yup, we got gas." He rubbed his face. "Shit, we gotta go in full bug suits. My people'll die before they even get here, just hiking up that ridge dressed out. Think I'll set up the zone right here. Christ, I wonder if snakebite goes through rubber." He glanced at Soliano and dimpled, briefly. "All right, no worry, I got it."

Hap lowered his fedora. "I ain't worrying. Course, I ain't going in."

Scotty stalked off along the ridge.

"Let us lend a hand," Soliano said, to Hap and Ballinger. To me and Walter, he said, "You rest, in the eventuality your skills are needed."

Walter and I sank against the hillside. I said, "He expects us to go in."

"It's not his call."

"Right."

"If we do decide to go in," he said, "there's no need for the both of us."

I let that hang in the hot air between us.

We watched Scotty and his crew hauling equipment out of the vans. Soliano, Ballinger, and Hap began ferrying the stuff up the ridge. Hap took the lead, laden with silvery suits. He was whistling—heigh-ho, heigh-ho, it's off to work we go. He appeared to be having fun. Just when I think I can predict him, I can't.

I glanced at Walter. "I don't mind snakes, per se."

His eyes were closed. "Rattlesnakes."

I studied his flushed face. "Big ones, I'd think."

"Mean, certainly."

"Cranky, anyway."

He said, "I go in."

"Let's wait and see what Scotty finds before we take on snakes."

"You're of child-bearing age," he said. "I go in."

He will never, ever, let the subject go. I said, "You're at an age where your cells are not so resilient."

"Thank you for the reminder."

"Thank Hap."

We all waited, stacked against the hillside, while Scotty paced and his three RERT colleagues rested. Scotty had sent in the smallest of his team, a wiry woman with a purple punk 'do named Lucy who, it struck me, looked of child-bearing age.

The heat was a bath, submerging us. We could drown in this heat. I watched cloud shadows tongue along the ridge and strained to detect the drop of a degree Fahrenheit or two.

Fifteen minutes later Lucy emerged, looking like her next stop was Mars. Scotty metered her at the hot line then helped her skin off the heavy suit. She pushed back her hood and spat out the respirator and rasped out a word.

I thought she said *fuck* and didn't blame her.

"Went right," she rasped. "Nothing."

Oh, *fork*. Shit.

Scotty raked his hair, spiking the wet strands. "Okay, I get to go." A tall thin RERT guy named Tim grumbled to his feet to help Scotty dress out.

We waited, sucking our water bottles dry. I believed I saw bees buzzing a great sunflower but it was only heat waves flaming off an orange hill.

Twenty minutes later, by my watch—hours, by my fried brain—Scotty reappeared. When Scotty was stripped to his shorts, when he had downed half a bottle of water, he gave Soliano the thumbs-up.

Now we know, I thought. Okay, it's better to know.

Soliano got to his feet. "In a cask, or loose?"

Scotty tried to speak, and then just mouthed it. Cask.

"Contents?"

"Hot."

I licked my cracked lips. The real deal, this time.

"And so we account," Soliano said, "for one of two missing casks."

I wondered which one. The swap cask, which Jardine recovered from the talc mine? Or was this the rainy-day cask? Then again, what did it matter, which one? What mattered was what it held.

Scotty cleared his throat. "Another thing. Mud on the cask. Spattered."

I sat up straight. "What's it look like?"

"Mud."

"Well did it look like it came from the surrounding soil?"

He lifted his palms.

Whether it was the swap cask or rainy-day cask, it could have been stored at Jardine's depot before being brought here. I looked at Walter, and he nodded. We wanted that mud.

"Geologists." Soliano toed the soil. "*This* could be Mr. Jardine's depot?"

I doubted it. Couldn't swear to it. If we hadn't lost our soil map, if we weren't playing catch-up, we could say something with some heft. I said, instead, "It's not consistent with the soils we've analyzed so far."

"Then this is *what*? A demonstration, that Mr. Jardine has the hot resins and can place them wherever he wishes?"

Scotty answered. "I'm convinced." He ran his hand through his hair. "Could be something more, some kind of taunt. I mean, it's sure the right place for it. Borax mine."

"This means...?"

There came a strangled sound, from Ballinger. I thought he was going to be sick. Hap leaned in whispering, the brim of his fedora eclipsing Ballinger's glistening scalp. Then Hap got to his feet. "Milt just recalled a little incident that might tie in here."

"Yes?" Soliano said.

Ballinger hunched, silent.

"Sorry Hector," Hap said. "Milt doesn't have a fully developed sense of irony."

"I have," Soliano said. "Explain to me this irony."

Hap shrugged. "Like Scotty said, this place makes a point. Borax ore contains the element boron. And boron, Hector, is a crackerjack neutron absorber. They put it in the reactor control rods to slow the fission process—keep that chain reaction under control."

"Yes?"

"So, Milt's little incident began with the boron-recycle system at the nuke plant. Once upon a time plant's getting decommissioned and sends the dump the resins they'd used to clean the system. Low curie-count, so casks get buried in the trench."

Soliano frowned. "I thought resins were hot. Or hotter."

"Depends what they pick up. Pick up hot clides, they're hot. Boron resins are low-rad."

"Mild salsa," I said.

He nodded. "Anyhoo, couple weeks later a guy's digging a drainage ditch—and he's a mite hungover—and he sideswipes a row of containers. Including the boron resin casks. But he doesn't notice. Couple months later somebody sees the trench is slumping. Now, they have to regrade it." Hap sighed. "Woman by the name of Sheila Cook gets nominated. Gets her backhoe stuck. Gets out to inspect, sees she's tramping around in beads. Dang. She calls in the cavalry. And when they frisk the beads, surprise! Triple-X hot." He winked at me. "Been used to clean the spent-fuel pool. Turns out somebody at the nuke plant loaded them into the wrong cask and it shipped with the low-rad load."

"Christ," Scotty said, "nobody caught it before it got buried?"

"What you gotta understand, Scotty, is trucks were backed up half a mile waiting to unload. Busy time at the dump. So they frisked the resin truck and the overall dose rate was under the limit and they were under-staffed and all those high-rad trucks were waiting." Hap smiled that curbed smile of his. "And that story came to be known in the dump oral history as Boron-gate."

"Very witty," Soliano said. "And Ms. Cook?"

Hap sighed again. "Starts woofin her cookies couple days after the incident. But she recovers, so the question becomes what're the long-term effects? She gonna win the cancer lottery? By gum, she do. About seven years later she gets leukemia." Hap whipped off his hat and held it over his heart. "Now, I didn't see the poor woman get crapped up—this all happened afore I found my fortunate way to the dump—but it's one of them legendary stories what get told to the new guy." He glanced down at Ballinger. "That's what Milt's feeling a mite sick over right now."

I fixed on Ballinger oozing sweat and thought, he's doing the math.

Soliano said, "Mr. Ballinger, you were manager at the time of this incident?"

Ballinger nodded.

"You gave the order to hasten the disposal?"

Ballinger started to speak, and then just nodded.

"This was CTC policy?"

Now he spoke. "Policy is avoid delays and make a profit. Safety first, and all."

"Did CTC bear liability for Ms. Cook's contamination?"

"Paid workers comp till she recovered."

"And later? The leukemia?"

"No proof that one-time incident caused it. Lotsa things cause cancer."

"The cancer lottery," Soliano said, with distaste.

"Yeah, that's what it's called around here. You know, black humor."

"I will wish to contact Sheila Cook."

Ballinger wiped his skull. "She's dead."

I recoiled, as though I hadn't expected that.

"She died....when?"

"That would be, uh, two years ago."

"And you learned of her death...how?"

"Grapevine."

Soliano squatted in front of Ballinger. "And Mr. Jardine? When did he come to work for you?"

"That would be, um, three years ago. Same year she left. You know, when she got, uh, sick."

"So their employment overlapped?"

"No, he came later in the year."

"Then Mr. Jardine would not have encountered her?"

"Not at the dump."

"Meaning what? He encountered her outside the work place?"

"Girlfriend, I'm thinking," Hap said.

Ballinger looked at his shoes. "Sister."

Soliano cursed softly in Spanish.

I cursed silently, in English.

"Mr. Ballinger." Soliano gathered himself. "You did not recall a grievance he might hold against you, in regard to his sister?"

"Just found out she *was*. She's listed as his emergency contact on the new hire form. Sheila Cook. Sister. Guess it was her married name." Ballinger wiped his oiled face. "And I guess after she died, Roy never bothered to change his info. Point is, I didn't know. I mean, who reads that stuff anyway—unless you need it?"

Soliano said, "I read that stuff."

"Okay, see, I looked it over before I gave it to you and it kinda broadsided me—her being his sister. So I, uh, deleted it." Ballinger took on a tight unwilling look. "Didn't see any point in the FBI digging up ancient history. I mean, what difference does it make now?"

Soliano said, icily, "Motive."

"So he's got a bone to pick."

"Two bones, Mr. Ballinger. Let us not forget the prank that scarred his face. He might, perhaps, blame you for a...culture of lax management?"

"Well he never complained to *me* about it."

Hap looked pained. "Uh, what if he's sending a message now, Milt? You know—boron, control rods, chain reaction? And we're at the wrong end of a chain reaction. Let's see, nuke plant shuts down, got no more use for all the gear but you can't sell the gear on eBay because the gear's crapped up, so the gear gets shipped to the dump, but the paperwork's effed up and the backhoe driver's hung over and then poor Ms. Cook steps in it and gets contaminated and wins the cancer lottery. Then brother Roy gets a feather up his and decides to put it to you, brother Roy's got access to all those rads—and brother Roy's gonna pull the rods and let that chain reaction go critical. Metaphorically speaking."

"Christ," Scotty said, "so that diagram he drew on the truck —skull and bones, the guy running away? That's supposed to be you, Milt?"

I stared. My stick figure?

Ballinger said, "That's a buncha crapola."

"No Milt," Walter snapped, "that's revenge."

My thoughts took off along the chain of events. Brother Roy takes a job at the radwaste dump where his sister got crapped up. Maybe he's looking to gather evidence of mismanagement—a lawsuit. Then his sister dies. And the prank is just one more grievance. So he settles upon revenge. He plans the swap. He enlists Chickie and her talc, or he just steals it. He enlists the truck driver; maybe he sells the plan as extortion, offering a cut. The pothead buys it. They siphon off radwaste for who knows how long. Then something goes wrong. Maybe Ryan Beltzman learns Jardine's real motive and wants no part of it. And there's the fight, the chase, the crash, the shooting. And that changes things...how? Where does the chain reaction go from there? Metaphorically speaking.

If the running figure is Milt, he's not running alone any longer. We're right there with him.

Soliano moved to me and Walter. He looked haggard, his face more bony than aristocratic. "This mud on the cask—this could be from his depot?"

I nodded.

"Go get it."

"Which one of you?" Scotty asked, rummaging through the suits.

Walter started to speak but I clamped his arm. "I'm smaller."

Walter shook me off and headed for the suits.

I followed and said, "And I'm healthy."

He shot me a look I would not like to see again.

I pulled him aside and said, harshly, "You're flushed. Try wearing one of those bug suits. Get halfway into the tunnel and pass out. Somebody has to come in after you. Go ahead and push yourself real hard and see if you can bring on another stroke. Then you'll be in the hospital and I'll be here doing this job without you and that's damned unfair."

Walter looked at the others. They hadn't heard, or pretended not to. He gave me a brusque nod.

Feeling like the biggest shit in the world, I went to Scotty. "It'll be me."

Scotty had offered to go back in himself and scrape some mud but I needed to see it, undisturbed, in situ. Read the pattern of deposition before ruining it to take a sample.

So now it became my show.

Scotty opened an ice chest, pulled out a plastic vest filled with something that looked like blue ice, and then wrapped it like a gift around my baked husk. I had a moment to enjoy that and then Scotty worked me into the rubberized suit out of hell. I asked, "How much does this bug suit weigh?"

He said, stern, "I call it a bug suit because I've worn it more times than I can count." He packed me into the air tank and harness assembly. "You're gonna call it a fully-encapsulated suit with self-contained breathing apparatus because I don't want you to forget why you're wearing it."

Hardly likely.

"Weighs about sixty pounds."

I would have said a hundred.

"I already metered for background radiation," Scotty said. "We're at eleven micro-Roentgens per hour. That's what we'd expect around here, so no worry. You know, rads from rocks and..." He dimpled. "Well, rocks, that's your department. Right-O?"

"Right-O." There's some uranium and thorium in most rocks and soils, but around here it'd be down to point oh-oh parts per million. No worry. About the rocks.

Scotty rummaged in his box of meters and brought out a Geiger counter. "This one's for you. See the rate chart? Tells you rads based on clicks per second—alpha, beta, gamma. You get inside the tunnel, should sound about like this." He snapped his fingers, paused, snapped again. "When you reach the fork, your reading's gonna pick up a little." He snapped a little faster. "When you see the cask, should sound about like this." Faster. "Don't get any closer than you need—Lucy's making you a tool. And you wanna limit your time. Just grab your dirt and go, real fast. Got it?"

"Got it."

"Your Geiger sounds like a machine-gun, you make that Titanic face and get the hell out."

I swallowed. "Got it."

Lucy came over with the tool. It was the type of telescoping wand the woman at the dump had used to meter the cask at a respectable distance. Scotty had, I assumed, used it in the adit here, to similar purpose. Now it was my turn. Lucy had duct-taped a small scoop to the end of the wand. Very clever. She made a fist and after a moment I understood and balled my free hand and we bumped fists. Very cool.

Scotty moved back in. When I was fully encapsulated, he connected the breathing hose and opened the valve. "Gimme a big inhale." He hung the Geiger around my neck, attached the headlamp, and tapped the hood. "We'll stay in touch."

There was nothing for it now but to get on with the show.

I moved, elephantine. Walter intercepted me and fastened the belt bag of tools around my bulky girth. I extended my fist. He pretended not to notice. He said, "Watch out for snakes."

As I passed Hap, he outlined a cross over me.

I remembered. Go with low dose.

I entered the adit. Already sweating. Turtling along in my thousand-pound rubber shell. The floor was furred with decomposed borates. If I tripped and pitched face-down I doubted I'd be able to right myself. My headlamp lit the near view, the hacked throat of crumbly gold and milky white. Further on, the gullet was pitchy black.

I followed the tire tracks.

There was a sudden glitter at the edge of my vision and I thought bat eyes, but of course it was just my light sparkling off faceted ore.

"How you doing?" Scotty's voice, jovial, came in my facepiece speaker.

"Fine," I lied. Back ached, sweat leaked, cool vest chafed, mouth metallic, and I was already hallucinating bats.

The Geiger clicked leisurely. Snap...snap.

I returned my attention to the tracks. They grew spotty as the soil thinned and the floor showed its base rock.

Up ahead, the gullet split in two.

For a wild moment I couldn't remember which fork Lucy had taken, which fork I need take, and I didn't want to take the wrong fork and spend one extra second entombed in this suit in this place. The tire tracks were unreadable—Scotty and Lucy had made such a mess that it was simply hopeless. I was making a bigger mess with my own shuffling bug-suited feet.

I squeaked, "Left fork, right?"

"No, not right," Scotty boomed in my ears, "go left."

Something skittered in my beam. My heart lurched. A small naked form turned tail and disappeared into the left fork. Some kind of rat. So the air in that fork was rat-safe, anyway. Can rat teeth go through bug suits?

Bile came up into my mouth. I forced it down in dread of retching into my self-contained breathing apparatus.

And now my Geiger counter was growing chattier. I checked the rate chart. All was as Scotty said it should be.

Okay, just keep going.

I forced myself into the left fork, following the rat.

Following Roy Jardine. Had he worn a bug suit? Surely a veteran of the radwaste dump knew what to wear in here. I hoped, fervently, that he had ached and sweated and chafed. I felt no sympathy for him, none at all. I felt a sorrow for his poor dead sister. And for the rest of us.

Up ahead, my headlamp beam caught on a roadblock of silver.

The cask seemed to fill the adit. It was the same make I'd seen at the crash site, and at the dump—that hefty tin can of a cask—and down here stuffed into the gullet of the mountain it looked monumental.

I heaved my weighted self to a stop. "I'm looking at it," I told Scotty.

"Okey-doke. You got twenty minutes air left but you might wanna hurry it up."

My Geiger chattered gaily. I checked the chart. All was as it should be.

I stood where I assumed Scotty had stood, at a telescoping-wand's distance. I played my beam over the skin of the cask and saw what Scotty had seen: patches of dried mud, like the cask was molting. A dark gray mud. Not—just eyeballing it—the same species as the native soil around here. Not—a reasoned leap—acquired here. The mud was spattered across the lower reaches of the cask. I thought that over. Let's say this cask was stored at the depot, until Jardine decided to bring it here. And in the process of loading it for transport maybe he spun the wheels of a telehandler or trailer in wet soil, and spattered the cask.

I wanted that mud.

I tucked Lucy's tool under my arm and opened my belt bag, fishing for the specimen dish. I couldn't tell a dish from a hand lens through this clown glove. Come on come on. You wanna limit your time. Just grab your dirt and go. Whatever I'd been fingering slipped away. I swallowed a curse. Scotty was listening. What if he told Walter I was stressed? And Walter's already berating himself for letting me bully him into staying behind, and he's got Soliano's noblesse oblige dogging him, and if there's anything Walter hates more than letting himself down, it's letting others down. He's out there telling himself he feels just fine, and he's never happy unless he can put his own eyes on the scene, and it's not out of the question that he'll bully Scotty into dressing him out and sending him in here to help.

I secured the specimen dish and set it on the ground.

I untelescoped Lucy's tool and held the thing like a fishing pole, fishing for the spot just above the cask's base collar where the largest mud patches clung.

The scoop banged against steel and it made a big sound.

And then there was a long moment when I didn't understand, when I thought the sound came from my headset—Scotty banging his microphone into something—and then I thought I'd somehow dislodged a rat nest and it was rat turds spewing out. And then I focused on the yawning rip in the cask. Did I do that? With Lucy's tool? And then I recoiled. The cask shat out beads, and beads geysered through the tunnel and spattered me and pooled at my feet and before I could backpedal out of their path, beads buried my booties.

I must have screamed.

Scotty yelped in my earphones.

I paid no heed to my ringing ears, to Scotty's babble—I paid heed, rather, to my little Geiger counter that was clicking its fool head off.

I prepared to step out of the shower but Scotty stopped me. "Lemme get those hard-to-reach places." He had a long-handled brush. "Lift the suit."

I pulled it up so that the leg wrinkles smoothed out, like I was hiking up a pair of sagging pantyhose, and Scotty scrubbed. Water was pumped from a RERT van up the ridge, and the hose connected to a PVC-pipe frame, and a nozzle rained the water down on me, and it pooled at my feet in a bright yellow catch basin that looked like a blow-up wading pool. I concentrated fiercely on the ludicrousness of this scene, of a toy shower stall outside a mine adit in the desert, of me in my bug suit being scrubbed down by Scotty in his suit. Some kind of kinky scene for hazmat fetishists. I focused on the soapy water that sluiced off my suit into the catch basin, on the hose that pumped the contaminated water out of the shower and down the ridge to the waste tank in the van.

"Raise your arms."

I complied, numb, so Scotty could get at the hard-to-reach

alphas and betas, but it was what he couldn't get at, what my bug suit couldn't keep out, that kept me sweating.

I saw Walter, who had come to the edge of the decon corridor and was staring at me like I was from Mars. Soliano touched Walter's elbow and said something I could not hear over the hiss of my tank.

"Damn you," Walter said.

I heard that. But I didn't blame Soliano for the exposure because I would have chosen to go in no matter what he said, and so would Walter, because there was the chance we could get a jump on locating the rest of the radwaste—although that chance had been blown to dust—and I knew Walter would not be blaming Soliano if Walter were the one standing here being deconned.

Scotty moved between me and them, blocking my line of sight. He shut off the water. He went over me hood to boots with the Geiger and this time, unlike his frisk before the shower, the counter relaxed. I relaxed too, a fraction. Scotty opened my hood and removed my facepiece. I sucked in sweet hot air. He disconnected the regulator and took the tank off my back. I felt so light I could float away.

He doffed his own breather. "Doing okay?"

I nodded and turned my face to the sky, to the low brutal sun, and for a moment the solar rays on my liberated skin felt simply like a beachy summer afternoon.

"Okey-doke," he said, "we're gonna peel you outta that suit."

I said, "Do I have a problem?"

"About?"

"Gammas."

He said, grim, "Puppies throw off some gammas."

I shifted in my two-ton suit. "Any lead in this? Like the dentist's bib?"

"You can't wear a suit with enough lead to protect against gammas, and still move."

"What's my dosimeter say?"

"Says you picked up some gammas. And I'm real unhappy about that. Rules say a civilian shouldn't be exposed to more'n a hundred millirems a year—above and beyond the background dose."

"How safe's the dose limit, Scotty?"

"Depends what you mean by safe."

"The numbers they put in the equations. That correlate millirems to likely effects. Hap says it's a guess."

"Hap's a clown."

"So you trust the numbers?"

"Gotta have *some* guideline." He shifted. "Anyway, we go by alara."

"What's alara?"

"A-L-A-R-A. As low as reasonably achievable. It means, let's not take the dose limit as a goal. Let's lowball the exposures. If we can."

But we hadn't.

"Hey Cassie, what you got...there is nothing to worry about."

He didn't say 'no worry.' I didn't like 'there is nothing to worry about.' It was too formal for Scotty. It sounded like it came from some manual: there is nothing to worry about so long as exposure is kept below the dose limit. I glanced at the scowling RERT crew, preparing to start the cleanup of Jardine's mess. "What about them? How's ALARA let them go in there?"

"ALARA for us isn't the same as ALARA for you."

"Come on, Scotty, you're made of the same stuff I am."

He reddened. "Look, nobody on my watch goes over their set limit. I time them. Keep track. That's why we have dosimeters. Somebody gets close to dosing out, I'm gonna limit their exposure. It's real simple." He looked down at my boots. "Time equals dose."

It had taken me, I calculated, about five seconds to ID the resin beads as not rat turds, and run.

He squinted, although the sun was not in his face. His skin crackled around the eyes. He looked weathered—surfer dude soaked too long in the brine, in the sun, soaking up too many cosmic rays. Surfer dude in hazmat that doesn't protect against gammas, that doesn't protect against the revenge-soaked unpredictability of a man with access to the rads. He said, finally, "We follow the rules best we can."

"I know you do."

He absently touched the good-luck medallion at his neck, then saw me looking. "Hey, we're not gonna have you sucking up any more dose." He peeled off my gloves and dropped them in a plastic decon bag. "I mean, it's cumulative."

Scotty had taken my place in the shower, vigorously going after his own hard-to-reach places. I thought, it's old news to Scotty. He's done it before. He'll do it again. Get contaminated. Decon. Rub the medallion for luck, or grace, or habit. Go on his way.

Lucy had disappeared into the adit.

Walter had gone to fetch me a chilled soda from one of Scotty's ice chests.

Hap joined me, clutching his EMT kit. "Probabilities, Buttercup."

"Not now, Hap."

"Don't knock it. The radiation track is all about probability—whether or not it hits the cell. Odds are it didn't. You're not your grandma."

I glared at him. How about just: chin up, Buttercup?

He knelt and opened his kit.

My scalp prickled, like I'd spent a day at the beach and come back with sand in my hair. I watched Hap—the top of his fedora, his red-freckled hands rummaging in the kit. Probability, which means the cancer lottery. Probability, which means the genetics lottery. Step yourself right up and take a guess. You might win or you might lose but no worry Buttercup. Nobody knows how to score anyway and you won't find out how you did until somewhere down the road apiece.

Hap stood, opening a pill bottle. He held it out to me.

"What is it?"

"Good old ibuprofen. Ease up those sore muscles." He passed me his water bottle. "Sorry I can't offer a nuke-dodgem pill."

I took the pill and washed it down.

"And next I prescribe a long hot shower."

I glanced at the yellow stall.

"Back at the Inn." He grinned. "A real shower where you get naked and use soap. Soothe them aches and pains." He added, kindly, "You have had one piss-poor day."

24

Roy Jardine was a happy man.

He lay on his belly on a ridge top, binoculars to his eyes and earbuds in his ears, watching the aftermath at Twenty-Mule-Team Canyon. He wanted to savor every last moment.

Three hours already on his belly, monitoring *The Trial*. The arrival. The dressing-out. That female with the purple hair—was she supposed to be ace? And then the going in and out, one after another. Right past the little hole Jardine had bored into the ground to hide the microphone. Oblivious. And then there'd been the payoff.

He just wished it hadn't been the female geologist who got caught. He'd expected it to be one of the hotshots. If he'd had his choice, it would have been that Bastard Ballinger who went in—that was the original mission plan—but he understood the hotshots had no reason to send in Ballinger. Even if they had reason, Ballinger was a dirty coward.

And evil.

The Trial had proved that today. Ballinger was convicted. Today, everybody found out what kind of murdering coward Ballinger was.

And Ballinger's problems were just beginning.

Jardine estimated that Stage Two could commence within a day or so. He wished he could be more precise but he had to wait for the trigger event. If it triggered sooner rather than later, he'd send another email, move up the deadline. Meanwhile, he'd wait. And he wouldn't be waiting alone. The enemy was waiting along with him.

And if the enemy threatened, there was that cask in Vegas with their name on it.

He was riding high now on a day of great success but he had learned his lesson about riding high. Keep watch for surprises. The geologists were the ones he really had to keep an eye on. Still, after today's events, how many surprises did they have left in them?

He'd have to make a phone call soon. He needed to get information.

He was suddenly bored with the flunkies down below. He scooted back from the vantage point and got up, stretching his stiff self. He packed his gear. He planned, when he got to *Hole-in-the-Wall*, to treat himself to the freeze-dried Shrimp Creole for dinner. A celebration. He would eat outside on that hidden outcrop and watch the sunset.

He left the ridge and headed upcanyon. The chances of meeting anyone here were tiny because this was a rough and remote canyon, not in the guidebooks.

His mind raced ahead of his feet.

After the female again. All in all, he guessed the female getting crapped up was a good outcome. Make her stay out of mine tunnels in the future. But he sure hoped she hadn't sucked up much dose. He was embarrassed, now, about how he'd reacted watching her in the decon shower. He'd wondered what she'd look like in his shower at home. He'd buy her strawberry shampoo and that girly soap. Maybe even get in and soap her up.

The canyon narrowed. He felt a breeze. He looked up. Clouds were coming in fast.

He thought about what Miller said to her, the sneaky way it sounded in the earbuds: *I prescribe a long hot shower*. Getting naked. That took some real nerve. Jardine couldn't see their faces but he was sure Miller had leered when he said it. Miller was a cad.

Jardine was sure the female felt the same way.

The breeze quickened, moving his ponytail.

He stopped. There was a sound, in the distance. Ahead? About a dozen yards ahead, the canyon took a turn. The sound came from upcanyon, he thought, although in these narrow canyons sounds and directions could fool you. He listened. Still as post.

He tried to hold on to the female.

The sound was louder, coming downcanyon—coming straight for him—roaring now, and now he thought about the clouds, hells bells it was a flood and he was in a canyon. He looked around wildly. No way out. The walls went straight up. He threw himself against the nearest wall, flattened his skinny self until he was just a bump on the wall.

The sound was deafening. The thing came around the corner and if he had not been pressed against the wall the thing would have gone right through him. Spinning, shrieking, speeding down the canyon like it had wheels.

When he could breathe again he said her name.

He watched the dust devil whirl along the ground until it came to another turn and it pivoted and went around that corner like it knew what it was doing.

If it had been a flood, he'd be drowned.

When he could speak, he told himself: let this be a lesson. That whirlwind was a message, surprising you like that. Just like the female. The female is a whirlwind spinning your head to where it's facing the wrong way and you better straighten it out.

25

WALTER SAID, "You're not eating, Cassie."

I lifted my fork and bit into my rattlesnake.

Soliano had been first to order the rattlesnake croquettes because he always ordered the local delicacy, and Scotty and Ballinger recoiled and ordered steak, but then Hap brought up primitive tribes who eat the enemy to absorb their power and so Walter had ordered the snake and I thought *why not* and followed suit. I swallowed. The snake seemed to stick in my throat. Bats for breakfast tomorrow?

Going a little mad, tonight, at the Inn.

I hunkered down. We sat around an oak table in the corner of the dining room. I had an adobe wall at my back and a picture window at my flank, and from my hard oak chair I could keep watch on the twilit desert outside and the mad sunburned visitors inside who kept looking our way.

We're making them nervous.

We should have made them gone. After today's events, Soliano had wanted an evacuation but all he got was the borax canyon roped off until the cleanup's done. His superiors bowed to the Park Service, who bowed to the businesses at Furnace

Creek who feared publicity and the loss of dollars. And so we remain the EPA monitoring team, which has discovered illness in a colony of nesting bats in the borax mines. And so the mad summer visitors who came to Death Valley for sand and salt and heat just might—if we don't stop Jardine—get more than they came for.

Soliano laughed.

"What?" Scotty said, alarmed.

"The music."

We strained to hear over the buzz of talk in the cavernous room—guitar licks as haunting as background clicks of the Geiger counter.

Soliano wore a dreamy look. "The piece is titled *Fantasia Para un Gentilhombre*, which translates to..."

"Fantasy for a gentleman," Hap said.

Soliano showed his surprise. "You speak the language."

"Some. Don't get the funny part though."

"No? It is you who calls unstable atoms *the gentlemen*. I hear this music and wonder what fantasy Mr. Jardine entertains for his gents." Soliano smiled. His teeth showed white as bleached bone in the light cast from the brass coyote candlestick.

I thought, some sense of humor the FBI has.

"I'm not laughing," Scotty said. "Add C4 to resin beads and I'm scared."

"That what he used?" Ballinger asked. "Plastique?"

"We await the lab," Soliano said. "The lab awaits the decontamination. A shaped charge certainly fits Mr. Jardine's profile. He is not a wasteful man. Plastique is not a wasteful explosive. It can be shaped to fit the need. It can be placed unobtrusively. And, we will assume he attached some sort of motion sensor, which triggered a blasting cap to detonate the plastique."

Yeah, we could assume that. I bump the cask with Lucy's tallywhacker scoop, the motion sensor reacts—and boom. My hand, now, shook. I feared I'd drop my fork. Walter was eyeing me. There he goes again. Since this afternoon he's taken on a watchful look, overseeing my every move. Now I know how he feels when I watch him eat a sugar donut. How many donuts is safe? How do we know? Is one donut ALARA? Two, three? One donut for him is not the same as one for me. He's already on the list. And it's cumulative.

Walter's focus switched to Soliano. "Will we assume Jardine acted alone, today?"

"Or in concert with Ms. Jellinek, who is not yet located, or with another, or others, not yet identified." Soliano glanced around the table, then flipped a hand. "Currently, I confine myself to Mr. Jardine. My fantasy is to divine where he will strike next. Thoughts, Mr. Ballinger?"

"Why ask me?"

"Because we learn today that you are the object of his attention. He airs his grievances against you at the borax mine. Where next?"

"Ask him when you find him."

"I ask you. He demands payment, to his bank account in the Caymans. After today's demonstration, your superiors at CTC consider negotiation. But he also, it appears, intends to get his pound of flesh. He does not appear to care who gets in the way. He has a stockpile of resins yet to unleash. And so, Mr. Ballinger." Soliano's voice went very soft. "I do not wish to be blindsided again. You knew about his sister. What else do you know, and do not say, that will help us identify his next target?"

Ballinger's skull bloomed in sweat.

"There is something more? I will find it, but it behooves you to save me the trouble of looking."

"Just the, ah, side effect of the resin spill. Nothing to do with Roy."

"What is this side effect?"

"It's old news."

Soliano said, icily, "It will be new to me."

Ballinger hesitated.

Soliano slammed his palm onto the table.

Ballinger jumped. "Okay, so the resins that got spilled in the trench? The trench was torn up, it rained a lot. We get a kinda monsoon season in summer. Lot of thunderstorms. Like now."

"And so?"

"And so rainwater made leachate."

"What is leachate?"

"Stuff in the water."

Walter set down his fork, hard. "Milt, the man asked what leachate is. Not everyone is versed in hydrology." Walter turned to face Soliano and said—using the tone he takes when he's explaining what gabbro is to a jury, the tone that says lack of information is not a moral failing—"Leachate is a liquid that percolates through soil and picks up soluble substances."

Soliano gave an almost imperceptible nod. "And these substances were... What, Mr. Ballinger?"

"Radionuclides."

"Dios mio."

"Hey," Ballinger said, "we reported it to the Nuclear Regulating Commission. Got a fine. Notice of violation. No big deal. We're not the first to get fined for a leak."

Scotty snorted. "You're damn lucky you didn't get shut down."

"Well we goddamn cleaned up. Soon as we found the spill."

"True," Hap put in. "Two months after the fact."

"You weren't even there, Hap."

"True, Milt. But like I said at the borax mine, it's one of those stories get told to the new guy. I get it wrong?"

"We cleaned up. End of story."

Soliano turned to Hap. "What further do you know of the

story?" There was a new edge to Soliano's voice, of grudging respect. Maybe because he'd learned that Hap understood Spanish. Maybe that was Soliano's fantasy, to have others search for the translation.

Hap shrugged. "Just what I heard."

"Did you hear if the cleanup recovered the contaminants?"

"Ahh...ever try to put the toothpaste back in the tube?"

"No I have not. What happened to the contaminants?"

Hap folded back the white linen tablecloth, gathering our attention. He reached for his water glass. The glass was cobalt blue and it was impossible to tell how much water it held. Hap tipped it over. Not much water, it turned out, but enough to find its preferred path in the wood grain and channel to the table's edge and trickle down to the carpet, where it was absorbed into the deep blue pile.

I stared.

Hap righted his glass. "Water moves. And if nuclides get into the water, they move. Tritium darn near does the backstroke. Mr. Plutonium hitches a ride on clay particles and rafts away."

I went cold. "You're saying they got down into the water table?"

Hap nodded.

"At what concentration?"

Ballinger answered. "Below regulatory concern, missy."

"Oh?" I regarded Milt Ballinger. I didn't know if he could be found criminally negligent in the death of Sheila Cook. In the contamination of the water. What I did know was that this cocky little man was a moral pygmy. "So, if it's below X number of parts-per-million, then everything's copacetic? Above that line and somebody's going to have to get upset about it?"

Ballinger's sharp chin tilted. "Didn't crap up anybody."

"Ahhh," Hap said, "we don't rightly know that yet." He put a finger in the little stream on the table, then touched his tongue.

He made a face. "Thing is, plants take up the water from the aquifer and animals eat the plants and drink the water, and then people drink the water and eat the plants and animals. And in the process of moving up the food chain, the clides get concentrated and us apex feeders get a richer dose." He eyed the snake on Soliano's fork.

Soliano set down his fork.

"Fact, some of those other leaks Milt mentioned got connected to cancer clusters."

I watched the water find its way over the edge of the table. "Cancer again."

"Ain't it a bitch? Everything gives you cancer these days."

"Let us confine ourselves to this leak," Soliano said. "Which appears to parallel the contamination of Mr. Jardine's sister, yes? One more grievance to lay at Mr. Ballinger's door?"

"Well he didn't threaten *me*," Ballinger said, "he threatened *the priceless*, remember? So why don't we frigging drop this leak crapola?"

"Why don't we follow the evidence," Walter said, "and see where it leads."

I ached, suddenly, muscles sprung from slouching through a tunnel in a sixty-pound bug suit in pursuit of mud on a cask. But I'd do it again tomorrow if I thought I'd get the evidence. Because Walter's right, that's what's going to get us to Roy Jardine and I wanted that sick bastard got. As Walter taught me back when I was learning the ropes at his bench, a crime does not happen without leaving its mark. One of the golden rules of forensic geology says that whenever two objects come into contact, there is a transfer of material. The methods of detection may not be exquisite enough to find it, but nonetheless the transfer has taken place. That means if you don't find it the first time, you hold it up to the light and look again. And you keep looking until you see what was hidden. Like a flash of mica in granite that suddenly catches the sun. And if your evidence soils are stolen and you have to start all over again, you suck it up and keep looking. Because that's what you signed up for. Because a sick bastard has got hold of lethal shit and is playing god with it. Because I don't want him crapping up anything, priceless or pricey or overlooked or underprotected or just plain unlucky. I had a bad taste in my mouth, redolent of rattlesnake and canned air. I said, "We'll find the place, Hector."

"I await. Meanwhile, let us consider *the priceless*, which he threatens to contaminate. What is it? Where might it be? What can we extrapolate from his choice of locations so far? His cask-swapping setup is in Death Valley. His first attack comes in Death Valley. Death Valley appears to be his chosen venue. Thoughts, Mr. Ballinger?"

"Christ on a crutch," Ballinger said, "I...don't...know. Figure it out yourself. Or ask somebody else for a change." He turned to Hap. "Like Mr. Know-it-All here."

"Very well," Soliano said. "Thoughts, Mr. Miller?"

Hap cocked his head. "You asking me to speculate, Hector?"

"I am asking what attracts Mr. Jardine to Death Valley. Yes, do speculate. It may help if you use his perspective."

I thought, that role-playing thing again, like Soliano used with Ballinger in the talc tunnel. Very effective.

Hap chuckled. "Should get me a Roy mask. Anyhoo, let's see. I'm Roy, with a shitload of hot resins. What I have to do is find a worthy place to threaten. Think I'll call it *the priceless*. Nice ring to it, and it'll sure grab everybody's attention."

"Where, Mr. Miller, is this worthy place?"

"Well it sure ain't the dump." Hap sat back and laced his hands behind his head. "Sooo, what else could I contaminate? There's the Nevada Test Site down the road—that's where Uncle Sam buries his waste. That's been contaminated since the atomic tests." Hap glanced at me.

I met his look. Go ahead.

"Anybody gonna notice if I crap up NTS? Nah. Over the hill from the dump is Yucca Mountain, which is where they keep changing their minds about if they're gonna put the spent fuel rods, if they ever quit bitching about earthquake faults. Anybody care if I crap up Yucca? Nah. Well then, how about Death Valley? Compared to the neighbors she's a downright virgin. And if I crap up a virgin—long as she's called a national park—I'll get somebody to sit up and pay attention."

"And why do you wish attention?" Soliano asked.

"Remember, I have a grudge or two against Milt. Sooo, attention's going to come back around to Milt—like it's doing right now—and the old news is going to leak out. Then John Q Public's going to read about it with his morning coffee and have a cow. Holy hell, all them nuclides in the water table, that's where I dug my well! And here's where John Q is going to ask what Milt's plutonium is doing in John's coffee."

"As you phrased it yesterday morning at the dump."

"As Hap phrased it. When Buttercup here asked what happens if the resins get loose in the environment." Hap shrugged. "But I'm still playing Roy, right? Sooo, once I get all this attention, with John Q screaming and all, I figure the Nuke Regulating Commission is going to have to step in again, get tougher. And then Milt's going to get his radioactive materials license yanked, or get fired, or get tarred and feathered." Hap unlaced his hands and folded his arms, decapitating Homer Simpson. "So whaddya think? That why Roy chose Death Valley?"

"It is plausible." Soliano considered. "And yet, Death Valley is a very large target."

"Anywhere in the virgin's gonna turn the trick." Hap grinned. "So to speak."

I thought, suddenly, we're asking the wrong question. Forget the *where* for a moment—what about *how*? I watched, electrified, as the last drops of water plinked down from the table into the carpet. I saw Walter scratching his ear, looking where I was looking.

Ballinger said, "Well I think you're full of it, Hap."

"Well thanks, Milt." Hap's cave-pool eyes darkened. "Because Hector asked for my help and I just tried to give it. Because, you know, it's my ass too. It's all our asses, because dog knows how Roy's fixing to unleash his stockpile. So you might be a little more forthcoming, Milt."

"Why don't *you* be forthcoming, Hap? Why don't you tell them all about the nickname you got when you worked at the nuke plant?"

Hap rolled his eyes.

Ballinger turned to us. "They called him Doc Death."

Scotty stared. "Wait a minute...he's *that* guy?"

26

WE HAD A NEW VISION, glimpsed in a spilled glass of water.

After dinner we'd returned to Walter's room and downloaded USGS reports on the leak from the Beatty dump. The hydrologists had been having a cow, as Hap might say.

And then I had to wonder how I could have any idea what Doc Death might say.

I shook that off. Right now, it didn't matter what Hap did at the nuke plant.

It mattered what Roy Jardine had done with the radwaste.

It mattered whether we could follow the trail he'd left.

I stared at the coffee table I was using as a workbench. Dishes of fender soil lined up, layer one through layer six. Walter and I had built ourselves a new map—patchy, riddled with unconformities. It took us where we'd been two days ago, considering a dozen or so candidates. And there we'd be right now if not for the new vision. It was one part onageristic estimate and three parts hydrology.

And I liked it. Not least because it pared the candidates down to two.

Which one, Brother Roy? Where'd you go? Either way, I'm

with you from the get-go. You leave Chickie's talc mine with your offroader rig and its nasty cargo and at some point you abandon paved road to drive up a fan across a wash into a canyon. You follow that canyon until you pick up layer six, the final layer. Point D, we're calling it, for destination. And then you do your dirty deed, and then drive back to the talc mine. You make the trip again and again, dozens of times. I can't say precisely how many because of the patchy nature of the layers. But ultimately, Roy Jardine, you left us a freaking map.

Once we find Point D, we'll see where we go from there.

There was the sudden clatter, outside, of hard rain. I looked up. More hurricane spin-off? Still, come hell or high water, we're going into the field tomorrow. We're going to find your address, pal.

"I read about a mine over in the Tucki Wash," Walter said. "The story goes that the owners quarreled and shot each other and the skeletons are still there, arms extended."

"They're gone now," Pria said.

I thought she'd fallen asleep—she'd been silent for so long. She was folded into a wicker chair and her head rested on its broad arm but her eyes were open. She met my look and then her black eyes skated back to Walter. We'd found her stationed outside Walter's room when we returned from dinner and Walter invited her in for a lemonade. Isn't someone expecting you at home? he'd asked. Nobody's home, she'd said, and asked if she could stay awhile. He didn't appear to know how to refuse.

She said, now, in that high girlish voice that seemed too young for her, "Grandfather, you wanna go see where Walter Scott had his hideout up a canyon?"

"You're talking about Death Valley Scotty?"

"That's a bad name. His name was Walter, like you. You wanna go?"

"I certainly do," Walter said, watching the soils settle out in his test tubes. "When I'm not quite so pressed for time."

"He never found any gold. He was a faker."

"That could be said of a good number of people who came here."

She giggled.

He smiled.

"You wanna go see where a prospector cut his name on the rock where there's old drawings that tell stories?"

Walter said, "We appear to be concocting a tour of killers and frauds and petroglyph-desecraters."

Well you started it, I thought, you just had to bring up those skeletons.

"A lot of them's came here," Pria said.

Walter turned to look at her. "You know the area well?"

"I got coyote eyes."

"Do you?" He thought a moment. "I may want to go see a mine but I haven't quite figured out where it is. If I could describe the surrounding territory, could you help me?"

Her head lifted. "Really?"

"Really."

She raised a clenched fist, pinkie extended. "Roger, Grandfather."

He did not smile. "I'll tell you what. Let me finish my work here and then tomorrow after I'm back from the field, we'll look at some maps together."

"I could come along," she said. "To your field."

I took in a breath. I used to say something like that. Come on Walter, take me with you. It would be fun.

He said, "I'm afraid not, Pria."

"There's mines not on maps," she said. "I need to come."

He rubbed his chin.

I held my breath. She had a point. What if Jardine had

chosen a mine that's not on the maps? How many dozens of unmarked prospects and shafts and adits were there in Death Valley? Nobody knew. Did she? I came over to Walter and whispered, "She's a kid, we can't take her."

Pria shot me a look with those black coyote eyes and then seized hold of her large feet and tucked herself deeper into the chair.

Walter whispered, "You were just a kid."

I said, "You should start a club."

27

MIDNIGHT AT THE POOL.

The thermometer on the stone wall beside the stacked lounge chairs read ninety-one and the underwater thermometer read eighty-eight. The silky water left the faint taste of minerals on my lips and dissolved the ache from my shoulders.

I corked along under stars so bright they radiated haloes.

The night was mine. The rainstorm of two hours ago had vanished. Pria had vanished. Walter had called it a night and tucked in. Everyone at the Furnace Creek Inn appeared to have called it a night. Sunburns and bellies full of rattlesnake and soft beds. No stargazers, no lovers, no partiers. Just me and the sky and the water.

A coyote screamed.

I dove, dolphining underwater.

There was an explosion.

I saw a water-sheathed torpedo and then flailed for the surface and came up gasping and seconds later the torpedo surfaced and assumed the features of Hap.

"Nice suit, Buttercup."

Treading water, heart pounding, I reflexively looked down at my bathing suit. Big flowers. Small suit. I'd borrowed it from the maid. When I could speak with a steady voice, I said, "Why are you here?"

He flipped on his back and crossed his hands beneath his head. "Get me some exercise." His trunks were long and loose and floated like purple jellyfish around his pale legs.

"You said you were going to bed. When you left dinner."

"Couldn't sleep." He righted himself, treading water. He was so close our feet brushed. His wet hair was hematite red, already curling in the hot night air. He smiled. "Next question."

All right. "How'd you get your nickname?"

"You're curious as the cat."

He tucked and dove under and surfaced at the far end of the pool. He climbed onto the deck and I thought he was going to leave. He didn't. He took a diver's stance. Despite the ludicrous purple trunks, he had the look of a real athlete, long and leanly muscled. He dove, easing into a smooth crawl that took him the length of the pool in the time it took me to reach the side and hang on. He jackknifed and went under and emerged halfway and backstroked to the far end, then came back my way in a butterfly. I watched, mesmerized, as he did his laps.

On the eighth lap he angled over to me and then he hooked an arm on the tiled ledge. "So," he said, barely winded. "My nickname."

I nodded.

"Fifth grade. Music class. We were learning folk songs and there was this one called *The Happy Miller*. All about an indolent fellow who's happy to sing and dance all day and not toil like the other drudges at the mill, although I never did see how he got any milling done if he spent all day dancing. And you can imagine—me having the last name Miller—what happened. All those little dickenses start calling me Happy. Of course I hated it. What kid doesn't hate what the other kids call him? But then my daddy heard the kids calling me Happy and that jess pained my daddy. See, daddy's the one picked my given name—which is Brendan—even before I was born. Brendan ain't jess a name, see? It's a calling. It means, in old Celtic, from the fiery hill. Don't that give you visions of a manly man striding down out of his Celtic castle to fight the good fight against the incoming hordes? Well," he tugged a curling lock, "I got the fiery *hair*. But I wasn't ready to take on the incoming hordes of fifth-graders. And my daddy told me flat-out he didn't wanna never hear nobody calling me Happy, I guess because that made him Happy's daddy—Chuckles or Goofy—and my daddy wasn't much of a chuckler. Still, I did have the last laugh because I got to fuck over my daddy without doing anything to get in trouble. Alls I had to do was beg the kids *not* to call me Happy, which gave them license to double down." His eyes shone. "God my daddy hated a victim." He flicked the water. "Kids eventually shortened the name to Hap. And I did come to get used to it. That satisfy your curiosity?"

I looked away, across the water to the stone arches that rose like Roman aqueduct bridges on the far side of the pool deck, framing a view of blackness that was the night desert. I had to fight off a wave of sympathy that threatened to pull me under.

Hap splashed. "Well, I've had me my exercise."

I looked back to see him lever out of the pool. I said, "I meant the nickname at the nuke plant."

He stood dripping. He looked down at me. "Milt told you. About five hours ago. In the dining room. Memory not so good?"

"Milt told us what he knew. Scotty'd sure heard about it. I'd guess it's one of those legendary stories in the nuke industry. I'd like to hear your side."

"Whyever for?"

To know if I need to be watching my back. I said, "It's a nasty story."

He shrugged.

"Okay," I said, "since you left the table in the middle of it, let me recap. You were working at the nuke plant, keeping watch on a diver in the spent-fuel pool."

"RC, Buttercup. Radiation Control. In the SFP. You tell my story, you need to talk like the in-crowd."

"I'm not in the in-crowd." I didn't like having to look up at him. Neither did I like the idea of climbing out to face him in my skimpy suit, so I stayed where I was and spoke to his feet. "There was a diver—Drew Collier—installing fuel racks."

"Fuel rack support plates. Precision, Buttercup."

"Whatever. Anyway, somebody misread a smudged work order and transferred a spent fuel rod to the wrong place, which was near Collier's work area. The dive contractor surveyed the area before the dive but didn't pick up a reading. He said later that the survey meter had been behaving erratically."

Hap snorted. "Isn't that what I've been going on and on about? A little eff-up here, a little eff-up there."

"And Collier got too close to the fuel rod."

Hap nodded at the pool. "Water's a great shield but you need to watch out for the dose gradients."

"But you didn't watch out."

He folded his arms.

"Collier wore teledosimeters set to alarm at your surface monitor if his dose rate went too high."

"That's right. I monitored the readouts and relayed them to Collier on the intercom. Readouts looked a little hinky—I didn't know why, I didn't know some inbred effed up the work order and put a rod in the wrong place. All I knew was I didn't like the readouts so I relayed to Collier to move into a lower-dose area. He relays to me he *is* in a low-dose area. By the time he stopped arguing, the monitor alarms were going off. So I relayed the standard what the firetruck you doing down there, get TF out."

He shrugged. "You get yourself into a high-rad field and it only takes seconds to get yourself a nasty dose."

"Your readouts were too low. You should have warned him sooner. Your surface monitor was faulty."

"Wasn't mine. Was the dive contractor's."

"You didn't check it before the dive?"

"Sure did. Checked out fine."

"When Security examined it, afterward, they found NFG written on it, in permanent ink."

"Youse *is* in with the in-crowd. Youse knows what NFG means."

"No fucking good."

"I didn't write it. You want my guess? Somebody wrote it after the fact."

"By the time the dive master got Collier out, he had a lethal dose."

"Not for a couple months. Probably wished he'd gone right away."

I said, "That's a little cold-blooded."

"Didn't cry for him. Doesn't mean I wished it on him."

"That's all you've got to say?"

His toes curled, as though he was trying for a better grip on the water-slicked pool deck. He had long big-knuckled toes. "Nobody listens."

"That's it?"

"That's it. You swim in the SFP, you better take care."

"Didn't he?"

"He's a dumb lunk thinking about getting laid over the weekend instead of what he's got to look out for in the dive. I give him the spiel but he doesn't listen. He's in a hurry because the plant wants the maintenance done yesterday because they're off-line and it's costing plenty, so the prevailing mindset isn't ALARA—it's ALACA. Keep your exposure as-low-as-cheaply-achievable. Anyway, he gets into his dive suit—kind of like your bug suit—and that's when he asks me what I already told him that he wasn't listening to. So I repeat the advice, only he can't hear too well with a face pump going, so who knows? I tried. He goes in." Hap suddenly leapt over my head and cannon-balled into the pool.

I waited.

He surfaced and hung in place. "Go under and look around."

"Why?"

"Because I'll add a purty please onto it."

I ducked under. I saw Hap's long legs languidly treading water. He was silhouetted by the pool light. I surfaced and wiped my eyes.

"See much?"

"Depends where I looked. You were blocking the light."

"That's the thing. The visibility down in the SFP isn't always what it should be. Especially when you got a bubble on your head and no peripheral vision. And you're not expecting an irradiated fuel assembly next door."

"And the surface monitor's not calibrated right."

"Was." Hap lifted his palms. "Maybe it slipped after I calibrated it."

"The NRC investigated you for tampering."

"NRC investigated the incident up one side and down the other, fined the plant operator, held a lessons learned meeting." He slowly sank. "I wasn't cited. No proof."

"The plant fired you. The District Attorney filed murder charges."

He went under.

I waited.

He came up, onto his back, and expelled a spout of water. "I was cleared."

"You had a motive."

"Didn't like him. You like everybody crosses your path?"

"You fought him. At some bar."

"Wasn't a bar, was a tavern. Precision, Buttercup. Didn't fight him. Didn't get to lay a hand on him. He didn't appreciate the way I excused myself for accidentally knocking over his glass of ale and so he beat the stuffing out of me. And then he brought out his dingie and whizzed on my poor battered self—right in front of my fellow workers, who jess knocked theyselves out laughing. Daddy woulda cringed, iffen he'd seen."

I cringed. I said, "So you bore Collier a grudge."

"Yeah. Flipped him off real good behind his back."

"So the SFP was an accident?"

"Isn't that what Milt said?"

"He said the DA dropped the charges."

"She did, indeed. Still, I did get me a new nickname around the plant. And daddy would have liked that one." He waved at the sky. "Nothing wimpy about Doc Death, eh daddy?" He straightened. "Whoops, I's looking the wrong way for daddy." He rolled face-down, into a dead-man's float.

Goosebumps broke out on me. I wondered if it had been what he said, just one little eff-up after another and nobody's to blame. He couldn't have planned it because somebody else smudged the work order, somebody else transferred the fuel assembly to the wrong place, somebody else did a survey of the work area with an erratic meter. But somebody else wasn't reading the surface monitor. He was. He could have sabotaged it. He could have delayed his warning. Just takes a few seconds, when a diver gets too close to recently discharged spent fuel. Opportunity knocks and he answers, like encountering somebody who's humiliated you on the edge of a crowded platform and the train's coming.

I got out and went for my towel. I heard him come up onto

the pool deck with a grunt. I heard his wet feet slapping the concrete behind me.

I heard him start up again.

"And that's why I'm here with the cool kids in Death Valley. Ain't that something? Chain reaction. I get smeared at the nuke plant, but that's okay, I'm sick of being a house tech anyway. I hit the road and take on temp jobs, only the life of a road whore isn't so hot, and besides my deadly nickname keeps catching up. Then good ole Milt comes to the rescue. Milt didn't mind my checkered past. Fact, he was glad to get somebody who wasn't shooting for a job at the nuke plant. See, everybody who's anybody wants to work at the nuke plant. Them boys and girls at the nuke plant is so full of theyselves they think they pulled the rods on the sun."

I felt his wet arm go around my shoulders. I ducked away and wrapped in my towel.

He crossed his arms. "I'm like those unstable atoms. Start out at the nuke plant doing my business, get spent, end up buried at the dump."

"You could leave."

"Where'd I go?"

"I don't know. Go flip burgers. Go to art school."

"Yeah." He turned to go.

I hadn't meant it to sound so harsh. "Wait."

"Yeah?"

"What's so wrong with keeping people safe?"

He cocked his head. "About a minute ago you were thinking I'm a killer."

"You didn't specifically deny it."

His face tightened, visible even by the castoff lights of the pool. "Cassie, you think I'm going to kill somebody because he makes me look like a fool?" He looked at the sky, then back at me. He produced a brief grin. “Hell, I make me look like a fool six days a week.”

I laughed.

“Take a break on Sundays. Wait and see.”

Maybe I will, wait until we’re not hunting a madman with a lethal stash, wait until we’re done here—if we’re done here by Sunday—wait until we’re out of this liquefying heat that’s making my head swim, wait until Sunday to figure out what I think about Hap Miller.

He uncrossed his arms. “Sunday’s four days away.” He moved closer and anchored my chin with his thumb and forefinger.

Startled, I froze. Maybe not startled.

He leaned in and kissed me. His lips were silky, like mine, tasting of alkali. I dropped my towel. We crowded together, sealing the hold of our mouths. His hands went down to the hiked-up border of my too-small swimsuit. He slipped his thumbs beneath the elastic. My attention jumped there, to the pressure points of his thumbs. He fitted his hips into mine. For a moment, for one long moment in which my heat flared, I stayed planted in place, and then I intertwined my fingers in his and tugged his hands free.

He pulled back. “You no like?”

Oh yeah, I like. I adjusted my suit.

He expelled a breath like it was a spout of water.

I found my own breath. “Can we just back up a bit?”

“Ain’t never no way to go but forward.”

“Okay.” My heartbeat ramped up again. “Sunday’s still coming up.”

“That it is.” He picked up my towel and handed it to me. “Thing is, Buttercup, I’m near spent. Had one fiasco marriage, got a woman I visit now and then. Fraid I gave you the wrong impression here. I’m not looking for a sweetheart.”

I said, after one more long moment in which to cool back down to stone, "Afraid I'm not looking for a roll on the pool deck."

28

FIELD DAY.

The morning sun already savaged us. I slumped against the Jeep. Walter shifted, sweating, stirring up dust. Soliano wiped his brow.

Pria hugged herself, fixing her hopes on her aunt.

The gray-haired woman with the sour face—Ruth Weeks—was on Soliano's cell phone. She listened with a tight mouth.

I expected the answer to be no.

It was surely a no-looking kind of place, of dusty trailers and adobe cabins, and the only thing good I could say was that it seemed temporary. I looked across a short stretch of desert to a wall of palms and tamarisks and caught a glimpse of green green grass. A small white ball flew above the trees and I imagined a curse in German. I turned and squinted uphill at the Inn, which docked at the head of the fan like a cruise ship in palm-green water. I turned back to this sad outlier of the village of Furnace Creek and thought, everybody around here has water to spare, but them. Even their mesquite looks thirsty.

Ruth Weeks returned Soliano's phone like it was contaminated. "Jackson says you're one of them." She eyed our borrowed

Park Service vehicle, a Jeep Cherokee offroader. "His car. He's responsible." She shifted her lawn chair so that it faced her mobile home, giving us the back of her head.

Pria bounded to the Cherokee. It will be fun.

Walter slid into the front passenger seat as if by choice, and I took the wheel as if by default, and Pria piled into the backseat beside Soliano.

I drove past the sign at the end of the dirt road—Timbisha Shoshone Tribe, and below that, Radio 91.1—and Walter reached for the radio and Pria said, "You won't get nothing. It's Thursday. You could try tomorrow."

Soliano, in my rearview mirror, nodded as if he'd known. Maybe that's the way it was where he grew up, stations on and off the air unpredictably so all you can do is shrug. Shooting victims in the road and all you can do is wait for them to die. Soliano was on Pria's wavelength. He'd made his pact with her earlier when he found her waiting outside his room. Undoubtedly looked at his watch. No time, and here's Miss Desert Alien who knows this area like none of us could know it, who volunteers her services. Dios mio, this is her homeland. What can one do? Refuse the offer?

Well—Walter had said to me on the way to the parking lot—*she's nearly fifteen.*

I'd been twelve when he first took me into the field.

I hit the asphalt and and took the road back up the fan and dropped Soliano at the cruise ship and picked up our escorts, two FBI agents in another Park Service offroader.

Our third escort, Hap, took Soliano's place in the backseat beside Pria.

Something was wrong with Hap.

He didn't ask me why we were heading for talc country. He made no dire warnings to take care out here. No yak, no Buttercup-baiting.

No apology for last night at the pool. Then again, he'd been frank about what he wanted last night. Brutally so. It was me who'd been slow on the uptake. I really should paste a warning label on my forehead: romantically needy but touchy as hell. It seemed like a dream now, anyway, in the brutal light of day. The night, the stars, the heat. Fantasyland.

Walter seemed not to notice Hap's tense silence. Walter was explaining the passing landscape to Pria. "Look Pria," he pointed at a black ridge, "what do you think carved out those rocks?"

She looked; star pupil. "Timbisha?"

"It would have happened before your people came along—but it is an ongoing process." He kinked in his seat and inflated his cheeks and blew.

"Wind!"

I waited for Walter to call the rocks by their name, ventifacts. Teach her the Latin, *ventus*, for wind. That's the way I recalled the lessons back when he was teaching me—in between instructions on extracting soil from the shoes of a murder suspect—straightforward and no-nonsense. Certainly, no cheek inflating.

I waited for Hap to step in with a snarky comment. Blowing some hot air, Walter? Hap was mum.

Maybe Hap wished he was overseeing the borax cleanup with Ballinger and Scotty, instead of babysitting us.

Maybe he'd picked up a chill at the pool last night.

Or maybe his weird silence had something to do with whatever he was reading on his cell phone.

At Chickie's talc mine, our trip officially began.

If we have it right, here's what happened, time after time: Jardine and Beltzman made the swap, and the radwaste driver took the cargo with the dummy cask to the dump. And then, when the time was right, Jardine drove the offroader rig with its hot cargo from the mine down the dirt road to the highway.

Our itinerary, today, was this: follow Roy Jardine.

We took the dirt road, sampling along the way. Layer one of the fender soil map.

Then, there was a break in the map as Jardine traveled on highway pavement.

We, too, turned north onto highway 127. Two days ago, we'd traveled this highway southward on our way from Beatty to talc country.

I checked Hap in the rearview. Pale, silent. Phone now in his T-shirt pocket, a slight lump over Homer Simpson's right eye.

Who the hells knows. It's Hap. I refocused on the highway ahead, on the pools of water shimmering in the distance. The kind of mirage I like. No running figure. No creeping bat.

We passed the cinder block town of Shoshone and everybody's heads turned, because it was Chickie's town. Which one of the squat tin houses was hers? I spotted a white SUV pulling out of a Dairy Queen parking lot and twisted for a longer look.

"That's not her," Pria said.

"Her?" I said.

"The one people say messed you up."

"You know Chickie?" Walter asked, a tick before I could get it out.

"She's my mother."

We passed from California into Nevada. We came to the town of Lathrop Wells, and turned northwest onto highway 95.

We came mostly in silence, digesting Chickie and Pria.

Pria hadn't had much more to say, other than that Chickie and Pria and Ruth had all lived in the trailer with Peter Weeks—Ruth's brother, Pria's father, Chickie's husband. Peter had died of lung cancer when Pria was six. Chickie then left the village because she was not Timbisha. Pria, who was half-Timbisha, remained with Aunt Ruth. Pria had no more to say, other than that Chickie was the devil and that's why people said it was Chickie who had left us to die.

Hap's eyes had widened in surprise and then narrowed. "Devil's play," he'd said, when Pria finished. His first comment of the day.

I agreed. Whichever devil it was who'd bushwhacked us.

Highway 95 shot straight through the high wide plain of the Amargosa Desert. Keep going on this road and we'd come to the crash site, and then the dump. A lifetime ago we'd been there, wondering what we'd got ourselves into.

Pria said, "The school bus goes this way, to Beatty."

I checked her in the rearview. She was watching Walter, twisting a strand of hair into a cord. It shone like obsidian. If she didn't have the devil for a mother and a sourpuss for an aunt, someone might have put that hair up in a cool French braid. She was waiting for Walter's response. High school's not his strong suit, so I stepped in. "So, Pria, what's your favorite subject?"

"Softball," she said, grudging.

"What position?"

"Pitcher."

"Cool. I played soccer in high school. Midfield." I waited for her to acknowledge the coolness of soccer and when she remained silent I looked again. She yanked the cord of hair so that it bisected her face, then crossed her eyes. I yanked my gaze away from the wild child back to the highway.

Walter said, "Up ahead."

Up ahead, to our left, an ungraded road snaked up the gentle fanglomerate of the eastern flank of the Funeral range to its rough-hewn summit.

I slowed. This was it: the road we figured Jardine took. This route had been on our list from the get-go, along with many others, but Hap's spilled glass of water last night jumped it to first place. I said, "You know that road, Hap?"

"No." Second comment of the day. In my rearview, he was studying it.

Well, we were betting Roy Jardine knew that road. If we were right, here's where he left the pavement. Why he took this route was a matter of speculation but we speculated that he preferred to re-enter Death Valley by the back door, the route no ranger patrolled. Because he didn't want company.

Neither did we. I was glad to have the FBI on our tail, instead of the devil.

Soliano had given us a new toy—a satellite phone—so that we could stay in contact while in the canyons. Walter used it to phone our escort and tell them we were about to go off-road.

I turned onto the fan road and the FBI followed. I stopped to sample the coarse-grained alluvium, layer two of the fender soil.

From here, Jardine's itinerary led up the flank of the Funerals. So did ours. We crossed an old railroad grade, climbed gently, then dropped into the wide pebbly wash of the Amargosa River. Layer three—playa mud and sand. This time, we all piled out.

The FBI kept watch, submachine guns nodding.

Hap leaned against the Cherokee. Nothing for him to do until, unless, we encounter something requiring a Geiger check.

While I sampled the soil, Walter resumed his lessons.

Pria stared at the dry riverbed. "You said we were chasing the water."

"We are." Walter smiled. "When this river floods, water ends up in Death Valley."

I wondered if she'd get the significance of the river's course. It runs through this desert along the eastern border of Death Valley, then cuts down to its southern tip—talc country—and thence takes a hook northeast to exhaust itself three hundred feet below sea level on the Badwater saltpan.

I pictured the dinner table last night, Hap's spilled water taking its path along the wood grain and then over the edge. That had sent my thoughts along their own path: if Jardine was trying to nail Ballinger for the leak at the dump, maybe he was following the path of the leak. That path led down into the water table, and thence into the flow system that brings water into Death Valley. On the hydrology website I'd learned there are two major flow paths. One is the Amargosa River, whose riverbed runs somewhat in line with the radwaste truck route. It also runs close to Chickie's mine. Maybe it had led Jardine there. Maybe he'd been scouting for a site to stage his attack. He'd certainly found a place to stash his equipment and a use for the talc. I wondered if Pria knew we had visited her mother's mine.

Walter stood behind Pria, pointing upfan to the crest of the Funerals. "That's the water we're chasing today."

That's the other flow path into Death Valley. That's the one we're betting on.

Hap looked where Walter pointed. I wished I could read Hap's face but it was shadowed by the fedora.

Pria sighted uphill. "Water goes downhill."

"So it does," Walter said. "Then how do you think water crosses the Funerals?" He gave her time to knit her brows and then he took a chisel from the field kit and stuck it into the ground. "Wiggle it."

She knelt and wiggled the chisel. Star pupil.

"You feel the give?" Walter asked. "Where the chisel finds a crack in the soil? Way down beneath us is an aquifer. It's a big tub of water that flows through cracks in the underground rock. And because Death Valley's elevation is the lowest in the region, that's where the water goes."

"Look out!"

Pria dropped the chisel. We spun around.

The two FBI men were backpedalling. The trim black guy named Darrill Oliver now morphed into that primal stance that needs no interpretation, and the blocky sunburned guy named Stan Dearing was grabbing Oliver's gun arm. Oliver shook him off.

"What is it?" I said, "what's wrong?"

Dearing jerked his subgun toward the scrub brush. "Snake."

Walter tensed.

"King snake." Dearing hissed, then grinned. "I happen to know they're harmless but my bro here thinks they bite."

Oliver lowered his weapon, a flush darkening his obsidian face.

Walter threw Oliver a look, fellowship of the phobic. "Good eye."

The scrub brush shimmied and a thick banded shape disappeared down a hole.

"Should have shot it," Hap said, to Oliver. "Snakes eat bats." Third comment of the day.

29

SILENCE in the car as we continued up the hill.

Thanks to Hap, I was thinking food chain. Bats get contaminated, snakes eat bats, snakes carry the scourge as they creep along their way. What eats snakes? Hawks. And then they fly away.

Hap, in the rearview, had his phone open again.

The Cherokee jolted and I whipped my attention back to the rough road. A new ground cover sprouted among the creosote and sage—stone and tin. Stone foundations marked vanished buildings, stone cairns stood watch over pits and shafts, and you would have thought that tin was mined here, for the earth was rich with rusted cans. If Jardine wanted a mine handy to highway 95 he could have thrown a dart in any direction and hit one. But the fender soil said he kept going, and so did we.

Above the Town of Stone and Tin, the road entered a narrow twisting canyon and then we crested the Funerals and descended past another ghost town, smaller and sadder than the first. Walter rubbernecked.

Pria said, "If you go off this road there's lots of mines."

Is that what Jardine did? If he selected a mine on this road, one he could drive his offroader into, didn't he take the risk of some weekend warrior driving his tricked-up offroader into the mine for a little sightseeing? The soils would tell. *If* he came this way.

The road narrowed and it was no longer a road but cascades of sheeting rock. I wrestled the Cherokee to a stop. "Did we miss a turn?"

"No," Pria said, "this is the way."

I had to admit, Soliano was right, she knew this area like we did not.

"Chickie's drove this," she said. "It's not that hard."

So Chickie knows the way, too. I filed the fact in my expanding mental folder marked *devil.* I gripped the wheel. If Chickie, and presumably Brother Roy, could drive this astonishing excuse for a road then so could I. Walter watched me. I hit the gas and tires latched onto rock and lurched us forward, and as sweat cascaded down my flanks I understood why Jardine needed that high-clearance offroader with its beastly trailer.

We came to an exposure of Pliocene sedimentary deposits and I stopped, gratefully, to sample. While Walter explained to Pria that a few million years separated one layer from the next, the FBI checked their tires, and Hap headed for the canyon-wall shade.

I followed him. "Who were you texting?"

"Just checking messages."

"I don't think so. I think something's going on."

He leaned against the canyon wall. "Like what?"

"You tell me."

He held my gaze, first time today. "It's personal."

I flushed.

He gestured at the ground. "Don't let me interfere."

"I won't." You can bet on it. "So, you know what we're after here, right?"

He cocked his head.

"Nuclides from the dump leak are into the Death Valley flow system. Like you told us at dinner. And the nuclides are coming this way."

"More or less."

"Okay, yeah, the contaminant plume wouldn't precisely follow the road, but if Jardine wanted to mimic the leak, this is the way he'd come."

"I get it."

I watched him. "You get what?"

"Here's where he gets into the virgin."

"How?"

"How should I know? He ain't my homie, I's jess the guy what frisks him."

Hap suddenly sounded like himself—first time today. I said, "So give me a wild-ass guess."

He pushed back his hat. "Haven't got one, Cassie."

It was getting tight.

The canyon squeezed steeply into a cavernous gorge and we funneled down into the narrows.

The rocks were tilted and pitted in somber shades of purple and green. I craned my neck to follow the walls upward to the spires that tortured the clifftops. In places, windows had eroded through rock, framing roiling clouds.

"Ghosts," Pria said.

The road gentled and I gave myself over to reading the formations, and when the banded layers of the Bonanza King fully commanded the walls, I stopped the Cherokee.

Layer four.

Hap paced while we sampled, keeping watch he told us, on what I did not know because he did not bring out his meters, and then finally he halted in front of Dearing and Oliver, who were parked against the wall. "Good place for an ambush," Hap said, loud enough to startle the agents and bounce an echo off the walls.

Ambush ambush ambush.

The agents swung their submachine guns upward and we all tilted our chins but I saw nothing on the clifftops but Pria's ghosts.

By the time we pushed on downcanyon, the clouds had congealed.

We stopped to sample an exposure of trilobite trash beds because we had fossil fragments in layer five.

And finally we came to the end of the line. Point D, for destination.

As we piled out, I brushed close to Hap and said, "Actually, *here* is where he got into the virgin."

Hap gave me a tight smile.

Well, it was somewhere around here—this was a very big neighborhood. Layer six was a sandy shaly zone that extended a good long stretch through the main canyon, and the canyon pouched into offshoot sides that mostly dead-ended within a few hundred yards. We wearily sampled two dozen sites, conferred, and then called it a day.

"Was ready an hour ago," Dearing muttered, trudging to the FBI jeep.

Oliver eyed Walter's bulging field pack. "Get what you need to track the rat down?"

Walter said, "If not, we'll get more."

"Good man."

Rain caught us on the way out, drops bulleting the roof of the Cherokee. The thin canyon soil began to saturate and I fixated on the ominous ledge of mud plastered twenty feet up the wall.

The last place I wanted to be, right now, was pinched in this narrow gorge.

We exited the canyon, and I exhaled.

We exited onto a modest shallow fan, unlike the giant on which Walter and I had been marooned.

As we bumped downfan, thunderclouds gathered themselves and headed east. The sun angled in through the windshield to steam us. It steamed raindrops off the Cherokee's hood and the alluvial gravel beneath its tires.

I took note of a steaming jutting outcrop. I waited for Walter to start up again with the lessons. Look Pria! You notice a difference between that layer of rock and the gravel it sits upon? Where could that rock have come from? Well Grandfather, she says—knitting her brows—I'd say that's where a thrust fault is exposed. That's my girl, says he.

We reached the toe of the fan, and highway 190.

We'd traveled 190 yesterday, to Twenty-Mule-Team canyon. Turn left onto the highway right now and we're almost there. Real convenient, I thought, for Brother Roy to transport a cask from Point D to the borax mine.

I turned the Cherokee right, heading for the Inn. Back to the barn.

We passed the crumbly white travertine I'd noticed yesterday, bearding the Funerals fan.

"Look Pria," Walter said, pointing out his window, "where it's white."

I knew it. He couldn't resist.

"Those deposits," he said, "are from old dry springs."

"Aliens used to camp there, Grandfather. There was water then."

I just had to join in. "Look further, Pria—at all that mesquite. There's water here now."

"Well *yeah*. Like, bighorns drink there?"

Well duh, like this is only the second time I've been on this road and I didn't see any bighorns yesterday. All I saw now was a covered flume paralleling the highway. Aliens built that, I thought. Aliens to the desert.

"Mr. Miller," Pria said, "it's not nice to keep texting when people are talking."

The car went thick with silence and then Hap gave a rough laugh. "You're right, Pria. Can't come up with a good reply anyway."

I heard the snap of his phone shutting.

I pulled off the highway and shut down the engine and kinked in my seat to look Hap in the eye. "What the hell is going on?"

He met my gaze. Second time today. He opened his phone and thumbed the keypad and passed it to me. "Message came just after we left the Inn."

I read the text, at first not getting it, then I passed Hap's phone to Walter. He read, and after a long hesitation, he passed it on to Pria. Because it's sure not nice to exclude her.

She read, scowling. "Is this from the bad guy?"

Who else? I thought. Still, we'd be wanting Soliano to trace the message—to the re-sender in Bulgaria or maybe, this time, directly to Roy Jardine's phone. I wondered how Jardine had gotten Hap's number. From the dump directory? Or the online white pages, easy enough. Or maybe he had Hap's number on speed dial.

Hap might not be Jardine's homie but it looked like Hap had, somehow, come to Jardine's malignant attention. He'd texted: *You're on my list now, Doc Death.*

30

WHAT ROY JARDINE admired about C4 plastique was its risk-to-bang ratio. No risk, big bang. Dudes can handle it. Dudes can roll it into a ball and hit it with a bat. He'd heard somebody tried that once. It made a lousy baseball.

Add a blasting cap and it made an explosive.

He'd learned to use it in crap job number nine, road demolition. The plastique was ace but the work was hot and dirty. At least he hadn't had to work dressed out.

He was in full hazmat now.

He opened his pack and took out the stubby sausage. It was wrapped in cling wrap, like cheese. Cheese—he must be hungry. He was so sick of freeze-dried. When this was all over he was going to find himself a trucker's diner and order sausage and eggs with cheese melted on top. His stomach roared.

He looked around, in case his gut sounds made him miss the sounds of somebody approaching. That was not obsessive. That was careful. It was two-thirty a.m. Friday but he would not count on the dark or the night. He would keep his eyes and his ears wide open. The new audacious Roy Jardine was audacious in vision but he was not a fool.

He was at a stage where the risks were coming at him fast.

Yesterday afternoon, the risks came way too close. He'd been up on the ridge above the canyon, as usual, keeping watch. He'd hoped the geologists wouldn't recover enough to do their job. But they did. And they came with a whole party. Miller the cad. Some girl—who was she? And two FBI men—what else could they be?—with FBI submachine guns. If Jardine had had one of those weapons he could have opened fire right then and there.

He had his Buck knife and his pistol. Not a fair fight.

Watching, he'd gotten distracted again with the female. Look how she paid attention to her details! Even though she was tracking him, he had to admire her. In fact, he'd wanted to have her. He could admit that. He wanted her to admire him but even if she didn't he still wanted to have her. He'd even have her right down there in the dirt. By the time the enemy left the canyon he was all tangled up. Worried about being tracked, retreating to his hideout, thinking about the female so much that he got way ahead of himself. In the privacy underground he'd had to abuse himself to get her out of his head and that was humiliating.

But it worked.

He'd cleared his mind and considered his situation. He'd lost his breathing room but he couldn't hurry things up. The trigger event had not yet come and he could not launch Stage Two of the mission without it. What he needed now, he saw, was to throw something big at the enemy. And he had that something big waiting in storage at Vegas. He got to work. He'd sat at his makeshift desk with his notepad and pencil for hours and when he got up he had a detailed plan. It was—no reason to be modest—brilliant.

It was also risky.

First had been the risk of hiking down to the Ranch and getting into his rental car. It was almost midnight Thursday by then and the only people around was a couple arguing about if they should complain about the torn screen door in their room, and they hadn't cared about him. The next risk came in driving to Vegas. That went good too. The next risk, parking at the self-storage and driving away in the pickup, had given him a headache. All that adrenaline. But it went good. Driving back with his cargo had been both scary and exciting. Every time he'd seen headlights—five times—he'd nearly died. Every time the headlights disappeared, he'd howled.

When he'd turned onto the service road behind the Inn, he'd actually prayed.

When he'd backed his pickup right up to the target, he'd gone calm. That was a surprise. Here was the biggest risk of all. Him out here in his suit. No way did he look like a post. And when he'd unhooked the lead-curtain tarp in the bed of his pickup, the cask stood out like it wanted to be seen. It was mostly buried in talc but even some tourist who didn't know a cask from his ass would look at that and say what the hell? Jardine remained thoughtful. Anybody came along now, he'd have to use the knife. He'd already used it to cut through the polyvinyl of the target and it lay blade-open on top of his pack.

He returned his attention to the plastique. He unwrapped it. He moved to the bed of the pickup. His next moves had to be fast, to keep his exposure down.

That's the way he'd done it back in the borax mine—attaching plastique to the cask in that dark cramped tunnel. Fast fast fast.

That's the way he moved now. First he attached the plastique to the cask and then he stuck the blasting cap into the plastique. Fast fast fast. Next he ran the wires to the detonator. Then he got in the cab and turned on the engine, cringing at the noise. He pushed the lift button. He got out to watch the pickup bed rise—he wouldn't miss this sight for a million bucks—well maybe he would but nobody was offering. He watched the talc spill out.

He watched the cask tumble out and hit the target. He moved to the detonator and pushed the button. There was a muffled sound, far quieter than the engine noise.

The great thing about the target was that the noise of the explosion was muffled and the concussive effect was increased.

He wished the female could be here to watch with him. He wasn't ashamed to think about her now. She would see his handiwork and even though she was working with the enemy she would be impressed, and that was enough for him.

Of course, the whole point of this target was to surprise the enemy. He pictured them, right now, sleeping like they didn't have anything to worry about. They didn't have a clue. Come tomorrow, they would see that the Long Lean Dude could strike right in their own backyard.

Even though this operation was not part of the primary mission, he thought it was worthy of naming. He put on his thinking cap and then he took it right off again. The name came to him that fast: *Watering Hole*.

He edged close for one last look. He thought the beads in the water looked like fish eggs.

31

FRIDAY MORNING DAWNED bright and clear and hot.

Three days ago I'd seen dawn break at the radioactive waste dump.

Now, over a room-service breakfast, Walter and I began our fourth day. We'd nearly finished analyzing the soils we collected in yesterday's journey. We'd worked through a room-service dinner until midnight and then we'd slept and then at dawn we put our eyes back to the scopes.

And now, under the twin lenses of the comparison scope, I reached Point D.

The layer-six samples we'd taken in the canyon had slight variations and there was one in particular that stood out. It contained a yellowish chalcedony that matched the yellowish chalcedony of the fender soil. Hue for hue, chroma for chroma, a dead-on match according to Walter's Munsell color chart.

With some reverence, I moved the Point D specimen dish to its place at the end of the line of dishes I'd laid out on the coffee table. Then I slouched in the wicker chair to admire the map we built. It took us from the talc mine all the way to the echoing depths of a funereal canyon and then it branched into a side canyon and came to an end.

Point D, end of the line for Roy Jardine's offroader.

From there, he'd borrowed a team of mules to drag the trailer or strapped on a jetpack and flown, and in another moment I'd turn my attention to the fact that we had no way to complete the map. We did have the glop from the trailer tires but it was an unilluminating mix. In another moment I'd admit we were in the neighborhood but had not found the address. Meanwhile, I enjoyed this moment.

Walter glanced up from the polarized light scope.. "You're not busy?"

I pointed out the chalcedony.

He came over to study the map. He breathed on my neck, smelling of lemon drops. At least it wasn't donuts.

"Well?" I said.

He smiled. "Why don't I give your minerals a gander under the polarized scope, and why don't you go collect Hector and tell him we're narrowing it down."

I left Walter's refrigerated suite and plunged out into the morning furnace, on the hunt for Hector Soliano.

Soliano answered his door with the phone pressed to his ear and mouthed *wait*.

I nodded and headed for the nearest lawn table. And then I saw the table at the far end of the lawn where two people were, to my astonishment, taking morning tea.

I changed course and walked past an abandoned croquet set to the linen-set table. Hap had his nose in his sketchbook and Pria stared stolidly at her clasped hands. Big hands with broken nails and a dirty bandaid on the right thumb. Brown hands on white linen. He could title his sketch *Fish Out Of Water.*

"Morning Buttercup."

"Morning."

"Sit yourself down."

I took a chair, nodding to Pria. She nodded back. Progress.

"Cherry coke?" Hap indicated the pitcher I'd thought contained iced tea. "Or might we tempt your palate with those croissants? Do, howsoever, leave the chocolate eclairs for Miss Alien. I'm bribing her."

I stared. He was Hap again. "Is everything okay? With the, ah..."

"The mash note from Roy?" Hap kept sketching.

"Yeah."

"Hector's checking into it."

"You figure out why Jardine's targeting you?"

"Boy's real touchy. Never joined in the banter at work. Never appreciated my humor." Hap shaded in Pria's bandaid, adding the dirt. "Might have pissed him off. Might be he aims to settle all his grudges."

"You don't look too worried now."

"That's because I ain't stuck in a car going down ambush canyon." He threw me a grin. "Hector and I are confining me to quarters. Safe and sound, here at the Inn."

Pria said, "Are we safe here?"

Better be, I thought. This is heaven. I bypassed the cherry coke and poured from a sweating pitcher of water into a cobalt-blue glass.

Pria watched. "It's okay to drink?"

I hesitated, glass in mid-air.

"What if the water's not happy?"

I set down the glass.

"Like, we were chasing it yesterday?" She lifted a hand and pointed. "Like, *here's* where it comes?"

Hap groaned. "Nooo, don't move, I'm not done with your pattycakes."

She dropped her hand but I stared in the direction she'd pointed. Up toward the Funerals, highway 190.

"That's better," Hap said. "Clasp them like before. Bend in that pinkie."

I said, "The thing about the aquifer is..."

"Okay *fine.*" She clamped her fingers. "So drink it. You guys up here hog it anyway with your big fancy glasses just sitting around and then nobody even *finishes* it, and your fancy grass and all like you can't even walk on the regular ground like normal people, and them down there," she broke the clasp, ignoring Hap's protest, and pointed downfan toward the village, "with their swimming and their golf—and they even got lakes to golf around—and in their campsites they got running water and they wash their *hair* in it."

Hap had given up drawing. He just listened.

I thought of the flume we'd seen yesterday, paralleling 190, running down the Furnace Creek Wash toward the Inn. I hadn't noticed any other piece of the water collection system but it had to be there. I said, "Doesn't the water system serve the Timbisha, too?"

"We don't have *grass.*" Her high voice pitched higher. "We don't have a *pool.*"

Hap gestured to the pool on the terrace below. "Jump on in. Buttercup'll borrow you a suit."

I wanted to fling my water in his face.

She hissed, "I don't know how to swim."

"Well I'll teach you!"

I stared down at the pool where the lap-swimmers had taken over, where a bronzed blond man swam a beautiful butterfly, and I remembered a pale redheaded man doing a more beautiful butterfly, and a less-pale brunet treading water, preparatory to making a fool of herself.

"The water doesn't even want to *be* in your fancy pool," Pria said.

Hap widened his eyes. "Where does it want to be?"

I made a guess. "It wants to be watering the mesquite and the bighorn." Instead of the palms and the midnight swimmers.

She shrugged.

I picked up my glass. "You said the water's not happy. Why'd you say that?"

"The bad guy's putting atoms in it."

"He is?"

"Well *yeah*, I'm not stupid, I know why you're all so weirded about the aquifer."

She got that right. We were definitely weirded. If Jardine wanted to mimic the leak at the dump, all he had to do was dump his stolen resins every time he made the swap for a new cask. Dumping them *where* is of course the question—somewhere within the vicinity of Point D, I'd say. Spill the beads into some hidden ditch or glory hole and then every time it rains, the beads are washed down into the groundwater. Toward the aquifer. I'd say that's how Roy Jardine is getting into the virgin.

Pria said, "And what if the atoms get pissed off?"

I regarded my water glass. I wished it wasn't tinted, although if there was something to worry about in the water I wouldn't be seeing it. I said, carefully, "Travel time of a contamination plume in groundwater is measured in years. Lots of them. So this water's safe to drink."

"Buttercup speaks truly." Hap stuck his pencil behind his ear and passed the sketchbook to Pria. "You like?" He poured himself a glass of water and tipped it to us. "To your health."

Soliano joined us and I rose to lead him away, to tell him about Point D in private, but he paused behind Pria's chair for a look at the sketchbook.

I leaned in to see what had caught his eye. It was not the sketch of Pria's hands. She'd flipped the pages to another sketch, another pair of hands. She was studying it, feathery hair brushing the page.

Soliano said, "You know these hands?"

"Maybe the ring."

I came alert.

Soliano took a seat, gingerly, the way you'd move around a skittish cat. "Tell me about this ring."

It was the sketch of Jardine's hands, the one Hap had made two mornings ago in Walter's suite. I looked anew at that puzzling Rorschach ring.

Pria said, "That Badwater race."

Hap peered anew at his sketch. "Well I'll be darned."

Soliano's face sharpened. "Tell me about this Badwater race."

"It's a bunch of fools what come here in the heat of the summer," Hap said, "and for no good reason under the blistering sun they runs theyselves from Badwater halfway up Mount Whitney."

Reflexively, I looked. I couldn't see it because the Panamints were between my line of sight and the Sierra Nevada, but I knew it was there. Mount Whitney had to be more than a hundred miles from here.

"Big deal is, Badwater's the lowest elevation in the continental states," Hap said, "and Whitney's the highest."

Soliano frowned. "That is a feat, but..."

"It's stupid," Pria said.

"But you have seen the race? You know the ring. What is this, a prize?"

"My cousin got one. He didn't win. He just ran. He's stupid."

Soliano turned to Hap. "I find this odd. Roy Jardine allowed you to draw his hands, and he was proud enough of his feat to wear this ring, and yet he did not tell you about his race?"

"Boy ain't a braggart. One of his endearing qualities."

Soliano's gaze fell to the sketchbook. "What does this tell us about him?"

I said, "He's into extremes."

"Worse than that," Hap said, "he's into irony. Badwater. Baaaad water."

32

"There is a saying I learned my first year at Quantico." Soliano glanced at his watch. "Close counts in horseshoes."

I said, "Only."

Soliano's attention shifted to a woman in a peach uniform coming our way across the lawn. I recognized her. Gloria. Tiny, pretty, looked about twelve. I'd borrowed a tiny swimsuit from her.

"What?" Soliano said to me, eyes on Gloria.

"Close counts only in horseshoes. But there's another saying, one I learned my first year in the lab..."

"Que?" Soliano said, to Gloria.

She halted. She spoke fast.

Soliano leaned forward. "Aqui?"

She pointed beyond the terraced edge of the lawn.

We both looked. There was nothing.

"What is it?" I asked Soliano.

"Somebody is hurt."

I looked around. I saw Hap and Pria, artist and subject, once again engrossed in her hands. I saw no one else.

Gloria raised her palms to the sky. "*Por favor.*"

Soliano and I headed toward the far end of the lawn where a stone monolith rose from the stone wall. Beyond the monolith were more walkways. My foot struck something hard. I looked down. A green croquet ball was camouflaged in the grass.

Soliano did not slow. "What saying did you learn?"

It took me a moment. "You don't get there unless you get close first."

He laughed.

"*Alli,*" Gloria called, behind us.

From behind the monolith, a shoulder and stretch of leg came in and out of view. Someone was approaching, jerky. The lower arm bent inward. Someone was hurt and cradling a wound. And then she lurched so suddenly out from the monolith's shadow that it seemed she'd been tossed. She doubled over, face to knees.

"Dios mio," Soliano whispered.

She looked up grinning.

There was no wound. The only marks on her white shirt and white jeans were streaks of dirt and something yellowish that reminded me of the egg yolk stain on my shirt before Hap sent it to be laundered.

She was grimacing, not grinning. The lax skin bunched around her mouth.

"What'd you *do*, Chickie?" Pria was suddenly beside me.

Hap joined us. "Hold onto the girl."

I circled her waist. She twisted and yelped. I glimpsed, beyond the struggling Pria, Walter rushing out of his room. He came up on the other side of her. I let her go and she tunneled into him.

Chickie made an animal sound.

"Hector," Hap said, "you better call Scotty and tell him to get his RERTs on the scene."

Soliano was already dialing. He kept his eyes on Chickie, the same way he'd fixed on the radiation-sick bat on the garden lawn. "Might she carry contaminants? On her person?"

"I'm sure gonna assume that." Hap picked up the croquet ball and tossed it a couple of feet in front of us. "Listen up, boys and girls, that's the do-not-cross line. Everybody know about the inverse square concept? That's the one where just a little distance from a point source makes a big difference in dose. Give the gents some space."

Pria said, "*She's* moving!"

Chickie was struggling to get to her feet.

"Miss Chick," Hap said, "you'd best stay put and we'll fix you up."

I didn't think so. Her eyes widened, lifting the loose lids to show the bloodshot whites. And then she crumpled and retched yellowish stuff into the emerald lawn. I didn't think we were going to fix her up.

"Yuck," Hap said, pulling on latex gloves.

Soliano said, "Wait." His gaze settled on Chickie. "Ms. Jellinek. What happened to you?"

She spat. Yellow spittle webbed her chin.

"Ms. Jellinek. You have been *where*?"

Hap said, "Uh, Hector, interrogating a subject who's woofin her cookies is kinda a no-no." He snapped his gloves down tight. "Ain't it?"

Soliano said, icily, "This is not the flu." He made another phone call and I caught the word "lockdown."

I felt the heat. The sun was out from behind the clouds, sucking me dry. The smell of Chickie's vomit washed our way. I gagged. I noticed that nobody was in sight but us. The swimmers had left the pool. Gloria had disappeared. Where were the gardeners? Where were the sunburned Germans? Had everyone abandoned ship but us? Or maybe the lockdown was already in force. Chickie was on her haunches. Her mouth squirmed and she doubled over again only this time there was no egg yolk, just dry heaving. And here we stood staring like we'd stopped at the scene of an accident. All we could do was wait for Scotty with his shower and long-handled brushes. I recalled how that shower felt, only I'd worn protective clothing. Chickie wore white cotton and raw skin. She straightened, hands braced in the grass, like some white bulldog.

Soliano said, "You went *where*, Ms. Jellinek?"

I said, "Do we need to do this now?"

"If this will move us closer."

"It's not goddamn horseshoes."

Walter said, "Cassie," and when I looked he mouthed *boots*. I got it—her boots were caked with mud, and there's geology to do. Still, I waited for something more, like, after she's been deconned and treated and she's not disintegrating in front of us, let's by all means get hold of those boots, but Walter only lifted his eyebrows and tightened his grip on Pria. His concern, I saw, was for the child and not the disintegrating mother.

Soliano tried again. "You encountered some...beads...Ms. Jellinek?"

I looked then at Chickie's boots and like it's been bred in the bone I thought, maybe we'll get lucky and find distinct mud layers preserved in the waffle soles.

"Help us," Soliano said, "and we will be able to assist you."

Chickie extended her middle finger.

Pria hissed at her, "*Stop* it, you."

Chickie faced the lawn and retched.

Hap fished a syringe and small brown bottle from his kit. He tore the plastic wrap off the syringe. He needled the the bottle and sauntered across the croquet line.

Soliano snapped, "Stop, Miller."

Hap threw us a grin. "Time equals dose. I'll be quick." He caught Chickie's right arm and yanked up her sleeve.

"*Stop*. I do not wish her sedated."

Hap froze, needle raised.

And then all at once as if it had been choreographed Hap let go of Chickie and retreated across the croquet line and Scotty came running and a Beatty Sheriff chopper slipped out of the clouds and ranger trucks appeared on the road below and began the climb up the fan.

Chickie collapsed in the grass. For a moment I thought she'd died. Then her eyelids flickered and reddened eyes gleamed through slits. She spoke, just audible above the incoming grumble of the chopper. "I got somethin you fuckers want."

33

RAIN CAME ALONG WITH RERT, big fat drops that panicked Scotty because if there were resin beads on Chickie's person he did not want Mother Nature washing them into the lawn, and so Lucy in her suit held a big Wal-Mart umbrella over Chickie.

The rest of us huddled under the roof of the walkway while rangers and deputies patrolled the perimeter.

RERTs in hazmat rushed in equipment and raised the decon corridor. They started the pump and the yellow plastic unfolded itself into a shower. They connected the hose to the PVC pipe and ran it into Soliano's room, to the bathtub faucet. They ran the outflow hose across the grass past the monolith in the direction of the parking lot. Two of them began to meter the walkway, should Chickie have left a radiation trail. Another turned to Chickie and ripped open her shirt.

Pria gasped. Walter escorted her to his room.

Chickie fought feebly. It took three RERTs. They yanked off her boots. They unzipped her pants. They stood her up and peeled her to the skin. She hung between two of them. The third lifted her feet and they high-stepped into the yellow catch basin.

The water went on. The nozzles sprayed all four of them, the RERTs in their slick white suits and Chickie in her loose white skin.

Soliano, decorous, turned away.

Hap watched, matter-of-fact.

I sank against the wall and studied my boots.

When it was finished Scotty came over, skinning off his hood and mask, blond hair spiking every which way. "Okey-doke, Hector," he said, grim, "you get ten and then she's on a chopper to Vegas. They got doctors trained for this."

"No," Soliano said, "you will fly your doctor here. In the meanwhile, Mr. Miller will render medical assistance."

It was hot in Soliano's room. The air conditioner was off because Chickie had the chills.

She lay on the bed. The blanket covered her from the neck down but her naked arms and doughy shoulders were exposed. The skin of her arms was reddened, raising in patches like crackling pastry. Her eyes were shut. Beside her pillow was an aluminum bowl.

Hap eased the needle into her arm, then massaged the IV bag.

I was waiting my turn for a closeup under her fingernails. I heard Walter, just outside, arguing with Scotty about a shielded box of contaminated clothing and boots. Although the decon shower had not flushed any observable beads, Scotty—and the rest of us—were not taking any chances.

Soliano said, "Ms. Jellinek?"

She lifted, and the blanket slipped to reveal stringy breasts as she twisted to bury her face in the bowl. She retched loudly then collapsed onto the bed.

Hap adjusted the IV tubing then pulled the blanket back up to her neck.

"Mr. Miller," Soliano said, "how long does this...indisposition...last?"

"It's the prodromal phase, Hector. Lasts a couple days or so. Then she goes latent for awhile."

Soliano moved closer to the bed, gazing down at Chickie. "Ms. Jellinek, the quicker we proceed, the quicker you can rest through this difficult phase. You say you have something we want?"

He put me in mind of a raptor examining its prey.

She glared. "What you fuckers do to my desert?"

"You refer to Mr. Jardine?"

She was silent so long I thought she'd said her last.

"Help us find this man who threatens your desert."

She held up two fingers.

"*Two* men?"

I thought, she doesn't know that Ryan Beltzman is dead.

"And you are what?" Soliano asked. "A partner?"

Her eyes narrowed. "Just sold 'em my talc."

"And attacked my geologists."

She grinned. Grimaced. Then twisted, this time clutching the blanket, and retched into the bowl. When she lay back there were tears in her eyes.

The sympathy I'd been feeling evaporated in the overheated room.

Hap held up a bottle and syringe. "Anti-emetic, Hector. Stop the vomiting."

"And make her drowsy, yes?"

"Could."

"We will delay medication." Soliano shrugged. "Ms. Jellinek, help us and then we will help you."

She whispered, "Get Pria."

Soliano smiled. When he'd left the room I watched Hap massage the IV bag and my skin puckered where he'd run saline into me, and then Chickie caught my eye and licked her finger and mimed touching my cheek, and then Soliano opened the door and ushered in Pria.

Chickie raised her head to nod at her daughter. The blanket slipped slightly, revealing the fibrous roots of her breasts.

Pria's brown skin went crimson. "*God.*"

Chickie jerked up the blanket. "Pree." Her voice was raw. "A million bucks, you an me. I'm sellin—he's buyin." She jerked a thumb at Soliano. "You make sure he don't weasel."

Pria wrapped her arms around her chest.

"Ms. Jellinek," Soliano said, "this is not taking us where we need to go."

Chickie's tongue flicked out, wetting her cracked lips. "Awright. There's pellets." She cleared her throat. "Lot of em."

Soliano said, softly, "They are loose?"

"Fuck yeah."

A current seemed to run through the room.

Soliano said, "Where are they?"

"Ain't gonna tell you, am I?" Chickie winked at Pria. "Not till you pay up."

"Perhaps you do not know."

"Callin me a liar?"

"I am calling your bluff."

She grinned. "Well I took some of them pellets. Whole pack full."

I went cold. The thought that triple-X resin beads were accessible, that this woman had found her way to Roy Jardine's depot and simply helped herself, made the hairs stand up on my arms. I was simply agog at the ease with which the beads had passed from the jurisdiction of one thief to the hands of another. I suddenly wanted Soliano to tighten the screws.

"Where is the pack now?" was all he asked.

"Took it to Vegas."

Hap whistled his falling skyrocket. Ooops.

"Where," Soliano asked, dialing his cell, "in Vegas?"

She rubbed her thumb against her fingers.

"In a public place?"

"Hid it in the closet in my room. Vegas is full of fuckin thieves."

I sat stunned, listening to Soliano relay the information to his agents. Not only does she help herself to Jardine's stash, she then takes that pack of hot beads to Las Vegas. Which room? Which maids? Which motel, hotel, of the hundreds in Vegas? What if she didn't register under her own name?

She let it run, then said, "Hey dimwits, pack ain't there now. Go look in your fuckin parkin lot. White SUV. Under the seat."

Soliano gave her a long look, then phoned Scotty.

Chickie's lips skinned back. Grin, grimace, hard to say.

Hap leaned in. "How long since you took the beads?" He looked her over. "I'd say your exposure started in the last twenty-four hours or so." He studied her blistering arms. "You load the beads by hand?"

"That why I'm sick?"

Hap rolled his eyes. "Ooooh baby. Yowza."

She swallowed. "Wore one of their fuckin moonsuits."

"Just the suit?"

"The whole thing, tank and all. An I know how to use a fuckin air tank cuz I took a mine safety course so I knew what I was doin so why the *fuck* am I sick?"

"It's not enough," Hap said, almost gentle. "Unshielded high-rad beads—you got too close. For too long." He studied her face. "How about the facepiece? You seal it up tight? Breathe in anything that felt like dust?"

I cut in, "Beads can be inhaled?"

"Yowza. Small ones can go aerosol. Don't wanna inhale Mr. Alpha—he's partial to the lungs." Hap smiled a pained smile. "Tell me, Miss Chick, how long'd you wear your moonsuit?"

"Long as I had to, loadin the pellets." She looked, suddenly, a little desperate. "But I wrapped my pack in one of them silver sheets they had for...whaddya call it?"

"Shielding," Hap said. He did not add: it's not nearly enough.

Soliano closed his phone and moved back in. "Ms. Jellinek, how far did you carry the pack?"

Her eyes filmed and I thought, she's calculating. You don't have to calculate distance if your car is nearby. She walked a good ways. And she'd worn her moonsuit only to load the pellets, which means she'd removed it before leaving the place, which means she'd removed booties as well, which means that's good clean uncontaminated mud caked in her boots. I wanted to read it.

"How far, Ms. Jellinek? From the place you got your pellets?"

"You tryin to trick me, Mr. Fucker?"

"I am trying to get *through* to you," Soliano snapped. "You have no time for this childishness. You are going to get sicker."

Pria sucked in her breath.

"Hang on, Pree." Chickie's inflamed eyes slitted. "We're negotiatin."

Soliano grew a thin smile. "Then give us something. When did you see the two men?"

"Long time before you fuckers came."

"Who did you see? Mr. Jardine?"

"Fuck him, yeah, Jardine."

"Who was the second man?"

"Blond fucker."

"Was the blond man named Ryan Beltzman?"

"Didn't get introduced."

"How did you come to find the place with the pellets?"

"Followed the blond fucker once."

"Why did you return? This time."

She let out a snort.

Greed, I thought. Jardine paid her for talc and the use of her mine, Jardine no doubt paid her to strand us in the desert, so after gauging the interest of the FBI, why not see if she can sell something else?

"Was Jardine there?" Soliano asked. "*This* time?"

She snorted again.

No, I thought, or she'd already be dead. Then where was Jardine?

Soliano pressed. "Did you see anyone at the place where you found the pellets? This time?"

She rasped, "Elvis fuckin Presley."

"You act the fool."

"Fuck you." She grinned. "You all gonna get fucked. A real ranger-fuck. Enough play-dough for it."

"What does this mean? Play-dough?"

Pria spoke. "Stuff to blast tunnels."

Plastique. I recalled its effect on the cask in the borax tunnel. If there was enough explosive to reach us and the rangers, what did that mean? It's nearby? Or maybe she just meant any of us who get too close. FBI, RERT, Sheriff, cops, geologists—we're all rangers to her, we're all fuckers trying to shut down her mine.

"Ms. Jellinek. I repeat. *Where* is this place?"

She shifted her bulk to point to her rear.

Pria turned for the door.

Chickie hissed, "*Wait* girl. I'm countin on you. Your daddy's mine ain't gonna pay a nickel. Fuckers won't let it. This is our due." She extended her hand. "I ain't never hit you. Do it for me."

"You're acting *stupid*, Chickie."

Chickie rolled onto her side and put her face in the bowl, dry heaving.

"Stop her," Pria said, "*make it stop*."

Hap said, "She's going downhill, Hector. For the love of your soul let me stop it."

Soliano brought his hand to his forehead, that gesture of his. "Mr. Miller, you have perhaps Pepto-Bismol in your satchel?"

"The cheapo generic. If she can keep it down."

"Give it to her."

Hap brought out a bottle. "Here you goes, Miss Chick, courtesy of Doctor Hap." He put a pink tablet to her lips. "Tastes jess like bubble gum."

Chickie took in the tablet.

"Give it a minute or two, Hector."

Soliano checked his watch, then turned to me. "You wished to inspect the nails? While we wait." He hiked a shoulder at the bed.

I did not know if Chickie was worn down by her ordeal or just trying to digest the tablet, but she watched dully as I knelt beside her with my kit. I opened a specimen dish and placed it on the bed. I told her I was going to scrape under her nails. Her eyes narrowed but she made no objection. I took her right hand. She had a wide flat hand and skinny forearm that brought to mind a ping-pong paddle. Her puffed skin felt tender as a baby's. Her fingertips looked as though they might pop. The ragged nails sat deep within the reddened flesh. Scotty had scrub-brushed those nails but the decon left a thin line of dirt. Maybe old dirt, from her mine. Or maybe newer dirt. She'd been a busy desert rat, what with sabotage and theft, and maybe a telling grain or two stuck with her. Maybe not. But my fingers, as they say, itched. I chose the pointed file from my kit—a tool I've used to pry grains from a nail hole, mud from a knotted rope—and now, aptly, a tool made expressly for its job. I popped out a crescent of soil from her thumbnail.

Hap said, “You make a good manicurist, Buttercup.”

I glanced up.

He was examining Chickie’s hand in mine as if he’d like to draw us.

34

The doctor had come and Hap had left. The rain had stopped. The shower and hoses and pump were gone. Out here on the lawn it looked as though nothing untoward had happened. Scotty and his team had disappeared, to the parking lot I assumed. Walter was nowhere to be seen so I guessed he'd claimed Chickie's boots for analysis.

Ballinger was here, though, rooster-pacing the walkway. "She talk?"

Soliano shook his head and squatted in front of Pria, who sat against the wall hugging her knees. "Miss Weeks, help your mother by helping us. Tell her we agree to pay. Tell her you will watch out for her interests."

Ballinger halted. "Pay?"

"Five minutes, Miss Weeks. To think. And then please I will need your help." Soliano headed back to his room, saying to me as he passed, "Talk with her."

I took in a deep breath.

Ballinger sidled close. "How much the old lady want?"

"One million."

"Getting expensive."

I glanced at Pria, to see if she'd caught that. Of course, she might not know that Ballinger was the radwaste dump manager, that his company had already been extorted once this week, that he himself had no authority to pay out any million of CTC funds. As if Soliano, for that matter, did. The FBI was, in the end, a bureaucracy and certainly a field agent—even one as hotshot as Soliano—was not allowed off-the-cuff to dispense one million dollars. It was a bluff. And the girl Soliano was trying to bluff might be a fourteen-year-old from the rez but I'd bet she'd been raised by her daddy and her Aunt Ruth on tales of promises and threats and bluffs from generations of government agents who said let me help you but first you help me.

I didn't know how to get through to her. Maybe if I'd practiced on other kids I'd know what to say, but I'd been pretty much tied up in my own angst, which kids could smell on me like bad cheese, and this kid more than any kid I'd ever run across made my head want to explode. But minutes were passing and Soliano was waiting. I said, "I'm sorry about your mom, Pria. I know you're upset."

"I want Grandfather."

"Grandfather's busy looking at your mother's boots so we can find out where she went. Where she got into the radwaste. You don't need Grandfather."

Pria got up, leveling on me a look of closeup hate.

Just that quickly, I flipped. I became Soliano's creature. "You know what, Pria? You can save us the trouble. You get your mother to tell us where the stuff is and we can send the experts to clean up the mess." I waited. I was not reaching her. "What you have to do, Pria, is go in there and tell her she's going to get what she wants. And I can't tell you she is. So you'll be telling a lie. And that sucks. Believe me, I work with a man who will cut out his tongue before he'll tell a lie—unless it's going to prevent a greater sin. You know, like murder? Or like crapping up your desert? Once this stuff gets loose, you know, it hangs around. You know what a half-life is? That's the time it takes for half of a radioactive element to decay—to throw off *half* its radioactivity. So let's see, Scotty says we've got cobalt-60 in the resins. Nasty stuff. Got a half-life of five and a half years." I realized I was doing a Hap on her. Well sure worked on me, sure got me reviewing my radionuclides table. "Or maybe you've heard of plutonium-239? Hangs around a little longer. Gives up half its radioactivity every twenty-four thousand years." I waited. "Let's put it this way. How about your water? You want it to stay happy? Then get in there and tell your mother whatever she wants to hear."

Her black eyes went flat.

It began to rain again, thunderstorm loud, as if I'd called in special effects. Water please, and make it hard and loud.

Ballinger spoke. "Look here, I can maybe arrange for the company to pay a reward. You know, if everything turns out. If we get the material back."

I doubted that. He can't have much credibility left with CTC. And if word of his diddling Jardine's paperwork hasn't yet reached them, it will in the end. So what's Ballinger doing? Helping out Soliano? And then, quid pro quo, Soliano helps out with his ethical and legal dilemmas?

Ballinger said, "Not a million, but..." He seemed to calculate. "Thousands?"

Pria shook her head.

I said, "No? No, you won't help? No, it's not enough?"

"*Her*," Pria said. "She wants the money now."

"Look, she knows we don't have a sack of money under the bed, that's why she got you into this. She thinks if we make a promise to you we're more likely to keep it." Yeah, and I've got a treaty for you to sign, too. "So you have to decide if you want to help us or not. I know you don't want someone else getting contaminated."

She compressed her mouth. The ultimate daughter decay product.

"What do you want, Pria?"

"I want you to leave me alone."

Alone alone alone. The word buzzed in my head, like we were back up the echoing canyon, an echo of me, stiff-necked teenage me with my mom—you don't care, you hate me because I'm alive and Henry isn't, leave me alone alone alone. Good job, Oldfield. And now you can tell Pria to go to her room.

She was already moving. She started down the walkway toward Soliano's room.

I said, startled, "You're going to help?"

"I'm going to the rest room."

She was heading toward the main building—the lobby—not Soliano's room. I reached in my pocket and brought out my key. "Use mine."

She looked at the key as if it were crafted of cobalt-60. She looked out toward the lawn, and the walkway that led to the lobby. Raindrops bulleted onto the concrete, and bounced. Her face closed. She took on an almost crafty look. Another echo. I nearly put my key away. She snatched it from my hand before I could.

I turned my hopes from the girl back where they belonged, to the geology. I found Walter in our lab examining a plug of boot soil under the scope. He grunted. I knew that grunt—an expression of interest, if not quite satisfaction.

Half an hour later we heard a door slam and footsteps pounding and, distinct, a curse. *Dios mio.*

We went out to investigate and saw Soliano loping toward the parking lot.

35

THE BLUE FORD pickup stood alone at the far end of the parking lot.

It was washed clean. The body rain-washed, the fenders scrubbed. There was no mud to sample; Walter didn't even open the field kit. Scotty pronounced the vehicle not contaminated and put away his meter. Soliano didn't need to call in the plates because he'd memorized Roy Jardine's license number.

Now we just stared.

What got to me was the hose. The pickup was parked beside a planter box and a coiled hose. I pictured Jardine pressure-washing under the fenders, in the tire treads. No worry, then, that the geologists would build themselves a soil map. Hosing made sense. What didn't make sense was that he'd taken the time to neatly coil the hose after use. That, I found creepily obsessive.

Walter broke the silence. "This truck wasn't here yesterday when we returned from the canyon."

I agreed. "So it arrived sometime in the night."

"Or this morning." Soliano checked his watch. "Prior to Ms. Jellinek's arrival."

We looked, as one, down the parking lot to the white SUV in the yellow hot zone. Suited RERTs were examining Chickie's truck. FBI agents, Sheriff deputies, and park rangers milled—all keeping well clear of the coned-off zone.

The action was down there but the mystery was up here. Scotty voiced it. "So where'd Jardine go?"

One by one, we turned to scan the red tile rooftops and the reddened hills behind the Inn. Nothing out of the norm, or what had become the norm. Clouds had bunched again, though, throwing down fat shadows.

I had another question. I moved for a closer look at the tarp covering Jardine's pickup bed. It looked like one of the silvery drapes I'd seen in the talc mine 'garage.' Leaded, no doubt. I dredged up the scenario we'd spun, how Jardine learned at the dump—courtesy of my bragging—that I could follow the talc trail, how he rushed to Chickie's mine to get the resin cask. I expanded it now: he couldn't just drive off with the cask visible and unshielded. So he covered it with the lead tarp. And off he went. And ended up, finally, here. With a tarp, but no cask. I studied the tarp. Where it puckered, rainwater pooled. That said it had rained since the cask was removed. Not much help. It rained last night. It rained this morning. It's been raining on and off since we got here. He could have ditched the cask anytime in the past three days—although if he was going to ditch it then why take it to begin with? I wetted my lips and asked the obvious. "Where's the cask?"

Soliano yanked on the driver-side door handle. It was locked. He withdrew his pistol from his waistband holster and with the butt-end smashed the window. He unlocked the door and climbed inside. He rooted around, and when he finally swung out of the truck he was unrolling a sheet of paper.

We gathered around.

It was a map—a schematic drawing—and you had to study it

a moment before recognizing the razor-thin lines and sharp angles and precise arcs as a water distribution system. At the top of the diagram was a water storage tank. A pipeline ran downhill, to the Inn, to its bones, its framework, its pipes and faucets and inflows and outflows, its sinks and toilets and tubs and showers, its pool, its lawns, its sprinklers, its stream-cut gardens and water-rich palms.

A post-it note stuck to the map said *$10 million—water water everywhere.*

Water water everywhere. What if he's already contaminated it?

My mind raced, inventorying. Water in the glass on the lawn table this morning. Hap drank it. I drank it. Was it bottled? Wouldn't they serve something like Evian at a place like the Inn? But earlier, breakfast in the room, Walter and I drank coffee and they surely didn't use Evian to brew the coffee. And before that, a quick shower, water on my lips. And then brushing my teeth. My stomach curdled.

The others, too, looked glazed, looking inward, thinking back, reviewing—what'd I have for breakfast, what'd I have to drink, where and when and in what circumstances have I come in contact with the water over the past twelve hours or is twelve long enough? How long do I need to work backward?

What if the water's not happy?

Soliano recovered first. He was on his cell. "The water main. *Shut it off.*"

"We have the target," Soliano told the small crowd he'd assembled. "Proceed on the assumption that it has been hit. If it has not, assume that it will be hit, if not now, then one minute from now."

"Hit how?" a baby-faced agent asked.

"Radioactive material, either in a cask or loosed. You will divide into teams, each team consisting of my agents and RERT members who will monitor for radioactive traces. You will search every nook and cranny of the Inn and its grounds—most specifically, the water system." Soliano addressed the baby-faced agent. "Andre, you will coordinate, with the concomitant objective of locating Roy Jardine."

Andre scowled. "What if he's poofed?"

"His vehicle is here," Soliano snapped, "so you will proceed on the assumption that he has *not* poofed."

Andre moved.

Soliano said, "Full ninja."

My chest thumped.

Soliano was on the phone again. "Secure the annex. Every room. No person goes in, no person goes out."

The teams fissioned. Soliano and Walter and I made up our own team, with the object of doing a room check.

There was no one in sight on the annex walkway but Special Agent Stan Dearing, a sunburned monolith with a peeling nose and a Sig Sauer in hand. Nobody'd come out, he said. Not since the doctor came and Hap Miller left, about an hour ago. Miller, whom Dearing would trust about as far as he could throw him, had said he was going for a walk.

"Going for a walk where?" Soliano said.

Dearing shrugged.

Soliano phoned Andre and told him to put out a BOLO for Hap Miller.

Be On the Lookout—that one I knew. Try a lounge chair somewhere, I thought, or the sauna room. I looked at the lawn, at the table where Hap told me a couple of hours ago that he's staying put, safe and sound here at the Inn. Only, looks like the Inn is Jardine's target. I doubted Hap would appreciate the irony. Then again, maybe Hap knows the Inn is the target. Maybe he's in on it. Maybe that's why he left.

Soliano brushed past Dearing and opened the door to his room.

I glimpsed, inside, a doctor in hospital scrubs with a saddlebag gut, adjusting the IV that fed into Chickie's inert arm.

Soliano moved to the next room and banged on the door. "Mr. Ballinger!" He tried the knob. "Milt?" He drew his pistol and broke the window. He looked inside then spun on Dearing.

Dearing's sunburn radiated. "Didn't know he wasn't in there."

I said, "What about Pria? I gave her my key."

Walter shot me an incredulous look.

Dearing went purple. "Nobody came out of nowhere."

I looked around. No Hap, no Milt, no Pria. No Roy. Empty lawn, empty walkways, empty rooftops. Everybody's poofed.

We took off. Walter went for his room and I stopped at mine. I knocked, then Soliano shouldered me aside. He banged on the door and shouted, "*Open up*," as if Pria had barricaded herself inside, as if Jardine were holding a gun to her head or a glass of water to her lips. Before Soliano could bring out his gun and break my window, Walter opened my door from the inside. He had to have come through the adjoining door that linked our rooms into a two-room suite.

I said, "She's in the bathroom."

Walter and Soliano stood aside.

I opened the bathroom door. She was not there but she oh-so-clearly had been there. Even as I shifted to allow them a look,

I could not take my eyes from the bathtub with its porcelain scummed almost to the tiled rim.

She'd taken a bath.

Shit.

"Where is she?" Walter asked, eerily calm, as if there were some logical progression from the tub to the place she would naturally go next. To Soliano's room? All scrubbed for her mom, only to find her mom sedated by the paunchy doctor? And so she went elsewhere.

I hoped for that.

Soliano was on the phone, trying to reach Aunt Ruth.

Walter said, brittle-calm, "She had to have left through my room."

He led Soliano through the adjoining door. I stayed behind. I figured they'd find the sliding door unlocked that led from Walter's bedroom out to the tiny veranda that had so impressed Hap, and bordering the veranda they'd find a stone wall that any one of us could scale on the first try. And on the other side of that wall they'd find the walkway that led away from the main walkway where Dearing stood useless guard. Which was why Dearing in all honesty could say nobody came out of nowhere.

She'd left unseen, but had she left alone?

I braced a hand against the doorjamb. How would Roy Jardine know she was in my room? How would he know who was in what room? And if he did, why not go into Soliano's room and take care of Chickie, who knows what he does not want told, along with the doctor who is trying to save her life?

Because he'd have to go through Dearing, the monolith with the Sig Sauer.

But still, why go after Pria? Does Roy Jardine know Pria from Adam?

Well, it's my room and he knows me.

I heard Soliano and Walter stampeding through Walter's suite and then I heard Walter's door crash open and slam shut.

I stared at the bathtub. How long had she soaked? I feared I was going to be sick. I moved for the toilet. I had to kick aside the wet towels humped on the floor. The toilet seat was up. There was no paper left on the roll. I changed my mind and went to the sink for a tissue to wipe my face. There were none left. Soiled tissues papered the counter. Her used bandaid clung to the mirror. I turned away. The tub was worse. Gels and shampoos drained their last and made a purple slick along the bottom. The drain was plugged by a nest of black hairs.

She'd used everything. She'd gorged. She'd finally got a room at the Inn.

Pity convulsed me.

I stared into the tub. I could see the path made when the water drained. It had cut a channel through the purple slick. My vision suddenly jumped, to the giant fan Walter and I had hiked after being stranded. I saw again the fan rocks coated in black desert varnish and I felt again the heat they threw off. I felt the relief when Walter and I took shelter in the coolness of the channel that was unvarnished, that had been washed clean by floodwaters. I saw how the unvarnished channel ran down the fan and then snaked out onto the saltpan. My legs cramped, now, like I was wading again across the white floodplain.

And then that vision morphed into another that beggared belief.

I ran out the door.

Soliano and Walter and Scotty were lined up like ducks at the stone ledge, looking down at the pool. As I sprinted across the lawn I heard Soliano shout "break the lock." Down below, I saw

Andre's team on the hunt. They were armored and padded and helmeted and booted, hugging submachine guns. Full ninja.

"Yes?" Soliano said, spotting me.

I lifted a hand, panting. I felt, suddenly, unsure. This was an absurd idea. But they were waiting so I began. "What if this is a diversion?"

Soliano held up the rolled map. "Until you find me another target, I am diverted."

Walter eyed me. "Diversion from what?"

I waved at the clouds. "This is all an offshoot of that hurricane off Baja California. Right?"

They glanced at the sky. Scotty turned, stiff in his suit.

"According to the weather report, the storms were forecasted to start hitting us Monday and continue through the week."

They waited.

"What if the forecast was a trigger? So Monday night Jardine's ready to go. He does the last swap. But Beltzman gets cold feet—maybe he doesn't want to go offroading with major storms on the way." I took in a deep breath. "But major storms are just what Jardine needs."

Soliano stared. "Why does he need storms? For cover?"

I saw Andre's team, below, fan out to the pool house and the fireplaces and the banquet room. They were cautious, mincing their way, big ninjas on tiptoe like they didn't want to find what Soliano had dispatched them to find. Unlike the ninjas, I plunged ahead. "How about for a delivery system?"

Scotty's phone rang.

I clarified. "A flood."

Soliano frowned. "He needs storms to create a flood? And this flood will deliver the resins to...his target. This is what you are saying?"

"Yes. He's been waiting for a flood. And now the storms from the hurricane are going to give him one."

Walter's eyebrows lifted. "No. A flood is not predictable. At a set time. In a set place. He has to have chosen his site a good long while ago."

"Okay but what if he checks out the Park Service Doppler radar system every time there's a storm? And he gets a pattern, where the risk index is high. And he maps out likely areas. Then all he has to do is wait until a big enough storm hits."

Walter was shaking his head.

"He's got to move the resins from the mine to the target. How's he *do* that?"

"He releases them in situ," Walter said. "And your rains wash the resins down into the groundwater. Toward the aquifer. As we discussed."

"There's a better target."

"Hector." Scotty closed his phone. "That was Lucy. My RERT, with your man Andre. She says we got hit."

We took the service road that ran up behind the Inn. RERTs and their vehicles formed a wall. Ninjas hovered. I couldn't see anything. Scotty barreled ahead.

I tried to hold on to my bathtub vision. I had carried it like a cup of smoke and already it was curling away. I caught a glimpse of a RERT edging toward a field of black vinyl. The ninjas backed up. Somebody swore. I heard *beads*. I heard *crapped up*. And now I could see that the vinyl overlaid a water tank sunk into the ground. The vinyl was ripped. The RERT dipped his tallywhacker through the hole. Like ice-fishing. Crazy ice-fishing in the desert in a pool of crapped-up water.

My mind raced, inventorying. What did I have to *drink*?

Scotty joined us, unmasking. "This tank's an auxiliary."

Soliano opened the map. "For?"

"For watering the lawn."

I gaped. So this tank's not the main water tank on the diagram Soliano found in Jardine's truck. This tank doesn't supply potable water. We didn't drink the water from this tank. Pria didn't take a bath in this water. We all gaped at the auxiliary tank. All that worry. Out it went. Gushing out. Soliano expelled a breath. I sagged. Walter put his arm around me.

"And," Scotty added, grimly, "it's piped to the swimming pool."

It took us a long moment, to move from relief to horror. From us to them—the lap swimmers who got in the pool in all good faith for a little exercise, a little fun. And what they got was a big taste, courtesy of Brother Roy, of what's to come. My skin crawled. But beneath the skin, beneath my outrage and my horror, I still swam in my own relief.

"Scotty," Soliano said, "check it all. Re-check. Every place the water flows."

"We're already on it," Scotty said.

I stared at the exposed water in the auxiliary tank. Water water everywhere. Not really. I looked down at the dry fanglomerate soil. The rain squall of half-hour ago had left no liquid trace. The world again steamed dry. I watched Scotty run his hand through sweat-plastered hair. Blond filaments dried before my eyes. I turned to look at the service road, which ran from the Inn uphill to where we stood, and thence further up to the main water storage tank. Water water everywhere. Now you see it, now you don't. The sun glared. My bathtub vision came back so strong I had to squint. I spun to Soliano. "It *is* a diversion, Hector."

"This?" Soliano glanced at the tank.

"This is a bucket. He's going to poison the well."

Walter understood. He turned to look upfan, up toward the Furnace Creek Wash. We couldn't see it from here but we'd sure seen it yesterday. The mounds of travertine. The stands of mesquite, dotted along the fault trace for nearly a mile. The thrust fault that channeled water up from the aquifer, through the alluvium, spitting out that line of bighorn-attracting springs.

I said, fierce, "Springs."

Soliano looked directly at me, for the first time. "They supply water to the Inn?"

"Yeah. And the Ranch and the rangers and the Timbisha and the golf course and the campgrounds and all the rest. The whole village. And the bighorns and the coyotes and the bats and the snakes and the mesquite and these amazing little daisies that pop up when it rains and... The whole ecosystem, Hector."

"I see."

Not yet you don't. I said, "How about if he craps up the water supply for national park headquarters? How's that for a symbol?"

"Of what?"

"The virgin."

"Yes, I see." Soliano swept a hand. "An oasis."

No you don't see. My tongue seemed to harden, down to its roots. "Do you know how hard it is to find *water* out there?"

"I have not had to look."

I looked at Walter, whose jaw was working like he was sucking on a pebble.

"I see," Soliano said, this time like he did.

"You see what?"

"The priceless."

"Yes."

"No," Walter said, finding his voice, "he can't hit the springs."

I knew. We had a map that said he didn't, that said the geology took his offroader only as far as point D, well upcanyon from the springs. But Pria changed my mind. Pria in her bath. The draining water had carved a channel through the purple shampoo slick that coated the tub bottom. That bathtub vision reminded me of the giant fan where Walter and I took shelter, and how floodwaters had carved a channel through the desert-varnished fan. Pria's bath had left me a demonstration—the power of a channeled flood. I said, "Maybe he could hit the springs if he had a damn delivery system."

Soliano said, "The flood again?"

"I hope you're wrong," Scotty said. His hand was at his neck, at the medallion. "Because if you're right, we're S-O-L."

Soliano frowned.

"Shit-out-of-luck," Walter translated.

"You gotta remember," Scotty said, "they're dewatered resin beads."

I went cold. He'd never mentioned that.

Soliano's frown deepened. "What are dewatered beads?"

"Dried out, for disposal. Locks in the rads."

"Locks in? But I thought the beads were dangerous."

"They are—nasty hot. But at least when they're dry, they keep the nuclides from escaping." Scotty's face tightened. "Put the beads in water, they rehydrate."

"And they do what?" Soliano asked. "When they rehydrate?"

"They swell. Maybe crack. Degrade."

Walter said, alarmed, "Aren't the radionuclide ions chemically bound to the beads?"

"Bond's weak."

"This means *what*?" Soliano asked.

"Means keep the beads away from materials that can break the bond."

I got a sudden taste of the water in the hole beneath the mesquite. I thought, Badwater. It's why they call that water bad—it's saltier than the sea. But then all Death Valley water is high in sodium. Even an oasis like the springs has some salt. And that's how he turns an oasis into bad water. I said, "Sodium breaks the bond?"

Scotty nodded. "Get the beads in this groundwater and they..."

"They do what?" Soliano asked.

"They release 'em." Scotty rubbed his rad-weathered face. "Every damn nuclide."

And then, I thought, the nuclides raft away in the water, and the plants suck them up and the animals eat the plants and drink the water, and then the animals creep and crawl and wing their way out of Death Valley, carrying the radionuclides into the wider world.

36

It's a *diversion* Hector.

Hector you're not taking me seriously. Hector I'm not just an airhead female.

And then she'd made some sound that Jardine could not identify—since it was too risky to get close enough to watch he'd had to listen in remotely. And so he'd had to use his imagination. When the female geologist said *Hector* in that pissy tone of hers, and there had been that sound, Jardine imagined the female was stamping her foot.

He liked that. Hector's ignoring her and she's just so pissy about it. What she needs is a good spanking.

He saw he was still twisted up about the female. He thought he'd taken care of that. He wished he could take care of it the right way. Her and him in a meadow. Out in the open. He didn't mean out in the open where people could watch, he meant open like no shame. She'd have grass in her hair because they'd been rolling around.

Instead of the meadow he'd had to embarrass himself in the privacy of the mine.

So *excuse* him for making fun of her now.

He needed to remember who had truly loved him. Jersey. And look what he'd been forced into. A dude could love his dog and with a heavy heart leave her behind forever. A dude could do the hard thing when he had to.

He took the pistol out of his pack.

The timetable was speeding up. *Watering Hole* was a great victory. Put the fear right inside them. Pinned them down at the Inn. Jardine didn't know how much time this diversion would buy him. Going on what he'd overheard, plenty. Hector, you're an idiot. Your people are idiots. I outfoxed you all. My pickup sat in the parking lot half the night and half the morning before you found it. Took you half an hour to find the tank. Take you hours to check out all the vulnerable points in the water system. Hector, you're an...

Jardine stopped himself. "Stop it Roy." Don't count on hope. Count on a good plan. And practice.

He put the pistol in the holster. The holster sat low on his skinny hips. That's the way gunslingers wore it. Looked ace. Yeah—the ponytail and the shirt and the jeans and the boots, and now the holster with the pistol butt sticking out. If only somebody could see him now. Dudes, females. Any females. They wouldn't even notice his face.

He held his hand loose, near the gun butt. One, two, three...

Hector was saying something in his earbuds about the pipeline. Hector was asking somebody where all the access points were. Hector obviously never held a crap job like plumber's assistant.

Jardine listened to the ignorance. He wondered if anybody was going to find the little radio transmitter he'd planted last night in the scrub brush near the water tank. Didn't matter. He'd heard plenty. He smiled.

One, two, three... Slap the butt, close his hand, draw—and now the gun was in his hand and he was aiming it at the tin can.

It was already full of holes. Not much of a stand-in for a live target but it made the point. Firearm's a serious weapon. He wished he had one of those FBI shooters but what he had was plenty. He liked the pistol because of the holster—he could admit that. He liked firearms in general better than the knife but the knife was in his pack for a reason. Redundancy, the lesson he'd learned in job eighteen. Never count on one layer of safety.

A lesson he'd give that Bastard Ballinger.

The female was talking again and Jardine got sucked in again. She sounded worried. Jardine was glad that cad Miller wasn't there to tell her to get naked in the shower or something. Miller deserved a lesson in manners. A lesson he was going to get.

Lessons. Jardine needed one right now about the female. He needed to remember that she was coming after him. He needed to remember why. She was doing her job. She was doing it so good she was dangerous. So was the old fellow. That's what he needed to remember.

Because he had come to the Grand Finale. Nothing must interfere.

Jardine ripped out his earbuds and holstered his pistol. He had things to do. He had to go check on the progress of the trigger event, in preparation.

Stage One of the mission, at the borax mine, had been *The Trial* and Ballinger was found guilty.

Stage Two was going to be the mission climax. The Grand Finale. It would be a full and deserved punishment. The name for Stage Two said it all: *Death Penalty*.

37

We sat with the engine running at the mouth of the parking lot.

Walter snapped off the satellite phone. "She's taken her aunt's truck."

Relief hit me. "Where'd she go?"

"Aunt Ruth won't say." He grunted. "Perhaps because a fourteen-year-old is behind her wheel."

"You taught me to drive when I was thirteen."

"That was in the empty Von's parking lot." He looked out the window. "That was then."

And this is now. Now I'm the designated driver.

He cleared his throat and, for a micromoment, there was the chance that he'd ask me to swing the wheel to the right—downfan to the Timbisha village, down to interrogate Ruth Weeks and give chase to Miss Alien Underage Driver—but he simply said, "Shall we?"

I swung the wheel to the left onto highway 190, upfan to go to work.

The highway took us past the Inn and up into the trough cut by the Furnace Creek Wash, and as the Black Mountains closed in on our right and the Funerals reared up on our left, I shifted my worry to what lay ahead.

"Which spring," Walter asked, "would your flood target?"

My flood? I let that pass. My theory, after all.

But I'd fact-checked my theory on the map and plotted the line of springs that extends for nearly a mile. I glanced, now, at the riparian outposts along that fault line. "Maybe he's not targeting just one. All he has to do is hit the alluvium. So some of the beads go directly into the springs and some go into the gravel—both here and upgradient—for a later round." I wiped the sweat off my neck. "The gift that keeps on giving."

"If we knew which spring, we could work our way upcanyon from there."

"Oh."

We reached the turnoff and I nosed the Cherokee off highway 190 onto the ragged road up the fan. As we entered the canyon mouth, I peered up the wall at the reddish mud and cobblestones caught in the declivity some twenty feet above. Some flood that had been.

Walter was looking too. He phoned the Park Service Doppler radar guy for an update and learned that the precipitation pattern had not changed since the last call, in the parking lot.

The gunmetal sky had not changed, either.

I slowed, and the FBI behind us slowed, and we turned into the branching side canyon where we'd sampled yesterday and found the telling chalcedony. Point D. From here, we'll be entering an unknown neighborhood. From here, we'll be following the soil Walter extracted from Chickie's boots.

I said, "Want to call Hector and let him know we're here?"

"Let's wait," Walter said, "until we have something to say."

Instead of: you're wasting your time, Hector. Thing is, we couldn't prove that. If we hadn't lost a day to sabotage and wandering in the desert, we might have found our way here earlier and maybe Jardine wouldn't have had the chance to pull that stunt at the Inn. But he did. And Soliano's now busy with the target at hand. So don't call unless we can offer him another.

I had a mining map and red marker in my pack. Soliano had its twin. Within a two-mile radius of Point D, there were eleven mapped mines and uncountable prospects and glory holes. We call Soliano when we cross a mine off the list. We call Soliano when the evidence or the Geiger counter says we're there.

And then we get out of the way.

Of course there's always the hope Soliano will call us first with good news—that he has cracked Chickie, or the ninjas have found Jardine hiding in the bushes at the Inn and Soliano has sweated the location of the mine out of him.

Otherwise, we're on our own.

We stopped midway up the dead-end canyon, arbitrarily choosing the spot. Point D soil extended the length of this little draw. Evidence said Roy Jardine's offroader rig had parked in here, and so did we. End of the line—by vehicle anyway.

I stowed the sat phone and Geiger counter in my pack and shouldered it.

Walter stowed the field kit in his.

Dearing slung the strap of the FBI sat phone over one shoulder and wrestled his submachine gun over the other, wincing as the strap caught his sunburned neck.

I said, "Try some aloe vera on that sunburn."

Oliver nudged Dearing. "Sucks to be white, hey bro?" He slipped on his own subgun like it was a ceremonial sash.

We began the steep climb up the northern side of the canyon to the ridge above, to get the lay of the land.

The land, far as I could see, was riven by a tangle of steep canyons and skinny ridges. In the afternoon sunlight—pencil-thin shafts breaking through the smothering cloud layer—it was a shadowland.

Oliver and Dearing watched our backs while we put our noses to the soil.

Weathered quartzite and schist. Consistent with some elements of the soil in Chickie's boots—and in the glop from the trailer's tires. Inconsistent with other elements. I wished the boot soil had shown distinctive layers, like the offroader fender soil. Then we could have said: she walked hither thither and yon in these boots, picking up soils as she went, and we are most interested in the outer layers. But boots are like tires, not fenders, and--depending on the timing and conditions of acquisition--the soil they pick up can get mixed with the soil already lodged there. We couldn't say if the minerals we were tracking had been acquired in the last couple days on her way to and from the mine where she got the beads, or a month ago tramping through quartzite and schist on her way to and from the local tavern. We couldn't even say that the quartzite was acquired the same place as the schist.

We were analyzing on the fly, armed with hand lenses and Walter's encyclopedic eye for minerals.

The one unique mineral in the boot soil—a lucky find—was a silvery flake that Walter had ID'd as sylvanite, a telluride sometimes found in conjunction with the heavy metal ores. We were hunting a mine with a streak of telluride in its veins but first we had to find our way there via quartzite and schist.

As I pocketed my hand lens I was struck on the cheek by a pellet of rain. Within moments the ridge soil was cratered.

I phoned the radar guy.

The rain ceased. I looked up at the sky—where blue met the black leading edge of the next wave of thunderstorms—and I wished it would make up its mind.

Oliver and Dearing covered the mouth of a tunnel while Walter and I sifted through the soils around the one-stamp ore mill.

We crossed off another mine and reported in to Soliano.

I stopped. "What's that down there?"

Walter glanced down at the cars.

We were threading our way up the narrow spine of the ridge. It ran easterly and dropped precipitously on each side down to narrow canyons. To the left was Disappointment Canyon, as we'd named it after striking out at the one-stamp mill, and to the right was the canyon we'd named Cherokee where our vehicles steamed dry in a passing blaze of sun.

"Under your feet," I said, "in the brush."

Oliver, just behind Walter, jerked back.

But it was not a snake. Walter toed aside the brush and bent to examine the thing. It was a metal spike, looking like a large needle with a rusted eye. Walter tugged but the spike was anchored in the bedrock. It looked like it had hung on there for a very long time, longer than the creosote bushes.

"Um," Dearing said, "you gonna let us in on the secret?"

Walter stood. "It's a guidepost. For a cable."

"Do we care?"

Walter would not say and so we pushed on and within a few dozen yards came upon another spike, also scaled in rust. I began to care. We passed more and more spikes and then finally a length of cable rusting along the ridge. My interest stirred. I glanced down at the Cherokees, up to our ridge, down the other side. I saw a tunnel burrowing into the far wall of Disappointment Canyon, and the scar of a road running from the tunnel across the canyon and up to our ridge. I saw the knobby heads of rusting spikes, along that road scar. I let my thoughts run. Roy Jardine comes to dead-end Cherokee canyon and parks and now he faces a steep climb to get up to the ridge and onward. A climb hauling whatever equipment he needs to build his own little waste dump, and then hauling the casks to fill it. But the casks are large and very heavy. As were the ore containers the long-ago miners presumably hauled up and down these ridges. I eyed the old cable remnant. Jardine would have had to bring his own. I recalled the winch and cable drum mounted on the front of his offroader. So Jardine parks, unhitches the trailer, winches it up the ridge, cables it however far he's going, then lowers it down the other side. Winches up an extra drum and engine, if gravity alone won't get the stuff where it needs to go. I proposed my theory.

"You gotta be shittin me," Dearing said, peering down the steep wall.

"It's doable," Walter said. "Gold miners used to fill Mack trucks with ore and winch them up walls steeper than this."

"You gotta be shittin me."

We weren't. Down we went, Oliver and Dearing securing the way. Down there, however, the geology said no. I phoned Soliano and told him that Disappointment Canyon had yet again justified its name.

We followed the cable spikes and Chickie's soil along the ridge. I watched for gouges in the earth that would say something was hauled along the cable line here, but any and all markings had been erased by days of rains.

We reached an intersection of sorts. Below, Cherokee Canyon dead-ended. Ahead, our ridge bent northeast and arched across the head of Disappointment Canyon to reach the drainage of the next canyon east.

Cable spikes led the way. Old road scars crisscrossed the canyon.

This new canyon, at its head, was broad where an alluvial fan spilled down between the framing ridges from an upper canyon I guessed at, but could not see. Below the fan, the main canyon narrowed as it descended the Funerals, its skinny body slipping into shadow. The canyon walls gleamed where rain had slicked outcrops of green and silver schists. Get enough rain and that skinny part looks like a flood waiting to happen. My eye traveled back upcanyon, just shy of the fan, and came to rest on the steep northeastern hillside. Pockmarking the flank were black-eyed hollows. Heaps of ore tailings spilled across the slope. Below, scattered across the valley, were the tumbledown workings of the mine camp.

"I got a name for this one," Dearing said, arching his back. "They-Don't-Pay-Me-Enough Canyon."

We shifted into the routine.

Oliver and Dearing went first to secure the area. They followed the cable road down the canyon wall and across the valley floor to the mine camp. Now Oliver unholstered my Geiger counter and took the lead, sweeping the wand the way I'd taught him, the way Scotty taught me. Dearing looked more comfortable with his weapon. They sidestepped quartz tailings and rusting rail tracks. They probed collapsing buildings and an iron tank. Dearing peeked into a big stone oven, while Oliver disappeared into the rotting mill that climbed three stories up the hillside. Finally, they signaled, and Walter and I trudged down to the Town of Wood and Iron.

We sampled a patch of ground and found it not inconsistent with Chickie's boot soil—good enough to want to sample the mine entrance.

There were three entrances, actually, climbing the hill. The lowest opened onto a long wooden ore chute, which dumped into the slope-hugging mill. The second was obscured by rubble, perhaps a past collapse. The third was deeply recessed, with overhanging outcrops like Walter's eyebrows.

Cable roads made separate ascents to all levels.

We switchbacked up the steep hill to the sturdy ledge of the lower entrance. We ran the scenario: can he winch a trailer up here? Check. Can a telehandler, or some similar beast, fit into that tunnel? Check. Is there room on the landing to transfer a cask in and out of the trailer—and for tires to spin and spatter mud on the cask? Check. Check—this site fits the criteria, as did three other sites before it.

This was clearly the business entrance. Rail tracks came out of the tunnel and ran over the edge on an elevated bridgework that ended in mid-air. The way inside was barred by a locked gate. We'd brought the master Park Service key but it didn't fit.

Oliver said, "Rangers could've changed the lock."

Dearing said, "Or the perp did."

They gripped their subguns while Walter and I sampled the soil, which proved inconclusive.

As we resumed the climb, it began again to rain.

The second-level entrance—once we'd skirted the rubble of the old collapse—was gated, locked, and inconclusive.

We switchbacked up. I scanned the valley below. Nothing moved but rainfall.

The topmost entrance was the most inviting of the lot, a horseshoe arch bored through blue-gray schist. I eyeballed the quartzite-schist soil and envisioned it attaching to the crevices in Chickie's boots. Walter, already sampling, grunted. He liked it too.

My pulse quickened. If she indeed walked here, then how had she got inside? I moved to the gate inset in the tunnel walls. I took hold of a crossbar and leaned into it.

The gate swung open.

38

WALTER SHINED HIS FLASHLIGHT. "That's worth a closer look."

We stood at the open gate. His beam had caught a bull quartz vein, creamy and white, deep in the throat of the tunnel. Where the tunnel took a turn, a streak of silver intruded the white.

"Look all you want from here," Oliver said. "Soliano says you don't go in."

Walter waved his flashlight. "I believe he meant, don't go exploring. I don't believe he'd say, don't nip in there and collect a critical mineral sample."

I said, "I'm willing to stipulate that's a telluride."

"You'll stipulate? When the proof is within sight. It can't be more than fifty yards up the tunnel."

I said, "We don't have a gas detector."

Walter shifted his flashlight beam to illuminate a shaft that cut through the ceiling like a stovepipe. "The tunnel is ventilated."

"I don't care if it's air-conditioned," Oliver snapped, "you don't go in."

"Mr. Oliver," Walter said, "my feet hurt. I've been running around all morning. So you'll understand that I want to sample that vein, and if there is any justice to be had we will ID this place and turn it over to Scotty so he can clean up the damnable mess and we can go back to the Inn and soak our *feet*."

"Amen," Dearing said, lifting the toes of his boots.

Walter opened his pack and retrieved his headlamp.

I sighed and got out my own headlamp.

Oliver stiffened. "Hold on just a goddamn minute." His obsidian face turned rock-hard. "Why am I here? I'm here because you're looking for the mess. You go in there, I've gotta go too."

Walter shook his head. "I'll just nip in and out."

"I've seen guys like you. They make it personal."

Walter fitted his headband.

"You're not the goddamn bad guy," Oliver said. "You got nothing to do with the mess."

Walter considered. "Strictly speaking, I do."

"The hell's that mean?"

I fitted my headband. It means Walter makes it personal. It means he's Walter. I said, "He consumes power. Nuclear's part of the nation's power grid."

Oliver just shook his head. He told Dearing, "Take the watch and call Soliano." He switched on the flashlight built into the forward grip of his submachine gun. He shoved around Walter to take the lead. "So you wanna live in the Stone Age?"

No we don't, I thought. They didn't have French press coffeemakers and scanning electron microscopes in the Stone Age.

Or Geiger counters. I got the meter out of my pack. Just in case. We'd brought it along because Scotty told us to monitor outside every mine tunnel and if the count rose above background to get the hell away. We hadn't expected to be going *into* a mine, which was why we hadn't brought hazmat suits. And even if we'd wanted to bring that heavy equipment we'd have needed a couple of RERTs to haul it, and RERT was tied down at the Inn.

Well, we'll just nip in and out.

We entered the tunnel, abandoning day for night. At first the rain-gray light seeped in along with us but within a few yards it yielded to the dark. We traveled on three thin beams. My hair stirred as we passed the ventilation shaft. As we penetrated deeper into the tunnel, I glanced back. The entrance seemed to have shrunk, like the mine was shutting down for the day. Closing time, everybody home to soak their feet. I turned to peer ahead, estimating—it'd take maybe half a minute to the bend, couple minutes to sample, then another couple to get the hell out. That Clementine song started up in my head. In a cavern, in a canyon.

"Here we are," Walter said.

Oliver pointed his light and his ammo uptunnel while Walter inspected the silver-flecked vein and I sampled a stretch of thin ground soil. I did not take the time to search for grains of sylvanite in the decomposed quartz. I did think mechanics. Chickie comes in here with wet boots and wet soil plugging the waffle soles. She is a walking glue stick.

Walter peered over my shoulder. "Well?"

"Maybe."

"Good."

"We'll see."

"Outside."

"I think..."

"*Shut up*," Oliver snapped. "Listen."

We listened. I could hear nothing but my breathing. Walter's and Oliver's breathing. And then, a thudding. Thud thud thud thud. Silence. Thud thud thud thud. Rhythmic. It was not the sound of somebody walking. Nobody walks like that. It came from around the bend. Deeper within the tunnel. Thud thud thud thud.

"*Out*," Oliver hissed, "*now*."

We tried to move on cat feet so as not to telegraph our position but then we just gave in and ran. Oliver followed, covering Walter and me, and I would have to say they don't pay him enough.

I thought, running, heart pounding, it had sounded like some kind of machine with some moving part that caught every so often on something it shouldn't—thud thud thud thud—and then it worked itself free until it caught again, but if there was a machine running somewhere in this mine, that said there was somebody who started it, only why didn't he hear the thuds and come fix it?

Walter reached the entrance first and stopped short, blocking me.

Not, however, before I saw what he had tried to stop me from seeing.

First I saw the feet, the boots toes-up, and then I moved and saw the rest of Dearing. He had come just inside the mouth of the tunnel. Maybe he'd tried to get free. His arms splayed, like he'd been startled. His head tipped, sunburned nose in the air. Mouth open to argue. Chin jutting. The cut was neat, wide and deep, splitting the band of white muscle. Blood still ran, leaking at the corners. The soil beneath his neck was saturated with red leachate.

I fell to my knees and held my head.

I saw Oliver's boots, rooted.

When I looked again, I saw the satellite phone. Dearing

must have begun to unpack it from its protective case, to make the call to Soliano. The caved-in sat phone lay against the gate post. A grapefruit-sized rock lay nearby.

Dearing's submachine gun was missing.

Oliver said, voice thick, "Bro."

39

OLIVER SHOVED US. And then we found our footing and ran ahead of him back the way we'd come, back down the throat of the tunnel toward the thudding machine.

"I'm carrying an MP-five submachine gun," Oliver bellowed, "and I'm prepared to open fire on anyone who does not announce his presence loud and clear and he goddamn well better announce it on his knees with his hands in the air."

Air air air echoed down the tunnel.

I ran sickened. Walter in front of me ran hunched over and I knew as well as I knew anything what he was carrying. A load of guilt. And that psycho outside was carrying a blade and that's what I fixed in my mind, instead of the memory of Dearing's peeling nose.

We came to the ventilation shaft and Walter abruptly stopped to peer up but there was no ladder and no one larger than a child would have fit.

Oliver crowded me up against Walter. "*Shut off your lights.*"

We killed our lights and listened. No thudding. No footsteps. Just heartbeats. And then there was a shusshing sound.

I went queasy with fear.

Walter grasped my arm.

Oliver's light flicked on and his subgun swung up and steadied on a timber bracing the air shaft. A small figure clung there, wings hanging like an open coat. Its eyes gleamed milky in Oliver's light. We backed away from the air shaft. No need to bother analyzing the telluride soil. Bat's telling us what we want to know. Its nesting ground is fouled. It found the mess.

The bat shrieked and its teeth suppurated blood. Like Soliano, I knew I was going to have dreams of teeth.

The thuds began again.

Oliver muttered a curse and took the lead. We advanced uptunnel toward the rhythmic thudding, which was only slightly less insane than retreating downtunnel and exiting to the ledge where the blade-wielding psycho had perhaps settled in.

If he hadn't already come into the tunnel.

We passed the telluride vein and turned the corner and Oliver led us into a side tunnel that ran leftward. He stopped us there and shut off his light.

The thuds were louder, here. I wanted to scream for somebody to fix the damned machine. In the pitchy dark, I couldn't tell forward from backward, up from down. I went dizzy. I reached for a wall. My hand closed on air. I needed to see. Where was Oliver? Where was Walter? I could not hear their breathing over my own. I found Oliver by his smell. I could differentiate his smell from Walter's. We all shared a wet dog sweaty smell but beneath that Walter smelled of lemon drops and Oliver smelled of gun oil. I knew what I smelled of. Raw fear.

And then Oliver's mouth was at my ear. *No lights*, he breathed, *no noise*. I breathed the message to Walter. And so we moved on, my hand on Oliver's waist and Walter's hand on mine. Quiet as mice, blind as bats. Slow as snails, feeling out the bumps and cracks of the ground.

My hair stirred.

Oliver veered to the side of the tunnel and we snaked behind him. The breeze was stronger now. Oliver put on his light. We'd found another shaft, this one with a ladder. Oliver aimed his beam downward but the shaft swallowed his light before it reached bottom. We listened to the thuds. There was no longer any question where they came from. My heart pounded in sync. My mind raced. Whatever thudded down there was a mystery. What stalked behind us was not.

We put our heads together, whispering.

"Winze must go down to level two," Walter said.

"Winze?" Oliver said.

"Shaft's called a winze when it descends."

"Who cares?" I hissed, "it goes down."

"Winze ladder look solid to you?" Oliver asked.

"No obvious rotting," Walter said.

"I did ropes and ladders at Quantico."

"I've handled firearms, forensics ballistics testing."

After a moment, Oliver said, "Good enough."

"And you."

They swapped—Walter's headlamp for Oliver's subgun—and guilt and blame over Dearing's death seemed to go by the wayside. I hoped that mattered. I moved to the edge of the winze and switched on my headlamp to spot Oliver down.

Oliver inched his way, dipping a foot to test each rung.

Walter stood watch, feet spread, holding the weapon like it was his garden hose.

At long last Oliver called, "Come down."

Down down down echoed as I got on my knees and fished a leg down. My boot connected with a rung. I glued my eyes to the wall behind the ladder, comforted by old rock if not by old wood. The winze took a long time to swallow me and when my feet at last connected with the floor I called up to the pinpoint of light "okay." I lit Walter's way while Oliver stood watch. It was not until they'd exchanged gun for headlamp and we'd moved from the winze alcove into the new tunnel that I noticed the thudding had stopped.

We hesitated. One passage branched left, one branched right, and between them tongued a third.

I brought out the Geiger and painted the walls with the wand, picking up only background noise. I was putting it away when the thudding started again. It came, distinctly, from the right-hand tunnel. It grew louder, less rhythmic. It grew frenzied. Clearly, no machine.

Oliver shouted, "I'm carrying an MP-five and I'm prepared to open fire if you don't knock off that goddamn noise."

The thudding stopped.

"Stay put," Oliver whispered. He advanced into the right-hand tunnel and disappeared around a bend.

It doesn't want to get shot, I thought, but it definitely wants to get found.

"Come ahead," Oliver called. "You won't believe this."

40

He lay on his back, bound with silver duct tape. Ankles were crossed, knees pressed together, hands taped in prayer at the waist, mouth gagged, eyes squeezed shut against our lights. No need to wrap the eyes, down here in the dark. Otherwise, it was a thorough job.

I got my pocket knife and started at his ankles. He wore river shoes and no socks and his feet through the mesh were icy to the touch. I sawed through the tape, postponing the mouth and its Buttercup-baiting yak. I freed his knees and then his hands, and he flinched when I pulled off red wrist hairs along with the tape. I fingered the duct tape on his cheek. The mouth was going to hurt. I said, "I'm sorry," and pulled.

He flinched. He rolled to one side and pushed himself up to a sit. His arms trembled and he went no further.

Oliver moved in. "You got a bulletproof reason for being here?"

He rasped, "Water."

I unholstered my bottle and gave it to him.

He nodded a thanks and drank, greedy. He cleared his throat, eyeing Oliver's weapon. "I'm the victim."

Oliver grabbed Hap's arm and twisted it up behind his back, forcing him forward over his knees. "Cut the crap. Who did this?"

Hap gasped. "Roy."

Oliver released Hap's arm. He placed a boot on Hap's calf, securing it in place. He reached down to Hap's right ankle and tugged at the severed duct tape. It clung to the parachute pants. He repeated the experiment on the left ankle, as if there could be any doubt that the tape had in truth been binding. He removed his boot. "Now tell your story."

Hap curled his legs away from Oliver. He took a sip of water, holding it in his mouth like a rare wine.

Oliver snatched the bottle. "From the get-go, Miller."

Hap's eyes narrowed as he swallowed the last of the water. "Get-go's at the Inn." His voice cracked. He cleared his throat, tried again. "Vegas doc comes so I bug out. Run into Milt. We're hungry. Whole place is locked down so we find our way to the kitchen and make sandwiches. Take them to the garden for a picnic. All of a sudden here's Roy. Armed. I'm more than on his list now. I'm in his sights." Hap gave a helpless shrug. "Roy takes us to this service road. There's a ranger truck. Roy gets in back with Milt and tells me to drive. Key's under the seat."

Oliver said, "There was no ranger truck anywhere in the canyon."

"Didn't come that way. Took a utility road. Hiked from there."

"You try to run?"

"And get shot? Roy was talking hostages and that sounded better to me."

Walter said, "Where's Milt?"

"Down some tunnel?" Hap cradled one wrist, then the other. "Milt's a joke most of the time but I do hope he's alive."

"My partner is dead," Oliver said, coldly. "Somebody cut his throat."

Hap paled.

"You'll lead us on every goddamn step you took with Jardine."

Hap rolled to his knees and, cautious as a cat, rose to his feet.

Walter said, "What about Pria?"

Hap's attention remained on Oliver's gun. "What's she got to do with this?"

"Did you see her on the road? *Anywhere*?"

Hap lifted his palms.

Walter's stony face said he did not believe in Hap's ignorance. I had to differ. Like Hap, I couldn't understand what Pria had to do with this. It made no sense. Hap's story made a certain sense. I believed in Jardine, because of Dearing. I believed Jardine had bound Hap, because it was a physical impossibility for Hap to have done it to himself. Beyond that, I was not willing to go.

Nevertheless, I found myself in line behind Hap and Walter —with Oliver bringing up the rear—following Hap through the rocky maze.

We filed down the tunnel to the intersection and Hap without hesitation took the left fork tunnel. The rocky floor here was lined with timbered rails capped with iron straps. This raised my hopes. I hoped the rails went out. In another few yards I had my answer. The rails fed into a shaft with a wooden ore chute. Walter looked in, as if it might still contain yesteryear's ore.

We continued past the chute.

I concentrated on the noise we were making. Too many feet, too little care. Sound travels, as we'd learned from the thuds. Even whispers travel. I remembered a family trip to Washington

DC—I'd stood on a spot in the rotunda of Congress and whispered, and the people nearby did not hear but my dad standing on the sweet spot across the rotunda heard me perfectly. I pictured Jardine, standing on the sweet spot in another tunnel, listening for us. I tried to tread more softly. I focused on my feet. My socks rubbed. Like Walter, I yearned to return to the Inn and nurse my feet.

We passed a little alcove and like Walter, I rubbernecked. I saw a crushed cardboard box with faded lettering that said *Trojan*, and then *dynamite*. My thoughts jumped from decaying dynamite to modern plastique.

I began stepping with more care.

Within a few yards the rails reappeared, in broken lengths, and we navigated cautiously around the dagger ends and the splintered cross-ties. Something skittered underneath. I heard Oliver stop. I smelled his metallic sweat. I listened for the rat. Or the snake. I heard Oliver's wet palm slap his subgun. Oliver and Walter, fellowship of the phobic. We moved on but Oliver's footsteps slowed now, cautious ninja on the lookout for snakes. Soon the rails improved and my hopes spiked again. Our tunnel and the rails took a hard right and as I followed Hap and Walter around the corner I saw another shaft, this one descending from level three, above us. I spared a cursory look at the large storage bin on the floor of the shaft, then my attention snapped back to the rails. Sooner or later, I hoped, they'd lead us out.

But as I turned away, something registered. Something I'd glimpsed. Had I really seen that? A shadow cast from my headlamp, stretched across the back wall of the shaft, distorted by the rungs of the shaft ladder. A shadow rising from the storage bin in that micromoment when I'd looked away. Stretched and distorted, but had that been a head? A ponytail?

Reflexively, stupidly, I looked again.

I looked him full in the face.

Just below, at chest level, his arms rested on the top of the bin and the muzzle of Dearing's subgun looked me full in the face.

I focused on his shirt, behind the gun. The beam of my headlamp caught on his breast-pocket shiny buttons and they gleamed like eyes.

When I moved my gaze back up to his face, to the real eyes, I was shocked to find them moist. Like he was deeply moved, so overcome he was about to cry. His small mouth pursed. He put a finger to his lips. As if I could speak, or cry out, in my frozen state. He lowered his finger and smiled at me. A shocking smile. Full of warmth. Like he was so glad to see me here. He bobbed his head, encouraging me to agree. So glad we meet again! For a moment I was lulled. Wanted to believe in his benevolence. Wanted to be lulled. When he smiled, his tiny mouth stretched and his cheeks bunched up and the crater on his left cheek wrinkled and deepened. I followed its transformation. His mouth suddenly tightened and he moved his head leftward, just enough that the crater disappeared from view. I jerked my head so that my headlamp beam hit the wall to the right of his face. But I could still see that mouth compress to fury, oh shit he thinks I turned my light away because I can't stand looking at him but I'd only turned out of raw fear.

I didn't yet fully know fear.

The gun muzzle swung away from me. Uptunnel. It pointed at Walter's back.

I turned back to Roy Jardine, *don't shoot don't shoot*, please I'll do anything just don't shoot, and he smiled again, he saw he had me, and he put his finger to his lips again and then gave his head a jerk to the left. Instructions clear. Move on. Keep quiet. And I won't shoot Walter.

I wanted with my whole heart to follow those chilling instructions.

But I could not forget Dearing. Dearing's neck, opened to the windpipe.

This man with Dearing's submachine gun would not keep his bargain. He was going to wait for me to move on, following Walter and Hap up ahead, in the dark, and wait for Oliver to finish hunting for snakes and come tiptoeing around the corner behind me. He had to wait for Oliver, who had shouted for the whole mine to hear that he was carrying an MP-five submachine gun and was prepared to open fire. Otherwise, Jardine would have already mowed us down.

I went calm. I bought frozen seconds in which to formulate a plan before I had to move, to appear to honor our bargain. Maybe there was a better plan than the one I concocted in five seconds but this is what I went with.

I gave Jardine one last look and a nod—yes yes I understand I'll do as you say—and he returned to me a look of such approval, such a soft yearning smile like he wished he could embrace me to seal the bargain, that I almost honored it. I turned face-front and started to move. I heard Oliver behind me, finally, coming around the corner. Oblivious to the man in the storage bin. There were only two things that would improve the odds for Oliver. One was the flashlight built into the grip of his subgun. When he swung the gun to point it at Jardine, his light would hit Jardine in the face. Just as my headlamp had done. But it wouldn't be a vanity thing for Jardine this time. It would be a distraction. A light in the eyes. Maybe a micromoment of blindness. Just the tiniest edge.

The other edge I gave to Oliver myself.

I moved my right arm—on the side facing away from Jardine—stiffly, up twenty degrees, a semaphore. *Stop.* At the same time I stuck out my thumb and jerked it leftward, toward the bin.

Look. After that, I could do no more than put faith in Oliver's Quantico training and trigger finger.

As the shots came, I screamed, "*Down down down*," and hit the floor and Walter and Hap uptunnel must have caught the terror in my voice because they hit the floor too.

41

"Holy crap," Hap said.

I looked up. I'd been tugging on my boot, which was caught under a cross-tie. Clumsy. Amazed to be alive.

Hap moved to the storage bin and grasped Roy Jardine's dangling left wrist. He fingered the pulse. He shook his head.

Relief flooded me as blood poured out of Jardine. He hung over the lip of the bin. His arms draped down as if reaching for the submachine gun he had dropped on the rails. His head was bent, showing the crown. His black ponytail hung down, funneling blood.

"*Come help*," Walter yelled.

Walter was kneeling uptunnel over Oliver, who lay with one knee bent. Looked like Oliver, too, caught a boot. I yanked my boot free. Hap turned from the bin and helped me up. As we rushed forward my headlamp caught a dime of blood on Oliver's khaki shirt front. Oh no, I thought. No no no.

Walter freed Oliver from the sling of his gun and laid the weapon on the ground. I glanced back at Jardine, at the subgun on the rails. Oliver and Jardine had shot each other.

Walter snapped, "Do something, Hap."

"Don't have my gear."

I came alive. "I've got first aid." I unslung my pack.

"Needs more'n first aid." Hap knelt and put his hands on Oliver's chest, which rose and fell fitfully. He ripped open the shirt, exposing the hole in Oliver's gut, just below the rib cage. There was a seep of blood, almost no blood at all compared to the stream draining from Jardine.

I knew that meant little but I held onto it nonetheless.

Walter passed Hap gauze and tape from the first aid kit. Hap's long fingers danced around the wound, patching it, and then suddenly traveled up to Oliver's neck to find the carotid.

I went cold.

Hap's fingers moved again, up to Oliver's face, and pulled back an eyelid.

I watched, fixated.

Hap sensed me. He looked up, like he was taking my measure in preparation for a sketch. But he does not draw faces. He draws hands. I could not help looking again at Oliver's face cupped in Hap's hand. Hap wore a ring on his right pinkie.

I turned to look at the storage bin, shining my headlamp at Jardine's dangling hands. He wore no rings.

When I turned back to Hap, he had released Oliver. "Nothing more I can do." Hap's hands had disappeared into the capacious pockets of his parachute pants.

It didn't matter. I knew what I'd seen. It was a flat-headed gold ring and the signet bore the engraving of a desert scene. I'd seen Hap sketch that ring in Walter's room, when he drew Roy's hands.

"Then here's what we're going to do," Walter said, getting to his feet. "We're going to make a sling out of our shirts and we're going to carry Mr. Oliver outside and phone for help."

"Okay," Hap said.

I thought, Hap must have taken the ring from Roy, when he checked Roy's pulse. But why? Some kind of souvenir?

Walter was already unbuttoning his shirt. Hap put his left hand flat on the floor, preparing to get to his feet. His right hand remained in his pocket.

I stood, fingering my top button. I suddenly took note of Hap's shirt. Last I saw him at the Inn, he'd been wearing Homer Simpson. But now he wore Blinky the three-eyed mutant fish that lives downstream from Homer's nuke plant, where the water's contaminated. I suddenly didn't like it that Hap had changed shirts. Why'd he do that? I always change into a pantsuit before I testify in court. Walter puts on a tie. Hap changes into Blinky. And now he puts on Roy's ring. Why's that? Hap caught me studying his shirt. He winked. He smoothed it out and took his right hand from his pocket and scooped up Oliver's subgun. He leveled the muzzle up at me. "You can keep your shirt on after all, Buttercup."

I still gripped the top button. I could not get my fingers to move, one way or the other.

Walter froze, half out of his shirt. "What do you think you're..."

"Think I'm giving you a chance to cooperate." Hap got to his feet and backed against the far wall, where he could cover us both with the flick of a wrist. He ducked into Oliver's gun sling. "Finish taking off the shirt, Walter."

"Hap," Walter said, evenly, "let's think this through. Whatever your plans, you can let us go. We won't try to follow you. I give you my word."

"Don't rightly know the worth of your word."

"It's solid."

"Take off the shirt."

Walter, stiff, removed his shirt. His bare chest showed the rails of his ribs.

"Cassie, go get it." Hap tracked me with the subgun. "Now bring out your pocket knife and cut the sleeves off at the shoulders."

I glanced at Oliver.

"He won't be needing it."

My heart squeezed. I'd been clutching the hope that we were still making a sling to carry Oliver.

"Wouldn't matter anyway. Can't carry him." Hap added, "Not where we're going."

I asked, faintly, "Where are we going?"

Hap pointed the gun downtunnel then recalibrated it on me.

I made clumsy work of the sleeves.

"Now shut the knife, wrap it in one of the sleeves, and toss it to me." My toss was wide; he had to reach. "Cassie, you want to be more careful." He pocketed my knife and draped the sleeve over his shoulder like a tailor. "Now use your sleeve to tie Walter's hands behind his back. Take off your wristwatches, first. Don't want anything interfering with a nice clean knot."

We undid our watches. Piece by piece, we were losing our tools.

"Make it a square knot. Don't want no sneaky taut-line hitch. I know my knots—scout's honor. You know your knots, Cassie?"

I nodded. I'd earned that badge. I tied Walter's wrists with a true square knot but I looped it loose.

Hap moved in to check. He slid a finger into the knot. "Aw, Buttercup." He shook his head and laid the gun butt across my back.

The blow knocked me to the floor.

Walter swore.

There was a thud and a grunt and Walter came down beside me.

I lay stunned, as much from the shock as the pain, because against all good sense I'd held onto the idea that a man who'd run saline through my veins had a strain of humanity running through his, that Hap would not penalize us for trying, but I came to my senses and saw there was no scout's honor here.

Hap climbed onto my back and tied my wrists with a boyishly brutal knot.

Then he moved to Walter.

I kept stupefied watch. This EMT runs terror through the veins and cuts off oxygen to the brain. I feared the effect on Walter. Another mini-stroke. And then Walter, like Oliver, could not be carried.

42

HAP HAD to help Walter to his feet.

We went single-file, first Walter then me then Hap. Hap had retrieved Dearing's subgun and he wore it slung across his back. Oliver's subgun rode in his hands, as I discovered when I slowed and its hard mouth bit into my spine.

Walter stumbled once but all Hap said was, "Watch your step."

We came to a junction and bore left into a larger tunnel, a tunnel with a cathedral ceiling and four-square timbering and intact rails. An important tunnel.

I oriented myself. There was daylight at the far end. We were on level two, heading for the exit where, beyond the locked gate, was the rubble pile, and beyond that was the path leading down to level one and the valley, and beyond that the ridges and then Cherokee Canyon and our waiting vehicles. And beyond that, the way back to the Inn to find Soliano and then soak our feet.

I fought down the vision.

We nearly made it to the exit. Hap stopped us a dozen yards short, where a side tunnel branched off. It was gated. I angled my headlamp to illuminate the metal sign wired to the bars: *No entry. Hazardous. Deteriorating explosives. Broken machine parts.* Hap stood us against the far wall. He brought out a key ring from his capacious pants pocket.

I focused on the problem of the locks, desperate to occupy my mind. Hap or Roy had changed the Park Service locks because they did not want any patrolling rangers to come in here and find their stash. But Chickie turned up instead, come to find out what Jardine had been hiding, come to get in on the blackmail. Single-minded in her greed. Methodically, I ticked off the gates we'd seen, the locks we'd tried. Two entrance gates had been locked. The top-level gate had been unlocked. Either Chickie had picked that lock, or Hap or Roy had been sloppy. I didn't much care. I cared about this gate, this lock, and what lay beyond.

Hap didn't need his key.

The side tunnel was unremarkable until we passed an alcove containing a winch and a spool of neon purple cable, both on wheeled dollies. The growing knot in my stomach tightened. Up ahead was a larger intersecting tunnel. Some kind of fat snake crawled out of that tunnel, into ours—and Walter stiffened—but as we drew nearer I identified the snake as a bundle of wires. The bundle ran along our tunnel wall then snaked to the right, into a room.

Hap directed us to follow the bundled wires.

It was a cavernous room filled with rusting machinery. It took me some moments to sort the tangle by the light of our headlamps. I identified the twin flywheels of an old drum winch. A cable spool lay flat with its guts unwinding. Wheels and gears were scattered about, like the sprung works of a giant wristwatch. Hap followed the bundled wires to the corner where a small generator sat. It too was rusted but Hap brought it to life, illuminating a string of bare light bulbs.

I had to squint.

Hap directed us across the room. We skirted crates of supplies no miner would have dreamed of: bottled water, freeze-dried food, sleeping bags, hazmat suits and SCBA gear. And then there was a box of putty-like cylinders that any modern-day miner would presumably recognize. I thought, so that's what plastique looks like—play-dough, like Chickie said. It should look scarier.

Hap told us to take a seat on the cable spool.

He turned to the splintery table against the wall. He removed a rotting burlap sack to reveal a machine no miner would have dreamed of: a laptop computer. Its cable joined the wire bundle. He switched on the machine. He sat on a crate in front of the table and rested Oliver's submachine gun across his lap, snout to us. He tapped the keyboard. He angled the monitor. "Look around the corner."

The creepy thing was, we could.

Around the corner was the large tunnel. The picture on the computer screen was a long shot, looking uptunnel, which was lit by bulbs that hung like bats from the ceiling. The camera, as well, must have been ceiling-mounted because we had a bat's-eye view. I oriented myself, first, by locating the wire bundle which powered the room. Traversing the tunnel were rusting rails where ore carts used to run, but clearly Hap had no need for carts to haul his loads. A beastly telehandler squatted beside an ore shaft. Attachments were at the ready: tools to unbolt and detorque the cask lid, invertible forks to hook into the cask lifting lugs. The telehandler was ready to empty the next load of resins, but the swap had ended. The stockpile was, de facto, complete.

My attention shifted to the ore shaft.

As if Hap understood, he changed the picture. The bat's-eye view closed and then a new window opened onscreen. It was a view inside the shaft, a view that brutally tied off the knot in my gut.

Resin beads filled the shaft, lapping nearly to the top. So that's what they look like. I'd seen them in the borax tunnel but they'd been coming at me like cannon-fire and I hadn't paused for a good long look. I took it now. Looked more like sand than beads. Or, even, bath salts. They gave off a warm amber glow. They should look scarier. They should sound scarier—*beads* was too benign a word. There should be better words. Triple-X shitload of mayhem carrying cell-destroying gentlemen.

There were no words. There was only fear.

I averted my gaze from the screen. It fell on the crate of hazmat gear, next to Hap. The lid was propped open but I guessed it had been closed when Chickie found her way in here. I guessed she'd had to fight the latches to open the lid, picking up the grains of rust I'd scraped from beneath her nails. Here's where she'd found her moonsuit. And then, suited up, believing she was good to go, she'd gone looking for Jardine's cache. And there, in the shaft, she'd found it. She'd known we were hunting for it, and now she could take a pack full of beads to show Soliano she'd found it, and bargain for her million-dollar reward. She certainly worked hard for it. It must have been an awkward job. She must have been on her hands and knees, reaching down into the shaft to scoop enough to fill her pack. Maybe she stirred up the beads enough to go aerosol, and if her facepiece wasn't snugged up real tight, maybe she breathed in the murderous dust. I hoped not. From what I'd seen, she was already paying dearly for her crime.

I whispered to Hap, "What do you want?"

"Compensation for my hard work." He swiveled to face us. "Speaking of which, you can't get good help any more, can you?"

I could not think what to say. Yes? No? I could feel well

enough—the rough wood biting into my backside, the shirt-sleeve throttling my wrists—but I could not think which answer would satisfy Hap. Nor, evidently, could Walter.

"This tying your tongues?" Hap hefted the subgun. "We're just going to talk. About lousy help. You paying attention?"

I was paying exquisite attention.

"Problem starts with Ryan when I tell him tonight's the night."

My attention focused on Ryan Beltzman. What'd the radwaste driver do? Can Walter and I avoid doing it? I spoke, asbestos-tongued. "He tried to back out?"

"He smoked too much damn dope." Hap rested the weapon across his knees. "Too wasted to do his bit, so Roy gets incensed and then there's the fight and the chase and the crash—you two know that bit—and then Roy turns out damn near useless as Ryan. Sits in his pickup wringing his hands. Which leaves me no option but to take care of Ryan myself."

So it was Hap, not Roy, who shot Beltzman. Shit.

Walter said, "I see your point."

"What's my point?"

"Your partners botched it."

"You got that right. But that's not my point." Hap fingered his ring. All that showed now was the gold band. "After the fiasco we've got problems. I tell Roy to go home and stay put. Knew we'd have the Feds on us soon enough—told him I'd play along, decide when it's safe to make our move. Afraid I didn't anticipate a couple geologists following talc and mud and whatnot." Hap gave us a rueful smile.

I returned an icy look. "Who sent Chickie after us?"

"That'd be Roy. Seems he thought I mighta been thinking of selling him out. Boy starts going freelance on me. Still, he didn't do half-bad—stealing your soil samples, that is. Don't rightly approve of stranding you out there. You could've died. I wanted you dead, I'd have taken care of that myself."

Walter said, voice brittle, "C4."

"I didn't plan it for *you*. That was Roy. Again. Overkill, you ask me. Borax mine was set up for Milt—original plan was to send him in, let him find the cask. That irony thing, let him know where he stood. Of course, nothing went exactly as planned, what with you and Hector and Scotty getting into it."

Walter said, "And the water tank at the Inn?"

"Pure Roy. Bragged about that one, on the way up here. Damn his eyes, I mighta gone for a *swim* last night." Hap gave me a long look, then winked.

I sat dense as rock.

"Tried my best to rein him in. Chatted on the phone, now and then. But I was kinda pinned down, keeping watch on everybody. And it turns out being on the team was a real bonus. Got to volunteer tidbits, like the boron-gate story, to keep Hector's focus on Roy. Tried to keep *your* focus on the radiation risks—tell me, did that work? Undermine your confidence, just a wee bit?"

Yeah that worked but damned if I would tell him so.

"My concern was real, Buttercup. Hate to see good guys like you and Walter get crapped up."

Walter grunted.

"Must admit, though, I mostly hated the idea of you finding this place before CTC agreed to pay."

I sat up straight. "So it *is* about money?"

"Ain't it always?" He nodded at the computer. "Streaming live to CTC."

"The extortion email? That was you?"

"Was the both of us." Hap sighed. "Thing is, Roy wanted to settle his grudge along with his payday and I guess that made him a mite unstable. Sure turned on me. Anyway, like I told you, I end up trussed like a turkey, he goes Rambo and collects himself the FBI shooter." Hap unslung Dearing's subgun. "Not the way I envisioned getting here but all's well that ends well."

I said, "Why didn't he kill you?"

"Two hostages were better than one."

"Where's Milt?"

"Down some tunnel. Like I told you."

"Why should we believe anything you tell us?"

He shrugged. "You can pick it apart afterward, for inconsistencies."

My heart turned over. Afterward?

"Caught that future tense, did you?"

"Then you're not going to..."

"Kill you? What if the cavalry comes?" He gave a slight smile. "Two hostages are better than none." He raised the subgun. "Now get down and kiss the ground."

I held onto the thought *we're of value* as we floundered down. With my cheek to the rock, I watched as Hap put aside his weapons. He took the key ring out of his pocket. He moved to the hazmat crate and I watched, sick, as he began to dress out.

I said, "What about us?"

He put on booties and gloves and taped himself into the suit. He hunched into the SCBA harness and cinched the waist belt. He hooked a large pouch to the belt. He clipped a multi-tool knife to his key ring, and clipped the key ring to the belt with a big carabiner. He considered the two subguns. He selected Oliver's, snapping on Dearing's magazine to double his ammo supply. He used a carabiner to attach the subgun sling to his right shoulder strap. He gave himself a little shake; subgun and belt pouch and key ring held fast. He muttered, "Effing Christmas tree." He picked up the last item of equipment—the facepiece. He put it on, adjusted the head straps, then pushed it up to rest on top of his head, electrifying his hair.

He looked nothing like a Christmas tree.

He swung his attention to me. "About you? Take care. Don't end up getting zapped like Grandma."

43

WE STOOD at the lip of the winze.

Hap untied Walter. "Down you go, wait at the bottom. Keep in mind, one hostage'll do."

Walter said, "You'll have two."

When Walter was down, Hap untied me and we descended together. Hap first, then me, acutely aware of the marksman on the ladder below me. I recalled my first winze descent and the fear of rotting wood, a fear that now seemed quaint. I heard the thud of boots on the ground and then I, too, hit bottom.

We ran the re-tying drill, with true square knots. The tingling started up again in my hands. And then Hap set his facepiece and brought up his hood and connected the regulator hose, and I was no longer tingling, I was numb.

I moved numbly in the direction Hap pointed, following Walter, following a narrow tunnel which took a right turn and fed into the widest tunnel yet. The final tunnel, I figured, because this was clearly the main haulage level. Drop chutes stuck out from the walls at regular intervals, the rail tracks here were unbroken, and three rusting ore carts were parked downtunnel. Daylight beckoned at the end but my heart no longer lifted at that sight. When we exited, it was going to be Hap's way.

The subgun nuzzled my ribs and I picked up my pace.

I oriented myself. I'd become a cave creature with underground senses and I judged this tunnel to be beneath the level-two tunnel with the wide view. So I judged which drop chute ahead was cause for worry—the chute midway. Hap confirmed my judgment when he stopped us there, stood us against the far wall, and tapped a wired keypad that was mounted on the chute gate. The keypad lit up, glowing red.

I pressed into the rock, putting another inch between me and the exposed shaft.

A crude metal hopper was fitted inside the shaft, bolted to the walls, braced with two-by-fours, standing off the ground on metal legs. A black ribbed hose was attached at the bottom. Hap grabbed the hose and began to play it out. "You want to move now."

That we did.

I glanced back once, to see fat coils springing free.

By the time we reached the ore carts I was thinking, just finish it. Set up your demonstration, if that's what this is. Stream it live with your laptop cameras. Strike your bargain with Soliano or CTC or whoever in hell will pay your price and if Walter and I survive this to bear witness, then I'll feel surprise.

Hap stopped us, disconnecting his regulator hose and pushing up his facepiece. That surprised me. That engendered a spasm of hope, that the health physicist was now willing to share our air.

"Walter," Hap said, "I need your counsel."

That floored me.

Walter's eyebrows lifted.

Hap pointed to the last ore cart.

Walter moved to have a look.

I took note of the hose clamp bolted to the cart's rim. I took note of the black ribbed hose that Hap had snaked from the hopper in the shaft to where we now stood. I took note of the red cord wrapped around the cart's brake handle. I figured I understood. This was the demonstration that required Walter's counsel. Fill the cart and threaten to send it into the world. The cart was rusted bloody red. I tried to recall the shielding properties of iron. The cart was chest high, maybe three feet wide and a good four long. I tried to work out the volume, how many cubic feet of resin beads it would hold. Walter swore. I stopped doing the math. Walter turned to Hap, face set. "You know my counsel."

I came up beside Walter and looked in the cart. My heart fell. Surprises within surprises, sucking me down. I thought I might fall in.

Hap joined us. "You've been asking. Here's the man himself."

Milt Ballinger was stretched on the floor of the cart, bound and gagged with duct tape. Ankles crossed, wrists in prayer, mouth sealed, eyes squeezed shut against my headlamp. I'd seen this handiwork before. "Roy did this?"

"I did this, while Roy held a gun on me. But that's all in the past. Roy's not here. Milt's here." Hap leaned in the cart and ripped the tape off Milt's mouth. "Damn, I know that hurts, Milt. Buttercup did the same to me."

Milt whimpered.

I said, "Stop it, Hap."

"Soon as we run a little test." Hap held his hand so that our lights shined his signet ring with its desert scene, so that Milt could fully see it. "Milt, you figures out what the ring means, you gets to wake up tomorrow."

Milt croaked, "Roy's ring, right?"

"Somebody give him a hint."

Walter said, "This is sadism, Hap. We don't know what you're getting at."

Milt's eyes found mine but I had no hints, I'd fail Hap's test, we were all going to forfeit to this freak out of hell. Milt blinked back tears. I dredged up all I had, for Walter's enlightenment as well as Milt's. Neither had been there at the lawn table this morning when Pria identified the drawing on the ring. "It's a race. Badwater to Whitney. Maybe a play on words." They nearly choked me. "Bad. Water."

Milt sucked in air. "It's the *leak*? At the *dump*?" He turned from me to Hap, who waited soberly. "And Roy got mad..." He cleared his throat. "Okay then, so Roy ran the race and..."

"Not Roy," Hap cut in. "Sheila Cook ran the race. *Her* ring."

I gaped. Not Roy's ring, not Hap's ring. Roy's *sister's* ring.

"She got it for participating but she DNF'd." Hap glanced at me. "Sorry Cassie, I know how you hate those cryptic initials. Did...not...finish. Collapsed in a heap, to be precise. First clue she'd won the cancer lottery. About a year later she DNF'd for real. Didn't get a ring for that."

Walter said, "Dear God."

"God doesn't give a fig, Walter. So give Milt the clue. The one about helping. Somebody? Test isn't optional."

I said, faintly, "You can't get good help."

Hap beamed at Milt. "That's you. Youse is the star of the show."

Milt was crying now.

"Everybody know why?"

Nobody spoke.

"Sheesh." Hap sighed. "Weren't you listening down at the borax mine? Nobody *listens*. Milt's the star because of Sheila."

Milt shook his head.

"No? Let me jog your memory. We were discussing revenge?"

Walter snapped, "Why now?"

Hap pointed at me. "You remember, Buttercup. How revenge is like a runaway chain reaction?"

I remembered. "But Roy's dead."

"Well I know that. I saw him get shot."

"Then why avenge his sister?"

"I'm not."

"You said it's because of Sheila."

"It is."

In all its horror, the truth dawned on me.

"Not *Roy's* sister." Hap reached down and hooked Milt under the armpit and hoisted him to his feet, a brutal one-handed yank. "Mine."

44

IT SEEMED to have grown darker. Our headlamps were dying. Faces were dimming. My senses were going. Arms numb, hands dead. Ears plugged. I heard Milt's mewling like he was far away, buried. I heard Walter's voice like he was talking through dirt. Words filtered up. Right. Wrong. Justice. Prison.

Hap watched Walter, intent. No cartoon eyes. No wise-up smile.

I cast about in my woolly mind for pleas, rebuttals, anything —because for those heartbreaking minutes it really did seem that Hap wanted to listen.

But in the end he did not take Walter's counsel.

It was not going to be ALARA.

Hap opened his belt pouch and brought out a handheld remote. He punched the buttons and the dusty light bulbs overhead flickered on. He threaded the ribbed hose through the clamp so that its mouth fed down into the cart. Milt's eyes followed the hose from the cart back uptunnel to the shaft. He appeared to understand. His eyes—animal-in-quicksand eyes—flicked in desperation to Hap. "New-hire form said she's *Roy's* sister."

"Forms can be altered."

"Then no way I'd know she's *yours*."

"That your philosophy, Milt? Ignorance? Sure ticked off Roy."

"But if she's *your* sister ..." Milt cast about. "Why'd Roy care?"

"Roy was already unhappy with you, Milt, about that cesium-source prank. He thought you were covering up so nobody'd be arrested—because that would shine the spotlight on your management history."

Milt's scalp leaked sweat.

"Since we're clearing things up, Milt, here's another FYI—I'm the one who planted that source under Roy's pillow. Needed a recruit. Somebody who'd share my outrage against you. By gum, Roy did. Real helpful, until he went wacko." Hap sighed. "Murphy's Law."

I blurted, "That's why Roy turned against you? The prank?"

"Nope—he never found out. Like I told you earlier, he turned against me when I joined up with the team, thinking I might sell him out. And then he got touchy about you, Cassie. Thought I was 'courting' you. Said I wasn't worthy."

I went sick. Roy's moist eyes. Roy's yearning smile.

"*Hap*," Milt said, "I'm sorry about your sister."

"Been carrying my sister's ring for two years, Milt. Always in my pocket, hidden away. It was my own private connection to Sheila. My own private declaration of war against you." Hap fingered the ring. "Time to go public."

"But Sheila wasn't my *fault*."

Hap unwound the red cord from the brake handle.

"Wait," Walter said.

Hap cocked his head.

"You told us it's about money," Walter said. "You dump the beads now, you lose your bargaining chips."

"Bargaining's over. Deadline's come and gone."

I said, "Try them *again*."

Hap smiled. "They're still gonna pay. Spotlight's going to shine real bright on CTC's indulgence of Mister Radwaste. Money would've been icing on the cake, but I'm here for the cake." He gave Milt a long look.

Milt whispered, "Please."

"We're gonna mosey on out now, Milt. My guests ain't wearing protective clothing." Hap turned his back, urging Walter and me forward with the subgun. We set off downtunnel. Behind us, the screaming started. At the tunnel mouth we hugged the wall while Hap unlocked the gate. He swung it wide and we emerged into the day as if it were the most natural thing in the world.

It was raining again.

Hap turned us to face back into the tunnel. We got a raw tunnel vision of the frantic figure in the rusting red cart. Hap worked the remote. I imagined I saw the keypad on the shaft turn from red to green. I imagined the chute gate opening, allowing the load in the shaft to flow down into the hopper, and thence into the black ribbed hose.

And then I did not have to imagine. I saw the hose ribs expand to accommodate the bulge, like dinner passing through a snake. I saw the spew of resins begin, into the cart. Milt tried to jackknife over the edge but he had no leverage. His attention shifted downward, toward his feet. I imaged they were already covered. He cried out. Animal in quicksand. Hap yanked the red cord and I saw the brake handle move, and the cart wheels began to roll, and my fears switched from Milt's fate back to our own.

Hap said, "Let's get out of the way."

He herded us along the narrow ledge that hugged the hillside to a wide spot, like a roadside turnout. We watched from there.

The fickle rain had stopped. Sun shafted through black clouds.

The ore cart nosed out of the tunnel, trailing the uncoiling hose. Milt rode like a flagpole in front. Pinned by the rising tide of beads, immobile. Hap began to whistle—heigh-ho heigh-ho—but he only whistled one bar before he let it die. The cart rolled onto the elevated track that bridged the steep drop-off. It came to a stop against wood blocks bolted to the rails. The front wheels hit a lever that pulled the pin on the dumping mechanism, and the side gate opened to release its load. The load spilled into the ore chute, which angled down to the ore-processing mill below. But this load was resin beads, not ore. Milt slowly lost his footing and joined the flow of beads and, like a log at a waterfall, he went over the side and down the chute, disappearing into the mill. And still the beads flowed. We watched for agonizing minutes while the hose spewed beads into the cart and the cart dumped beads into the chute, down into the mill. And when the flow turned to a trickle and then to a stop, I guessed the stockpile in the shaft had been emptied. And the mill down below us was full.

Hap said, "Down we go."

We started down the switchbacked path we had climbed hours ago with Oliver and Dearing. We crept, boots sticking in the fast-drying mud. But it was not the poor footing that unnerved me—it was the mill, slumping halfway down the hillside like its old frame could not contain its new load. We descended to the final switchback before our trail ended below, in the valley. I turned to look across the fall line to the butt end of the mill. It seemed about to burst.

If it burst, the beads would run free down the mountainside.

Hap opened his belt bag and withdrew a putty disk with a wired metal stub at its center. He brought out a spool of red-sheathed wire. He used the multi-tool knife on his belt to strip the insulation off the end and then he spliced it to the stub wires. He said, "Wait here," and then in afterthought, "you move, I shoot." He caught me staring at the facepiece on top of his head. "Mind's somewhere else." His eyes were turned inward, deep-diving cave-pool eyes. He pulled down the mask, connected the regulator, raised the hood. He started off, traversing the fall line toward the mill.

He turned to look at us once, unclipping the subgun from his shoulder harness, holding it at the ready.

I looked beyond him—where Walter was looking—to the mine camp with its tumbledown shacks, and across the valley to the canyon wall that rose to the far ridge where we had come in.

Walter turned back to me, and shook his head. We'd never reach it.

I focused on the near view. Hap had reached the mill. He hurried, shouldering the gun sling, slapping the putty against the mill's butt-end, and then he retraced his steps, unrolling wire from his belt bag. By the time he reached us he had the wired detonator in hand. It looked like a garage door opener. He depressed the button. There was a concussive jolt from the mill, and then it yawned open.

Gravity finished the job.

I wished for veils of rain to shield us from the sight of the spew from the mill. Resins ran free, carpeting down the slope. It was only at the end of the resin-fall that the mill disgorged Milt, who seemed to have momentarily jammed the works, but then the beads like ball bearings greased his way and carried him along with the avalanche.

The avalanche threw off a dust cloud—golden resin fines going aerosol.

Walter bowed his head. I did not and so I witnessed the recapture of the resins in the stone reservoir at the bottom of the hill. Some ran wide, some stopped short, some spilled over the concrete lip, but when the final bead had come to rest, the reservoir was topped.

Milt lay on his back, legs half buried.

I watched the poisonous cloud settle over the reservoir, powdering Milt. His right hand lifted, then fell. I held my breath. Unlike Hap—still masked, still breathing canned air—Walter and I were without protection. I worried about that poisonous brew down there, about those unshielded gammas. We were a good long distance and I'd learned by heart the inverse square law—radiation intensity decreases as the inverse square of the distance from a point source—but I nevertheless edged behind Hap, putting him between me and that point source. He did not appear to notice. His attention was riveted on the scene below.

Walter whispered, "Keep your head."

I turned to ask why.

He jutted his chin. "Above that pile of rock..."

I lifted my face.

"*Don't look.*"

But I already had.

45

"ALMOST THERE," Hap said, softly.

I barely heard him over the hiss of his breather but as he unmasked I fixed my gaze squarely on his drawn face, taking scrupulous care not to look up at the hillocks of waste-rock ore tailings so as not to direct his attention toward Pria, who had appeared from who-knows-where and then disappeared behind the nearest hillock, and who knew where she'd turn up next. Miss Alien Apparition. I had trouble believing she'd been there at all.

Hap peered up at the sky. The clouds were closing back in.

In that micromoment, Walter's eyes met mine and we settled upon a plan.

I said, "Why are you checking the sky?" and when Hap's focus drifted back to me, I tried to hold it. "You need more rain?"

He eyed me and then his attention shifted again, to the reservoir.

And now there was a feathering of black hair at the base of the nearest ore heap and Walter shook his head and lifted his feet in a mime—*run* Pria, run to tell Soliano and then run home to hide under the bed—but she had already disappeared again so she didn't catch Walter's drift.

Hap was now scanning the hillside above the reservoir.

I said, "Hap."

Mercifully, he turned.

Walter said—as if he did not think my theory was hogwash —"You need a flood, Hap?"

I thought, it is hogwash. This may be a floodable canyon but how is Hap going to summon a flood? Here? Now? Walter and I were correct with our first scenario—the rains will wash the nuclides down to the aquifer. That's bad enough. I took my turn: "I'll play your game, Hap. I know what else the ring means. Means you're going turn clean water into bad water."

Hap listened, like he had listened to Walter's counsel.

I caught Walter angling for a look up the hill. I angled too. Had Pria run, after all?

Hap shifted to look.

I said, "Milt's legacy, right? Crap up the virgin. Like he crapped up your sister."

Hap's attention snapped back to me.

I saw Pria then, sidling out from behind the ore tailings hillock. She put her finger to her lips. I tried not to flinch and give her away. Walter started in again, yammering about the aquifer, voice rising in outrage, covering the sounds of Pria's approach. She came in a low crouch, straight and true, right for us.

Walter braced, as if for a blow.

She straightened and cocked her arm. She held a rock the size of a softball and she pitched it in a skilled overhand pitch and it didn't have far to travel. Hap turned, unslinging the subgun but it was too late to do anything but catch Pria's rock full in the chest. The gun slipped out of his hand and he came down hard on his back, turtling on the air tank. He rolled to his side, gasping. Before Walter or I could begin to come alive, Pria had dashed forward and snatched up the subgun.

I watched stunned. She comes out of nowhere and saves the day. No, she comes in her aunt's truck and drives to point D and hikes from there only how in the world does she find this place? Some alien magic. I didn't care. I wanted to hug her.

She shouldered the weapon and went to Walter, untying the knot that bound his wrists. Hap started to rise. She yelped, "Don't move, *you*," and came at Hap, aiming the weapon at his chest. "You used my *mother*."

Hap froze.

Walter caught my eye, and tipped his head. He wanted us to stand in her way, some kind of blocking maneuver. I had no faith in that. She's defending her mother—if that didn't amaze Walter, it sure amazed me. What I don't know about daughters could fill an ocean. I didn't know if she could operate an MP-5 but if she could we had to stop her from shooting Hap. That's a heavy burden for anyone to carry, much less a fourteen-year-old, and in any case Hap was no threat right now. I watched her fingers playing on the gun stock. Walter had edged in close to me, untying my wrists, but I could not have curbed a kitten right now, much less this girl. I said, "Pria, you can't do anything for your mom now, but *look*. Look down there, that's Milt down there and he's still alive."

She looked.

I said, "You saved us, you're a hero, and you can help us save him. There's a phone in the mine—we can call Soliano. He'll send help for Milt. He'll arrest Hap. So you can give Walter the weapon now."

She said, still looking at Milt, "Is he sick?"

"*Hey*," Hap said, "Milt's not the victim."

She turned to Hap. "What do you mean?"

"I mean it's your mom who's the victim."

Walter said, "Pria, listen to..."

"In a minute, Grandfather." She jabbed the gun at Hap. "Say about my mom."

Hap plunged ahead. "She had no idea what she was getting into. My partner was scouting for a place, she surprised him, he bought her off. I never even met her, Pria, until a couple days ago at her mine. Next time I saw her was this morning. Never dreamed she knew about *this* mine, much less she'd come up here. And I'm real sorry she sent you."

"She *didn't*." Pria lifted her chin. "I figured it *out*. About the ranger fuck." She flushed. "Chickie calls it that when they say what we can't touch. Like bat nests. And drawings on rocks. And Grandfather said what kind of rocks we're looking for so I figured it *out*."

Walter looked stricken.

Pria glanced at me. "In your bathtub. I liked your bathtub."

I nodded, faint, in reply.

"Chickie showed me drawings on that kind of rocks once, up here. But it was a long time ago so when I got here I had to go looking." She nodded at an outcrop downcanyon. "Then I had to go find something to show that policeman, so he'd let my mother go."

I blurted, "You went inside the mine?"

"You think I'm *stupid*? I was looking for footprints. Only then I heard you guys come out, and all that noise, and I hid."

"Not stupid at all," Hap said, "just trying to help your mom." He cautiously sat up. "I tried to help her myself, when she was sick. Remember?"

"No Pria," I said, "he wanted to give her the medicine to put her out, so she couldn't talk."

"I wanted to stop the torment," Hap said. "I saw my sister go through that."

Pria looked stunned. "Is that true?"

"Yeah that's true. Thanks to Milt."

"Is your sister sick?"

"Dead."

Pria's hand went to her mouth. The weapon bobbed in her hand.

"So how about a little justice? For my sister and your mom. The victims. Let me go and I'll tell their story."

"You just did," Walter said. "You're done. Pria, whatever Milt did, he'll account for. But now he needs help. That's radioactive material down there—same thing that hurt your mom. Hap did that. And he's the only one in position to undo the wrong. So I need you to let me take care of this."

I went cold. Take care of this how?

"Give me the weapon, Pria." Walter put out his hand, and when Pria didn't pull away, he took possession of the gun. He said, "Get up, Hap."

Hap, wary, got to his feet.

"Take off that belt bag. Set your facepiece. Connect your breather."

I said, "Walter *no*."

"I'm with Buttercup, Walter." Hap's face was white. "You got a conscience. Use it."

"I am. There's human life at stake down there. Go get him."

Hap was rooted.

Walter leveled the muzzle at him.

"Your firearms training teach you how to use that, Walter?"

"We'll see."

Astonishingly, Hap smiled—that curbed toxic smile I'd seen in the RERT van the night he warned me to go with low dose. "Guess I lose." He unclipped the bag and tossed it to the ground. He masked up and his smile disappeared behind the polycarbon shield.

I grabbed the belt bag and yanked open the zipper and

rooted inside but there was no cell phone, and I considered running back to the mine to try to find my way to the tunnel where I'd left the pack with the satellite phone, but how long would that take on my rubber legs? And once I'd brought the phone back out and called Soliano, and Soliano and Scotty and his RERT team got themselves up here, how long would that take? Too long, for Milt anyway. I remembered Scotty's words to me, two days ago at the borax mine: time equals dose.

I dropped the belt bag.

As I watched Hap trudge down toward the reservoir, my veins seemed to fill with poison. There was no clean way out here. This was the hopeless frontier between wrong and more wrong. I moved to stand beside Walter.

Pria folded herself down to sit, hugging her knees, watching.

From where we stood it looked like a real rescue, a real hero in PC wading into the spent-resin pool to aid his unlucky coworker, plunging his hands into the poisonous beads to hook Milt under the arms. Sending up a new cloud of resin fines. All the while ticking off seconds and sucking up dose. If there'd been a health physicist on radiation control, counting the gammas, he would have surely screamed *get out*. Hap was trying. Milt was feebly protesting, not understanding. Hap tried to drag Milt to the rim but he sank with every step. It must have been like walking through quicksand. At last, he just dropped to his knees in the shit and got Milt around the waist and humped him over the shoulder in a fireman's carry. He levered to his feet and staggered out of the tub.

We watched in silence as Hap carried Milt up the hill, well clear of the reservoir, well clear of us. He went down on his knees and unshouldered Milt, laying him out flat. He rose and started to move away.

Walter shouted, "You're not finished yet."

Hap looked at Walter. At the gun. He turned to finish the job.

He brushed himself free of beads that still clung, hood to boots. He bent over Milt. He thumbed away the resinous crust on the gash on Milt's skull. He whisked Milt's eyebrows and lashes. He scoured Milt's ears. He wiggled a forefinger between Milt's lips and swabbed inside his mouth. Milt gagged, then lay still. No protest now. Hap sat back and examined his gloves. They glistened with beads. He wiped them clean on Milt's torn shirt.

Pria spoke. "What's he *doing*?"

"Decon," I said.

Hap untaped Milt's wrists, unbuttoned his shirt, cradled his torso, and stripped him to the waist. He laid out the shirt, stuck the tape to it, and then wiped his gloves on it. He moved down to untape Milt's ankles. Milt's loafers were gone. Hap rolled off the socks. He undid Milt's horseshoe buckle and snaked off the belt. He lifted Milt's hips, unzipped the slacks, and tugged them off. Milt's black bikini briefs stayed snugly in place. Beads nested in the elastic waistband. Hap yanked off the briefs and tossed them in the pile.

Pria looked at the sky.

Hap turned to the pile of crapped-up clothing, wrapping it in Milt's shirt. He wiped his gloves clean on his own suit. And then, scrupulously clinical, he whisked Milt's body, head to toe. He examined his gloves. He held up his hands, showing us. The latex shone clean in the fading sunlight. Decon finished. He hooked Milt under the arms, dragged him away from the decon zone, deposited him in the uncontaminated soil, then walked away.

"That's far enough," Walter yelled.

Hap halted. He took off his SCBA gear and heaved it toward the pile of Milt's castoffs. He untaped booties and gloves, stripped off his suit, balled it, tossed it. He turned to face us across the fall line. "Walter," he called, "I did what you asked and I got me a dose so let's call it even."

Walter held the gun steady.

"Nobody's life at stake this time."

Pria leapt up, edging in close to Walter. "That's *true*, Grandfather."

Walter said, "Pria, stand back."

Hap shifted. "Way I see it, Walter, you've got no reason to shoot me now." He lifted his hands and slowly turned and set off in a measured walk upcanyon.

He gave us his back like he was putting his trust in us, believing we'd see it his way, and like he'd programmed me I started ticking off reasons why we had to let him go—he's done his worst and the priority now is to undo the damage—and that was true but what got to me was Hap giving us his back, and Walter with the gun, eons ago shooting paper targets in forensics ballistics training, only now it was a man in his sights, and Walter was going to have to shoot him in the back to stop him. I hissed, "*You can't.*"

Walter said, "We surely can't catch him."

There was a moment when I calculated distance, the two dozen yards or so between us and Hap and the likelihood of me covering that distance, but now he was into a sprint and he sprinted as well as he swam. I said, "Soliano will get him."

"And he's gonna get sick," Pria said, "so it's even-steven."

I said, "There's nothing more he can do."

Walter glanced at the reservoir.

I said, "We need to get Scotty here fast."

"And help," Pria said, "for that hurt guy."

Walter grunted. "You two can save your breath. I'm conversant with the concept of appropriate force." He lowered the weapon.

I sagged. Relief, resignation, I did not know.

"Then here's what we're going to do," Walter said. "I'm going into the mine to retrieve our sat phone. And the first aid kit. I'm going to check on Mr. Oliver, who..." Walter looked away. Looked back, face set. "Nevertheless, I'm going to check on him. Meanwhile, you two are going to wait here. If Milt revives, reassure him." Walter considered me a moment, and then held out the submachine gun. "Cassie, you're going to keep this. Should Hap return."

I stared at the thing. Should Hap return, I point it at him and tell him to stay put? Should Hap not obey, I shoot him? I said, "I don't know how to use it."

"Hap doesn't know that."

And then I was left with Oliver's subgun slung over my shoulder and Pria eyeing me skeptically. I watched Walter head up the switchbacks, and then shifted my attention to Hap's retreating back.

He was still heading upcanyon.

It was raining again, the kind of storm cell that goes from drizzle to downpour in seconds. Rain curtained Hap. As he moved up the mine valley I tracked him by the orange flag of his parachute pants. He was approaching the alluvial fan. He turned to glance up at the ridge, where we'd come in. I thought, he's going to access it from the rising fan, escape to Cherokee Canyon, maybe hot-wire our Jeep. No matter. Soliano will track him like a dog. Scotty will come and take charge of the tub full of beads. I wished Walter would hurry. I turned to watch Walter trudging up the last switchback to the top level, where Dearing's body guarded the mine entrance. I hoped, against reasonable, that Oliver, inside that tunnel, would benefit from Walter checking in on him. I shivered in my sodden clothes. And now the storm cell was passing and the rain eased off and sun shafts punctured the clouds. I looked again for Hap and found him halfway up the fan, following a deeply incised channel. You could hide in a channel like this—the way Walter and I had hidden in our deep channel on another fan. But Hap wasn't hiding. He glanced back at me and then climbed out and crossed the fan, catching the faint trail up the canyon wall to the ridge top. The sunlight intensified and I began to sweat. My mouth was horribly dry. I wished for a pebble to suck on. I turned to the fan yet again, studying the channel Hap had taken and then abandoned. Something was off. There were no gray pebbles. The pebbles up there were too dark. This channel was not, after all, like the channel Walter and I had hidden in. I whispered *shit*.

"What's wrong?" Pria asked.

Me. For believing Hap had already done his worst. My sweat turned to chill. I snatched up his belt bag and dumped the contents—detonator, wire spool, remote control, keys, flashlight, wristwatch. I picked up the keypad remote, the one he'd used in the mine. Wondering about lines of sight. Wondering about range. Wondering what the hell I think I'm doing.

"What's that for?" Pria asked.

I said, voice tight, "I think he's not done."

"He's *went*. What can he do? If he needs that clicker he doesn't have it."

That was precisely the problem. "When Walter comes out, tell him to tell Soliano if he has search teams down at the springs to get them out of the way. Tell him to have Soliano send choppers up there." I pointed to the top of the alluvial fan, and the unseen canyon above.

"Where are you going?"

"Up there."

"Grandfather said wait *here*."

Now, she obeys. I thought, with brutal calculation, if Oliver is indeed dead, if Milt is beyond first aid, then Walter has no reason to stay here. I said, "Just try to keep Walter from following."

"How?"

"Tell him Soliano will need his guidance."

"Tell him yourself."

I watched Hap. He was nearly at the ridge. "There's no time."

"If you can go, why can't Grandfather?"

"He's been sick."

"Then if he can't go he won't go."

I met her coal-black stare. It was impenetrable, like her reasoning. I didn't know what else to say so I just told her the truth. I told her what I suspected, what I knew. I armed her with the geomorphology. I told her to stay out of the valley, to stay high on the hillside. I gave her the keypad remote, and told her to show it to Walter. I strapped on Hap's wristwatch, a clunky diver's model. I put Hap's flashlight in my pocket; Girl Scout law. I reset the subgun so that it rode tight against my flank.

She eyed me. "You said you don't know how to shoot it."

"Did you?"

She shook her head. "It's got a lot of parts."

46

I STOOD at the base of the alluvial fan, recapturing the vision I'd had staring into the dregs of Pria's bath. I saw again the giant fan where Walter and I had been stranded. I felt again the heat thrown off by the fan rocks with their dark coating of desert varnish. I felt again the relief of taking shelter in the channel that was unvarnished, washed clean by floodwaters.

That bathtub vision had led me to an idea that beggared belief and I'd abandoned it because logic said Hap could not summon a flood.

I saw, now, that he could.

Studying the dark channel on this fan, I knew three things:

First, the dark channel was deeply incised and so it must have been carved by a significant flow.

Second, the flow path led directly to the reservoir below. Perhaps the miners had built it there to collect runoff water. That runoff, now, was only a localized trickle.

Third, desert varnish darkened the channel, which meant it had been many years since floods came this way.

These things told me what had happened here. A once-major channel had been abandoned by forces unknown and now it was largely inactive. I did not know the main thing—why. Maybe a fault scarp had broached its head. Maybe an obstruction had diverted the water flow, up in the canyon above. I'd find out, somewhere up above.

Hap, wherever he was, already knew.

I started up the mysterious channel. As I climbed, the incision deepened until only my chest and head were above the rim. Somewhere around here, Hap had spotted me watching him and climbed out. I scanned the curve of the fan—nobody. I scanned the bowl of the sky—nothing. Not a man, not a cloud, in sight. The sun baked the dark rocks and heat boiled up my legs. As fast as my rain-wet clothes dried, I wetted them again with sweat. My spongy socks had never dried. My eyes stung in the bright sun. I wanted my hat. I wanted my shades. I wanted my water bottle. I picked up a pebble to suck on, and tasted bitter manganese. I flung it away.

I returned my attention to what lay up ahead, puzzled. My channel seemed to lead directly into solid rock.

Ahead, at the top of the fan, the framing ridges met to form a face of high-rising walls. I scanned that face, searching for the break in the rock that would lead to the upper canyon—the canyon that must have once fed its waters down to build this fan. I wondered if a rockfall had blocked the watercourse, if the closed rock face was the end of the line. And then my climb topped out and, suddenly, I saw what I had not seen three steps back. There was a joint in the wall, a ragged slot with its edges offset so that if you looked from any viewpoint other than dead-on, you would miss it.

This was not the end of the line. I spent a minute staring at the slot, cataloging the things I knew:

First, the slot fed the dark channel.

Second, the slot, like the channel, was stained with desert varnish.

Third, flood waters had not come through the slot in a very long time.

Should they come now, I did not want to be here. This slot was like the nozzle on a fire hose, only the hose was obstructed somewhere up ahead. And if that obstruction was removed, this nozzle would shoot a high-pressure jet stream down the dark channel to hose out the tub of beads below. Only one way I knew to remove a geological obstruction and that was to blow it the hell up. With C4 and a remote control. And if you don't have your remote, then you come do it in person.

I glanced back at the cable ridge, where I'd last seen Hap. He'd been moving slowly, maybe beginning to get sick. He'd been traveling as though intent on escape but I figured he'd changed directions once out of sight, and the good thing—the main thing—was that it was going to take him some serious time to traverse the rugged terrain to reach the canyon above the slot. Actually, I knew a fourth thing. There must be another route to that canyon. Otherwise, Hap would not have abandoned this one.

Either way, I had a head start. I wasted thirty seconds of it wondering if I had the nerve to continue. If I cut and run, if Hap completed his work, then that fire hose was going to sweep the beads down to the oasis at Furnace Creek and crap up all life that drinks there.

My palms grew slick on the stock of the subgun.

You're armed. He isn't.

You can figure out how to shoot this thing, if you need to.

I moved like I'd seen the ninjas do, leading with the subgun, and passed through the slot. Nobody was waiting in the narrow canyon, although my imagination gave itself a short run for its money. I settled my nerves scanning the rock crevices for nesting snakes.

It was a sinuous canyon, sidewinding its way deeper and

narrower with every yard I advanced. By the time I'd advanced a few dozen, the walls had risen so high they reduced the sky to a thin blue strip. At first, I welcomed the shade. I cooled, I dried, my mouth found its spit. But within another dozen yards I was straining to pierce the gloom. The rimrock, in places, blistered out to close my sky-strip, darkening the walls beneath the overhangs. The walls were inky dolomite, their folds so entangled I could not read the strata. They began to squeeze in. Ahead, in silhouette, the walls undulated like the bosoms and bustles of Victorian ladies. The ladies were draped in a rough brocade, pocked with erosions and studded with pebbles. As they crowded me, I had to press my arms to my sides so their curves would not slice my elbows.

And then the canyon kinked again and I squeezed around a corner and nearly whacked my head on a tree branch wedged between the walls. It looked to have hung there for ages, stripped bare and bleached white. Hung up to dry by some long-ago flood.

A saying came to me about floods in narrow canyons: more water than you want in less time than you have.

I checked Hap's watch. Eight minutes gone.

Reflexively, I scanned the walls up to the rims, searching for escape routes. There were none to be had. The sky-strip still showed blue but what did I know of thunderstorms up ahead?

The varnished walls gave me comfort and the will to move on.

I passed beneath the deadwood bridge and continued up the hallway of Victorian ladies, who passed me along in stony silence.

Lady Canyon, as I christened it, began to climb in earnest and within a few dozen yards I met the chute of a dry waterfall. The chute-rock was polished but on either side the roughened rock provided handholds and footholds. It was not much of a dryfall—six feet, at most—but I had to sling the subgun across my back and let it ride, unreachable, as I inched up the rock. Now's the time, I thought. Nobody ever jumps out at you when you're ready for them. Of course, Brendan From The Fiery Hill would need wings to get here fast enough to swoop down on me while I'm pinned on this rock. Nevertheless, I was glad to achieve the top. Nobody awaited me there but my ladies. I ninja-cradled the subgun and within another dozen yards came to another little dryfall and had to do it all over again.

It was around another bend, at the foot of the third little fall, that I first heard the hiss of running water. I stood frozen in the dolomite gloom. I stared so hard at the dryfall that it seemed to flow, like dripping candle wax.

Ten more minutes gone, by my watch.

Hurry. I slung the subgun across my back and scrambled up the fall.

When I achieved the top and approached the next kink in the canyon, the hiss fractured. It seemed to come from here, from there, from above, from below. A trick of acoustics.

I went reluctantly around the bend, subgun at the ready—for what that was worth.

Nothing.

47

THERE WAS nobody to wave the gun at.

There was nowhere to go.

So I just stared at the obstruction.

My path dead-ended at another dry waterfall, an end-of-the-liner. It was a good forty feet high and its slick chute was edged by vertical strata that I was not equipped to scale. And even if I'd had the ropes and guts for it, achieving the top of this fall would bring me to the bottom of the true obstruction. It rose above the dryfall at least another forty feet and jutted out like a defiant jaw. Its rough gray face filled the canyon from wall to wall, like it had been born here, but there was no crater in the walls from which it might have been torn. There was only one way it could have got here. It had to have come from above, carried downcanyon in some past monstrous flood, and here, unable to shove its jaw through the narrow slot, it had come to rest. It was a keystone, locking the canyon shut. It was the biggest mother chockstone I had ever come across.

I listened to the hiss of water. There was no longer any question where the water hissed—up above.

When I regained my nerve, I searched for a way up. There

was a narrow ledge on the right side of the dryfall, maybe eight feet up. The ledge slanted steeply and led to a fracture in the steeper canyon wall. I continued to search for a better route but there was none to be had.

I waited, for Soliano's helicopter to appear, for the good sense to send me back downcanyon. But the fastest way out was in front of my nose. Backpacking the subgun, I began to frog-crawl up the chute. Two feet up, I slipped back down, leaving some skin on the rock. Nopah Formation, I judged, upper Cambrian. I didn't give a shit. I started up again. When I'd passed the bloody palm-streaks I figured I was committed.

The ledge was worse.

I no longer had to worry about slipping. I worried, instead, about toppling off. The ledge was so narrow I side-stepped, kissing the dryfall, heels hanging in air. I looked up, once, to the underside of the jutting chockstone chin. There was a stain of travertine, where water had once leached.

The steep wall was worse yet.

I glued myself to the rock, fingertips probing chinks in the brecciated dolomite, toes curling in my boots as I edged along the fracture. At last, the scarp widened and I exhaled in relief. My thin footpath now accommodated a heel-toe walk and as it angled up the wall, the wall flared inward and I could lean away from the edge. I chanced a look down and saw the chockstone directly below, where it bulged into the lower wall. I went queasy and snapped my eyes back to the business at hand. Ahead, where the scarp angled more steeply, the faint trace of a trail intersected. The trail followed a soft stratum of rock that had been eroded, creating a relatively flat bench. But this was no Park Service footpath. This was fit only for native creatures. I eyed the corrugated horns of the skull on the trail and, in the end, threw in my lot with the bighorn.

It was not until I found a wide enough pocket to collapse

that I realized I was crying. I wiped my face and blew my nose, then reset the subgun and scanned the canyon, searching for Hap.

Nothing moving. Nothing orange, trying to blend in.

I turned my attention to what lay below.

It was long and narrow, like a lap pool. It nearly filled this section of canyon but for a shelf of rock that ran alongside the water below me—the decking of the pool.

I thought of the pool at the Inn. I thought of Hap diving into the deep end, doing lap after lap in his purple trunks. I thought no further along that line.

This pool was fed by a large waterfall at the upper end of the canyon. At the waterfall's base, the pool was shallow. Then, as the canyon descended, the water deepened, plunging to unseen depths by the time it met the chockstone.

No doubt this waterfall would dry up once the hurricane-spawned rainstorms that fed who-knew-how-many-square-miles of this watershed stopped.

But for now, it fed the abyssal pool.

My attention moved to the chockstone. It domed maybe fifteen feet above the water line. It was the lumpy back-head of the jut-jawed face I'd seen from below. It plugged this canyon and backed up this water as surely as a knot obstructs a fire hose. Undo the knot and the water flows free through the hose to the nozzle, which compresses it into a jet stream. I didn't know how much water was needed to create a large and rapid enough flow to flush the beads from the reservoir and take them all the way down to the springs, but if I'd wanted to make that kind of flood I guessed it could be calculated. And if I wanted to keep track of the water level, I guessed I could rig up a depth gauge that transmits a signal.

I scanned the canyon rim and spotted what looked like the desiccated spine of a cactus, only it was nothing so indigenous.

It was an antenna and it rose from a cairn of rocks and it was well positioned to relay signals. Which meant there must be a box around here to send—and receive—them. Where? It didn't really matter. Hap no longer had his remote.

Thunder sounded somewhere beyond my patch of blue sky. Somewhere, perhaps at the head of this watershed, the rains were beginning again.

I decided to have a closer look at the pool while I still safely could.

The slope below the bighorn trail was steep and crumbly with talus. I had to scramble down, nearly losing my footing in the rocky debris. When I reached the pool decking, I realized my viewpoint had changed and so I scanned the canyon yet again.

Nobody in sight.

I turned to study the water. There was a strong current right now, fed at the inflow, puckering the surface. I peered into the depths. The water was opaque with suspended sediment, concealing the bottom. I broke out in a sweat, fighting the temptation to take a dive.

Another crack of thunder brought me to my feet. I looked upcanyon and spotted a newcomer—the fat gray lip of thundercloud above the waterfall. And then I spotted a second newcomer—curled into a red-headed knob in the deep notch to the right of the fall.

48

My first thought was, I wish I'd come in that way.

I'd come in the hard way, via the chockstone and the ledge and the sheep trail, and now I stood at the deep end of the pool and stared upcanyon at Hap.

He'd come in the easy way.

The notch was almost a stairway, cleaving all the way down the canyon wall, paralleling the tall waterfall, intersecting the bighorn sheep trail, continuing down to the shallow end of the pool.

The notch was so recessed that I couldn't have seen it from my end of the sheep trail, on my way in. So recessed that Hap couldn't have seen me.

But we saw each other now.

I found my voice and yelled, "*Stand up.*"

He rose slowly, like an unfolding petal, bracing his arms against the notch walls.

I thought, jolted, he's already sick. How long does it take between exposure and symptoms? Or maybe he's just playing me. I grew uneasy. But what could he do? I reminded myself, again, that I was armed, that figuring out how to use the subgun wasn't rocket science. I reminded myself that I had a plan.

I yelled, "*Come down.*"

He didn't move. I raised the gun. He spidered down the notch stairs to the sheep trail.

No, not sick.

"*Keep coming,*" I yelled, wondering precisely where I wanted him to go, but he moved at my command so I did not have to decide just yet. I watched him walk that sheep trail as impeccably as if he were, himself, a bighorn.

When he approached the skull, he paused.

Plan was, I'd make him take off his shirt and kiss the ground and then I'd use his shirt to bind his arms behind his back. First, though, I wanted him away from that skull. "Step over it. Don't even think about kicking it at me."

He cleared the skull with an exaggerated step and lost his balance in the process, putting out his hands to catch himself on the trail. He held there in a crouch. A tremor started up in his right leg. I waited for his back to arch, his gut to convulse. His right leg flexed, and now suddenly he looked like a runner in the blocks, waiting for the start gun. I figured why he was crouching there. He was ready to make his move. All the while, watching my hands on the gun.

I knew what he was wondering. Does she know how to shoot it? Did she learn, watching the FBI? And if she did, will she or won't she? And if she's undecided, can I move fast enough to interfere? Throw a rock, like Miss Alien. Slide down and tackle her before she makes up her mind.

I yelled, "*Lie on your belly.*"

He sank smoothly to the trail like the athlete he was.

I saw now that I should never get close enough to tie his hands. Okay then, what's the plan? Just keep him believing. He already thinks you might shoot. Or, he's not ready to call your bluff. Just keep him away from any place that could be hiding the explosives, and hold him there until Soliano comes. You've got him under control. Now increase the odds in your favor. I said, "Roll onto your back."

He turned over.

"Take off your pants."

He rotated his head to peer down at me. "Hey Buttercup, change your mind?"

I said, coldly, "I know what you were after that night at the pool." Blow a fog of romance into my eyes so I don't see clearly. "It won't work now, either."

"Was after a little bit of life."

My heart hardened. "Take off your damn pants."

He put his legs in the air and peeled down the parachute pants. He wore the purple swim trunks underneath.

I filed that piece of information. "Wad the pants. Slide them down to me."

The bundle rolled down the slope and I put out a foot to stop it.

"Roll on your belly and clasp your hands behind your head. Arms out like wings."

"Like in them cop shows?"

"Damn you *do it*."

He rolled, and clasped.

I squatted beside the orange bundle. There was no danger of radioactive beads being caught in the pants because Hap had worn hazmat when he'd waded into the reservoir to get Milt. There *was* a danger that I'd fall into the pool while trying to multi-task here. Balancing the subgun on my knees, holding my aim on Hap, I freed one hand to unwad the pants and fish in the deep pocket to retrieve my field knife. I returned it to my own pocket, glad to put it beyond his reach. The familiar weight threw me, like I'd pocketed the knife for the field and come up here for the rocks. Some joke. I leaned back to dip the pants in the water, then slapped them flat on the decking, tugging the ankles to spread them wide. Orange parachute flag.

Hap called down, "What if nobody comes looking?"

I said, "They're on their way." Sooner or later Soliano was going to shift his attention from the search for Jardine and the mess at the Inn, and notice that we hadn't checked in. Surely, I thought, he's already noticed. He's surely already sent choppers. Only, the searchers missed us earlier because we were inside the mine so long, and Dearing's body would not have been visible. So they widened their search grid. But that's okay. Walter's going to come out of the mine and Pria will tell him where I went and he'll phone Soliano. Maybe he already has. So the choppers are on the way, right now. Or ten minutes from now. And if they pass anywhere in the neighborhood they're going to spot my orange flag.

Hap groaned. "Arms're cramping."

I bet they were. "Tell me where the explosives are and you can drop your elbows."

"Have a heart."

"You need to blast the chockstone, right? To let out the water."

"You had one an hour ago."

"That was pity."

He grimaced. "Then extend it."

"Here's my heart. It won't let you contaminate anything or anybody else."

"Not even to wake up John Q Public?"

"Not even that."

"I'm hurting." His elbows dropped.

So was I. My legs ached, crouching beside my flag. I sank to the smooth rock deck. I propped the gun against my knees, keeping it aimed at Hap. He watched me. I watched him. He was flat out pasted onto the sheep trail. Still as death. And then his eyes closed. I thought, any moment now he'll shove up into that runner's crouch and head for the place where he's set the explosive. And then what will I do? What I did, now, was take the moment while he was playing possum to study the submachine gun, to figure what's what. And then, when he did not move, I began to relax. I gave in, catching the heat from the rock and the warmth from the dying day's sun. Minutes passed. His eyes flicked open, and then closed again. Neither of us spoke. Too drained to re-engage, like an estranged couple on vacation distracting ourselves with hiking and sunning and spatting and now, exhausted by our day in the sun, wary of the evening ahead.

"Cassie," he said at last.

Here we go. I tried to rally.

"You recall the SFP?" His voice was thin, but steady now.

The spent-fuel pool. I glanced down into the silty water. Not this pool. Another pool entirely.

"Recall that dude?"

Collier. Drew Collier. Guy who beat the crap out of Hap over a spilled glass of ale. Diver at the nuke plant who got too close to the fuel rods. Guy who died, which gave Hap a new nickname. Doc Death.

"Listen."

I listened—to Hap's raspy breathing on the sheep trail above me, to the hiss of the current in the pool below me, to my own shallow breathing as I took in the heated air. I could sit on this hot rock forever.

"Waited too long," he finally said. "Watching on RC."

Radiation Control—initials no longer cryptic. I remembered well enough. Hap waited too long on radiation control, didn't warn Collier soon enough that he was in a high-dose area. "By mistake?" I stirred. "On purpose?"

"Outcome's the same."

Death. He was telling me something now. I clutched the gun harder.

"Too late, Cassie."

"For what?"

"Initiator's in the box." He drew in a breath, expelled it. "Box is down a hole where ain't nobody gonna reach it. Timer's set."

I said, "You're lying."

"Fraid not."

"You left your remote in the belt bag. You'd have to do it by hand and you got here after I did."

"Was climbing out," he said, "when you caught me." He curled almost into a ball. He'd started to shiver. "Got here before you. Shortcuts, Buttercup."

I prayed that he was lying. I whispered, "Where were you going, climbing up that notch?"

"Up. High. Where I could watch."

I did not have to ask what he wanted to watch. The explosion, the release of the water, the flood. I jerked my head to look at the chockstone because that's where the explosives had to be if he was going to let out the water. I scanned the chock for a crevice where explosives might be jammed but there was nothing marring the back head of the stone. I looked back to Hap.

"You got the time?" He was still shivering. "Since you got my watch."

I looked. "Five forty-two."

His lips moved, counting. "We got nineteen minutes."

I froze.

"Go."

"You go."

"Count on it. Be a sorry thing for a man to miss the culmination of his hard work."

I wanted him to move first. I wasn't certain he could. But if the explosives blew, he was not in a bad place, up on the sheep trail. I was in a bad place. A shock wave of water could lap the pool deck and sweep me in.

He said, "Walter's waiting."

"*What*? What do you mean?"

"Means I saw Walter down below, when I was climbing up out of the canyon." He shook so hard his shoes knocked. "Means he's in a bad spot, down in the slot. Means you're on watch. Don't wait too long."

I thought, Walter *can't* be down there. All the warmth went out of me. He can.

Hap said, "T minus eighteen and some seconds."

I screamed *run* and the canyon walls bounced my scream back to me. There was no point screaming down here—I had to get up high enough to scream down the slot canyon for Walter to hear me. And the fastest way to get up high, with a view down the slot, was to climb the chockstone. I got to my feet and ran along the pool decking to the huge stone and started up. The angle was gentle but I nevertheless gave thanks for the rough graspable skin of the dolomite.

It was not until I'd topped the chockstone and got a million-dollar view that I saw Walter down there, above the third dryfall. I gaped, stunned that Hap had told the truth. Walter didn't see me. He was looking straight ahead, no doubt hearing the hiss and wondering what lay around the next bend in the slot canyon. He looked like a desert rat, wet hair striping his scalp, torso bared in the heat, pants ripped at the knees. He disappeared into the bend. I found my voice and screamed.

He emerged with his head thrown back. Open mouthed.

I screamed, "*Go back*."

He didn't. It would take a moment, I knew, for the shock to sink in. You come around the bend and here's this giant stone head blocking your way and you hear that hiss from the canyon above and you know what the chockstone is blocking, and then you see your partner on top of the stone like some drowned-rat ninja with a submachine gun across her back.

He found his voice and bellowed up to me. "Get down off that thing."

Of all things, I waved. I was spinning the scenario—scramble off the chock and up to the sheep trail and across the ledge and down the face to join him and drag him out Lady Canyon before we run out of time. I checked my watch. T minus seventeen and some seconds. If one could believe Hap. I turned to look. Hap had not left. He was sitting now, arms laced around his knees. He sat sunning himself like a crocodile on a river bank. What's he waiting for? Maybe he *was* getting sick. Or maybe he'd lied—maybe we had more time. Or less. My heart gave a squeeze. What if there's not enough time to run?

Hap saw me looking and drew a finger across his throat.

I went very cold. Find out for yourself.

To blow the chockstone, he had to have set the explosive charges somewhere on the rock. The most accessible place was right here, on top. It didn't take me long to find it, on the far side of the crown. In a crevice beneath a shelf of rock was a metal can and short antenna, its spring-coiled base attached to nothing. No longer remotely operable. He'd had to take the timer out of the can and wire it to the initiator. And he'd told me where he put the initiator: *initiator's in the box, box is down a hole*. I found the hole—a fissure, really—in the network of cracks around the shelf. Box was down there, all right. Neon yellow, size of a DVD case. Like he'd said, jammed down deep *where ain't nobody gonna reach it*.

He'd wanted me to know it was a done deal, that I couldn't stop it. And maybe he even wanted me, and Walter, to save ourselves. I felt no gratitude for that, none at all.

The numerals on the box down the hole were bright enough to read from here. T minus sixteen, and thirty-five seconds.

I dashed to tell Walter I feared there was no time to run.

But he was already coming up.

Shit. Chute's like a slide. I held my breath. I held my tongue. Don't distract him. One word and he falls.

He didn't fall. He reached the ledge and anchored there.

I breathed. He's going to make it. He's already committed himself to coming up here, which means he could be of no help to either Oliver or Milt back at the mine, and Pria told him where I'd gone, which means he's got nothing on his mind now but making this climb. He's already made it up four dryfalls and all he has to do now is reach the scarp. I can meet him there and guide him to the wide spot on the sheep trail, where we'll watch in safety and despair the culmination of Hap's hard work.

But he did not move.

"Walter," I called softly, and when he looked up I said gently, "there's explosives up here. We've got sixteen minutes."

He stared up the face of the chock, shaking his head like he could not believe it. And then his face went taut. "How many?"

"What?"

He bellowed. "*How many charges*?"

I shook my head, I didn't know, how should I know, all I'd seen was the yellow box and I didn't see any wires so I guessed the wires came out the bottom so I guessed the charges were underneath. And what difference did it make how many?

He looked at the canyon wall, eyeing the scarp.

I died, as he began the sidestep across the ledge, and it wasn't until he reached the wall and began to navigate the pitiful path that I truly knew he was going to make it. He found the place I'd found, where the wall flared inward. He stopped there, turning to lean into the slant, pressing his backside against the wall. The toes of his boots met the edge of the scarp.

We stared at each other across the canyon gap. I could read the relief on his face. I tried to smile. It's a cakewalk from there, to where the scarp intersects the sheep trail.

And then I wondered what Hap was doing. I turned to look. Hap was gone.

I scanned the notch that cleaved up the wall beside the tall waterfall. Hap could be there, in the recessed folds. I guessed he could climb it. If he wasn't sick. Who knew? I didn't know. While Walter took his tortuous time climbing the chock, Hap could have made it to the notch. I wondered how high he'd have to climb to see the chockstone blow, to let the water out, to watch his flood do its work.

And in the time it took me to wonder, I understood Walter's question: how many charges? It made all the difference in the world. That's why Walter shook his head when he looked up the chock. It was dolomite, dense and massive, and Hap wasn't going to blow it up. He'd have to pry it open. And he'd need a shitload of charges and a focal place to set them. That's why the box was down in the fissure.

He was going to pry open the chockstone at the fissure.

I was a learner in explosives but I sure knew rock. A fissure is a weak point and a blast would direct its force along that plane of weakness, widening it. And the place Hap needed to pry open was down below, to let out the water. The only way that works is if the fissure runs at an angle, exposing itself down below in a surface crack.

So he feeds the wired charges down the fissure from up here, then goes down below and grabs the charges and sticks them along the exposed crack. Then waits for the big storms to fill the pool. I recalled the smooth back head of the chockstone above the pool. That surface crack was underwater now.

But still, someone could dive under and find those charges.

Was that right? I hoped so. I was about to wager on being right.

Walter found breath enough to bellow again. "*Move.*"

I checked Hap's watch. I had time to climb down the chock and up to the sheep trail. I had time to do more than that. Once I'd understood, I could not pretend I hadn't. I called to Walter, "I'm coming." I moved to the far side of the crown, descending enough to be out of Walter's view. He'd assume I was getting down off this thing in the most efficient way possible. I was. I sat and took off my boots.

The water looked deep down below but to be on the safe side I took Hap's flashlight from my pocket and turned it on and tossed it in and watched the light dim as it sank. Okay. I scooted as far down the rock as I could, and then stood and sprang off.

I'm falling, and then just before impact my vision jumps to the place where the chockstone intersects the pool decking. Hap's there, propped against the rock. I'm startled that he hasn't climbed out yet. And then I get why. He knows what I saw up top, that yellow thing down in the hole, He worries I'd figure where the charges must be. He's been waiting, on guard. And now, seeing me jump into the pool, he's moving.

I hit the water and my legs buckled and my arms whipped up and as I arrowed down deep the gun sling slipped off like someone had snatched away my coat.

Oh crap, *cold*. I gasped, cramping. Fighting my cramped self to kick for the surface. I came up and spat ice water. Where was he? I flailed, fighting the current, rotating myself, and saw him surface deeper in the pool. He looked in shock too, hanging by his chin on the surface of the water.

The current took us both toward the wall of the chockstone.

He fanned his arms, backstroking, going with the flow, pale limbs trailing.

I could ride this unrelenting current all the way to the stone but he'd be there first, waiting for me. I jackknifed and dove. Kicking my way blindly through the silt, hoping to avoid him.

I bumped against his leg.

He grabbed for me but I kicked away.

When I surfaced I had no more fight.

The current finished it, plastering us both against the chockstone. We were a couple of yards apart. He could have reached me with a lunge. He didn't move. He laid his cheek against the rock, wheezing. I mirrored him. My second wind had died. I waited for a third.

I needed to go back under. When I'd kicked free of him, my foot had grazed a crack in the chockstone.

I thought I heard Walter call. I could see, beyond Hap, a portion of the canyon wall but the chockstone's bulge blocked most of my view. I thought by now Walter must have reached the wide spot in the ledge and collapsed just where I'd collapsed, the place where your limbs go to butter and your mind goes to mush. But he'll catch his third wind and keep coming.

"Buttercup."

I took in a sweet breath, filling my lungs. I fixed my attention on Hap's blue-eyed gaze. The whites were reddened from too much sun. I was close enough to see that.

He whispered, "You're swimming in the SFP."

Oh no Hap, I'm not.

I dove. It was a world of silt, sparkling in the sun rays. It was so cold my eyeballs ached. As I wall-crawled along I found the crack that my foot had grazed. My rock sense told me where it came from. This was the fissure I'd wagered on. Before my air ran out I glimpsed a shadow in the crack and it put me in mind of snorkeling in Maui, glimpsing an eel snout in a reef crevice. But this was not the ocean. And this was not the spent-fuel pool.

Hap didn't follow me down. He waited until I surfaced and gulped a lungful of air and then he lunged.

He knew what I'd found.

He wrapped himself around me, clinging like the limpets I'd seen clinging to the reef in Maui where the eel lived. My hands were free and I pounded his back but I could not get him off. He held onto me as if for life. Our legs entangled, trying to tread water. I used my hands to help keep us afloat. We spun lazily in the current, bumping gently against the chock. His head was pressed to mine. We were cheek to cheek.

I looked past his red hair frizzing in the heat, up to the sheep trail, watching for Walter.

My thigh pressed against Hap's and I felt the pinch of the knife in my pocket. If I could just get to it. And then dive to find the wire that was going to electrify that eel—only of course there's a colony of eels all the way down that fissure because it takes a shitload of charges to rip open this rock—and so if I can find one wire I can cut them all and do the job I'd jumped in here to do in the first place. But first I needed my knife.

I arched, trying to throw us off balance.

He snuggled in tighter. Shivering. I shivered, too. We shivered in sync. His shivers were blows, his knees knocking mine, his fists digging into the small of my back. His skull rattled mine—the two of us reduced to essence like the skull on the bighorn trail. He put his mouth to my ear. Lips of ice. "Want to live?" Breath so hot it warmed my ear. I nodded. Want to live. Want my knife. The skin of my thigh prickled, every nerve focusing on that pinch of knife in my pocket, and then the prickling spread to include the feel of his thigh against mine. I held there a moment, almost relaxed, and I felt him relax, and then I brought up a knee and jammed it against his groin. He cried out and shrank away. I thought I was free and made to dive but he got me by the webbed belt that wove through my waistband. We were arms-length, now, attached at my belt. His face went livid. I'd done that, given him that pain. While he agonized I fumbled at my belt, trying to unhook it. Cursing him. He opened his mouth to answer but no words came. He convulsed and emitted a gutful of yellow liquid and it lay intact like oil on water and then the current broke its surface tension and washed it away. I stared at the receding plume, understanding. It wasn't me. It was the gents. He wasn't faking it now. The gents got him. He turned them loose and they got him. He lifted his head and his face showed panic. Not my problem, not my doing, I wallowed in my innocence but he would not let me be. He was crying. I could not believe that Hap and I have the same feelings but we must because we're both crying now. He put his face into the water, back humping up, and I felt his convulsions by the jerking of his hand in my belt. I went for my knife. He pulled himself close and wrapped around me and vomited hot stuff down my back.

I yelped, like it could burn through my skin and lodge in my cells.

"*Let her go.*" It echoed down from above.

I looked up and saw Walter on the sheep trail.

Hap clung now not like a lover but a baby, latched on for all it's worth. He had the strength of desperation in that grip. He was sick but the water was his medium. I said into his hair, "Let us help." He pulled his head back to look at me. Those radiant eyes shone between swollen red lids. I wrapped my arms around him, opening the blade of my knife behind his back. He felt it coming. He grabbed for the knife and I felt the buzz of steel on bone and then he screamed and I let go in horror. He curled away, cradling his hand. A rusty bloom colored the water. He spasmed and went under, taking my knife with him.

Walter was crabbing down the talus slope, bellowing at me to get out.

I couldn't, even if I'd wanted. Hap had surfaced between me and the deck, treading water. His right hand cupped over the knife, which entered the meat of his palm and jutted out between the first two knuckles.

All the pain of the day welled up, threatening to drag me under.

Walter was on the deck. Yelling. A broken record. *Get out, get out, get out.*

I shook my head and pointed at the chock, trying to get a word in, calling out, "*Extension fracture*," and then, "*Underwater*," and then finally Walter shut up and looked where I pointed, and I gasped, "*Wires*."

And then he turned back to Hap and his gaze rested on the knife.

Hap sank beneath the water.

Walter jumped in, thrashing like a big wet dog.

Hap surfaced beyond us both, swimming toward the shallow end. He was not the swimmer who had lapped the Inn pool time after time. He was fighting the current, and the depredations of the gents. I struck out after him but I was fighting my own depredations. Walter outpaced me and caught Hap around the waist. There was a boil of arms and legs and then Walter had him in a headlock. Walter reached for his arm, for the knife hand, but all he succeeded in doing was spinning them both. Hap went limp, head against Walter's chest, arms outflung.

Walter snapped, "I could use some *help*."

Leverage. Walter wants me to pull out the knife. I'll never be ready for this but my gaze catches on the watch on my wrist and I'm stunned to see that nine minutes have gone which means we've got seven left and I can't decide if that's a lot or not much at all. So I kick for all I'm worth over to Hap's outflung arm, to the knife hand coloring the water. I don't trust him, I won't get too close. I reach across the water, my fingers brushing his, and when his hand curls away I lunge closer and slip my hand into his palm. He gasps. My fingers freeze on the hilt of the knife.

Walter says, "*Now*," and so I shut my eyes and yank. The knife rolls. Hap screams. But the screaming fades and the sound that fills my ears comes from inside my head, a remembered sound, that wet crush when you twist the knife to core the apple and you hit the pithy heart and stall there. You can't push any farther or pull out the knife so you gently rock the blade until it frees itself.

I opened my eyes.

Hap lay still, anchored on Walter. Hap's hands cradled over his belly, one hand balled up like a squeezed orange leaking red-orange pulp, a blood-orange hand. His reddened eyes assaulted me. I raised the knife—already washed clean—in a salute. To life.

Walter eyed my knife-hand, my watch-hand. "How much time?"

"Seven minutes. No, six."

"Chopper's on the way. Be here any minute."

"With divers?"

Walter shook his head. Not likely.

"Then give me a minute." I know just where the wired eels live. Behind Walter and Hap, to the right, where that chert interbedding dips about twenty degrees north on the chockstone's back head. Right beneath it. Maybe three feet down. In the joint.

I gripped the knife and dove.

49

We lifted into the air, my stomach rising along with the chopper, my head spinning with the rotors.

Below, the pool rippled with rotor-wash. Otherwise, we'd left no observable trace. Soliano's divers were en route to dispose of the explosives. Good wilderness manners: leave only footprints, take only memories.

And then, almost before we had cleared the ridges, we bellied down toward They-Don't-Pay-Me-Enough Canyon. I pressed my face to the window and marveled at the scene. What a crowd. They seemed to have sprung up like desert blooms during my absence. Uniforms everywhere—sheriff tan and FBI black and ranger green and RERT silvery-white. They wore the canyon colors. They were clustered high on the hill above the hot zone. Up even higher, on the ridge above the mine, surveying the scene below, sat Pria, hugging her knees. She wore a ranger-green jacket, big as a tent on her.

Had she looked up, I would have waved.

What to say, if she's waiting outside our door at the Inn when we pack up to leave? You saved us, twice. How did you do that, at fourteen? Maybe we should sign you up. But, then, you pulled that teenage stuff too. You scared the shit out of me, disappearing from my bathroom. You should have told Walter what you were up to. And you didn't talk him out of coming after me. Okay, that worked, Walter coming after me. I didn't really get what you said—if he can't go he won't go. I get it now. He could, so he did. Bottom line, Pria, you didn't make my head explode, although it was touch and go. You let me talk to you, even though I don't speak alien. You made me surprise myself. So if you're waiting outside our door I guess I'll just say thanks.

The chopper banked and now I got a view of another chopper parked downcanyon from the mine. Milt was there, on a stretcher, attended by medics. So he was alive; beyond that, I could not tell. On the other side of the chopper, considerately out of Milt's view, lay three body bags. I thought, fiercely, Roy Jardine shouldn't be allowed in the same neighborhood with Special Agents Darrill Oliver and Stan Dearing.

Walter leaned close to stare out my window. I spoke, low, so as not to attract the attention of Hap on the gurney, although Hap lay with eyes closed, unconscious perhaps, in his own world certainly. I didn't worry about the medic who squatted beside Hap or the pilot because I'd never seen them before and didn't care if they heard me or not. Soliano, I cared about, but Soliano was up front and likely could not hear me over the racket of the engine. So I said, low, to Walter, "I never know how to tally the costs."

Walter settled back in his seat. "Don't even try."

The chopper banked again, cutting across the canyon to avoid flying over the hot zone.

Soliano's head swiveled, showing his profile. He needed a shave. His whiskers were salt-white and I had to wonder if they'd been that color at the start of the week. And then I, too, looked where Soliano looked—down at the reservoir. From up here the beads appeared liquid, like a desert mirage.

A RERT stood well uphill from the tub, hands on hips, studying the cleanup job below.

I guessed they'd have to airlift in bulldozers and loaders to recapture all the beads, and empty casks to put them in, and telehandlers to move the casks. I wondered how many beads had been washed by the rain down into the soil. I wondered how far down the cleanup crew would have to dig to remove the contaminated earth. I wondered if they'd get it all.

Soliano appeared to know what I'd been wondering. "EPA will make this a Superfund site."

I wondered how long it would take to remediate.

The RERT I'd been watching sank to the ground, draping his arms across his knees. I could now read the name on his air tank. Scotty Hemmings. He bent his head and clutched his face-piece in his gloved hands.

I guessed Scotty was wondering the same thing.

50

WE TOOK OURSELVES HOME.

Soliano offered to send us by chopper but we needed measurable time and distance in getting from here to there and so we rented a car. There was a tense moment when the clerk placed the keys on the counter. Who would pick them up? I told Walter, "Go ahead." Seemed to me he'd proved his abilities ten times over. But he declined. On the "minuscule chance," as he put it, that he'd have an "untoward event" on the drive home, he declined. He preferred to wait for the all-clear from his doctor, at which point he would resume his place behind the wheel.

And so I picked up the keys.

We crossed the desert and when we came to the Sierra and began the climb to the plateau on which our hometown sits, each degree drop in temperature put more shielding between home and the pools of Death Valley.

We fell, hopefully, into the routine. It was good to be back in our own laboratory with its view of trees and mountains. It was good to drink the snowmelt water of the Sierra.

It was good, even, to bury ourselves in the newest work, a straightforward and largely mindless case of sabotage at a plastics fabrication plant. I had just identified the crystal under the scope as amphibole when Walter came through the door. He came balancing the day's mail on top of a pink donut box. We've compromised. Donuts on Fridays. TGIF.

I wanted to get at that mail before he sorted it.

As he set the donut box on the counter in our mini-kitchen, I rescued the unstable stack of mail under the guise of helping out. Walter started the coffee. I took the mail to my workbench and put my eyes on the particulars.

"Looking for something?" Walter yelled over the grinding of beans.

Just when I think I've put one over on him I am reminded that he's still sharper than anybody I know. I called back, "Yeah, the rebate for that iPod I bought."

No rebate, just bills and catalogs and the latest issue of the *Journal of Forensic Sciences*. And, near the bottom, the thick envelope I'd been expecting. I hid it in my drawer. Wait until the coffee's ready so I can broach the subject when his mouth's full of donut.

Meanwhile, my attention caught on a large manila envelope with my name printed on a label and no return address.

"Glazed or crumb?" he asked.

"Crumb." I opened the flap and pulled out a sheaf of papers. A blue post-it was stuck on top, and the handwritten note read: *To Cassie, From Hap*. Cassie, not Buttercup. The formality of that greeting put me on alert. In fact, getting mail from Hap put me on alert. Last I'd heard, he was in the hospital. I wondered what he wanted from me now.

I pulled off the post-it and looked at the top sheet of paper. It was a printed form, the boxes filled in with the same neat cursive as on the post-it. My eyes skipped to the signature box at the bottom: Brendan F Miller, Licensed Health Physicist. The formal title chilled me.

My eyes jumped to the block letters printed at the top. NRC Form 5. Occupational Dose Record For a Monitoring Period. My mouth went dry. What the...? Name (last, first, middle initial): *Oldfield, Cassie E.* Monitoring Period: *8-14 to 8-19.* I rushed, a little wild, from box to box—Radionuclides, Intake, Doses. For crying out loud I had an entry in every box. I skimmed the numerals because I didn't really know if those numbers were high or low or ALARA, and so I skipped to the comments box. *The individual was exposed in the course of an emergency response to an incident. She has received above the recommended maximum yearly radiation dose. Long-term effects are not calculable. Recommend the individual limit future exposures.* Hap had added a postscript, at kindergarten level: *Recommend you take care out there.*

Walter set a donut on a napkin on my bench, sequestering it so as not to crap up the open dishes of soil with the crumbs. "What's this?"

I handed him the second sheet of paper, the form with his name.

Walter sat down, reading. "How could he..."

"Know the numbers?" Scotty's the one who had our dosimeters, and Scotty had phoned the day after we returned home to tell us, "No worry." Scotty promised to send the entire incident report, with our numbers, once the NRC review was complete. But I guessed Hap didn't need to wait on bureaucracy anymore. Hap could get on the net and download NRC forms and then run his own equations. How many rads in the point source, how close I stood, how long I stood there. Still, Hap wouldn't have exact numbers to feed into his equations. I said, "He took a guess."

"And why the devil is he sending them to us?"

I didn't want to know.

There were three more forms in the pile. I had the urge put them through the shredder. I had the urge to stuff them back in the envelope, along with mine and Walter's, and return to sender. Instead, I continued to read.

Ballinger, Milton P. The numbers were huge but largely irrelevant because the neat cursive in the comments box said it all. *LD. Lethal Dose.*

Jellinek, Christine C. Lower numbers than Milt's, far higher than mine. *The individual's shallow dose equivalent, max extremities, has required reconstructive surgeries of the hands and arms. Outlook for the individual's short-term recovery is guarded; long-term effects are of grave concern.*

Miller, Brendan F. Double-digit microcuries, triple-digit rems. I closed my eyes. Breathed in, breathed out, settling my stomach. When I gained the nerve to read the comments I had to follow the arrow and flip the page. He'd needed more room than the comments box provided. Under the heading *Long-term Stochastic Effects* he'd written *odds-on favorite to win the cancer lottery.* Under the heading *Thanks For Asking,* he'd made himself a diary:

Tuesday: Thought my latent stage would last longer but this morning when I rolled over I left my hair on the pillow. People think the hair falls out but what happens is it gets thinner and thinner and then you can't even roll your head on the pillow without breaking it off. Here's a health physics lesson for you—the parts of your body where the cells keep dividing are bullseyes for radiation. Like hair.

Wednesday: Still trying to maintain my morning schedule. Been reading the papers. Guess what? Our story made page one of the Vegas Sun *today. I know you disapprove of my demonstration, Buttercup, but you have to admit it made a point. Even interrupted. Wish I could sit across the breakfast table from John Q Public, watch him reading what nearly happened to the water. See how that goes down with his morning coffee. To be frank, not really feeling up to morning coffee myself.*

Thursday: Nurse put a diaper on me since I can't seem to make it to the john. The cells that are supposed to maintain my intestinal integrity aren't doing their job. Man in diapers talking about intestinal integrity—that strike you as funny?

Friday: Too bad it's not Halloween because I've got bloody fangs. Scared the nurse anyway when she made me go aaahhh. Mouthful of lesions. Yuck. Stem cells in my bone marrow went on strike—how's that for loyalty?

Saturday: Coughed up a hairball last night. (Jess funnin youse) Was the mucous membrane in my mouth sloughing off.

Sunday: Can't write much more. Nurse will get your address and mail stuff for me. She's a peach. Come tomorrow, only going to have one hand left. My drawing hand thank the good lordy. Right now I'm going to use it to sketch my left pattycake so I don't forget I had one. Infection's gone gangrene. Where the knife went in—you remember.

Monday: I'm scared, Buttercup.

I understood now why he'd sent the forms to us. He's scared, alone, and he wants company. And, I thought, absolution. I couldn't give him that.

I got off my stool and went to the window to shield my face from Walter. I stared out at the forested flank of the Sierra. If I was a kid I'd go up into the trees and hide. Do my crying there.

Walter made a lot of noise, letting me know he was picking up the forms on my bench. Then he went quiet.

When he had finished reading I headed him off, in case he wanted to discuss Hap. I said, "My numbers are okay. Just means I need to be careful in the future." Like I'd go anyplace near unshielded shit without full hazmat and a ten-foot tallywhacker. "And you're fine. You didn't pick up any dose." Thank Scotty, and even Hap—I'd thank the devil himself if he'd had anything to do with keeping Walter from sucking up dose.

Walter said, "Never again."

"Never again what? Never again take a case where we need to wear full hazmat?"

He nodded. And then he grunted.

I knew that grunt. It meant, never again unless a case comes along that cries out for justice, in which case we'll likely end up taking it.

We got coffee to go with our donuts and went back to work on the plastics case. I left the thick envelope in the drawer. We worked until one-thirty and then I suggested lunch. When he looked up I brought out the envelope and laid it on his workbench. "It's that conference," I said, "on soil forensics."

"It's too far. We don't have the budget."

"Yes we do. I got a deal."

"What kind of deal?"

"Internet special. It's off-season in Belize. And don't forget frequent-flier miles." I folded my arms. "So here's what we're going to do. We're going to that conference because it has a session on geostatistics that I'm dying to attend. And we're staying in this funky hotel I found—right on the beach. Meals included. And in our down time, we're going to learn how to dive. Don't worry, hotel's got a certified instructor." I leaned forward, nearly coming off my stool. "Walter, we're going to get back in the water. With breathing tanks and facepieces. Only this time it's going to be fun."

Walter opened the envelope. He paged through the lime-green hot-pink brochure, studying it as if he'd never heard of an Internet special. He spoke, finally. "This diving instructor? He's young and good-looking? And kind? And intelligent—you'll want someone you can have a conversation with."

I groaned.

He winked.

I relaxed. "And we're going to drink margaritas and eat lime-baked chips."

"With salsa?"

"Yup. I'm not giving up salsa."

He said, firmly, "No seaweed, though."

"Only in the water."

"Only when the conference is not in session," he amended. "I'll want that deduction on income tax."

I got off my stool and came to him and extended my fist, to seal the deal. But then, as we bumped fists, I could not help noticing the age spots on his hands. Suddenly I could hear Hap's voice, clear as if he were here in the lab assessing Walter. *Your cells are already in the decay mode.* I shook Hap off. I didn't need a health physicist to tell us to wear a hat and shades and sunscreen out there. SPF-50.

I said, firmly, "It will be fun."

THE END

I hope you'll join Cassie and Walter on their next adventure. For a preview, please turn the page.

PREVIEW OF BOOK 3: VOLCANO WATCH

PROLOGUE

TOWN OF MAMMOTH LAKES
SIERRA NEVADA RANGE, the land of fire and ice

Twice, the mayor of my hometown gave me advice.

The first time was when she joined my third-grade class on a snowshoeing trip to chop a Christmas tree. She was nobody's mom—just the town's busybody mayor who volunteered for everything. Her name was Georgette Simonies. *Call me Georgia* she'd boom to any kid who addressed her otherwise, and since she was barely five feet tall, kid-size, we could do that. Out in the wilderness that day, I got myself lost. Trees suddenly thick, shrouded. That snow-blanket silence. Georgia was the one who found me. *Next time wear a bell*, she boomed.

The second time Georgia Simonies advised me, I was eleven. My little brother Henry had recently died. He had hemophilia, wherein the blood refuses to clot. He'd gotten sicker that year, bleeding out again and again, and my parents stockpiled pressure bandages and I fed him pureed broccoli to replace the lost iron, but his luck ran out when he bumped his head and bled into his brain.

I had night terrors for weeks until my parents, cartoonists, did the only thing they really knew how to do. My mother drew me a cartoon-brother snugly dead in his box. My father wrote the caption: death by God.

My older brother added a comma: death, by God.

I knew better.

A week later Georgia dropped by our house and studied the cartoon and then took me aside. She asked, "You feeling guilty?"

I nodded.

"You couldn't watch him every minute."

"But I was in charge."

She put a gentle hand on my shoulder. "Nobody blames you."

"Nobody lets me say I'm sorry."

She picked up the cartoon and put it on the table in front of me. Gave me a pencil. "Say it that way."

It took me over a week, and an hour with a thesaurus, but I finally added my own caption: death by inattention.

When I turned thirty, it was halfway through Georgia's fifth mayoral term. She'd been in and out of office for twenty-five years, mostly in.

She's been missing almost five weeks.

I've been catching the talk around town. People grumble that she can't disappear on us now, when it's a question of the town's survival. A couple of jerks have made bets: accident, or foul play? A couple of wits say she'll be back, she wants a sixth term.

As for me, I'm paying relentless attention.

CHAPTER 1

It was an icy dawn.

The four of us huddled at the Red's Meadow trail head, nursing coffee, inhaling steam, hands stealing warmth from the mugs. Seemed like we'd continue nursing that brew until hell froze over, which appeared imminent. I drained my mug, slushed it out with snow, and gave the three men a look. They cleaned their mugs. I collected the mugs and stowed them in my pack along with the thermos. Always the female who brings the coffee.

And then there was nothing for it but to snap boots into bindings and get going.

There's a body up the mountain, and from the report made by the ice climber who'd found it, the body had been there awhile. Until proven otherwise, the police had to treat it as a suspicious death. This mission had already been delayed three days because of bad weather, and another storm was forecast for tomorrow.

The corpse, according to the ice climber, was female.

Could be Georgia.

Nobody wanted to postpone.

The climb was too steep for snowmobiles and the weather too iffy for choppers. We had to ski it.

The four of us strung out on the trail, packing yesterday's snow. We were a silent group but I chalked that up to the weather, to the stress we've been under with a missing mayor and our hometown existence touch and go. No need for talk, though, because I knew this team down to the ground. Detective Sergeant Eric Catlin took the lead, cutting trail the way he worked a crime scene, muscular and precise. Recovery team volunteer Stobie Winder followed, ski patrolman in winter and horse wrangler in summer, thickly muscled as one of his pack horses—and that's why he was hitched to the sled we'd use as a litter. I followed the sled: Cassie Oldfield, meeting although not beating the local athletic standards, gloomy for a time in adolescence and now only in her dreams, good with rocks like Stobie's good with horses, precise as Eric in her work, once-student and now associate forensic geologist to the persnickety old man following her: Walter Shaws, the backbone of her life.

Eric set a climbing pace but I set mine by the rasp of Walter's skis. I had to slow, and slow again, to pace his fitful stride. A gap opened between us and the others and within an hour Eric and Stobie had left Walter and me behind.

Georgia would have been slower, still, had she come this way.

It was a wicked climb. When the old sea floor lifted to become the Sierra Nevada range it tilted sharply westward, so this eastern flank rises without mercy. We live on a plateau of eight thousand feet at the base of an eleven-thousand-foot peak, and we consider a pass of nine thou low. But this climb goes up to twelve. There are those of us who'd hike it or ski it just for the thrill of it, but Georgia tackled the outdoors only by necessity. To take a school group snowshoeing, to ski to the market when the roads weren't plowed. She fought off her extra pounds on a treadmill, not on a mountain. It took three million Pliocene years to raise this range and it would take three mill more to convince Georgia Simonies to climb up here for fun.

Which could argue that it wasn't Georgia up the mountain.

Walter and I turned up the next switchback, a pleat of a trail that would lift us another hundred or so feet.

I glanced up. Eric was positioned on the cliff edge above, watching our progress.

We topped the switchback and found Stobie with folded arms, poles dangling from his wrists.

Eric edged down from the cliff. "Listen up folks, I phoned for a weather update and that storm's moving in faster. We've got to make time. Stobie and I talked about it and we can handle this. Cassie, Walter, why don't you two head back down."

Walter stiff-armed his poles for support, recovering his breath, eyeing Eric.

When my own breathing had steadied, I said, "What the hell?"

"Hey babe," Stobie chimed in, "getting snowed-in up there's no joke. Eric and I can boogie-woogie it a whole lot faster." He shook his rump, waggling the sled.

I regarded Stobie, who's called me *babe* since we were kids, me being two years younger than Stobie and Eric, the two of them part of my older brother's group. Stobie's always quick with a smile, kidding around, more a big brother than my own flaky brother. Now, he smiled but without any warmth. Perhaps it was the cold. I turned to Eric. Eric's always slow to make a joke, although easily amused. He has inky blue eyes, the left one glass. There's a delicate network of scars beneath that eye and when he's amused the skin there crinkles like crystallized ice. The skin stayed taut.

No, I thought, nobody's kidding.

"I'll bag your evidence for you," Eric said, evenly. "Don't be territorial."

"But we are," I said. "And you've worked enough scenes with us to know that."

There was a thick silence, all of us looking past each other and the air heavy with retained snow.

And then Walter smiled. He has a beautiful smile, in a rough seamed face. Walter himself calls it a geologist's face: it looks igneous. "Eric," Walter said, "I will get there when I get there, which I can assure you will be no later than twenty minutes after you get there, during which time you can busy yourself with your own duties, and perhaps you, Stobie, can busy yourself photographing the scene, and as long as neither of you disturbs the geology before Cassie and I can put our eyes upon it, all will be well."

Eric exhaled a long breath. "Your call." He did a kick turn and took off up the trail.

Stobie pulled a rueful face, and fell in.

And then Walter and I were left stony-faced, looking at each other wondering what just happened here, why had half the team acted like the other half was downright unwelcome on this trip?

But the first half of the team was already leaving us behind and so we fell in as well. Walter set himself an ambitious pace. I followed, taking note of the ease of his stride. A couple of years ago Walter had suffered a series of tiny strokes; according to his doctor he was now fully recovered. Nevertheless, I kept on keeping watch—and keeping it to myself.

It took me some time to find my own pace. There's a rhythm to be had on skis, even uphill, a rhythm that takes over the body and relaxes the mind, and I aimed for that.

A couple hours later we gained the last switchback and the land leveled into summit country. A wide snowfield lapped up to the jagged tips of the mountain range. The sole representative of the living was a whitebark pine, branches clawing the ground, battered into submission by ages of steady wind.

One by one, we stopped to add layers of clothing.

Eric started off again, leading the way across the snowfield.

We followed our own trails and our own thoughts.

In the distance, Eric stopped and faced up to the headwall of the range. As I neared, I saw what he was examining: a glacier cupped by a steep rock outcrop. This range was littered with remnants of the Little Ice Age, and this glacier was a larger one. Waves showed its progress, the spacing between the crests marking the amount of ice flow in a year. In places, the downflowing glacier had run over ridges and cracked open into crevasses.

The others drifted in. Walter was winded, but hanging on. I thought of the whitebark pine.

After a rest and power-bar snack, we advanced up the glacier. I anchored for a moment near a crevasse, peering at the bluish ice within, thinking what the world had been like when that old ice was water. Thinking how one could dive right down into oblivion.

"Here!" Walter called. He squatted at the head of the glacier.

We converged and looked down.

This was the bergschrund, where the downflowing ice separated from the rock headwall and opened a cleft. It looked to be fifteen or twenty feet deep. Down there on the floor of the schrund was a sprawled form, sheathed in ice but recognizable nevertheless as a woman. She was face-down, arms and legs askew, and a woman's generous hips humped up. Someone—I assumed the ice climber who found her—had scraped her clean of loose snow.

Stobie dug a spotlight from his pack and planted it on the edge of the schrund, illuminating the scene down below, highlighting the details.

She wore hiking boots. She wore pants, parka, and gloves, matted with mud and ice. She wore a wool cap, beneath which darkish hair hung out. She could be a perfect stranger. She could be Georgia. Georgia had bottle-brown hair. Georgia had disappeared five weeks ago, in early December. It would have been cold. Not a lot of snow then; the big Thanksgiving ski weekend had been a bust. Georgia had complained to God but it wasn't until mid-December, after she'd disappeared, that the storms came.

"Hiking accident," Stobie said.

"We'll know," Walter said, "when we establish the career of the body."

Eric's eyes ticked to Stobie, the glass eye a tick out of sync. "He means what happened to her, Stobe. How she got here."

The career of the body would be written in the soils she picked up. I glanced around. Certainly, the basin rock would feed minerals into the glacier, but down here on the schrund floor those soils were locked in ice. She could have picked up basin soil up top, around the glacier—walking, sitting, falling?—before she went into the schrund. Assuming the soil was bared then. There could have been bare patches in early December, before the storms hit. I realized I was already identifying her as Georgia. I stared down at her, my eyes aching with cold, as if she could be somebody else. Whenever, however, she got here, she'd come to the end of her career. The career of the body stank.

"Odd," Walter said. "The climber noticing the body down there."

"Nah," Stobie said. "Ice climber wants to get to that rock wall, he'd be checking out the schrund before he crossed."

Eric opened his pack. "Let's get on with it."

Walter and I began sampling the soil in the glacier basin, digging where it was thinnest beneath rock overhangs. Eric and Stobie rigged a rope ladder, climbed down to the bergschrund floor, and then set to work with ice axes. By the time the sky had hardened into a gray roof, enough ice was quarried to loosen the body.

Walter and I clambered down to join them.

And now that I was down there, I took note that the body was that of a short woman. Just how short was hard to tell, the way she sprawled. The face was obscured, planted nose down into the ice, hair fanned like a frozen drape. I had the urge to sweep the hair back, get a look. Bad scene protocol. I kept my hands to myself.

Eric moved in first, to collect evidence that might jar loose when we move her. He exchanged his ski gloves for latex. He plucked out a thick fiber caught in the waistband, and bagged it. Looked like rag wool—heavy-duty winter wear. Could have transferred from her hat or her gloves. Or could have come from somebody else's. It looked like the rag wool of my own hat. Or Stobie's gloves. Or Walter's socks. Eric moved to the right boot and plucked out something caught at the collar. He studied it. He took his time.

Walter said, "What is it?"

Eric said, finally, "Maybe a horse hair."

I glanced at Stobie, as if the horse wrangler might have an opinion on the matter.

Stobie was silent. And then, almost in afterthought he whinnied.

That was for my benefit, I thought. Showing me the old Stobie, kidding around when things got dicey. Somehow, it did not ease my mind. I said, "Could she have ridden a *horse* up here? That makes no sense."

"Her car was left at her office," Walter said. "However she got here, she didn't drive to the trailhead."

"Maybe she caught a ride," I said, "with somebody else."

Eric finished his collection and moved back from the body.

Now it became Walter's and my show. We gloved up. Walter examined her clothing, her hair. I took the boots. I was numb with cold, too cold to speculate whose feet were in those boots. I grasped the left heel, toe still locked to the ice. There was a generous layer of soil preserved in the waffle sole. With the small spatula I pried loose plugs, then with tweezers transferred the plugs to a sectioned culture dish. I shivered.

Walter cast me a sidelong glance. "Something?"

"Not a good match," I said, "just eyeballing it." It was a quick and dirty field guess, but the boot soil did not look much like the basin soil we'd collected. Which argued that she didn't walk here, that she walked somewhere else and picked up soil in her boots and then was dumped here.

I was talking murder, but yet not out loud.

I heard the ratcheting of Stobie's Nikon and glanced up. He was shooting a roll of the body. He aimed the Nikon at me, and snapped. "Beautiful."

On my best day—auburn hair clean and shining, gray eyes framed with liner—I'm not beautiful. Been called pretty. And now...nose red, skin bleached cold, eyes squinting, hair roping out from beneath my wool hat. Knot in my chest, although that wouldn't show in the photo.

I looked away, at the ribbon-like bands of blue ice on the schrund wall, shimmering in the glow cast by Stobie's spotlight. Beautiful. And then the wall seemed to lean in and all I wanted to do was escape.

But she was still bound here.

When Walter and I finished our collection, we all worked together to chip away the last bonds of ice. Then we eased our arms beneath the body. It was like lifting some valuable piece of furniture you dare not drop. And now that we held her I could not deny who she was. We eased her onto her back.

There lay our mayor.

My heart plunged.

Arms and legs askew, she looked as if she were trying to run. She was iced all over, smooth in some places and rough where chunks of her glacial bed still clung. Her face was abraded and there was damage to the forehead. The ice on the right side of her face was sheet thin and the texture of the skin there was apparent. White and waxy, like boiled fat.

Walter bowed his head.

Eric pulled out a notebook. His face was pale as hers. "Overt marks of trauma to the head," he said, voice not his own. "No apparent lividity in the visible skin of the face and neck. Suggesting she didn't die in the position she was found, face down." He grimaced, and wrote it down.

I said, fury rising, "Suggesting someone put her there, after she died."

"Aw shit," Stobie said. "Shit."

"Dear God," Walter said.

None of us took it particularly well.

We had made our collections on her anterior side—more wool fibers, another horse hair, a few more mineral grains—and we were easing her into the body bag when Walter noticed a bulge in her parka pocket. Eric unzipped the pocket, fishing out a small clutch bag. Shiny vinyl, wild tropical print, pure Georgia. I recognized it. She carried it in place of her big purse, when convenient. Eric unzipped the clutch, dumping the contents onto the ice. Keys, cell phone, comb, lipstick, micro-wallet, pen, small notebook.

Walter said, "What's the notebook?"

I looked. "Weight Watchers—her pocket guide. Calories and all that."

Walter indicated the pen. "She wrote in it?"

Eric picked up the notebook and flipped through it. "Yeah. What she ate, some kind of point system."

I asked, "When's the last entry?" thinking that might pinpoint the day she died because I knew Georgia damn well wouldn't have skipped a meal or skipped holding herself accountable, and I waited while Eric flipped to the last written entry and read it, while his face closed up tight. "What?" I said. "*What*?"

Eric passed it to me. Walter and Stobie crowded in. I read the inked notes, then read them again. It looked like she'd been trying different ways to word something. Mostly cross-outs. Nearly blotted-out, the way you'd slash your pen angrily because you can't get the words right. I could decipher *just found out* and then, at the end of the slashed-out section that nearly tore the page, she'd found the words she wanted.

No way out.

— end preview of Volcano Watch —

FROM THE AUTHOR

Thank you for reading—I hope you enjoyed the story. You might also like other books in the series, all standalone novels that can be read in any order. See a complete list with descriptions on my **website:** tonidwiggins.com

NEW RELEASES
If you would like to be notified of new releases, you can sign up for my mailing list: https://eepurl.com/GtdZn

JOIN ME ON FACEBOOK
facebook.com/ToniDwigginsBooks

LEAVE A REVIEW
Reader word-of-mouth is pivotal to the life of a book. If you enjoyed reading this story, please consider leaving a review. It would be much appreciated.

ACKNOWLEDGMENTS

"Writing is easy. All you have to do is cross out the wrong words."

— Mark Twain

I had some help identifying the wrong words.

I want to thank the following experts in their fields for information, reading the book, and terrific suggestions: Gregg Dempsey, Terry Fisk, David Lochbaum, Marvin Resnikoff, John Thornton.

If there are factual or technical errors in Badwater, they are mine alone.

Thanks to the following for reading and commenting: Jack Barnes, Lisa Brackmann, Russell Dwiggins, Dan Kolsrud, Patrick Price, Del Roy, Marcia Talley, Emily Williams, Sue Worsley.

An added note of appreciation goes to Emily Williams, for noting that 'playa' refers to a person who has enough 'game' to be a major player in a group. Still, I like the geological definition —a desert basin from which water evaporates quickly—and I'm sticking to it ;)

To Molly Williams, thanks for the enthusiasm, and asking how it's going.

To Chuck Williams, thanks for reading, supporting, being there, and a boatload of everything else.

No book is complete without a cover.

I'm fortunate to work with a talented cover designer—Shayne Rutherford at Wicked Good Book Covers. She has created extraordinarily wicked good covers for my books.

Many thanks, Shayne. I look forward to working with you on the cover for the next book in the series.

Printed in Great Britain
by Amazon

45075848R00209